CASCADE

CASCADE

Maryanne O'Hara

FIC
O'HARA
2012

VIKING

VIKING
Published by the Penguin Group
Penguin Group (USA) Inc., 375 Hudson Street, New York, New York 10014, U.S.A.
Penguin Group (Canada), 90 Eglinton Avenue East, Suite 700, Toronto,
Ontario, Canada M4P 2Y3 (a division of Pearson Penguin Canada Inc.)
Penguin Books Ltd, 80 Strand, London WC2R 0RL, England
Penguin Ireland, 25 St. Stephen's Green, Dublin 2, Ireland (a division of Penguin Books Ltd)
Penguin Books Australia Ltd, 250 Camberwell Road, Camberwell,
Victoria 3124, Australia (a division of Pearson Australia Group Pty Ltd)
Penguin Books India Pvt Ltd, 11 Community Centre, Panchsheel Park, New Delhi – 110 017, India
Penguin Group (NZ), 67 Apollo Drive, Rosedale, Auckland 0632,
New Zealand (a division of Pearson New Zealand Ltd)
Penguin Books (South Africa) (Pty) Ltd, 24 Sturdee Avenue,
Rosebank, Johannesburg 2196, South Africa

Penguin Books Ltd, Registered Offices: 80 Strand, London WC2R 0RL, England

First published in 2012 by Viking Penguin,
a member of Penguin Group (USA) Inc.

1 3 5 7 9 10 8 6 4 2

Page vii: Excerpt from "The Ruins of Time" from *Near the Ocean* by Robert Lowell.
Copyright © 1967 by Robert Lowell. Reprinted by permission of Farrar, Straus, and Giroux, LLC.

Art credits
Pages 248–249: Walker Evans, Library of Congress, Prints and Photographs Division,
FSA / OWI Collection (LC-USF533-006712-M5)
Pages 332–333: Courtesy of CardCow.com

PUBLISHER'S NOTE
This is a work of fiction. Names, characters, places, and incidents either are the product of the author's
imagination or are used fictitiously, and any resemblance to actual persons, living or dead, business
establishments, events, or locales is entirely coincidental.

LIBRARY OF CONGRESS CATALOGING-IN-PUBLICATION DATA

O'Hara, Maryanne.
Cascade / Maryanne O'Hara.
p. cm.
ISBN 978-0-670-02602-9
1. Marriage—Fiction.   2. Man-woman relationships—Fiction.   3. Triangles (Interpersonal
relations)—Fiction.   4. Life change events—Fiction.   5. Artists—Fiction.   6. Massachusetts—Fiction.
7. Domestic fiction.   I. Title.
PS3615.H37C37 2012
813'.6—dc23
2011043918

Printed in the United States of America
Set in Carre Noir Std
Designed by Alissa Amell

To Nick and Caitlin
Don trí mhuicín

*O Rome! From all your palms, dominion, bronze
and beauty, what was firm has fled. What once
was fugitive maintains its permanence.*
—Robert Lowell, "The Ruins of Time"

ACKNOWLEDGMENTS

To those who offered advice and encouragement during the long period when I first conceived *Cascade* as a short story and then a novel, I say thank you: Monique Hamze, Susan Conley, Lily King, Electa Sevier, Diane Whittemore, Katie Whittemore, Janet Tashjian, Don Lee, DeWitt Henry, Ellen Tarlin, Ellie Frazier, Pamela Painter, and members of my old writer's group: Ted Weesner, Jr., Nicole Lamy, Audrey Schulman, Tyler Clements, Dan Zevin. A double thank you to Ted for recommending me for a St. Botolph Club emerging writer's grant, and thank you to the St. Botolph Club for awarding me that grant, which marked the true beginnings of this novel getting off the ground. The Massachusetts Cultural Council also recognized *Cascade* in its early stages, and I'm grateful for the support.

I am indebted to those people who provided me with crucial details about art and the time period, about dams and winches and land assessments and Shakespeare: my mother Florence Bavaro and her extraordinary memory, the late, lovely Frances Poole, Evelyn Gates, Joe Antonellis, Rick Cullen, Clif Read at the Quabbin Reservoir Visitor's Center, Georgianna Ziegler at the Folger Shakespeare Library, and some extraordinary artists: my beloved brother Michael Bavaro, Bobbi Robbins, Jack Tremblay, and three former W.P.A artists—James Lechay, Alan Rohan Crite, and Paul Cadmus. I would also like to recognize the former residents of the Swift River Valley, whose sacrifice inspired this book.

I always had faith that when the time came, this book would find the right editor. Thank you to the elegant Kathryn Court for her grace and care with *Cascade*, and for assembling a superb support team, which has been so capably led by Tara Singh.

Stephanie Cabot is more than a wonderful agent; she's a remarkable human being, and I am fortunate indeed to have her, Anna Worrall, and the rest of the Gernert Company on my side.

Finally, I cannot imagine life without my brilliant daughter, Caitlin, an astute reader and natural editor whose insights and wisdom informed so much of this book. And for the love and support of my husband, the unique and generous Nick O'Hara, I am eternally thankful.

CASCADE

1

December 1934

AND SOMETHING BECOMES SOMETHING ELSE

During his final days, William Hart was haunted by drowning dreams. Every night, at the sound of his shouts, Dez came awake herself, always briefly startled to find a husband—Asa—sleeping beside her. She would dash across the hall, fearing another heart attack, but by then her father would be lying quietly, gazing at the plaster ceiling. Probably half the town was having drowning dreams, she'd say, reminding him that the reservoir was an old rumor and ticking off good reasons why it would never happen—the state had looked to Cascade before. If it was too expensive to build so far from Boston six years ago, then surely, in these hard times, nothing would come of it.

Usually that kind of talk made him feel better and in the morning he'd be rested and fairly optimistic, ready for whatever diversion she had planned for him—a new copy of *The American Sunday Standard* borrowed from the library, a coil of his favorite black licorice from the Handy Grocery, an offer of a game of chess.

But the night after Christmas, he hushed her irritably—"Desdemona!"—as if she were still a child. His white hair spread across three pillows, his eyes blazed. He was frail, but he was also a lifelong player of Shakespearean kings; he could still play the part of regal.

"There are so many ways of drowning, my dear."

They passed a moment without speaking. Downstairs, the banjo clock ticked, and across the river, a train blew its horn. William Hart's stage, where stars like Lionel Barrymore and Kathryn Tranero had taken bows, had been dark last season for the first time in twenty-five years. That darkness was all he thought about.

"We're not going to drown," Dez said firmly, and slipped from the room before she could confess that she, too, was under water. She had been since September, when the dean of the Boston Museum School called her in to say that her tuition had not been paid, since Rose wrote, *He's had to let Annie go, the yardman, everyone but me.*

The next morning, the diversion was French meringues, a first for her—she wasn't much of a cook. And she was dubious, eyeing the puddle of clear slime at the bottom of the copper bowl Rose said to use. Remarkable to think that this beater contraption would change all that, but Rose had said earlier, "Have faith," and so she gripped the red wooden handle with her left hand and began to crank with her right, beating air into the eggs, faster and faster. Don't stop, Rose said, even when your arm feels like it's going to fall off. Which it did, becoming separate, mechanical, a moving part thrusting forward and around, forward and around. She became conscious of the linoleum under her shoes, the countertop digging against her hips, arm crying out *stop*, but it was fascinating, too, to see how the nonstop forcing of one thing into another could cause such a complete transformation. Air into egg. Increasing in volume, expanding, until all at once the bowl was full of shiny white meringue, thick and lustrous as paint. Sweet on the tongue. She spooned dollops of it into Rose's canvas pastry bag, then—a whim—piped it into tiny sculptures: why not? A dozen pointy kings' crowns to make her father laugh.

She slid the baking sheet into the oven, where the meringues would spend hours drying out. Then she washed up the bowl, the beaters, the spoon. She set everything on the draining board and paused by the window to catch her breath. Outside, the day was grim and overcast, a few stray snowflakes starting to drift down from the sky. It was the kind of day that would turn to night without fanfare, with a gradual extinguishing of light, the kind of day that pierced you with melancholy and reminded you it was only December, that a whole winter had still to be gotten through.

And what would spring bring? What once seemed an interim, a transitory phase only, was dragging on into endless day-to-day existence. What the country had named the Depression wasn't getting much better, and a lot of people were starting to worry that maybe the United States of America was one big experiment that had failed. You could feel it in the streets, in the very air—no one had any idea what was going to happen. The future was one big void they were all stepping into. Every night, Asa came home with more bad news picked up in the drugstore: the Cascade Hotel had closed another floor, Warren Estes was closing the boating supplies shop for good, turning the Water Street property into a filling station. Their once-fashionable resort town with its pleasant waters was looking more and more like the ghost valley that was invading dreams and even the pages of her sketchpad. She had done half a dozen studies: the drowning person's blurred upward view from the bottom of a flooded place. The bleary, uncertain light. The smooth stones, long grasses, and someone struggling through thick river mud, Ophelia-like, trying to find a place to breathe.

The banjo clock began its low, rhythmic chiming and she turned from the window. Eleven o'clock. Her father would nap for hours now, Rose wouldn't be back today, and if she was lucky, she could make real, uninterrupted headway on her new piece.

2

At first she assumed he was a hobo. They sometimes hopped off the trains and mooched around town for food. The man on the porch had that same hungry look, but he was clean-shaven, wore a pressed gray suit, and carried a large satchel. A jalopy Dez hadn't seen for months sat in the driveway behind him: black with big fenders and bug-eye headlights, faded gold lettering on the door: *Sid Solomon Wares*.

Dez remembered hearing Ethel Bentonford in the Handy Grocery, back in September, clucking her tongue. *Did you hear the old Jew-man died? He was a nice man, too. I miss the truck coming around. You get to depending on them.*

The man on the porch introduced himself as Jacob Solomon. He didn't wear the stovepipe hat his father used to wear, nor the little black skullcap beneath it, but a gray flannel trilby that he removed and tucked under his arm when she said how sorry she was to hear about his father. He was slight and somewhat self-effacing, at first glance almost nondescript, a person you might describe by saying he had dark hair. But his eyes were keen and watchful as he took in first her face, and then her smock and paintbrush at the instant she realized her brush was about to drip. Then, a small commotion, laughter, cupping one hand under the other to rush back to her studio, where he examined her canvas, a winter study of the buildings facing Cascade Common, at twilight.

"If you add a layer of gesso mixed with a little powdered charcoal," he said, "you'll get streaky, translucent shadows that will really suit what you're doing, I think."

His advice was matter-of-fact, confident, and she turned to look more closely at him, to marvel, really, to see who in Cascade could possibly know such a thing. Then she remembered Sid, on his rounds, talking about an artist son. *He is in New York. He is in Spain. He is in Germany with his mother's people now, painting who knows what. Great things, that I know.* She hadn't paid too much attention to Mr. Solomon—so many people bombarded you with anecdotes about their sons and brothers when you told them you painted. But now she thought about it, she remembered he had also said that his son had *taught* art classes. In New York.

An hour went by like the wind, an hour that was a back-and-forth comparing of experiences—where they'd done their training, and with whom, and where they'd traveled. (After New York, it had been Spain, Amsterdam, then Germany for him; she had gone from Provincetown to Paris.)

And then, in the kitchen, over a pot of coffee and some stale cigarettes Dez found in a drawer in Asa's desk—while her father napped, while the meringues slowly dried, while the kitchen developed a remarkable coziness it usually lacked—they argued about who was good and who was great. Great was Goya, Jacob said, no question. Goya was the only reason he'd gotten on that crazy freight boat out of Brooklyn in the first place.

"Oh, but they're so brutal!"

That amused him. "But don't you see why? He's conveying everything that's usually so interior, so under the surface. He's a genius at it. And his use of light—" He stopped, lost in thought. "Well, you'd want to see them in person, of course, color plates can only convey so much."

He drew deeply on his cigarette, held the smoke, then let it out with a troubled sigh. "But who knows when any of us will see them again? Things were getting unpleasant all over Europe by the time I left." He stubbed out the cigarette as Dez thought back on Paris—how close that beloved place was to the unrest they were starting to hear about. You hoped nothing would come of it all—men had surely had their fill of war after the last one. Still, there was that nagging sense of worry.

A thump on the ceiling brought them back to the kitchen, to the cups of coffee, drunk down to dregs, to the saucer Dez had set out as ashtray, gray with ash, Jacob's open satchel sitting by the chair. He had sales to make; she needed to get upstairs to tend to her father. But first, she thought, well, they had to arrange to meet again.

3

"You changed your will?" Was that what he'd just said? Her father, back in bed after the exertion of a walk, was mumbling, and when she swung around from hanging his cardigan to look directly at him, he hemmed and hawed and finally admitted that he had given the playhouse to Asa, back in October, after their wedding. "As a dowry of sorts."

She blinked. She stood up a little straighter. "Are you joking? And the two of you kept this a secret from me?"

"No secret, my girl." He tried to speak matter-of-factly, jovially. "Just business between men."

With that, she walked over to the window and laid her forehead against the cold glass. Outside, the snow had begun to fall thicker, faster. The unexpected hour with Jacob Solomon had left her preoccupied; she'd let her father have his way when he insisted on taking a walk outside, even though Dr. Proulx had said no to outdoor ventures. He'd headed straight to the bench at the end of the lawn for a clear view across the river to the town common, where their old house and his theater sat diagonally across from each other. As he'd rattled on about the playhouse, she hadn't paid much attention, but now she realized he must have been looking for a way to break this news to her.

"You actually put the deed in Asa's name? Why would you do such a thing?"

His face flooded with blood. "I couldn't come here empty-handed," he said bitterly, "like some drifter, no better than a hobo. I am a bankrupt, Desdemona."

"Oh, Dad." In all these months, he'd never used the phrase. Not in spring, while she was still in Boston and he was scraping money together to pay the mortgage he had taken out after the first of the staggering financial-market losses. Not when he broke down and sold his beloved First Folio and everything else in the Shakespeare collection. Even after the foreclosure on their home, he had never used that phrase.

A bankrupt. He hadn't actually had to declare legal bankruptcy—by selling everything else he'd managed to skid to that precipice and stop before the playhouse went over the cliff, too. "First of all, you are not a bankrupt. And I can understand how you felt, of course I can, but to give it away after all you sacrificed to save it—"

"I hardly gave it away. Asa's your husband, after all. But I do have something else, just for you." He gestured to his bureau, where one of his theater props—Portia's casket—sat among a stack of books. Had Rose retrieved that from the playhouse?

Portia's casket was a small, leaden chest that he used for *Merchant of Venice* performances. When Dez carried it over to the bed, he pushed it back into her hands with purpose. "It's for you."

Odd, she thought. An odd choice of gift. In *The Merchant of Venice*, Portia is an heiress who is not free to decide whom she will marry—her father's will has stipulated that the suitor who wins her must choose the box—gold, silver, or lead—that contains her portrait.

"You've locked it," she said. Indeed, the lid was fixed tight, with a sturdy brass padlock.

Was she supposed to guess at its contents? What was inside had nothing to do with husbands, with Asa—that she could be fairly sure of. And it certainly wouldn't hold any treasure. Back in September, when she'd first come home, she'd been sent down the basement stairs of the playhouse to the safe—the Victor Manganese Steel Vault with Triple Time Lock and backup key, concealed behind a shale imposter's wall, so she could empty it of the last few bills that remained inside. That money had paid Rose's wages and kept them in food for a few weeks.

"What I've locked in there is something infinitely worth saving, though I can't tell you, right now, what it is." He spoke somewhat gravely. "But it's critical that you, number one, keep it safe," he said, counting off on one hand, "and two, don't open it until the night the playhouse reopens—however far in the future that may be."

"But you'll be there to do that."

He opened his other hand to reveal the lock's key, tied to a length of leather. "In case I'm not, my dear," he said, reaching to push the key into the deep patch pocket she sewed on most of her clothes. The small movement made him catch his breath, and when he lay back against the pillows, she looked on his face with fresh eyes: the bluish pouches on top of his cheekbones, the skin thin as rice paper.

"I'm not feeling right," he admitted, motioning to stop her from whatever she might instinctively scurry away to do—call Dr. Proulx, fetch medicine. "I've lived in this body long enough to know what feels right. But it's nothing I can put my finger on, nothing Addis can help." His ragged breathing evened out and he struggled to sit up straighter. *"The stroke of death is as a lover's pinch,"* he quoted, in his old stage tenor, *"which hurts and is desired."*

Then he held her gaze. *We've avoided straight talk for too long*, that gaze said.

"You're a painter. You know the plays. You can stage one. It's all about vision, putting a shape to things—you know that. You could get that friend Abby of yours to come out from Boston and help. You must stage a triumphant *Tempest,* I think—but regardless, do promise me that there will be an opening night. That no matter how long it takes, you'll open it again."

Dr. Proulx had assured them both that William Hart had plenty of years left in him, but she didn't contradict. He hadn't raised the subject of the reservoir, so neither did she. Maybe now he'd start sleeping through the night.

"Of course I promise," she said. "I love the playhouse, too."

He smiled for the first time. "And Dez? Asa's a good man."

She knew that. "I just wish he wasn't in such a hurry for children." On Christmas morning, Asa had mentioned that maybe, with luck, there'd be one more Spaulding next year. Or two. "There've been more than one set of twins in my family," he'd said. Dez's smile had been reflexive, full of alarm. Across the table, Rose had caught her eye with a discreet, sympathetic wink.

"I did stipulate, in the will, that the 'first child of the union' inherits."

Child. That was a word that plotted out her life like stage directions, even more than the words *I do* had. "But what if I don't have a child? Or want one?"

"Well, upon Asa's death the playhouse would go to you, and if you were gone, then to the town, in trust. That way I'm assured of some kind of continuity, don't you see?"

She suddenly saw very well. In the upheaval of leaving Boston, and losing their home and moving in with Asa, Dez had pictured her father's heart getting stronger, the world returning to normal, men going to jobs every day again. Her father reopening the playhouse, Dez showing her paintings in the vestibule and some gallery owner from New York exclaiming, *I must have these,* and Asa—well, things turned fuzzy when it got to Asa. Had she imagined they could return to the casual camaraderie of dating? *See you in a few weeks.*

Her mind flashed to Jacob Solomon. At one point, she had been telling him how they'd lost pretty much everything. "And then we had absolutely no place to live," she'd said, "except the playhouse, which was impossible, and so then—"

She had stopped short. She had been about to say *and then I married Asa*. But she hadn't. Because she had been enjoying the little frisson of attraction between them. Because she hadn't wanted to kill it with talk of her husband.

Her pulse began to slow, to thud thickly through her veins. The connection with Jacob had felt harmless enough, but there had been that little zap of attraction, undeniably, and Dez remembered, suddenly, a woman she had not thought about in years, a friend's mother, discovered to have been carrying on a relationship with one of the New York summer men. Ruinous.

"Dez—" Her father broke into her thoughts with a voice that was gruff with embarrassment. "Did you marry Asa so I could have this?" He gestured to the snug iron bed, the walls covered in rose-and-vine wallpaper, the casement window with its view to the Cascade River.

Of course she had. He knew she had. Their wealth had been nothing but vapor, and deep in the fog that was comprehension of that fact, Dez had felt the deepest kind of panic as she'd packed her steamer trunk and returned to Cascade from Boston.

"What were we supposed to do, Dad? Live in the playhouse?"

He looked toward the window, toward town, where the playhouse would be sitting in the dark, its eaves collecting snow. "I suppose I wanted to believe you'd have married him anyway."

She closed her eyes. She'd bought an apron. Brown and calico, twenty-six cents pressed firmly into Jacob Solomon's palm. To make sure the relationship started on the right foot, so they would both feel comfortable doing what she proposed: that he stop by on his Thursdays in Cascade. To talk about art, to swap ideas. Until now, *Art News* had been her lifeline, read cover to cover. Now each week would wait for Thursday.

"Marriage is serious business, Dez." But his voice lacked conviction. "Maybe I was too wrapped up in my pride, too worried about the playhouse."

Dez eyed Portia's casket and thought, *Maybe you were. And now you've gone and given it to Asa but expect me to be the one to save it.*

He looked at her as if he'd read her thoughts, and opened his mouth to speak. He coughed instead, a cough that developed into full-blown wet, phlegmy hacking. Dez hurried to the bathroom to fill his glass, then ran back with it, hoping the look on her face hadn't upset him. He sipped at the water, cheeks bright red, eyes running.

She waited while he cleared his throat and dabbed at his eyes with small, wiping motions; she waited while he drank more water and arranged his blankets and lay his head upon the pillows, skin barely there, barely even a color, just a veil over veins.

"Level with me," he said, and sank lower into the pillows. "Do you love him at all? The truth now."

"Of course I do."

He fixed his eyes on her, as if he wasn't sure whether to trust her answer. "I know that after all your training, it must seem like it's come to nothing. But life has a way of working out and, Dez, I do urge you to welcome children. Even one child will make a difference in your life that you cannot fathom. I promise you, my girl."

She thought of Asa, wanting his Christmas twins, with no idea that his wife was not at all ready for a single child. Asa, with his kind ways, his tall and solid presence. Asa, who was at that moment innocently going about his workday, who was likely in the back room of his drugstore, mixing prescriptions. No—the banjo clock had already struck four. Mrs. Raymond would have slipped home to fix her husband's supper before the evening rush. Asa would be greeting customers at the fountain, grilling franks and mixing Cokes. "Good to see you," he would say to each customer walking in. "Thanks for coming in."

Dismay is a small, quiet emotion. We say we are *filled with dismay,* when actually dismay causes us to pause and quietly check our consciences.

Dez always liked to think that if her father had not died that day, she would have wrenched herself onto the straight and narrow right then and there. She would have walked to town and begged Mrs. Mayhew to let the Harts live at the hotel for a while. She could have offered to wash linens, clean toilets, anything, and despite the secret satisfaction that that Cascade busybody might have felt to see once-grand people like the Harts laid low, Ella Mayhew was a good woman at heart. She probably would have said yes, they could have a room. They'd have called back Attorney Peterson to rewrite the will. In summer, they could feasibly have moved into the playhouse.

But her father did die. She left him propped up with a copy of Proust that they both pretended he had the energy to read. Then she went downstairs to fetch the deviled egg snack that Rose left on a white enamel tray for him each morning. Rose, who insisted on continuing on as his housekeeper, even though he no longer owned a house. "What else have I got to do?" she'd say. "And after all he's done for me."

Dez was lifting the tray, lacing her fingers around its metal handles, when she heard it, heard the odd, knee-buckling *thud*. Forever after in her memory the next instants would be a muddle of images: Portia's casket lying on its side on the floor, the Proust flipped upside down and resting beside it, the lamplight's long beams like fingers down the blanket that just minutes ago he had tugged on. Everything slowed down and she became both empty and heavy, as if all that made up her body was sliding through the floor.

She found herself downstairs, lifting the telephone, the calico apron and coffee cups sitting on the table like relics from another life, her fingers like rubber on the push button that wouldn't push, the crank handle that wouldn't turn, until she got Pearl, the high school helper, on the line and then Pearl didn't stop for breath: *He left here a good hour ago, Zeke Davenport came in all upset, well, they're all upset aren't they, the news from Boston isn't good.*

She managed to break in. Then she huddled by the back door to wait. The wind rattled the back door. The snow was turning to sleet. It tapped at the glass in a way she used to find comforting. She shivered and wrapped her arms tight around her until the Buick skidded to a stop outside and Asa came striding through the back door, shaking the snow off his shoulders, stomping his feet, Dr. Proulx hurrying to catch up behind him.

4

The morning Abby was due to stop by on her way to her new life in New York City, Dez woke with a thought running through her head: one of many, one of many. How did one stand out among many? Because one *did*, undoubtedly. But how to convey the idea with paint?

Asa was downstairs waiting for his breakfast, she knew that. His bedside calendar, which he flipped each morning the minute he opened his eyes, read April 24, 1935, Wednesday. Arthur Godfrey was on the radio and the milkman was on the back step banging bottles, which meant it was 6:30, barely enough time to slip the cool glass thermometer under her tongue and record the reading. But she lay still an extra few minutes, working out details for her idea, which was still filmy, still barely a vision, in need of being nailed down before it evaporated. *One of many, each unique.* Maybe raindrops, the emphasis on a singular raindrop sliding down a pane of glass, a juxtaposition of the natural world and things made by humans.

Yet—depicting water was one of her weaknesses.

What else? Something from the natural world definitely, maybe with some element added to suggest that this one truth applied to all truths. Trees? Grass?

Asa called up from the bottom of the stairs. "Dez?" She heard the concern in his voice, the hope that it was finally morning sickness making her late.

Grass could work—blades of grass, giant blades, two feet tall and filling the canvas, with one that grabbed the eye's attention. How, she did not know, but the idea was solid enough to get her out of bed and down into the kitchen to fix her husband's eggs.

Haven, refuge, harbor, sanctuary, studio. After the wedding, Dez claimed this narrow space, the house's former birthing room, as her own. The room then was cramped and dim, inhabited by the ghosts of Asa's female ancestors, and she had recoiled a bit, the first time she opened the door and peeked in. But she brightened it up, took away the gloom, dismantled the rickety iron bed and carried it down to the basement. Threw out the mattress with its ancient bloodstains, removed the dark green roller shades from the windows. Whitewashed the walls and floorboards.

Now the room offered decent light off the river. Portia's casket sat on a shelf where she could see it while she worked. Along one wall, she had pasted the stories the *Boston Evening Transcript* printed when she won the Cabot Prize and the Henderson First Place. A lumpy horsehair sofa, with a thick, soft quilt thrown over it, lined the inside wall where she slumped when she was feeling stuck or uninspired.

But that didn't happen today. By ten, the new work was off to a good start, underpainting done, composition in place with a transparent wash of linseed oil and paint in cool blues opposed to the warmer greens and yellows she would use later. As soon as Asa left, she'd sat down and sketched three thumbnails, deciding on the one with the best-defined sense of light: a from-the-ground, root-level perspective of tall bluegrass growing wild next to a fencepost, a kind of moment from childhood, when you got down on the ground to really inspect things. The fencepost was barely a suggestion—a bit of wood, a small length of rusty barbed wire. Grass was the predominant subject, the focal point the foremost blade, and different from every other blade.

She slipped out of her painter's smock, wiped her brushes clean with a rag, and set them in turpentine. In any event, it was one more thing to show Abby. *Abby.* The train she said she would be arriving on was only twenty minutes away, and she hadn't phoned or telegrammed to say she wasn't coming after all, that it really did make more sense to take the coastal train to New York.

I always said I'd see Cascade, last week's letter said. And now she would be here within the hour.

It was a ten-minute walk to town, down River Road, across the bridge, up Main Street, then left on the common. She was preoccupied with anticipation when, on the common, Dr. Proulx tripped her up with his cane and nearly knocked her down. His gaze was unfocused, and she smelled whiskey on his breath when he apologized. Addis Proulx was not the sort of man to drink during the day; something was clearly wrong. Dez almost followed after him, and would later wish she had, but the train was blowing its whistle, pulling into the station. *Abby.*

At the train station, Abby stepped onto the platform looking the same: pretty and rather elfin, with her bee-stung lips and nut-brown cap of hair under a smart little cloche hat. She was a bustling bundle of energy, arranging to leave her luggage inside with the stationmaster, then clapping her hands and saying, "Well, then," to give Dez her full critical attention. Immediately, Dez sensed disappointment. "Oh, my dear," Abby said. "What is it that looks so different about you?"

Dez didn't remember Abby being so hawkeyed, so critical. "My hair?"

The thick head of hair Abby always saw forced into short waves was longer now, untended and left to hang in a cloud around her face.

Abby cocked her head to the side and smiled the cheery-false smile Dez had also forgotten. "Maybe. Though it's lovely, of course."

Dez was conscious of vague disappointment, but she didn't want to be disappointed. She drummed up enthusiasm, exclaimed over Abby's hat, over the fact that she was finally going to New York. Where they had both planned to be by now. "What will you do down there?"

Abby studied the marble floor a half-second too long before looking up with the same fixed smile. And then it was as if she stepped quietly behind a glass wall.

"No job yet, no plans at all really, but I have a few ideas."

Dez wasn't sure how to react. You never knew why a wall had been erected; sometimes it was best to leave walls unmentioned. "Brave of you" seemed a right thing to say.

"Oh, I don't know about that." Abby put a hand on the station door. "All I know is that losing that job at United Shoe was a blessing in disguise." She gave the door an emphatic push. "It was the excuse I needed to finally *go*."

They stepped out of the station to the reality of Cascade in 1935, a reality Dez suddenly saw through Abby's eyes: a dog sniffing along the empty common, patches of snow under the elms; bare branches scraping a gray sky. Late April, officially spring, yet looking eternally winter, the gloomy light making even the best-kept structures surrounding the common look bleak and impoverished.

The Cascade Hotel was in obvious need of paint, and its rooftop sign, once so grand with tall, gilt letters, looked tawdry. Carson's milk wagon rumbled by, the hollow clop of horses' hooves fading down Elm Street.

"This is nothing like I pictured," Abby said just as Dez thought, *This is nothing like the stories I used to tell*. She pointed out their old house, a graceful, redbrick Georgian that a lawyer from Springfield had bought but never moved into. The hedge separating the house from the street had not been pruned and now was uneven and leggy; ivy grew wild along the walls.

And the playhouse—it looked small, shuttered, insignificant, as it never had during its August heydays. As they approached, Dez described the opening-night parties they used to have on the lawn, and how in summer those willow trees lining the river were like great canopies, but Abby did not really pay attention. She climbed the front steps to read the sign, hand-lettered by Dez and nailed to the front door.

WILLIAM ALOYSIUS HART

~ Duncan, Gloucester, Prospero, Caesar ~

passed away on December the 27th, 1934.

He built this stage in 1908 and offered twenty-five summers of theatre.

May flights of angels sing him to his rest.

To Reopen, Eventually.

Abby pulled her collar close about her and gazed around, her eyes flat. "Nothing's like it was, is it? Not here, not anywhere. And now Boston's serious about building that reservoir and you might lose it."

"Does Boston know something we don't know? Do you?"

"No, of course not."

"Because I can't lose the playhouse. I just can't let that happen."

"But what will you do, if it comes to that?"

Dez didn't know. She didn't know what she would do. She fumbled to unlock the door. A dry summer and renewed drought concerns had pushed the state to draft emergency measures in October. A new reservoir was vital, and, since it would take years to build and fill, the push was on to choose a site and start construction. "Until the legislature passes the appropriation bill, nothing's official. And if it does pass, it's only the river they're taking, not necessarily the town. There are two big valley towns on the river that can accommodate a basin—us and Whistling Falls, and Whistling Falls has a much smaller population. No public buildings to speak of. They'd have less to destroy."

She pushed open the door. Inside, there was the smell of mildew. Frustrating, the way a structure could seem to stand unscathed for years, yet as soon as life departed, rot set in. Always, there were signs of mice: a sharp smell of urine and black droppings along the baseboards. The costumes smelled musty, even though she had given them all such a good airing during that windy week they'd had in March. The morning sun, which used to shine through the upper windows and light up the rafters, seeped in through grimy glass. No one had gotten to those upper panes in—oh, at least two years. She hadn't been able to do much these past months. In the old days they had taken help for granted—there had always been handymen and cleaners, seamstresses, yardmen, cooks, and window washers. Now, with Rose gone, she had no help at all.

Their footsteps echoed in the paneled wood vestibule. She wished she could wave a hand and reveal, like a movie, a piece of the past. This was the very place, when she was nine, where the great, then-young, Richard Leslie knelt down to button her shoe. Did she plan to be an actress when she grew up, he asked, and she said she was going to be a painter like Mary Cassatt. Those were the years her mother was still alive, and she still liked looking at the Cassatt book of color plates, page after page of mothers and their children.

Now she pointed out the tiled floor, the way the titles of the plays were inlaid with white tiles into the perimeter. A glass display case dominated the center of the room, standing tall and empty. "This was where my father used to display his First Folio on production nights."

But many people didn't know what a First Folio was, and obviously, by the blank look on Abby's face, she was one of them, so the story had to start from scratch: William Hart's First Folio was part of the first published collection of Shakespeare's plays. His edition had been in excellent condition, with its original calf binding. Dez used her arms, measuring neck to waist, to describe how big it was. While he was still in his twenties, William Hart had purchased the first item for what eventually became a rare and valuable collection of Shakespearean memorabilia—a somewhat-battered 1685 Fourth Folio that he bought for $107.50 on thirty days' credit. But as his wealth grew, so did the collection—early playbills and props, dozens of miniatures. In 1906 he finally got his hands on the prize: a pristine copy of the First Folio that cost him fifty thousand dollars, and he didn't care that he'd had to sell nearly 80 percent of his U.S. Steel stock to pay for it.

"He usually kept it wrapped in protective cloths and stored in a dry vault, but on play nights, he'd set it on that." She pointed to the red velvet plinth, turned pink and even white in patches. "It was one of the things that made this playhouse so famous."

"Who bought it?"

"A collector, from Washington. He was building a Shakespeare library there."

"So it was the first one ever printed. Well, no wonder! And to think it was here, of all places."

"Well, no—'first folio' means it was part of the first printing, the very first run."

"Oh."

"But only about five hundred were part of that original printing, so they're very rare, very valuable, especially in the condition my father's was in. Only about a hundred are known to exist now. And if Shakespeare's friends hadn't published it, the plays would have been lost forever. Forever. Doesn't the idea of something lost forever just make you want to weep? I don't like the word *weep* but it's the only word that will do."

"Oh, Dezzy." For the first time Abby's eyes were kind.

"It's like the thought of them tearing down all our buildings. How can you just flood a place as if it never existed?"

"I don't know, Dez." Abby peered down the hall that linked the vestibule to the theater. It was still lined with the handsomely framed, autographed photographs of the movie and stage stars who once flocked to Cascade because the summer stage gave them a certain cachet that Hollywood alone did not. These managed to impress her but not much else did, and when they entered the theater itself, Dez saw it, too, through Abby's eyes: the weak light illuminating the rows of empty seats, the stark angular balconies, the bare wooden thrust stage. The rich tapestries that hung high on the walls, above the paneling and between the ceiling beams, seemed to have lost their luster.

How different from how it once was. Her father had believed in reaching all the senses, so his productions were filled with color and noise and, when possible, with smells: smoke, perfumed oils, even hay bales reeking of horse urine.

He had designed the theater himself: a carved wooden masterpiece with thrust stage, tiered balconies, and oak columns. Tudor paneling and amber lanterns lined the walls. A gilt lion roared down from the strap-work ceiling. Through the years, magazines and newspapers had made much of "New England's bit of Elizabethan England," stories that always recounted how William Hart visited Cascade as a young man, how he and his brother had just cast fishing lines into the river when a commotion in the reeds led them to save a three-year-old child, wandered off from her family. Years later, in 1906, a career in theater abandoned at thirty, he was eastern superintendent of J. P. Morgan's New Haven Railroad and one day sat beside a young widow on a train. They got to talking, and, truth being stranger than fiction, she turned out to be the same Caroline Haywood whom William and Edward had saved from drowning. William was then forty-four years old, unmarried and restless, with enough personal wealth to leave the railroad and live a dream: to run a theater dedicated to producing the works of Shakespeare. He married Caroline and together they opened the Cascade Playhouse in 1908, the year the Interstate Commerce Commission began its infamous investigation of the finances of the New Haven Railroad.

Fate had gotten William Hart out of the corrupt railroad in time; fate had led him to Caroline. Fate would save the playhouse, he had believed. It simply had to.

Abby dropped her head back to read the words printed in gilt on the ceiling above the gilded lion. *All the world's a stage; And all the men and women merely players.* She wasn't the kind of person who faked enthusiasm. "It's so dead," she said. "So dead you'd never—"

The shriek of the train's whistle drowned her out. William Hart always had to stage plays around the train's timetable, so as not to have such a shriek interrupt a soliloquy or pledge of lasting loyalty.

Dez began to feel irritated. What did Abby expect? They were in the middle of a national economic failure, after all. And a theater that had been sitting empty was nothing like the nights it had seen, every moment changing from one production to the next, never exactly the same show twice. So different from the movies. She described Kathryn Tranero as Cleopatra in 1925, how the crowd stamped its feet so hard all the frames hung crooked on the walls the next day. "We had her here just as her career started to go crazy. My father contracted her that spring, then in summer *Queen of the Nile* came out. When she arrived in August, the newspapermen took up an entire floor of the hotel."

But it was like looking at a very old woman and saying, *She was beautiful in her youth.* And they both knew it.

"I suppose it's hard on you without Rose."

Dez blinked back sudden emotion. "That goes without saying." *I might live twenty more years*, Rose said, once it was clear Asa wouldn't offer her a room. *Can't last on savings all that time, can't risk ending up in the poorhouse.*

"If we could, I'd do it," Asa had said privately to Dez. But they were going to need those rooms eventually. Better for Rose to move to her sister's now, while she still had her health.

Dez remembered Rose, stoic and dry-eyed until the hour she boarded the train to Chicago, then her face crumpled in a way that Dez could still see when she closed her eyes.

On Spruce Street, Lil Montgomery bumped into them, on her way out of the Telephone & Telegraph office where she worked. Her hair was rolled up under a drab hat that was doing everything it could to take away from the smartness of the bottle-green tunic jacket she was wearing.

"Abby, you remember me talking about Lil. We've been friends all our lives. Lil, here's my friend Abby, from Boston." Thinking, *Please muster up some enthusiasm, show Abby that Cascade still is, at heart, a vibrant, welcoming place.* But Lil asked, oh, was Abby a woman artist, too—not even remembering who Abby was, though Dez had certainly mentioned her enough times. Lil sighed and said it was a shame Abby had picked such a dismal time to come, and Dez realized that Lil was always sighing—sighing if someone on the other end of the line took too long to give her the telephone number they wanted to connect to, sighing if Zeke was out of the butter beans she was counting on for her supper. All those sighs had had the effect of giving her chest a slightly collapsed appearance, as if it were just steeling itself for more disappointment.

"I remember you talking about her," Abby said when Lil was out of earshot. She suddenly squealed, and clutched Dez's wrist. "Wait—was she the one—?"

Yes. Lil was.

It had all come out in a terrible burst just before the wedding, a lashing out, a detailing of everything about Dez that had always bothered Lil. It had come out because Frederick Marsh, Lil's date for the wedding, left abruptly for Ohio for a chance at a forty-dollar-a-month job with the Civilian Conservation Corps, and because Dez made the error of confessing to Lil her mixed feelings about her upcoming hasty marriage.

Lil's spew had boiled down to this: *What kind of woman wouldn't be happy to be marrying Asa Spaulding?*

Had Lil harbored secret hopes regarding Asa? It seemed so.

"She apologized almost immediately. She's just one of those people who keeps things bottled up until she explodes, then embarrasses herself."

But Dez had been more unsettled than she had wanted to admit. What was the nature of a friendship that could sour so easily? It was the nature of life in a small community. People chose friends and spouses from the small, available pool. It did not matter which small town you lived in. You would find a friend, a spouse in any old place. The next day, when she stood in the vestibule of the Round Church with her mother's wedding veil tied to her hair and looked down at Asa, waiting at the altar, his brother, Silas, by his side, she considered that maybe Lil had been right—she had no business marrying Asa, but one foot in front of the other took her down the aisle, and before she could really take stock of it all, there she was with a ring on her left finger, with no idea that Jacob Solomon was about to walk into her life, and that her father would die a mere two months after the wedding.

Outside Stein's, standing under the *Mens Ladies and Children's Wear* sign, Abby stood with her hands on her hips, looking over the display window—three wooden torsos clad in sensible shirtwaists. "I just can't believe this is Cascade. Rudolph Valentino came here! And Lionel Barrymore."

"There's a new golf course opening. Everyone thinks that's a sign that good times are coming again." Dr. Proulx and two Boston men, a pair of executives and friends of the Boston mayor—men one would think knew a safe investment when they saw one—had bought the Clark estate on Route 13, near Whistling Falls. Since last year, workmen had been turning the 165 acres into a golf course, the fieldstone mansion into a swank clubhouse. Dr. Proulx's partners were men known for turning straw to gold, even in these times—especially in these times. They were building while building was cheap, biding their time.

But Abby's glazed eyes were back. She looked down Main Street, at the Brilliant Lunch Bar, the Handy Grocery, the Criterion Theater, and the Endicott Bank, which cautiously reopened after Roosevelt passed the Emergency Banking Act two years ago. "Why, it's just a small town."

It was. And now Dez felt its smallness, its loss of its old glamour. Even the historic Round Church, always marveled at by visitors, considered so quaint, simply looked like a round white building with a belfry on top.

At the end of Main Street, they crossed over Lake Street and paused on the bridge that spanned the Cascade dam. Water rushed down the ten-foot drop, drowning out their voices with the obliterating sound that had, since childhood, filled Dez with a fierce mingling of longing and affirmation. The thundering was like the word *yes,* like the word *go,* like staying awake all night in a city bright with electric light. The past few months, walking to town or back home again, the falls had been a kind of secret friend, reminding her, in a strange way, that life was still going on outside Cascade, that it would always go on. But now that she really thought about it, what good did that knowledge do her? She had been passive, waiting and hoping things would change.

Up River Road, past the closed-up summer homes with their chipped columns and falling slate, red auction flags waving in the breeze, she listened as Abby talked about old friends. Nelly Lodge married that boy from Yale, and no, no one from school was invited. Their history instructor, James Whittaker, was a curator in Washington now. "At the National Gallery, I think. Remember what a fuss he made over you, being William Hart's daughter? He always went on and on about Cascade. If he could see it now."

Had Abby always been so flip? Or was Dez herself the one who seemed different now that she was away from the crowd? She looked down into the churning foam streaming from the dam. All her life, she had been part of boisterous groups of girls without ever being very boisterous herself. Much of what had been her identity were aspects that had nothing, really, to do with who she was. Moneyed. Well-traveled. Daughter of a man with some renown. You took all that away and what did you have?

She considered. You had a person who'd known, ever since she could hold a pencil, that she had an innate ability to draw, and who wanted to do nothing else. That's what you had.

———◦◦◦———

The Spaulding home was a solid white farmhouse, the last house on River Road before acres of forest formed Pine Point, the craggy isthmus near Whistling Falls. It was the only inhabited home on River Road. Stiff brown grass was finally giving way to green. On the river, fog rose off the last of the ice remnants and moved in wisps around the birch grove. How silent it was, how silent it always was! There were bird sounds, water sounds. Sometimes the rustling of dry leaves. Sometimes rain. Once or twice an hour, trains rumbled across the river.

"Asa inherited this house after his mother died, which was two years ago," Dez said, holding the back door open for Abby. "But I still haven't lost the sense that I'm living in someone else's space."

Inside, Abby shook her head at the sight of the parlor, dark and full of wood and china bric-a-brac. "Oh, toots. It's awful! Why don't you throw it all out?" Along the west wall sat three claret-colored velvet stools that looked like kneelers in a Catholic confessional. Abby gave one a kick. "What the hell are these?"

A jumble that had belonged to Mrs. Spaulding. "Asa's one of those people who really doesn't like change," Dez said. "But I have to say he was generous about this." She opened the door to the studio, as bright as the parlor was dark. "It's got the steadiest light in the house."

Abby stepped inside, her eyes taking the measure of the workspace—the three easels and the long table cluttered with stretching supplies, jars of linseed and poppy oils, tins of paints and china plates, brushes, badger tools. The wooden shelves that bowed with the weight of books and photographs, and supported the drying racks below.

One easel contained a finished portrait of two sisters from Worcester, nieces of the New York Pullmans. A rare commission she had managed to snag, Dez said, although whether she would ever collect payment was another story. Twice, the mother had called in to pick it up, but money was tight, even for people who had plenty of it. The mother wanted to be sure the portrait was exactly right, and she was picky. First, she said that the color of Marjorie's dress wasn't quite right, that in real life the velvet was a much darker green. And then the younger girl decided she wanted her doll painted into the portrait.

Abby gave the two sisters a long look. "I can tell exactly what kinds of girls these are; you've managed to capture that, haven't you? They're spoiled, but they're not bad girls, are they?" She turned her attention to the other, new canvas: the squared-off view of grass. Seeing it anew, with fresh eyes, Dez's enthusiasm for it sank a bit. It wasn't quite right. The blades of grass needed to challenge the canvas's small size, appear to *spill* out of the boundaries. They weren't quite tall enough. Something.

It was an awful feeling—discontent. Especially when it happened in the middle of a social time. Because all you wanted to do was get back to work and try to make it right, but you couldn't. You had to put it from your mind. Either that, or become some kind of eccentric who did whatever she wanted, regardless of who was around, and then what kind of life did you have?

"I remember this," Abby said, reaching for a small framed portrait of Dez. "Miss Farrell did this during demonstration. She liked you."

"I liked her." And she liked that depiction of herself, the mix of chrome red and cadmium yellow wax crayon for hair forced somewhat unsuccessfully into the wavy style everyone else had worn so effortlessly. Harsh black strokes illustrated the rest: her lean body, her too-broad nose, her way of biting her lower lip as she worked, bent forward from the waist.

"She was a tough old bird." Abby knelt down and looked through the drying racks. She pulled out the low-key study of their old home that Dez painted when Jacob suggested she attempt to paint the senses. What are your favorite smells? he had asked. *Wood smoke in November, wind that is full of rain. A busy kitchen.*

"I like this."

Dez had used a narrow color range and soft-focus effects to convey the moody atmosphere of rain and twilight on the common, working at eliminating detail—trying instead to *distill*, to convey tone by letting the dark colors impose some compositional authority on the softer hues.

"You want to look and look," Abby said. "I'm not sure why."

"I know when my paintings are right," Dez admitted, even though she knew she risked sounding silly, or full of herself, "when I can look at them and ache with a kind of wonderful memory I can't quite place."

"I know what you mean." Abby studied it again before sliding it back into its rack. "Oh, I like this, too!" She pulled out one of the abstracted drowning studies that Dez had turned into a narrow, claustrophobia-inducing painting. "And this!" *Spanish Flu, 1918,* a small, square study of sturdy Rose, head bent, tending to Dez's mother and brother. The three figures were dark and shadowy, much like her memory of that time, the flu itself a static of eerie yellow air. A burst of vermilion, off-center, suggested a bedside spray of roses.

"Are you doing this kind of thing all the time? Such range. Good work, my dear."

"I'm trying. I suppose I'd like more portrait work, to bring in money, but—maybe I'm lucky times are so hard, and I live where I do. If I had nothing but portraits to do, I might get too caught up in them."

"We should all be so lucky."

"I mean it."

"I don't follow you."

"I'm afraid I'd find them too safe, too much of an easy trade for myself, especially now that I'm a wife."

Abby smiled with approval. "Right. You'd be able to keep yourself so busy you wouldn't have time to dig into what you want to say, and because you were so busy, you'd fool yourself into thinking you were getting an awful lot done."

"Exactly." Here was the Abby she had missed.

"So this is it," Abby said, lifting down Portia's casket to inspect it, to turn it over in her hands and hold it to her ear and shake it. "Doesn't it drive you mad? I'd want to peek."

"Sometimes. Sometimes I don't think I can wait. But it's doing what he meant it to do—remind me I have to reopen someday. And keep painting these portraits when I can get the work. Save what I can."

———◆———

In the kitchen, Dez perked coffee and sliced the last of the corned ham for sandwiches. She set down their two plates, and Abby regarded her solemnly, red-lacquered fingertips poised on the coffee mug.

"So what happened?" she asked, one hand gesturing to include everything, her dark eyes too scrutinizing. "You were the one who won the Cabot Prize. You got that write-up in the *Evening Transcript!* You're doing some wonderful painting but it doesn't look like you're doing a whole lot of it."

"I work every morning. And those red fingernails don't look like you do much painting yourself."

"We're talking about you. You always talked about Cascade this, Cascade that. And it's obvious Cascade is old news now—"

"It's different in summer. Or it was. And it will be again." She wanted it so desperately: the theater lobby filled, on play nights, with New York summer people. Her paintings, framed and on display. That was her only realistic chance of ever achieving any notice again. "When the summer people come back—"

"Oh, honey." Abby threw her hands into her lap and made her face a squish of "let's be frank" compassion. "I don't think they're coming back. Even if they don't build that reservoir, you know what? The place to be will be somewhere new. I can see that now, now that I'm here."

"That's not necessarily true."

"It's the way it always happens. Look—magazines are full of stories about how people are driving. Cars. More and more. All these roads and bridges Roosevelt's going to build all over the country? Vacationers might never come back here. And I hear that Lenox is nicer, quite honestly."

Cascadians liked to scoff at suggestions that Lenox could overtake Cascade in general popularity, but Lenox had a similar cultural bent and long history of moneyed vacationers. Lenox, once known as the "inland Newport," peppered with palatial "cottages," had clear lakes and nearby mountains, and easier travel routes from New York and Connecticut.

Abby jumped up. "Hey, I'm sorry. Let's cheer you up, do something fun," she said. "Get your pencils and paper. Do you still carry a pad in your pocket? We'll draw while we talk and see where our minds take us."

Freudian parlor games had been popular back when they were in school—everyone bent on tapping into his or her unconscious mind. Dez fetched pencils from her worktable, pausing by the newspaper clipping Abby had referred to. Abby was right. Even if that particular clipping was yellow and dry now, she *had* once been written up in the *Evening Transcript*. She *had* won prizes.

"So we talk and eat and draw," Abby said, her hand hovering over the paper. "Now tell me about this husband of yours. Will I get to meet him? You never said much about him when we were in school—what's he like? Go ahead! Draw!"

Dez scratched at the paper. No, she'd never said much at all. *Because I never expected to marry him, because even though I really liked him, I always felt we were too different to ever become serious.*

She gave Abby the rundown—how, after graduating pharmacy college, while Dez was in Paris, Asa had turned his father's dusty storefront into a modern drugstore. He'd put in a grill, a fountain, and a fancy oak-and-glass cigar case with an antique, piped-in gas lighter. But all the while she was talking she was remembering how proud he'd been to show off the store to her. She'd been truly surprised and a little unsettled to know he'd been waiting for her. She tried to make light of it, tried to discourage him. She was leaving again, she said, going to Boston, to a four-year program, and she thought she wanted to try New York after that. Promise you'll date other girls, she'd said, and he'd said he would, and he did, she knew that. But she suspected he had been secretly grateful when their fortunes turned upside down. It gave him the chance to step in and save them. The day she said yes to him was the same late-September day the sheriff knocked on the door, removed his hat, and said he couldn't put off the Springfield National Bank any longer. Dez asked how long did they have, and the sheriff said he could give them three weeks. He was a lumbering man with big hands, and eyes that apologized for everything his mouth was forced to say. "I'm afraid I'll have to put this up," he said, and pushed a red auction flag into the small patch of front lawn, where it flapped in the chill breeze blowing off the town common. It was the day of her mother's birthday—Caroline Hart, who hadn't lived to see forty.

"We do well enough. People still need medicines. A Coke is an affordable treat. And he barters a lot, especially with the farmers."

"No family of his own left?"

"A brother down in Hartford. Silas. He sees him about once a month, when he goes down there for supplies."

"Well, how about some tidbits? Is he good-looking? You know, you've never really said, never sent a photograph, which—"

"He's good-looking, if that's what matters." Dez realized she had drawn a face. One eye had become two, had become Jacob's. She quickly penciled in the skin, rubbing the lead back and forth, back and forth, making it Othello-dark.

"Of course it matters. You mean to tell me it doesn't to you?"

Asa was ten times better looking than Jacob, so no, it didn't matter. "He's good-looking in that Lucky Lindy sort of way. Though not as lanky."

"He looks like Lindbergh? That's good! How is he between the sheets?"

It was strange to be around someone so free-speaking again.

Abby's eyes scraped Dez's face. "No good."

"I didn't say that."

"You didn't have to."

"He's a little too eager," she confided. "I mean, clumsy. I feel like he goes at it with too much gusto." She laughed a nervous, embarrassed laugh, but it also just felt so good to confide in someone.

"Gusto," Abby said flatly, then burst out laughing too, so hard Dez felt hot and ashamed.

"I'm sorry, Dezzy. I just had this image—He wasn't possibly your first, don't tell me that! What about that fellow in Paris you told me about, what's-his-name? Pierre?"

Pierre Denis. She could barely recall him now, remembered only her own skin, mouth, hips, and what had been a heady, defiant testing and tasting of Paris. "No, Asa wasn't, not really, no, but—" They didn't hear the back door open, didn't realize Asa was home until he called out hello.

He filled the door frame, spectacles and gray pharmacist's coat making him look older than his thirty-three years, despite his clear face and bright blond hair. He removed his hat and nodded to Abby. He was welcoming and friendly. He said, "You finally made it to Cascade" and "I hear you're moving to New York." And Dez remembered something she definitely never liked about Abby: her way of instantly judging people. Oh, she was pleasant enough but she was soon answering Asa's questions with the kind of clipped courtesy she reserved for people who bored her, for men, in particular, who didn't react to her.

Suddenly Asa made a short, choking sound, noticing what they were doing, or rather, what Abby was doing. Dez looked across the table. Abby had drawn a violent, slashing-stroke sketch of a naked woman, legs open to reveal an obscenely abundant nest of hair.

It was shocking and embarrassing. Yet—why was it shocking and embarrassing to look upon such a nude? Why did it feel so violent? It was honest, that was all. No gently rounded body, no play of golden light upon skin. Sly Abby. *Let's see where our unconscious minds take us*, she had said, when each stroke, each line of her sketch had been deliberate and well-executed.

"That looks like one of Egon Schiele's," Dez said, trying for unfazed sophistication.

Abby smirked, taking pleasure in their discomfort. She coolly asked Asa what he thought of it.

A blush mottled his throat, then spread up into both cheeks; he looked twelve years old. He wasn't much of an art critic, he said, and pulled his gaze away and coughed, looking over Abby's head at Dez, eyebrows raised as high as they could go. Then he busied himself opening the icebox. "Anyone need anything? This tray's overflowing, Dez."

He babbled about the ice, getting out the green delivery card for the iceman, setting it in the window sideways for a full block. "In case you forget. Jeez, it's all water. Do you think this milk's okay?"

"The milk is fine, Asa." She got up and put a hand on his arm. "It's okay," she said. "I'll clean this up later."

Abby was speculative, watching them. "So, Asa, you have a drugstore," she said. "Now, I've always wondered what you druggists are *really* doing in those back rooms."

He blinked, not quite sure what she was saying. "Nothing but our compounding."

"Maybe I'd better take a tour and see for myself."

He hesitated. "I'll be pretty stacked up when I get back. Unless Dez wants to show you around?"

"She doesn't really want a tour, Asa." Wishing he would just go, or that he would rise to Abby's bait and give her a taste of her own sass. Something.

When he finally did go, they listened to his footsteps on the back porch, to the Buick's engine turning over. Abby cocked her head. "He does look like Lindbergh," she said. "I'll give you that, but is he always so serious?"

"You weren't very nice to him."

But Abby had lost the smug look. She leaned back in her chair, pulled a cigarette from her purse, and lit a match to it. She inhaled deeply and blew out the smoke in a long stream, regarding Dez with puzzled sympathy.

"With your father sick and all your money gone, you were a muddle, poor baby. You just jumped into the fire, didn't you? Got yourself married when we all vowed we'd have our shows first."

"As if having shows is just a matter of wanting them," Dez said quietly. "I made the right decision."

Abby jumped up and tapped her cigarette ash into the sink. "Look, honey, I don't want to upset you, but I think you're in trouble here! You took a wrong turn, understandably, because your father was dying and needed a place to live, but now you're walking down Wrong Turn Lane as if you can't do anything about it. You don't have babies. No babies means you can *leave*."

It was as if some exotic, preposterous bird had flown in the window and started to speak. "I couldn't do that to Asa, hurt him like that!"

"You stick around, you're going to have a pack of kids. Name a woman artist who had children."

There was someone, she was sure, but Abby didn't give her a chance to remember who it might be.

"See? You can't. No one who does anything seriously is also a mother. Unless you *want* babies."

"The thought of having one right now scares me to death," Dez admitted. Every month it was the same: bad dreams and nail-nibbling anxiety as she waited for the proof that she had escaped yet again. But how long could she keep risking fate?

The temptation to confess was too much. She told Abby how Rose— "Yes, that sweet old lady Rose, of all people"—with absolutely no self-consciousness, taught her, before she left for Chicago, how to calculate dangerous days: lying quietly with a thermometer, keeping charts.

"On unsafe days, I keep Asa away with excuses. On safe days I encourage him because a few raucous mornings in a row usually keep him content for a good long while."

"Good girl."

"I don't know about that. I don't know that it's forgivable."

"Oh, you're too hard on yourself. What about that artist friend you wrote about? What's he like? Tell me."

"If you're looking for scandal, you're not going to find it. Honestly, he's just a friend. And very talented. He went from studying with Lincoln Bell—"

"He studied with Lincoln Bell?"

Incredibly, Jacob had. And that wasn't the half of it, Dez said. When he got to the Art Students League, in 1929, John Sloan and Reginald Marsh were there and they encouraged him to get out and paint the streets. People liked his work, it began to sell. He did a show at the Painters and Sculptors Gallery. The New York School of Art invited him to teach. "Of course, when things got bad, they had to fire him, along with all the other junior instructors, but he says he's thankful, in a way, because that forced him to do all the traveling he did. I honestly don't know how I'll stand it when he leaves."

"Where's he going?"

She told Abby about Jacob's goal to return to New York as soon as he'd sold off his father's inventory.

"You're stuck on him, aren't you?"

"I'm not."

"You are." Abby narrowed her eyes. "I hear it in your voice."

Dez felt herself close up, become prim. "Thanks to him I'm ridding myself of that Boston 'formula' I was working in so completely after all the informality of the Paris school. I've really begun to loosen my palette again."

"That's not what I'm talking about and you know it."

But how to answer? One day back in February, Jacob had brought ingredients for egg tempera: a bag of dry pigment and an envelope of thick, crystallized salt ground into powder. The instructions were simple, he said: separate the yolk from the white, pinch the yolk over a bowl, add the pigment, mix in a small amount of water, not too much. Keep it sealed and work with small amounts, quickly. Easier said than done. They'd laughed at the mess they made until Dez caught sight of the broken shells lying in the sink. They had wasted half a dozen eggs. Other women were making eggless cakes and crusts. Dez Spaulding had wasted three days' worth of her husband's breakfast with another man in her husband's kitchen. Even though the two of them were mutually, wordlessly, careful not to threaten their easy camaraderie with flirting or innuendo, Dez had been troubled. What kind of relationship wasted eggs? Wasted anything?

"I don't know how to talk about him. We have a friendship—a very good friendship. He's never tried to make it anything else." And he never had. If anything, he was the one who backed off when their conversations got too intense, who put up the wall of caution.

"Have you?" Abby waited. "Cat's got your tongue? Well, what does he look like?"

The truth came out in a blurt: "The more you know him the better-looking he seems to get." Somehow those subdued looks and quiet mannerisms added up to something startling, the embodiment of one of Shakespeare's truths—*Love looks not with the eyes but with the mind.*

"Does he see anyone? Never mind. I can see by your face that he does, and you don't like it, do you?"

"Stop it, Abby. You're making too much of this. He's a normal man, of course he sees someone." And no, she didn't like it but she had no right not to like it, and anyway, it didn't seem to be serious. *Ruth and I just happen to have mothers who are ardent matchmakers*, he'd once said.

"Well, I just don't understand how you live like this. You studied in Paris. You grew up with a maid and a cook and a yardman! Really, my dear!"

"And who has a maid or cook now? Every dollar I can spare goes into art supplies or the fund to reopen the playhouse."

"Sell the playhouse, or worry about it later. Focus on yourself now."

"I would never sell it, even if there were such a thing as a buyer nowadays. And besides—" She hesitated.

"What? Tell me."

Dez admitted her father's misguided intentions regarding the playhouse.

"Oh, my dear. He *gave* it to Asa?"

"Well, he put it in trust for our firstborn."

"Oh, Dez," Abby said. "Cut your losses. Come to New York. We'll live together like we always said we would. We'll find a flat in Greenwich Village, we'll be real bohemians."

"Listen to you."

"I just don't see you with him. I don't see it at all."

"I'm hardly going to leave Asa because you don't 'see me' with him after meeting the man for all of ten minutes."

"Ten minutes was enough. And I'm not being cruel or flip, just being your friend."

In her quietest moments, Dez sometimes let herself wonder if she could ever really leave. First of all, there would be the awful stigma, and she couldn't help it, she didn't want to be a divorced woman. And every imagined conversation with Asa, every explanation, regardless of the words she used, would boil down to the same hurtful confession: *I married you so we would have a place to live. I didn't think through the consequences, didn't think ahead.* "Well, Asa's my friend, too. And I can't leave Cascade. I promised my father I would never abandon the playhouse, promised on his deathbed no less."

"Too many promises to other people."

"Maybe so, but I made them. And it's not like I have any means of support."

"You could make money doing illustrations. You have that Rockwell kind of skill. Some of the best illustrators are female."

"Oh, come on. Unemployment is still, what, twenty percent? Thousands of men—men with families—are without jobs, and someone would pay me to draw pictures? I don't think so."

Abby ground out her cigarette and leaned in close. "Listen." Her eyes glittered like a gambler's. "Have you read that book *A Room of One's Own?*"

"I've heard of it."

Abby spoke slowly as if she were offering some gift. "*She* says that a woman has to have money and a room of her own if she is going to write. It's the same for painting."

"I have a studio. We have some money. We're fortunate. *I* am fortunate."

"*Asa* has the money. He has this house. He has your playhouse unless you have a baby—my God, don't you see? You are heading toward a choice: sacrifice all for that playhouse or do what you were born to do and meant to do. And once a baby is born, that's it, there's no going back."

Dez looked away from Abby's straightforward gaze. She knew the reality of babies. When they were awake you had to tend to them, and when they were asleep, they never slept for long, and could never, ever be left alone. A baby went through twenty diapers a day—diapers that had to be scraped and scrubbed and bleached and rinsed and wrung out and hung to dry on wooden racks and radiators. Every day you had to sterilize a dozen glass bottles, and this on top of the regular cooking and cleaning, the weeding, the canning, the hauling out of the creaky old washing machine that always managed to bang into your hip and make you cry out with a curse.

"People divorce," Abby said.

"Not around here." Even the word sounded ugly: *divorce.* "Enough. What about you?"

"What about me?"

"What are you going to do down there in New York?"

"Now's a good time to move. If not now, when? You see your life leaving you, day after day, and you think, if not now, *when?*"

Abby was talking the way she used to hear Dez talk, reciting words from Dez's own mouth. *I went to Paris because I didn't want to look back one day and wish that I had.* She had taken someone else's philosophy and so made it her own that she was unaware of having done anything other than be what she considered herself to be.

Well, good for her. I should be flattered. And Abby was the unmarried, the unfettered one, the one who didn't have a theater hanging around her neck. "Good for you." Still, there was a pang that was partly envy, partly resentment, wholly wistful. "You'll be able to join the Art Students League."

"Not only that, but there's this new program starting up—the government is going to hire people to work at all kinds of jobs. Building bridges and roads, but to paint, too."

"To paint what?"

"To paint paintings, murals! To 'bring art to the people,' they're saying. It's called the Works-something-beginning-with-a-P program. Works—something. It's on the tip of my tongue. Don't look at me that way, it's true."

"Even if it is, what's the guarantee you'll be hired? I'd say mobs would be after those jobs."

"Then I'll be front of the mob," Abby said, cheerfully. "Works Progress Administration, that's it. And I was born in New York, so—" She grinned. "I'll claim residency somehow."

The banjo clock chimed half after one. "Damn it," she said. "I'd better get to my train."

———

They headed back to the station through a west wind, balmy and heavy with approaching rain. At the station, they arranged for Abby's luggage to be put on the 2:25 to New Haven, then sat on a slatted wooden bench to wait. The waiting room was quiet, filled with the click-click-click of the minute hand on the brass clock high above the ticket window. Dez said hello to a woman from Whistling Falls, to a man whose name she couldn't remember.

"So where can I write you, Abby? Where will you stay tonight?" The thought only just occurring. "You have enough money to last awhile, don't you?"

Abby didn't have much, she could tell.

"Here." Dez took out what she had and pushed the bills into Abby's hand.

Abby pushed them right back. "You're sweet but I'll do what I have to. I'll model for food, for a place to flop."

To flop! The woman from Whistling Falls made herself very still, listening. "You wouldn't model. You're just saying that to shake me up."

"I'm not."

"Well, you'll need to eat. Please." She tucked the money deep into Abby's purse and this time there was no objection, just a wordless look of thanks.

"There are always bananas," Abby said, with a trace of bitterness. "You can get a bunch of green bananas for ten cents. Did you know that? A bunch of green bananas can last you for days." Her tongue felt for a bit of tobacco on her lip as she pulled out a tube of lipstick. She circled her mouth red and pressed her lips together with a smack. "What I'm saying is, I can't count on anyone to take care of me but me. And if I do have to model, that's all right. I'm prepared to do whatever it takes."

From the Whistling Falls crossing two miles away came the faint wail of the approaching train. It arrived with a screech of wheels and metal-to-metal scraping.

Abby stood up and straightened her hat, smoothed her hands down her coat. "There's a revolution going on down there in the art world. The last two decades were just the beginning. I want to be there."

Dez wanted to be there, too. She trailed behind Abby to the platform, where the train's gasping metal was intent on drowning out their good-byes. Boydie Shaw, the conductor on the Connecticut Rocket who had looked after William Hart on many trips to the city, promised to take care of Abby, too. Abby accepted the hand Boydie offered, climbed the steps, and turned to smile down at Dez.

The train fumes were engulfing, reminding Dez of coming home from that trip abroad, so full of exhilaration, so *ready*. New York the ultimate aim. Like Jacob's ultimate aim. He was making progress toward his goal. The months would pass. Autumn would come and he would go. He would return to New York with a bit of money in his pocket and try his hand at the art scene again.

And within minutes Abby would be hurtling through the countryside, arriving in New York, muscling her way into some arty crowd. *A revolution. Art News* was reporting a turning away from Cubism, the hard times triggering a return to Realism. Thomas Hart Benton was the man of the hour, celebrated for his scenes of everyday life rendered in a sinewy, pulsating style. He and his followers were breathing new life into a representational style that critics were starting to call American Regionalism. He was teaching in New York, at the Art Students League, a place Dez imagined with "everyone's there but me" despair.

"I wish I could come," she said. "I'd do anything to be able to do what you're doing."

Abby's face lost its smile. She grabbed hold of the rail and leaned down to look Dez straight in the face, so close Dez could smell the smoke on her breath, could see the tiny vertical lines on her lips where the lipstick clung darker. "Would you? What would you do?"

5

The storm started dramatically, with a darkening of the kitchen and thunder that rattled the shutters. Rain spattered the windows as Dez put away the sketches that she and Abby had drawn, as she washed their plates and cups, scrubbing where Abby's lipstick had left a stubborn mark. She had expected Abby's visit to be cheerful, nostalgic, a little gossipy. She had even expected a bit of envy—she was, after all, married and living in a fine house with a studio of her own. Instead, Abby had turned her unimpressed eye on Asa; she had made sly remarks about Jacob.

Dez's mother used to quote Abraham Lincoln whenever Dez was feeling sorry for herself. "Most people are about as happy as they make up their minds to be," she used to say. Dez had to make up her mind to be content, to not be a wistful person, a person with regrets. One good thing about being away from art schools and other artists and movements and everyone else's ideas was that you weren't overly influenced anymore, you could wake up in the morning with your own ideas, listen to your own instincts.

So she never got to move to New York with Abby. She would just have to make New York come to her. Maybe she could do a bare-bones production, a single week of a single show—something, anything—next summer. Or a couple of matinees only, so that people from around the area could attend without staying the night. She wouldn't be that passive waiting-around-for-things-to-change person she had been lately. *I'm going to make things happen, starting now.*

She opened the icebox decisively. Asa would be feeling bad and she would start by making him feel better. She would make a nice dinner, put some extra effort in. She took two chops out of the icebox, seasoned them with salt, pepper—and leftover apple peel, there was an idea—then slid the pan into the oven. In the larder were four potatoes starting to go soft, the last carrots from the root cellar, one onion, and a small head of green cabbage. She would boil the potatoes and carrots and mash them with the onion to make a filling for the cabbage rolls Asa liked. Early on, she'd noticed the recipe in his mother's Fanny Farmer cookbook, its page stained and creased. The rolls she made had been a happy success; she would make them again.

And they would eat in the studio for a change. Add a bit of the unexpected to the daily routine. While the pan heated on the gas ring, she dragged a small, fold-up table from the hall closet through the parlor and set it with the Devonshire linen, the good silver. She put out a jar of apple butter that Asa had received in a barter. A hurricane lantern and her *Twilight, Cascade Common* painting on one of the easels set a tranquil mood. For a final touch, she tuned the radio in the parlor to the Bob Chester Orchestra, then stood there clasping her hands, looking with satisfaction over the scene she had set. And as the orchestra played, as evening settled over the house, she envied Abby a little less. Being by yourself, at night, in a city, was a lonely thing. She was happy for the bright overhead circle of light shining down on her kitchen, for the smell of the pork chops sizzling in their pan.

She was removing the cabbage rolls from the oven when Asa arrived home, peeling off his dripping slicker and stepping into the kitchen warily, with some sense of amusement, pretending to duck. "Is she gone?" He shook his hair, letting raindrops fly, then took off his spectacles and wiped them dry. "Whew. A bit unusual, I'd say." He removed a package of Lucky Strikes from his breast pocket and tapped out a cigarette. "But I suppose they were all like that at art school."

"Like what?"

He lit a match, lips clamped around his cigarette. "Oddballs!" He waved the smoke away from his face, pulled out his chair, and sat down with the evening paper.

She couldn't help herself. "I was at art school, Asa. Am I an oddball?"

"No, of course not."

"But I'm not so different from Abby." In another life she, too, would be on her way to New York.

He gestured as if to say the subject wasn't worth an argument. "Smells good, Dez. What are you making?"

"I'm not so different at all." Something perverse in her persisting.

He laughed aloud. "You're nothing like her. That picture she drew! Jeez. You start drawing stuff like that and everyone will start to wonder about you."

"What would they wonder?" She forked the chops from the pan, spooned out the cabbage rolls. The colors were too irritatingly bland. The plates wanted a third, deep color; she should have opened a can of spinach. "What would they wonder, Asa?"

"What was wrong with you."

"Why?"

"What she drew was obscene."

"Why do you say that?"

"Oh, come on!"

"What is the difference between that and, say, that big painting Dr. Proulx has hanging in his waiting room?"

He cocked his head. "Which?"

"You know, the one with the girl who seems like she's been drenched in sunlight, the one with the big red poppy. You can tell she's nude."

"Come on, Dez." His eyes asked, why was she arguing? He *saw* that she had been made uncomfortable by the drawing, too, by the fact that it was so clearly meant to shock. "You don't have to ask. Taste."

"Whose taste?"

"Everyone's. People's. Jeez, Dez." He wanted her to let him off the hook. He still had deliveries to make, plus evening hours to put in at the drugstore. Conversation at their table was usually a simple review of the events of the day. "That thing she drew—it was degenerate. *In my opinion.*"

He held the afternoon newspaper high to retreat behind its pages. The front-page headline was blacker, deeper than normal. **STORM CLOUDS GATHERING IN EUROPE**, and she was reminded of the strained, anxious times they lived in. *Be grateful for what you have. Didn't you just decide to make the best of things?*

She forced her voice into a gentler register. "Dinner's ready," she said, lifting their plates and cocking her head for him to follow.

In the studio, he stopped short at the scene she had set. "What's all this?" His eyes going straight to her belly.

Of course. When a normal woman found out she was expecting, she made a special dinner to announce it.

"Asa, no. It's not that."

"But—" He looked around, at the silver, the apple butter, the painting on the easel, before appealing to her with eyes that had turned cloudy. "But you've made everything so special."

"I don't have news, Asa. Not that kind of news."

"Oh." He pushed at the wire rims of his spectacles, then sat down and touched the sides of his plate, a gesture that made her feel guilty. Who did he have in the world, besides his brother, Silas, anymore? He wanted children, roots of his own, a family.

He looked up and gave her a bucking-up sort of smile. "What, then?"

"I just thought we'd have a change. Do something other than eat our supper in exactly the same way every night."

"I see." He hid his disappointment. He praised the cabbage rolls, praised the chops. "Juicy." She looked down at her plate to suppress the irrational shudder that the word *juicy* provoked in her.

From the radio came the sound of an audience clapping. There was a pause, the murmuring of a voice introducing the next song, then "Temptation" tinkling into the room: *You came, I was alone, I should have known you were temptation.*

She jumped up. This song always reminded her of Jacob. It made her feel wild and full of crazy longing that was pointless and stupid and wrong. "Don't you love this song?" She positioned herself behind Asa and rested her hands on his shoulders. She closed her eyes to sway to the melody. She wanted to be in love with her husband. She pulled him to his feet, making him lead her around the narrow space between the table and the wall, putting his hands to her hips so they would rest there. She looked up into his face, and saw that even as he was baffled by her, he was still crazy for her, and wasn't that a lucky thing? *Let him be enough*, she thought, relaxing against him, moving with the music, until he closed his mouth down over hers and then it was there—the knowledge—too late, that all this, of course, would lead to him wanting to go upstairs, and her temperature had spiked four days ago. Unsafe, unsafe.

He let go. He took a few steps backward and studied her for a few moments. "What is going on, Dez?"

Nothing. *I'm just a crazy person.* "Nothing."

"That's right, nothing." He composed himself before speaking, obviously trying to be nice, trying to be reasonable. "Dez, we've been married six months and nothing is happening and you don't seem to want anything to happen."

Why not tell the truth, she realized? Why not just tell him? "I'm not ready for babies, Asa, I'm just not. And I've been talking to Lucy Winters." Lucy, who had delivered three children in just under three years and was beside herself. "There's a doctor in Worcester where I can get fitted for a diaphragm."

He flushed at her use of the word. "Excuse me?"

"It will help us wait until the time is right."

"Why would we want to wait?"

"Why are *you* in such a rush for a baby?"

The question took him by surprise. He opened his mouth then closed it again. But she could think of a dozen reasons. Because an immediate pregnancy said a lot about a man's virility. Because he just plain wanted one. Because maybe, unconsciously, he feared she would indeed leave, like Abby had suggested. A child would tie her to him forever, they both knew that.

"We're getting old," he said. "I'm thirty-three. I don't think it's smart to wait. When my mother died, she died worrying about me, worried that I was wasting my time waiting around for you."

Dez looked away. "That sounds so bitter."

"Well, you were always breezing in and out of town, and she was always reminding me that my uncle Nat and his wife waited too long, and then, when they tried, it was too late. And I think for the number of times we've done it—" He flushed again. "For the number of times, something should have happened. I think something's wrong. I think you need to see Dr. Proulx."

"It's common for first children to take their time coming, you know."

"No, I don't know."

"There's nothing wrong, Asa."

The telephone rang, two quick jangling rings. Neither of them moved to get it.

It rang again.

She listened to his footsteps across the carpet, the hallway, the linoleum, the persistent double jangle, his hello.

Zeke, it sounded like he was talking to Zeke.

A rainy breeze blew in through the window and she turned to it, wanting to turn herself into it, into something that could float out a window. The hard rain had turned misty, a veil thrown over the night. Hairline cracks of lightning etched the sky, one after another like new constellations until one turned rigid and blasted bright for a full few seconds. The room lit up, catching the gleam and luster of Portia's casket, high on its shelf. *A child will make a difference in your life.*

"That's the truth," she said aloud. And thunder dropped like a boulder in reply. It shook the house, the plates on the table, it turned the radio to static. She backed reflexively into the doorway, looking around as if she might see a ghost. *Dad?* Was this some kind of sign? That her deception was wrong, her glass thermometer, hidden in her bedside drawer, was wrong?

Of course it was.

And there was her answer: the least she could do was be honest, tell him the truth, tell him there was nothing wrong, that she had been keeping charts. He would simply have to accept that she wasn't ready, give her a few months.

She walked into the kitchen with determination, with a cleansed and contented conscience. When the end of September came, when Jacob left, life would be grim enough. She would revisit the idea of a baby in the fall.

6

A sa was standing by the telephone box, the receiver still in his hand, looking at it with disbelief.

"That was Zeke," he said. "He said it's official. The legislature has passed the bill, it'll be in the Boston papers tomorrow."

It took a moment for Dez to comprehend the news, to grasp it and grasp at straws at the same time. "The project could still stall."

"No, they're pushing on. For some reason, it's all speeding up. Now they're on course to make a decision on which valley, us or Whistling Falls. Zeke's called a special town meeting for next Wednesday."

He was dazed-looking, but only in the way of someone who was quickly taking stock of his situation. "Why did I let people doubt me? We've been waiting around for months, and haven't I been saying right from the start that we should have been fighting this thing so that Cascade would never end up as an option like this? Wasn't that my instinct?" In January, Asa had tried to organize a protest trip to the State House, but people like Zeke and Dr. Proulx had urged him not to stir up trouble.

People in general were having a hard enough time as it was, they said. The threat would blow over; it had before.

"You can't blame yourself. We all hoped this was going to just go away."

"Well," he said, "we stopped them in '29, we'll just have to stop them again."

"But—" Or maybe he didn't know. "You do know the real story of why they pulled out of Cascade last time?"

He looked up, suspicion in his eyes—he had heard the rumors, had suspected there was a real story, known only by certain people. "Tell me," he said.

"Well, you remember Richard Harcourt." In the early twenties, Richard Harcourt, a vice president of the New York Stock Exchange, built one of the Greek Revivals on River Road. His wife and children used to spend their summers in Cascade; Harcourt would train up from Manhattan on weekends. He was one of the Cascade Playhouse's biggest patrons, good for large donations and dozens of tickets. Now he was in prison.

"Harcourt put in a quiet word to the governor back when the water commission was doing that second round of surveys and recommendations," she said. "He got the state to back off Cascade. He didn't want his summer place destroyed."

Asa raised his eyebrows with amusement, with relief. "Oh, come on. I heard those rumors, but one person's word wouldn't have been enough to squelch a major plan like that."

"It's true." Her father had been privy to all of it. "Governor Fuller was an arts patron. He came to a performance here more than once. He cared about that sort of thing. I happen to know he owns a Renoir and a Boccaccino. And of course at the time no one thought it made a lot of sense to build so far from Boston."

"It still doesn't."

"No." But it was kind of like death after a long illness. This uncertainty that had been hanging over their heads like an ax; well, it would be a relief, in a way, to finally *know*, one way or the other. If the state did choose Cascade, the fight could start in earnest. Either that, or—or what? They could accept the inevitable? No.

"They'll take Whistling Falls, Asa. It simply makes more sense."

"Our elevations are lower," he said, as if she hadn't spoken. "Our water levels higher. Most of Cascade borders the river. Our valley is a more natural bowl shape. Except for that chunk on the east, and I bet they'd take just a bit of Whistling Falls to fill it all out. I bet they would. The site work's done, too. All those surveys they did in the twenties. Once they make their decision it won't take long for them to get down to work."

He was too agitated to sit with the coffee he normally enjoyed after dinner. He lifted his coat, still slick and wet, off the coat rack and opened the back door. The rain had stopped and the night air was fresh with the smell of earth and river water. He stepped out onto the porch and raised his arms, an appeal to the heavens. "It's impossible. They simply can't do this!"

The yard was cluttered with dead branches. Among the debris was a Baltimore oriole's socklike nest at the bottom of the steps. Asa crouched down to pick it up and set it on the porch railing.

"That same family of orioles has come back to that nest year after year," he said grimly.

"I hope it's not a sign—"

"Oh, hush!" He said it so harshly she felt slapped. He'd never spoken to her like that. But he didn't apologize, just started across the lawn, then turned to shoot her a savage look. "What's the attraction to people like that Abby person, anyway? Why don't you socialize with the women in town?"

"Well, I—"

"What's wrong with Lil Montgomery?"

"Well, she—" Asa knew she had gone to boarding schools, for goodness sake, that the local girls were nice enough, but they had grown up with Dez Hart out of sight, out of mind. And now they were all busy with babies.

"I want children and I want Dr. Proulx's opinion why they're not coming, damn it. I'm entitled to that! I'm a little sick of my friends looking at me like—The house a disaster." His voice rose. "My wife's only friend the traveling Jew-man."

Dez went still. Asa had never seemed to notice Jacob, never mind insult him. "The house is *not* a disaster" was all she could manage to say.

He didn't respond, didn't look back, just strode across the lawn, got into the Buick, and skidded away as if it were her fault the state wanted to drown them all.

She stood in the doorway long after the sounds of the car had faded. Did people know about her friendship with Jacob? Were they talking about it? Laughing? It gave her a pang to know that people would. As a child, she had once referred to old Mr. Solomon as the Jew-man, like she had heard people do. Her father had used the opportunity to pull out *The Merchant of Venice*. He'd condensed and clarified, and even though Dez was only eight, she'd followed the gist of the story. She had imagined the pound of flesh as something neat and square, wrapped in paper and tied with twine, like lard, and was delighted with Portia's shattering of that image, delighted with Portia's cleverness. She wanted to know why her father hadn't named her Portia instead of clumsy old, silly-sounding Desdemona, but he said only that her mother hadn't liked the name and reread Shylock's speech again, intent on driving home his point. *If you prick us*, he read, *do we not bleed? If you tickle us, do we not laugh? If you poison us, do we not die? And if you wrong us, shall we not revenge?* Her ears pricked up at the word *revenge*, thinking that her father was preparing her for some wonderful act of retribution that Mr. Solomon would perpetrate on Cascade. None came, of course. Mr. Solomon took no offense; the townspeople meant none. Innocents all, her father used to say, *but Dez, innocence is the excuse of the ignorant.*

———

She was in bed when she heard the car pull into the driveway, the back door opening, the sound of rustling downstairs. She opened her bedside drawer and gazed down at the thermometer, closing her thumb and forefinger around the cool glass. How easy it would be to snap it, to release the puddle of mercury, to say, yes, Asa, I'm ready for all that you want. But she shut the drawer and shut her eyes, slid under the sheets, and pretended to sleep until he came in and turned out the light and pretended to sleep, too.

She woke to morning sun and the scent of soap, to the breeze of his body standing over her. He sat down on the edge of the bed; he took her hand. The pads of his fingers were rough where they made contact with the stone pestle day after day.

"I'm sorry," he said. "I shouldn't have taken my frustrations out on you."

Thanks, she started to say.

"But here's the thing," he said. "I think it might be best if Jacob Solomon didn't come here anymore."

She moved to sit up, to look him clearly in the face. "Asa, we've done nothing wrong."

"I didn't say you had."

What, then? "Has someone said something?"

"I'm saying something, saying I don't think it's the best idea for my wife to be alone with a man who shares her interests. It's a recipe for disaster, and I think I've had my head in the sand about it."

"But it's our work we have in common. He's just a friend."

His eyes were steady. "I'm not stupid, Dez."

No, he wasn't. But neither was she, and she forced herself to hold his gaze, to show her innocence. She'd been careful. She hadn't done a thing wrong and there was no reason why she should have to give up her friendship. "You can think what you like but you're wrong. And he'll be gone soon enough anyway."

"I don't care. I don't want him here." He got to his feet. "And that's the end of the matter."

"But he's coming today. What am I supposed to say?"

"Say anything. Tell him—tell him you want to meet in town from now on. Maybe you could start something, Art Hour or something. Ask Betty if you can run it at the library. That's it. Get other people involved—school kids—send some kind of message to the state, do up some posters maybe." He looked to her for approval, pleased with the idea. "Now, there's a way you can help. We've got to fight this any way we can. I've actually decided to band a few people together to figure out a way to fight this. The men in this town who won't buckle under."

And then he was gone, turned on his heels, down the stairs, and out the door. And like echo was the memory of Abby's voice: *Asa's house. Asa's money. He even has your playhouse.*

7

She heard Jacob's knock vaguely, as if from under water. Then again, louder. "In the studio," she called, rubbing paint from her fingers with an oily rag, rehearsing what to say. *Asa's asked me to ask you not to come here anymore. Asa's starting to get concerned about the time we're spending together.* It all sounded so awkward; it would force them to imagine an intimacy that would embarrass them both.

And then there he was, standing in the doorway, hat in his hands. "Hello."

"Hello." It was always like this to start: quiet, cordial, eyes connecting. It was as if they acknowledged something they couldn't put into words or act on, then moved forward with civility, as modern people, a man and woman who could simply be friends.

Or maybe she imagined all that.

In any case, they were easy with each other. She stepped away to reveal her canvas, to ask what he thought. And as he studied the new painting, she, with the fresh perspective that even a few minutes could give, saw how the light would need to fall much more significantly on that foremost blade of grass. The viewer's eye needed to be drawn to that blade, forced to reflect on how alike it was to all the others, while still uniquely itself. She needed to add something, a drop of dew perhaps, glistening and fat.

"If you add some aureolin yellow to the undersides of that blade, some flake white to the tip, just there," he said, pointing, "you'll get the intensity you're after. Without the muddiness." He tipped his head as if to say, *Go on.*

She did what he suggested and the look of the blade changed—it became more dimensional, more emphatic, more what she was after. "That's it! I want the viewer to first look and see 'grass,' and then look closer and mull on the fact that this blade—here—is different. And to wonder why. But I have to make it stand out even more, don't you think? I thought of adding dew, and one of my thumbnails had the river as backdrop, but I have such a hard time with water." She gestured to the west window, with its view to the river as it curved sharply toward town. River water was ever-changing and now the weather had been mild enough that it was flowing freely, the last specks of winter ice evaporated.

"Water's hard." The sun peeked out and a patch of river briefly spar-kled white, as if to make his point. "And there's no 'right way,' of course. But what you want to do is look for its different colors," he said. "Differ-entiate them. There's the color of the sun's reflection, first of all, which will hit at sharper angles than the color of the sky's reflection, or the clouds'. You ask yourself, is the water transparent? Here, we're too far away to worry about whether we can see the bottom, but if we were closer, it would affect the color we chose. You ask yourself, what color are the shadows? Because each ripple casts its own distinct shadow."

How easily he made suggestions, articulated techniques. But he shrugged as if it were nothing. "Lincoln taught me about water."

"The image I have of Lincoln Bell is so far removed from 'patient teacher.'" No one had known Lincoln Bell, never mind studied with him, but Jacob's father had somehow finagled an agreement, driving his son down two hours of dirt roads and at least two flat tires a trip to Lincoln Bell's Connecticut studio once a week, from the time he was sixteen until he went down to New York in 1926.

"Oh, he wasn't nearly so ornery as the public believed." He went quiet, almost somber, and she wondered if bringing up Lincoln Bell had somehow been a mistake. "But people often want to believe the worst of people, don't they?"

"I suppose they do," she said uncertainly.

He looked away with an attempt at a smile. "Sorry. It's just that we got some bad news from my cousin Brieghel today."

Jacob never talked about Berlin—he had plenty of stories about the print shop in Amsterdam, and Spain, which he'd loved, and London, where he had stopped to earn traveling money. But about Berlin, where he'd spent months with Brieghel and his wife, he'd said almost nothing at all.

"What news?"

He shook his head as if he'd rather not elaborate, and Dez's mind turned to the latest stories coming out of Germany, the kinds of stories you read sidelong in the newspaper, sliding away from the words even as you took them in, telling yourself that things couldn't really be as bad as they were made out to be.

"So everyone's talking about the big meeting next week," he said.

"There's a very good chance they'll take Whistling Falls, but Jacob, is your cousin all right?"

He chewed his upper lip, as if deciding whether to speak. Then he said, "His wife wants to leave. She thinks they should get to England while the getting is good."

"It's really that bad? Will they go?"

"He's going to give it a few more months, through the summer, hope for the best. In the meantime, try to put money aside. That shop is everything to them."

"You must worry."

"He doesn't think it can go much further. I guess a lot of people don't. They think the Nazis are preposterous, and deluded if they think they can get away with all this. I was there during that boycott of Jewish shops and businesses, and it was all very unpleasant but no one really took it seriously."

Still. "It must have been terrible," she said quietly.

His face seemed to shadow. Dez would one day try to sketch that shadow—it was a certain lowering of his eyelids, a setting of his lips.

He walked over to the window, put his hands in his pockets, and looked out for a few moments. Then he spun around with an air of decisiveness. "Let's talk of pleasant things," he said. "Did your friend end up coming?"

"She did, and I was thinking this morning that it seems like more than just yesterday that she was here." When weather changed abruptly, transitioning to another season within hours, time felt altered. Abby arrived during what still felt like winter, and then in a matter of hours, spring had arrived with warm wind and rainstorms. Even now, the room was darkening with another spring storm.

"I'm a bit concerned about her. She doesn't have a job to go to, doesn't have any money."

"Brave of her. Or foolish."

"That's what I thought. Although, it almost seemed like she was hiding something. I don't know."

"Maybe she has a fancy man." He smiled at her surprise. "Is she that kind of girl?"

"She did say she would model if she had to."

"Well, there you go."

Dez wondered if she'd been naïve. Maybe a secret lover was the reason Abby had been so reticent. "She does pride herself on being a bit wild. Her only definite plan was to join the Art Students League."

"Is she talented?"

"A bit too derivative perhaps, but she's good, yes." She headed to the shelf where she'd put Abby's sketch, then stopped herself. Asa had nailed that right; she was a bit embarrassed by it.

"Dr. Proulx commissioned another painting," he said. "He seems to have taken an interest in me. I'm not sure why, I don't have the most colorful palette in the world, and his taste seems to run to the less gritty side of life."

Dr. Proulx's waiting room was filled with paintings, including Dez's *After Rain*. "Oh, he's such a big-hearted soul. I think he'd buy a scribble from the traveling man." She realized what she was saying before it finished coming out of her mouth. "Not you, of course—"

But Jacob laughed.

"You look like his son." Paul Proulx, killed by a sniper while stringing telegraph wire along the western front. She had only snippets of memory, but there had been something similarly smoldering and intense about Paul.

"Yes, he's told me. He talks about him a good deal. Well, he's asked me for a Jewish painting, whatever that means."

She smiled as if she was in on "whatever that means." But all this talk of Jewishness raised questions—simple, curious questions—that she didn't feel were polite to ask. What was it to be Jewish?

He walked over to the bookshelf and lifted down Portia's casket. "Maybe I'll paint him a Shylock, with all of Shakespeare's ambiguity." He gave the box a shake and turned it upside down. "I wonder where I'll be," he said, almost to himself, "the night you open this."

Why did she feel startled? "It would be nice if you were in the audience," she said, even as it struck her how unlikely that really was. In New York, he would be a world away. He would make the trip to see his family maybe once or twice a year. They lived in Springfield, more than an hour from Cascade. A visit to Cascade would have to be planned, fit in. It would never happen. They would lose touch.

"Well, I'll certainly try," he said, "and hopefully someday you'll attend some gallery opening of mine. Who knows? Maybe someday you'll move to New York too, like you always thought you would."

"Asa would never move to New York." The utter, depressing truth. And now was the time to say it, to tell him Asa didn't want him to come anymore. She couldn't get her tongue around it.

"He may have to move somewhere."

"It's still more likely they'll take Whistling Falls, don't you think? And Dr. Proulx and his partners have spent this entire past year building a golf course. Those men *must* know something. Why would they invest in it otherwise?"

"No idea."

"They must be certain—"

"Nothing in this world is ever certain, Dez." He said it mildly; he was simply stating a fact.

"Well, regardless, the clubhouse is already open. It's beautiful. Have you been up to see it?"

"No," he said, with a clipped chill in his voice that confused her until it hit her what it meant, and then she became an idiot who babbled. "I just don't think the kind of men who built it would have invested in something unless they knew the reservoir *wasn't* coming. Some kind of privileged information."

The subject needed changing. She jumped up and planted herself in front of her easel. "Add something," she said boldly. "Whatever you think. I'm curious—this canvas is just an experiment."

He stayed where he was, demurring, and she said, even more boldly— it was so unlike her to be this bold, especially with him—that it seemed important that if someone was trying to express a truth they couldn't quite get, well, if someone else could help, why not? "What is the point of art, anyway? To feel things only for yourself, or to somehow share these raptures and insights?" God, she sounded ridiculous. She pushed the brush, one of her Senneliers from Paris, into his hand. Their fingers met, and she had to look away to hide her feelings.

"Such a perfect brush," he said. The handle was extralong burnished wood, with cupped filbert hog bristles.

"Isn't it?" In Paris, she'd loved Sennelier, its cramped aisles, loved opening tubes of paint and inhaling them, fingers itching to squeeze them. Paris was a memory even more remote than Boston. Not quite real anymore, that year and a half of classes, the school's high-domed studio, sharing the tiny rue de Fleurus flat with the wry and wonderful Jane Park from Bristol.

Jacob would be like this, and soon: gone, turned to a memory, not quite real.

"Okay, then." He slipped his thumb through her palette and went after the tips of grass, the brush poised between his fingers, feathering the paint to the canvas. As he worked, he caught the tip of his tongue between his teeth. His lips were sharply cut, the lower lip full and dark, and watching him paint suddenly seemed the most erotic thing Dez had ever seen. She flushed instinctively, hard and red, then thought: *It's okay to look, to admire. I'm doing nothing wrong.*

When he stepped back, she was startled: the predominant blade of grass was the only blade of grass in the world. He could make a single brushstroke take the place of five.

"You're so good."

"So are you." He handed her the brush, the palette. "And you are much too hard on yourself."

She shook her head. She was thrilled for him, but he did so easily what she had failed at, so her thrill was pricked by—something. Not envy, maybe despair. She turned her face up toward the ceiling and briefly closed her eyes. Why was perfection so hard to attain? You had an idea for something, you clearly saw how it should be executed, yet your execution fell short of your vision.

"It was your idea," he insisted, amused by her reaction. "I only helped with a very small part. That's why I was a decent teacher, I suppose."

Surely there were people—like Pablo Picasso, thirty years of masterwork and still young enough to have decades ahead of him—who were geniuses from the first breath, who were one in a generation, who could do it all on their own. Yes, there was a bit of despair, to realize you were not like that, but there was some camaraderie, some relief in finding another person like yourself. There was still the possibility of the some-time achiever, or the person who managed to produce one grand work in a lifetime. Something being better than nothing.

"Dez, stop. You have a gift for composition that people either have or don't have. A natural ability to draw. An eye for color. I can't believe you're getting so upset."

He peered at her. "It's something else. What is it?"

This was the only Art Hour she wanted. They had so few left anyway. And once Jacob was back in New York, these Thursdays would seem remote, maybe even quaint to him. He had once caught the attention of Sloan and Marsh; it was only the fault of the Crash that he'd lost his job. He would make a life again in New York, no question.

She shook her head but he held her gaze, and something passed between them. *You are going to leave. And go to New York, where I was supposed to have gone.*

"You know," he said, "you sometimes remind me of a painting by Dante Rossetti. You just did, the way you looked up and closed your eyes. The light made a kind of halo around your hair."

"Really?" Hadn't the models for all the Pre-Raphaelite paintings been pretty much the same—ethereal, long-haired? Dez's hair contained the requisite red tones but it was unruly, shoulder-length now. And her features were modern-looking: strong nose and chin, clear eyes. Far from ethereal. In fact, she often felt like the subject of an early Picasso, the plate of which sat in a book on her studio shelf: a downtrodden woman slumped over an ironing board.

"Wait," she said. "Elizabeth Siddal?" The famous Pre-Raphaelite model Elizabeth Siddal had been Rossetti's wife. "Ophelia in the Millais? Dead? You think I look like that?"

He laughed. "Yes, her, but no, not that one. The particular painting I'm thinking of is *The Death of Beatrice*, from Dante's *Divine Comedy*. I saw it in London. Do you know it?"

She did not. He told her: how Dante Alighieri had idealized a Florentine woman named Beatrice who died young. After her death, he immortalized her in his *Vita Nuova*. Six hundred years later, when Elizabeth Siddal also died young, Dante Rossetti used her as the inspiration for a painting of Beatrice.

"It's a stunning painting, in person," he said. "It glows." He shrugged. "Beatrice glows. I couldn't take my eyes off it."

Was he flirting or simply making a statement? Something was happening and she wasn't sure it was real. Even so, her pulse began to race. She wracked her brain but couldn't come up with any memory of the work. "When I was growing up and overly romantic, I loved the Pre-Raphaelites," she said. "I loved all the Ophelia paintings, especially John Williams Waterhouse's. The Pre-Raphaelites loved Ophelia."

"Ophelia, the perfect subject. Content to lie still, hair streaming among lilies and frogs for generations of us painters."

She told him about the summer her father staged *Hamlet*, how obsessed by Ophelia she'd been that year. "I put on a filmy white nightgown and carried hydrangea blossoms down behind the playhouse and floated in the river, the blossoms all around my head until my father found me and yanked me out of the water. I was twelve, and I'd seen death and was trying to understand it, I suppose. It was one of the only times he got really angry with me." She began to laugh. "And he was especially angry that I would choose to impersonate, as he put it, one who 'lacked moral strength,' or something or other."

It felt good to laugh. He laughed, too. "You know," she said, "the only Rossetti painting I can clearly see in my mind's eye at the moment is one of a redhead combing her hair, and she was frightening-looking, as I recall."

"*Lady Lilith*. His wife didn't model for that. His mistress did. That's another whole story. The reason Lizzie Siddal died young was because

Rossetti was unfaithful. She overdosed on laudanum. Afterward, he was so consumed by guilt that he reworked the painting to make *Lady Lilith* look more evil. Or so the story goes. And of course the real Lilith *was* evil, anyway."

"Real Lilith?"

"According to Talmudic legend, Lilith was Adam's wife before Eve."

And what, she wondered, was Talmudic legend? "You're joking. I have never, ever heard of a wife before Eve."

"It's true. Supposedly she was cruel and beautiful and she had no soul."

"Well, I'll tell you the painting you remind me of. You look nothing like her except—"

"Her?"

"Except when you smile. You have an inscrutable, Leonardo kind of look to you."

He laughed again.

"It goes away when you laugh."

"Then I'd better laugh more often."

———

She walked him outside, barely aware of another approaching storm, of thunder rolling up from the west, of the wind on her face, of her bare feet. Old leaves blew and skittered along the grass. "I'm going to try water, thanks to you." She would paint a portrait of the playhouse on the river while it was still real, while she could still capture, precisely, how the river light fell on the clapboards and made the water reveal its depths.

"Good," he said. And he put a hand on her shoulder in a casual way that might have been its own sort of question, a question that she answered by letting the hand rest there.

"Well, then," he said, after a moment. "Until next week."

When the truck rumbled away down the drive, the sounds of starlings and blackbirds returned, the slopping of river water against rocks. Dez was left with the cold fact of herself, her feet on flattened grass that was fast collecting dew. She didn't know whether it was excitement she was feeling, or panic.

8

Whatever she was feeling, it was a feeling that wanted either release or it wanted constant stoking, like a fire. Left to burn out, it made for ragged nerves, for irritability and vacillating emotion, for a husband who hovered at suppertime, asking too many times whether she was feeling all right.

"I'm fine," she told him, and waited anxiously all through the meal for him to ask about Jacob. She was ready to make a stand, defend her decision and the friendship, but he never said a word about him, and that in itself was irritating. He'd simply assumed she would do as she was told.

He did finally ask about Art Hour, as he was putting on his jacket to return to the store. "Did you talk to anyone at the library about doing the posters?"

"No, I didn't," she said. "I think it's a little late for posters, personally."

He blinked at her sharp tone, and looked up from his buttons. "I suppose that's true," he said, reaching for her shoulder, giving it an absent-minded pat.

Don't *pat* me, she wanted to say, but then he'd think it was her time of month, which in turn might bring up more talk of a visit to Dr. Proulx. Best to say nothing and keep the peace.

———✦———

Wednesday night came quickly. At Town Meeting, people looked for space on windowsills, on stairs, they crowded five-deep in the back of the auditorium. The night was spring-humid, doors and windows thrown open to the earth-smelling air. It was a smell associated with giddy promise, and appreciation, with nothing to look forward to but summer.

But not this night, not this particular unsettled spring. Inside the hall, the sound of chairs scraping and the echoes of voices filled the rafters, everyone eager to get on with it.

Dez arrived late. She scanned the crowd for Asa but didn't see him. He was probably up front; he was the kind of man who arrived early and sat in the front row. If so, he would have saved a seat for her but she wanted to stay back, observe. Clutching her sketchbook and pencil, she squeezed into a spot by the rear wall, up against a radiator, behind a gaggle of young mothers, Elsie Smith and Lucy Winters, and Ginnie Miller, who tried to catch her eye. Dez pretended not to notice. Ginnie, still swollen from that baby she delivered in March, was one of those women who always made a point of resting her hand on her belly, regardless of whether it harbored anything more than breakfast, to ask if anything was new. And there was Lil Montgomery, standing uncertainly at the door— another one trying to avoid Ginnie. It was hard for Lil, being the only unmarried girl their age, though Dez had run into her two days ago and Lil, her hair freshly marceled, had gone on about an upcoming date with a man who sold ink ribbons to the telegraph office.

More people crowded into the room, the buzz of chatter growing louder. Heads turned this way and that. Word went around that the superintendent of schools had initiated a children's letter-writing campaign to the state house and that Johnson Post, the pastor, had announced that all services would now be opened with a prayer for the preservation of Cascade.

Onstage, Zeke, the chairman, hunched over a long wooden table with the two other selectmen, Hartwell Page and Peter Southwick. Clara Post, town secretary, bent over her notepad, scribbling, eyeglasses sliding down her nose, managing to seem both attentive to and oblivious to Zeke, who was talking in his animated way, stabbing at the air with a cigar, a stream of smoke trailing his gestures. Zeke had a gift for elegant gestures and elegant diction; he had once played the lovable, lying Falstaff in a production of *Henry IV,* the only time William Hart ever hired a nonprofessional actor. But Zeke had insisted he'd make a good Falstaff and he had, playing Falstaff comically, pathetically, brilliantly. At a few minutes past seven o'clock, he walked to the center of the stage and clapped his hands. A chain of coughs echoed around the room. Dez sketched him in a few short strokes, a caricature from a political cartoon—growling demeanor, fat cigar in his mouth, buttons about to pop off his vest. Shoes scuffled, chairs scraped, then the audience hushed and all eyes turned toward the stage.

Zeke spoke into the fat microphone. "Basically, my friends," he said, his voice booming out through the window where it was carried away on the evening air, "we are between a rock and a hard place. The bottom line is that 1929 and our once-illustrious summer resident, Mr. Harcourt's, once-influential political connections lulled us into complacency. Now Mr. Harcourt is cooling his heels in Sing-Sing and Cascade is facing abolition."

There were murmurs—Richard Harcourt's help had always been nothing but rumor. "Back at the New Year when the state announced they'd chosen the Cascade River, those of us in the know hoped that, with the economy the way it is and all, that the project, being so large, was going to be pushed back a few years, at least, and then maybe even forgotten. Until they passed the legislation, nothing was official. Well, now it's official. And except for those two storms last week, we have had another dry month," Zeke said. "The farmer's almanac is calling for another hot summer. There's a great deal of fear and anxiety over the water problem in Boston, and since a reservoir will take years to fill once it's constructed, there is a very big push to get this ball rolling."

A growly shout erupted from one of the rows. Dr. Proulx rose to his feet, one hand heavy on his silver-topped cane.

"I am seventy-four years old," he said, his reedy voice tight with anger, "and I have seen drought and never-ending rain and pestilence and every manner of storm, and let me promise the Commonwealth of Massachusetts that the law of averages always wins out. This drought will end and will be followed by the kinds of rainy summers that towns like Cascade lament."

He's right, he's right, everyone turned to his neighbor to say. Addis Proulx was always right.

Zeke raised a hand for the hall to quiet down. "Addis, I am sure you are right, and we all have high hopes that your golf course will change some minds, but unfortunately the Commonwealth of Massachusetts isn't listening, nor are we dealing with reason here. What we're dealing with is fear, always a formidable enemy. Fear and uncertainty that wasn't a factor in the twenties. Secondly, we are dealing with a bureaucratic elite that is taking advantage of that fear, dreaming up elaborate schemes to solve problems in order to provide jobs for their friends.

"Now, remember who our governor is, good people." Zeke stabbed his cigar into the air to make his point. "He is no patron of the arts, like his predecessor. He is Mr. James Michael Curley and the few piddling votes he can get out here don't matter much to him. And as I implied, there's talk that he not only wants to take our valley, but I've heard, through people I know I can trust, that he's been telling his local voters he'll bus them out here to get them jobs. This will be a political coup for the Boston politicians—oh, it will make them all look good. I can hear their slogans now."

So that was the real reason. Dez looked out over the crowd. Instead of anger and outrage, she saw quiet, defeated faces. *We've been living with bad news for so many years now,* the general silence said, *here is one more piece.* Bad news had simply been the stuff of normal life for too long, newsreels and radios delivering gloom nonstop: strife in Europe, dust storms obliterating the western prairies, city bread lines filled with the out-of-work.

From outside, a boy jumped up—high schooler Popcorn Webster, his face at the window for just a flash, hand cupped to his mouth. "Which will it be, though? Cascade or Whistling Falls?"

Everyone laughed; Zeke shook his head. "We just have to wait and see, folks. You'll be seeing the surveyors around town again, the engineers, working out of the old boys' camp. As you know, the 1927 legislature created the water commission and both the House and Senate passed the water bill back in 1928. So a good deal of the surveying has been done—but you all remember that." He gestured to a stack of heavy, thick binders behind him on the selectmen's table. He picked up one of the binders and dropped it with a heavy thud. "*Most* of the surveying, I'm afraid."

Again, there was silence, as everyone remembered how the water commission's engineers had, for a time, kept an office above Stein's store. They'd surveyed every square inch of town property and roads, they'd drawn up maps. After the water bill passed, everyone expected the bill appropriating the Cascade River would be next. Cascade appeared doomed. Then the Richard Harcourt rumors started, the threat disappeared, and once it was gone, everyone had been happy to forget about it.

"What's left is formalities," Zeke said. "Deciding which valley is best suited to a dam—which valley has higher elevations, less ledge, better whatever-they-are-looking-for. They say we'll know by July first, about two months."

There were cries of *Two months?* "Impossible," someone shouted.

In the front row, a woman's hand shot up and stayed in the air.

"Lil?" Zeke asked.

Everyone strained to hear Lil Montgomery.

"Can you speak up?"

"Whistling Falls has a smaller population, barely any public buildings. There's less disruption if they take Whistling Falls."

"True, Lil, as we just said." Zeke's gaze from the stage, toward Lil and everyone else who would state the same thing over and over again, was patient. "And we have to hope that factors into the equation."

"So is Midland really out of the picture, once and for all?"

Zeke answered her by speaking out to everyone. "Yes, folks, at last summer's hearing in Midland, there was such vigorous and organized opposition that the water committee was decisive in their decision to look westward again. My friend at the State House tells me they made an awful lot of noise."

Popcorn jumped again, his face at the window: "We can make noise, too!"

"*You* certainly can, Mr. Webster," Zeke called, eliciting another laugh. "But I have to say, I'm not sure it will do much good. They rather easily dismissed Midland because Midland is *not* an ideal location. The Cascade River has been officially chosen, whether we like it or not. Now we have to wait and hope that our town will be spared. Final tests will begin after the Memorial Day holiday."

It was already May 1. There would be all-around tension until the state made its decision. That tension was evident in the brief period of silence that followed before someone—was it Asa?—spoke out. "I say we fight it."

Dez felt her arm shooting up—she couldn't stop it. She didn't really like speaking in front of groups but she could never stay quiet if she had something important to say.

Zeke put a shading hand to his eyes. "Who's that?" Heads turned her way.

She jumped off her perch on the radiator too quickly, and in the tilt of her body, a feeling like vertigo hit her. The ground under her feet—she could almost imagine it giving way. She put a hand to the wall to catch her balance, but imagined flooding overhead, imagined herself at the bottom of a reservoir, unable to breathe, looking up, up through water, like the sketches she had done at Christmas.

She stepped into the aisle so her voice would carry clearly. "I'm thinking," she said, "that the smart thing is to prepare for the worst. I think we've got to plan how we're going to negotiate fair value for our land. I mean, my father's playhouse is worth much more than its timber and nails. And then if they take Whistling Falls, good, but we'll have been prepared, at least."

"Excellent point," Zeke said. On the dais, the other men murmured their agreement. "And if your father was here, we all know he'd have a quote for us. One that comes to my mind is the Duke of Venice: *The robb'd that smiles steals something from the thief.* Thank you, Dez."

She stepped back to the radiator and pulled her pad from her pocket, pencil flying over the paper, envisioning a new work. If the worst happened, if the reservoir was built in Cascade, she could record it all, maybe in a series of panels, explore what it meant to dismantle a town, to disincorporate it, to move everybody out and say *this place no longer exists.* In Europe, she had seen murals depicting the rape of Europa, the fall of Rome. You could tell whole stories with mural panels. In Paris, in the twelfth arrondissement, painted on the side of a courthouse, was a depiction of the French revolution, which began with early fires lit by insurrectionists and ended with Marie Antoinette's neatly guillotined head falling into a bucket.

The panel idea was good—with the playhouse as the central theme somehow. First the playhouse on a long-ago opening night, with excitement and some kind of foreboding in the air. Second, the playhouse of now, uncertainty evident somehow. Then the playhouse of the future, with a tone she was still unsure of. Water closing over everything?

In any case, a series of panels, yes. She closed her pad with the satisfaction that came from solidifying an idea.

Up near the stage, Bud Foster had raised his hand and moved nearer the stage to speak. He was looking downright skinny, his jacket practically hanging off his shoulders, and he kept his eyes cast down as he rubbed his hands together apologetically. "I have to say Elaine and I'd be grateful to get cash for our land. I've never farmed it, and I sure can't sell it in these hard times. With a bit of cash, we could start somewhere else."

Hartwell Page himself rose from his chair on the dais. "I have to confess," he said. "I'm thinking the same."

A few others admitted that they, too, might benefit from selling to the state. The buzz in the room swelled as everyone started to talk at once. Onstage, Zeke covered the microphone and bent toward the front row. He stood up straight. "Folks, Asa Spaulding has something to say."

Asa's fair head poked up from the crowd down front, from a spot right beside where Lil Montgomery's raised arm had emerged. He took a moment to regard the crowd soberly, then rested his hands on his hips and waited until all eyes were on him, until all the rustling and coughing and chair-scraping had ceased. His eyes found Dez and he imperceptibly shook his head.

"This is our home," he said, enunciating each word. "This is our land." As he spoke, he turned slowly, to address as many people as possible. "Most of us have been here for generations. We will get through these hard times, but if we sell our souls for cash, how will we live with ourselves?"

"It's easy for them who have cash—" A shrill woman's voice from the middle of the crowd. It sounded like Tilly Allison, and everyone knew she was a grudging sort.

Her remark was met with general coldness. Asa Spaulding was well-liked. Zeke banged his gavel and said, "Please let Asa speak."

"I hate to wish this on our neighbors, but we have much more to lose than Whistling Falls. Like Lil pointed out, we've got a much larger population, far more businesses. It makes sense for the state to choose Whistling Falls." Asa's eyes passed over Bud, then Dez. "But we can't just sit around and wait for that to happen. We have to *make* it happen."

On the drive home he was grim, a hard man she did not know. After the meeting, people had peppered him with questions, "What did you mean, Asa? What can we do?"

"We have brains, imaginations, voices," he said. "Let's use them. Let's think."

Driving, he scoffed at Zeke's *wait-and-see* policy. "Wait and see. In other words, sit like hunters' ducks until they decide to shoot us." And he was disturbed by the fact that Dez had spoken. "You got people into a giving-in frame of mind. You got them thinking about dirty money."

"I did nothing wrong. My point was well taken. Everyone thought so. People have no money, Asa. You're lucky to have a business of your own, one that provides things people need no matter what. And that bit of cash your mother put away. You're lucky! And I've got to think about the playhouse, don't I? I can't see it sold for pennies and torn down."

They turned up River Road, but he drove right past their house.

"Where are you going?"

"I just need to see," he said, vaguely.

See what? But she didn't say anything, though her fingers flexed with impatience. She had put off the ironing and now it was ahead of her.

At the end of River Road, past Pine Point, he turned left onto the old Amherst Road. They passed miles of dark fields with only the occasional farmhouse and arrived in the center of Whistling Falls, a simple four-corners. There were no streetlights, no public buildings, just a few houses and a grange hall. "Look at this," Asa said, braking to a stop. "There's nothing here. They've *got* to take this place. It makes so much more sense."

He was more relaxed driving back to Cascade, taking the long, round-about way, passing by the Cascade Golf Course, slowing the car as they rolled past. The handsome fieldstone mansion that had been the Clark estate had been transformed, with a double front door and striped awnings on every window, into the clubhouse. There were still signs of construction—some scaffolding near the chimney, and bushes with big root balls, not yet planted, but the club looked on course to open as scheduled in June.

"Makes no sense to build that then tear it right down," Asa said.

"Perhaps."

"What do you mean?"

"I'm skeptical. You heard what Zeke said about the governor. The man's a crook! Who knows what will happen? I'm against this as much as anyone, but I'm also starting to accept that it might really happen and if it does, well, then maybe it's a blessing in disguise. In a city like Boston," she said, "or New York," she added, carefully testing the waters, "I might get an illustrator's job. In any case, I'd probably get more portrait work than I do now. All I've had is those two little girls, and the mother sent her driver to pick up the painting last Friday, almost a week now, and I still haven't been paid. And you could run a drugstore anywhere. We could be happy in a busier place, Asa."

His face, lit by the moon as he turned to look at her, revealed deep distress. "Dez, I don't want to run a drugstore anywhere. I want to run my drugstore here, in my town. Raise our children here." He reached across the seat to pull her beside him, but the yank was clumsy, pinching the flesh above her elbow.

"Well, what if you can't?" she said irritably. "There aren't any more Stock Exchange vice presidents or governors to care about us anymore. Richard Harcourt went to jail! Everything's changed. Cascade isn't what it was and it may never be again. Maybe we need to realize that."

He stiffened; she'd gone too far. The car rolled down the driveway, its headlights throwing out two circular beams that winked out when Asa braked and turned off the engine.

He sat quietly for a moment. "What is it you want, Dez?"

"I'm just saying we might do well somewhere else. We might do *better* somewhere else."

"This isn't enough for you, is it? I'm not enough for you."

"Asa, all I meant was that it's not like this threat hasn't been hanging over our heads for years, and now the state's telling us we've got a fifty-fifty chance of losing."

"We're not going to lose," he said, and got out of the car.

She sat for a moment, then followed after him. Inside, she saw he'd headed straight for his study and shut the door. She dragged the ironing basket into the parlor, set up the ironing board, and plugged in the hot-iron. While it heated up, she pulled open the door of the studio to look at the half-rendered view of the playhouse, stark against the river, that she had been working on since last week. With memory of the vertigo feeling that had hit her in Town Hall, and with fresh eyes, she suddenly saw, as if it were already painted, a maple tree looming out over the river, gnarled and reaching, down, down into the water.

She had to start over.

The perspective needed to be the view *up* through the water, the drowning view *up*, like those winter sketches, like the dizzy feeling, the firmly planted tree reaching *down*, its form blurred and heightened by the water's distortion.

She could see the composition clearly, fixed within her pupils, and knew: she needed to lay the boundaries down before the image slipped away. She changed into her smock, scraped at the old paint, and began to knife out a selection of color: blue-black, ultramarine ash, lamp black. Shades of luminous, silver bark.

But her first dabs dispirited her; they looked false. She kept on, and, gradually, the trunk began to come to life on the canvas. *Not too bad.* Then—it seemed a sudden thing—what she always hoped for with oils, but could never count on, happened: the convergence of effort and inspiration into something that actually looked the way she intended it to look. She let herself go—it was such a gift when this happened—and the tree came alive, the air around it thick and ominous. She mixed madder lake and yellow ocher with white to add layers of luminosity, to show that despite the gloom, trying to get in, there was light. What seemed a minute later, the banjo clock chimed in that speeded-up way time had when it was altered by the pleasure of being engrossed in something, and Asa poked his head in.

"*What* in God's name are you doing?" Was he angry? He looked angry. He gestured toward the parlor, toward the heaped-up ironing basket, the ironing board and hot-iron, plugged in and forgotten.

She grabbed his wrist and pulled him to her easel. She had to make him see. She did her best to explain: that when she got this kind of vision, she had to express it immediately or risk losing it forever.

"I don't know much about art," he said. "This looks interesting, I can see that. There's a lot that's pleasing about it." She was relieved; she'd gotten through to him. "But can you come down from the clouds? Our house, our town, is drowning—literally—and you're in here painting pictures. Instead of trying to help, you're standing up at Town Meeting telling people to sell, and you're in here doing—this." He flapped his palm at the painting. The back of his hand smudged the bark details she had worked so hard to get right.

There was a stunned, voiceless moment, almost black. She wanted to tear into him even as she fast-formulated how she could fix it: scrape there, reapply the paint.

"You haven't been yourself since that crazy friend of yours stopped by, and I've lost my patience. Got that? Lost it!" He was yelling. She had never heard him yell. She hadn't thought he was capable of yelling. "Here we risk losing everything and I don't have any shirts for morning."

"But you do, Asa." She realized her face was wet. She realized she was crying. "There are shirts in the wardrobe."

He stormed over to the basket and pulled out the first one that came to hand—a white one, like all the others. "I want this one, though! *This* one!" Forgetting that there was paint on his hand, a splotch of brown that ruined the shirt.

"But you don't, Asa. You only wanted that one because it's not ironed. Why are you so angry?"

He was all balled up, hands clenched, face red, sputtering for words. He didn't like fighting any more than she did. But this fight was not about shirts. It was about not wanting the same thing, it was about a man marrying a woman and thinking maybe he'd made a bad choice. It was about realizing he'd ruined a favorite shirt. "And now it's a rag." He balled up the shirt and rubbed his fingers with it. "And this sonofabitch oil paint doesn't come off, does it?"

A harsh word she'd never heard him use, and which had the effect of a slap across her face. It stunned her.

They had been living together for months now. She knew what it was to turn in her sleep and feel the length of his bare leg; she knew the pharmaceutical smell of his skin at the end of a long day. She knew things she'd never cared to know about anyone, like how five minutes after eating breakfast he needed to spend ten in the bathroom. But she hadn't ever seen how they would react to problems, and a small part of her stood apart, grimly satisfied. Maybe a rift between them was what she'd wanted all along, she thought, fetching turpentine, handing it to him, then tearing off her smock and pulling the rest of the shirts out of the basket. Throwing them hard, one by one, onto the sofa.

"Okay, okay. Are you happy? Here I go, ironing your shirts. They will all be ready by morning. You will have your pick."

"Dez." Now he was the uneasy one.

She ignored him. She spread the first shirt over the ironing board. She felt him watching her, her arm slamming forward and back: collar, shoulder, sleeves, back, front, down between each button, so ironically like the Picasso painting she had thought of when Jacob was last here. *Jacob*. The thought of that kindred spirit a nugget of comfort.

His hand came down softly, briefly, on her shoulder. "Dez, come on. Let's not fight."

She twitched his hand away and licked her finger, tapped it to the hot-iron to get the *sssst*. She wasn't sure, at first, if he remained standing there or if he sat down on the sofa; she refused to turn around through three shirts, but when she finally let herself peek, he was gone.

What would she be doing, she wondered, if she had not married him, if she had moved her father into the hotel, if she had moved back to Boston after her father died? What would that other self be doing now? There were so many possibilities. To imagine them in parallel with the life she was living made her feel like she was stepping outside herself. It was like getting her bloods each month, and reflecting on the fact that a particular combination of circumstances that would have produced a singular child was gone. A girl or boy, his or her chance at life gone forever. You couldn't help but wonder who that child would have been. And where all her own other might-have-been lives would have brought her. Every single choice in life offering up a dizzying branching of options.

She heard Asa get up a few times, heard him at the top of the stairs, but she didn't call up to him, and he didn't come down, and as the pile in the basket shrank, she began to feel strong, self-sufficient. She opened a window to let in the night air and finished her ironing feeling more wide awake than she had ever felt in her life.

In the studio, she studied the canvas. The tree was good, but she would have to do more with the water. She would have to be patient with it, work toward developing a cascading look of floodwaters. Using the upper end of a pencil cut to a fine point, she dragged through the paint while it was still wet, while there was still a thick pull to it, creating distortion, the sensation of seeing under water.

She finished all she could finish and stepped back, satisfied. Tomorrow she would work on it outside, with the river itself as model. Thursday. Jacob was supposed to come, and she would let him come.

She set her brushes to soak, turned out the light, and was halfway up the staircase when she turned back around. She just had to give it one more look.

A push of the wall switch flooded the room with light, illuminating the easel in a way she perceived with a shock of pleasure—the harsh beauty of the tree dominating the unfinished floodwaters. She took her eyes away for moments at a time so that she could reward herself by looking back and getting the pleasing shock of a fresh look.

The end of a good session's work was the best feeling. You were still in love; you weren't yet critical; you could wholly admire what you'd done.

It was late, past three o'clock. Dawn was still a couple of hours away, but already the sky was growing milky. She leaned against the doorjamb and let go, let herself do what she'd never quite dared, but which the quarrel with Asa seemed to permit: to fully wonder what it would be like to be partnered with Jacob, to be able to talk about work while doing everyday chores like folding laundry or stirring pancake batter or sweeping. To have two easels side-by-side, to stay up late while the night air blew the scent of sweet woodruff through the curtains. She carried the fantasy with her up to the spare corner room and crawled into bed with it, imagining exquisite intimacy that took her breath away, made her realize how much she wanted it, made her exhilarated and brave, and determined to do something, say something to tap at their wall of carefully maintained propriety tomorrow.

9

The Buick entered a dream that wouldn't pin to memory, chugging to life, tires kicking up gravel. Details of the night flooded back, her defiant Jacob fantasy replaced by a grubby sense of guilt and shame. Just a few hours earlier she had truly felt that sleep was not only unnecessary, but an indulgence. That a rift with your husband didn't matter. Now the happy alertness, the expectancy that normally marked Thursday, was gone.

She climbed out of bed, her limbs dragging like sacks of sand.

She had never in her life, not once—not in school, not at home— woken up after having gone to bed fighting with someone close, and now she felt hollow and anxious. Asa did not usually come home during the day, but there was a chance he would now, after last night, and he couldn't find Jacob in the house.

Funny, she didn't even want him to come now. In the light of day, her fantasy became timid and shrank away. He'd never made a pass at her, never been anything but decent.

She would have to do what Asa had asked, tell Jacob that his presence had started to make Asa uncomfortable. In the meantime, prevent herself from thinking, stay busy: hang up the ironing, make the beds, wash out the coffeepot and wipe up Asa's toast crumbs, the spilled jam, scrub the pan he'd used to cook the eggs he would have been glum fixing for himself, mop the kitchen floor. She took a bath and washed her hair and didn't bother setting it in pin curls, like she normally would on a Thursday morning, but scraped it back into a bun, half a dozen pins to secure it. What mattered in life? Not hair, not New York, not a pointless infatuation.

You want, you want, you want; when you're so lucky to have, to have, to have.

She was outside and everything was ready—easel set up, colors laid out. But her hand couldn't quite decide where to start. She couldn't get going.

Sometimes that was her problem: doing too many chores too quickly to get them out of the way, then being so geared up she couldn't slow down and focus.

She paced, the grass stubby under her thin rubber soles, the ease of the night before not quite with her anymore. Suddenly there seemed to be so much noise! A constant bird racket and across the river, somebody hammering something, over and over and over again.

She knew better: when artistry seems most elusive is when you must focus, dig deep, and force yourself to think about how to give form to an idea that seems almost too vague to express. The worst thing is to give in to distraction, to chores that need doing, to anything that deludes you into pretending you are so busy you can't focus on your work. But giant weeds—how had they grown so quickly, with so little rain?—were choking the nascent poppies, silent green pods that would fatten, then split, in a few weeks time, to unfold papery splashes of red and pink.

She found herself weeding the poppy patch, relishing the physical satisfaction of pulling and shaking roots, of dirt packed into her fingernails.

She pulled gangly grasses and dried, overgrown stalks away from the raspberry canes, away from the rose border, until her palms bled from the thorns and prickles and then she threw up her hands. Gardening could easily be a full-time job; she would never be able to keep up with it alone. The ice wagon clopped down the drive, and she gave in to the cleaning fit that seized her after Happy Joe set the block into its tray and she saw, with new eyes, how grubby the shelves were, littered with flakes of dried milk, soft mold like a mouse's fur starting to spread on a Florida orange she'd been excited to get her hands on, then saved so long she'd ruined.

She gave in to a hankering for a cup of tea even though she knew that the idea of a cup of tea—sitting still, calmly sipping—was more appealing than actually sitting still and trying to calmly sip. She didn't even really like tea, she decided, watching it steep. She sat down with it anyway and spread out the morning paper. All bad news. There were two separate stories about the Dust Bowl "black blizzards" of April, witnesses describing how day turned to night, the thick dust clouds blanketing crops and sending birds and people racing ahead of it. Wet sheets in the windows, both articles said—everyone was pinning wet sheets over their windows to try to keep the dust from getting into their beds, their kitchens, their food, their eyes, their hair.

Wet sheets in the windows, a black sky raining dirt. Her mind began composing an image: left side of the canvas—a cutaway, diagonal view of clapboards. The primary focal point three wet, gray, spattered sheets.

Sometimes an image was enough. It was all about curiosity, in a way. Could you make *this* happen? Could you do with your hands and a brush what your mind's eye had already painted?

Can I make that view up through water convey, to the viewer, how frantic the grasping-at-life instinct must be, how precious the air on the other side?

It was enough to get her back to her palette. Then it was bristles into paint, paint onto canvas, over and over, and a good hour went by, maybe two, branches, bark, light, all claiming their place on the canvas and becoming something more than the sum of parts.

When the 12:30 train from Athol blew its whistle, she looked up. Jacob was late, unless the train was early, and the train was never early. *Maybe he's not coming after all*, she thought with relief that was quickly replaced by disappointment. Then she couldn't help but be expectant. She lost focus, putting brush to canvas only to realize she had no real intent, that her mind had wandered, that she had become overconscious of any noise that could be Jacob's truck coming down the driveway.

But he didn't come and didn't come. At one point she slipped into the house to check the clock. A quarter after one. He'd never come so late, never not come without phoning.

He did turn up, an hour later, stumbling out of his truck to deliver the news of Dr. Proulx's death, a death that was strange, that would have the town talking for weeks.

He found him, he said. Found him in his bed. "Dead," he repeated, as if she needed convincing.

He had gone to Dr. Proulx's office to deliver the painting. "Dottie said he was late and wasn't answering his telephone. She said he was probably caught up on a house call, but I said I'd stop by, make sure he was okay. His car was there. I knocked and there was no answer, so I went in and that's when I found him."

Dez was thinking it was sad, but a blessing, too, to die of old age and to die in your sleep, but Jacob was shaking his head as if she didn't understand.

"He must have taken it to bed last night," Jacob said, "this rag soaked with ether."

And that was the unfathomable shock of it.

Jacob explained how after finding him, he'd gone directly to Oberon's but Henry Oberon wasn't there so he went to the police station to find Dwight and Wendell. "They said he was upset at the meeting last night."

"He was."

"But surely not enough to do a thing like this."

"No," Dez said. "Although," she added, thinking back, "he was acting odd another time I saw him." She explained how she had bumped into him on the common on her way to meet Abby's train. She should have paid more attention, but she'd been in a hurry. "He'd been drinking. No question. And that wasn't like him, especially since it was morning. Ten o'clock or so. He was clearly upset about something."

No, she didn't know what. "Still. How does a person do such a thing?" Lie down knowing it was for the last time? What if there was panic, a too-late change of heart?

"Who can say what makes a person do a thing like that?" Jacob reached into his pants pocket and took out a package of cigarettes. He lit one and looked off across the water.

Random memories came: the wooden box of lollipops Dr. Proulx kept on his desk. The silver clasp in the shape of a badger's claw on his black bag. The flu mask over his face the day he emerged from the sick room, like he must have emerged from countless rooms that terrible fall, telling her that Timon was gone and her mother was not far behind, and that she would have to be brave. She'd wanted to kick him. She'd run crying to Rose, *I hate him, I hate him.* Aware that he could hear her and feeling guilty then, because really, all he'd ever been to her was kind, and his only son had died too, somewhere on the western front that everyone talked about, and his wife never came out of the house anymore.

From inside the house, the telephone began to ring. "Come in," Dez offered. Who cared if Asa came home now and found him there? Everything had changed. "Or sit on the porch there, whatever you want to do. I'll get us some water."

It was Asa on the line, his own dismay so thorough he didn't register Dez's lack of surprise as he filled her in. Since there was no family left to decide the funeral arrangements, Henry Oberon was organizing the details, he said. And a group of ladies were getting together in the basement of the church, to cook for the funeral. "They've already started. I'm sure they'd like it if you came in and helped."

"Right," she said in a noncommittal way. She would cook something on her own, bring it to the church later.

"Jacob Solomon found him."

She looked out the window to where Jacob sat hunched on the porch swing, looking down at his shoes.

"Terrible," she murmured, "what a terrible scene for anyone to discover."

He was quiet a moment. "Let's never go to bed fighting again."

"No," she said. She never wanted to wake up to that kind of sick remorse again.

Jacob set the glass of water she gave him on the floor without tasting it.

"Do you want something stronger? I can make coffee."

"No," he said. "I'm fine."

He didn't look fine. His eyes were vacant, fatigued.

"The shock of finding him will stay with you awhile."

"It wasn't the fact of finding him so much as it was realizing what he'd done. At first I thought he'd died in his sleep, and that sort of thing is a blessing, really."

Dez said that had been her first thought, too.

"I wouldn't have even found him if I hadn't done the painting so quickly. But then poor Dottie would have found him. It's better it was me."

"True. Where's the painting now?"

"In my truck. What was the point, I thought. He had no family and I hadn't taken any money. Not that that would have mattered, I just mean—"

"You don't have to explain."

"You look different," he said absently. "Your hair."

"Oh, that." Her hand traveled to it, lamely. Why did people always have to do that, touch their hair, when someone else commented on it? The scraped-back look made her face sharper, accented the arches of her eyebrows.

"It's nice like that. It does something to your face."

In his own face, she saw there was something she couldn't quite read. Some kind of weight that she instinctively knew was distinct from the news about Dr. Proulx.

"I was kind of dreading coming here today as it was."

She set down her own glass, sensing a great tide sweeping under her feet. Sometimes one bad thing followed another, over and over, and there was nothing you could do about it.

"I might be going to New York sooner than I planned," he said. "I am, I mean."

"Oh." It was all her voice could manage. It wasn't like she hadn't known this day would come. But it was only May, surely he hadn't sold all the inventory?

No, he hadn't, he said. But he had seen a newsreel over the weekend, one that announced the same program Abby had talked about: the Works Progress Administration. The W.P.A. "The ironical thing is, Dr. Proulx mentioned this to me only last week. He thought it would be a great opportunity for me." A similar, preliminary program in San Francisco had been so successful, the government putting artists to work painting murals on public buildings, he said, that the federal government was developing a broader program as part of the Emergency Relief Act. "You apply and if you're accepted, you're paid to paint. *To paint.* Easel paintings, sculptures, prints. It's a way to earn money and get back to New York."

She nodded with the restrained enthusiasm that good news, on the heels of news of a death, dictated, grateful for the excuse for restraint. Otherwise she'd have had to acknowledge how incredible it was to think that the government would actually pay someone to create art. Because it was incredible. "But how can you be sure you'd be chosen?"

"I think I'd get it. I've got the right background. I could make it happen."

"But if the government is running the program, all the states will do it, won't they?"

"There's going to be a New England division, but getting back to New York's always been my plan."

"Won't you have to be a resident?"

"My aunt lives there. I can use her address to start. I just need to come up with a proposal for my application, a good idea."

"What about the inventory?"

"Al Stein's going to take it off my hands. We made a good deal this morning. He gets a deep discount and I get enough cash to leave my mother in good shape for a while."

"Oh."

He gazed at her with something that looked too much like pity. Or maybe it was regret. "It's an opportunity I can't ignore, Dez. They're saying we'll be able to paint what we want. Of course, with the New Deal mentality, they might be wanting things that support patriotism, national pride, but we'll see."

Terrible how grief could bubble up like some compound in Asa's back room. She forced herself not to blink, so her eyes wouldn't spill. Through the blur, the fleshy middle of his lower lip looked the exact color of the mulberries that birds dropped on the back walkway, and she found herself wondering—anything to keep her composure—how to mix that shade.

"I know you're disappointed," he said. "I'll miss our days, too."

She was unable to manage a word against the rock lodged in her throat. How could she have thought she didn't want him here, that she would be fine telling him to leave?

"What am I supposed to do, Dez? There are a hundred reasons to go and the only one that could make me stay is an option I have no right to."

It was the first acknowledgment of what had been unspoken, and it was too much. She found herself running down to the river, mortified that she was running, that she had lost control of her emotions. She pinched the bridge of her nose to keep from crying, watching the river bubbling and sloshing over rocks and pebbles, like her painting, but not like her painting, which seemed so fine only an hour ago but looked nothing like this, suggested nothing like this.

She could sense him behind her. He was behind her on the grass.

"Dez."

She inhaled deeply—*Get hold of yourself!*—and turned around, hands clasped together, voice as pleasant as she could manage. Of course she was happy for him, just a bit envious. She even managed a laugh.

He looked skeptical. "Are you sure?"

She didn't know whether to admit her devastation or continue in the same prim, false vein. "What about that woman you see?" She couldn't stop herself. "Ruth Sondheim?"

His face registered a kind of resigned surprise that she had remembered Ruth's last name, could call it up so quickly.

"Ruth knows what's what." He didn't want to talk about Ruth Sondheim, clearly, but she had to know, had to ask.

"Is she going to New York, too?"

"No, Dez."

A lie? No, Jacob didn't lie. Or maybe he did, how would she know? "Will you visit?"

"Of course I'll visit."

But it was unlikely. She knew that, even if he did not.

She sat down on the bench by the riverbank, a place she hadn't sat since the day her father died. She sat on the bench and imagined her father beside her, talking and breathing then ceasing to exist less than an hour later. Nothing in life lasted, nothing stayed the same. You were a fool if you got to a certain age and still grieved about that hard fact, or railed at it. Maybe you had to at least look on the bright side of change.

He was standing a few feet away, looking at her uncertainly. She smiled at him with an apologetic shake of her head. "Maybe, at least, when I reopen the playhouse, you'll come?"

"That's something I wouldn't miss," he said, and there was relief in his voice.

They were all right then, for the moment. He joined her on the bench and they sat there in companionable silence, looking across the water. But weirdly, partly, it felt like he was already gone. He was right there beside her but her brain was already starting to adapt, starting to visualize what it would be like when he was gone, when there would be no more Thursdays.

"Listen," he said. "I've never sketched you and I'd like to. A sketch I've done myself will capture you more, I think, than any photograph could manage."

"Right now?"

"I don't need to work any more today." After Cascade, his Thursday route usually took him down Route 13 to Alderville. He removed a penknife from his breast pocket and began to pare his drawing pencil. "What do you think?"

She put a hand to her bun to remove the pins. "So I should take my hair down."

"Actually, leave it up to start," he said. "I want to get your face right. With your hair pulled back I can really see it. Although . . ."—and here he smiled wryly, a bit of their normal casual banter coming into play—"your hair is a subject in itself, and of course I mean that in the best sense, and I would like to get that down on paper, too. Just not yet."

———

And so he sketched her. He rummaged in his truck to dig out a drawing board and linen paper while she carried a stool onto the porch. He sat on the stool; she positioned herself on the swing. Then he studied her face, this way and that, while she sat perfectly still, letting herself become part model, part object.

At first, he just scratched at the paper, wordless. A delicate breeze began to blow up from the water and wisps of hair sprang free from the bun, batting at her eyes, her jaw. But she kept her shoulders motionless, conscious of her head perched on its neck, the effort involved in holding it up. She knew what it was to draw someone who had gone half-dead from the boredom of holding still. She tried her best to be still but fluid, alive. And she wondered if Abby was doing this, or would soon be doing this—holding herself still in some artist's studio in Greenwich Village, only in her case naked and draped in sheeting.

Sounds became amplified. She could hear the way the trees rustled. The soft breeze was full of bird music—short whistles and long caws, shrieks and twitters. One song sounded like *LEEV-ing, LEEV-ing,* it really did, it wasn't pathetic transference, or anthropomorphism, or whatever Mr. Freud would say.

Yet Jacob had admitted, he'd *voiced* that she was a reason to stay. What did that mean?

It means you're married and that in another life, things would be different. That's what it means.

"Addis Proulx," he said quietly at one point, giving each syllable emphasis, in the way that you say something you can't understand.

"It doesn't feel real."

"We had a nice bond. Maybe it was mainly because I reminded him of his son, but whatever the reason, we had some nice talks."

"Maybe he had some disease he never told anyone about."

"Maybe." He looked off toward the river. "I don't suppose we'll ever know. He didn't leave a note that I could see. I think people are off-base, though, if they think he did it because of the reservoir."

"Maybe it was the final straw. It's infuriating and it doesn't seem right, does it? Eminent domain. Not in a supposedly free country."

"Well, it's not really a free country, is it? It's a constitutional republic. We like to think it's the same thing when it's not."

Dez remembered a long-ago public government teacher who had always driven home that very point. But at least there was a sort of essential freedom here, unlike the autocracies and military dictatorships that were wreaking havoc on Europe. "The thing is, there are an awful lot of people who could use the money they'll get for their property. Maybe it could be a good thing. Force us all to move, make changes."

Jacob's hand, busy shading, paused midstroke. "Could you really see your father's playhouse destroyed?"

Of course she couldn't, but she might have no choice. So maybe now was the time to rid herself of sentimentality. "Oh," she said, and she acted like she was weary saying it, "what is it but timber and nails?"

"You don't believe that."

No, she didn't, but something unreasonable was rising inside her. Something hurt and therefore disagreeable.

"Because if that's true," he said, "then where's the soul in anything?"

"The soul? The soul is the art, the words, the totality of Shakespearean theater, which is in no danger of dying because of this."

"But we're not talking about Shakespeare's soul." His eyes met hers. "We're talking about your father's."

"I know." She felt terrible. "I don't mean it, but—but if there is an afterlife, which my father wholeheartedly believed in, then his soul is in no danger of disappearing. If he was wrong and there is nothing at all, then it will just be a matter of time before my father, before even Shakespeare is forgotten. Just who Shakespeare really was is in doubt anyway, and the thing is, it doesn't matter! The writer's gone. The words live. Fame doesn't really endure beyond the grave."

"I have a feeling we're talking about something else here."

"Well, basically, it's this: Do I sacrifice my own existence, my own art, for this myth of eternity my father believed in?"

"You're dwelling on abstractions, Dez."

"Not really."

"I think you are. The bottom line is, you *are* painting, and doing a fair bit of it."

She looked over to her easel, sitting by itself on the lawn. "But I always believed I was supposed to try to reach people, not just keep myself occupied. Who sees what I do? Who cares? Miss Farrell, in art school, she used to say, 'You are a human being living in a human world. People will want to interrupt your working time. They won't understand when you tell them you must work while the vision is in front of you, or while the light falls a certain way. They will think you are a silly, self-indulgent girl. You have to be able to live with that.' But it's hard advice to live by."

Especially when you lived in a place like Cascade where art meant pictures drawn by schoolchildren, and occasional trips to museums to see canvases painted by "real artists"—real artists being something mystical, something *other*.

"It's harder for a woman, I'll give you that, but it's hard for all of us now. It's hard for almost every artist no matter what time they're born into. That's life, Dez."

He was right. Her own mother never saw forty. "But if we only have one life, then we should live it fully," she said, rising unthinkingly to her feet.

She had forgotten that she was posing and moved to sit. No, he gestured, it was all right.

"That's true enough," he said. "And this life of a peddler, honestly, how did my father do it? This morning, this awful woman giving me the hardest time because I didn't have the color yarn she needed, and I'm hardly gone and I hear them all behind my back, *That Jew's just not the man his father was.*"

Jew. The word sounded so blunt to the ear, so impolite. It disrupted the air between them. She didn't know what to say, only, lamely, "Things have to get better."

"Isn't the great lesson of history that nothing ever changes? And what are we talking about anyway? I don't think the minds of people like Ethel Bentonford will ever change. And the economy? How can any economy suddenly improve without something happening?"

"It was like a blossoming, a cup running over, wasn't it? Back in the twenties, and everyone too giddy to realize it couldn't last forever."

"And now it seems we are being punished for our excesses."

"Now you sound like the pastor."

"No, just a Jew."

Her laughter was short. "I don't know much about your religion."

He took so long to answer that she assumed he had chosen not to hear. Then he said, firmly, in a summing-up sort of way, "I don't put much stock in it all, but it's my background and I can't get away from that, I know. But we're all born the same and the only divisions between us are ones we make ourselves."

He handed her the sketch. He'd drawn her face tipped down so that her hands, one over the other, assumed prominence. The cuticles were stained with pigment, the nails ragged, knuckles on the right hand scraped by the washboard. He even got the scar on her thumb right—she'd been drying a glass one evening, the first week they were married, and the glass broke with her hand inside it. It bled so badly and she'd been a beast to Asa, as if it were his fault. It was his milk glass, and she'd been so afraid that cartilage was destroyed, that her hand would lose dexterity. Dr. Proulx had pronounced it fine.

"It's excellent," she said. There was so much she could say about it, decided on "It's so true."

He shifted off the stool to crouch in front of her, looking at it upside down.

He was pleased with it, she could tell.

Their bodies had been this close before, but the wall was gone now, she felt it. His confession—*only one reason to stay*—had changed everything. She could smell his hair, sweaty from his hat but not unpleasant, mingling with the scent of his shaving soap—the same brand, Nason's, as Asa's. Asa seemed far away.

"I was thinking, last time, after I left," he said, "how you hold your brush a certain way. Very elegant. Like a teacup. But then when you actually hit the canvas—look out." He smiled and pumped his fists like a boxer. "You go at it with a vengeance."

She studied the sketch, for something to do, not knowing what to say. What he'd said could be received as intimate, or simply as an artist's detailed observation.

Then he did the unimaginable. He lifted the fingers of her right hand and bent his head over them. Her heart slowed and began to thud so hard and loud she was sure he could hear it.

He looked up into her face. "I know this breaks all the rules."

She would describe the scene to Abby in a letter that she would rip to bits and burn in the kitchen sink. She would say that she gave in to the exhilaration of what was going to happen. That death opened doors that were usually kept closed, and something about Jacob finding Dr. Proulx opened a door between them that day. That somehow she found herself backed up against the porch column, its hard roundness fitting into the hollow of her spine, and he touched a stray bit of hair, tucked it behind her ear. Across the river, a freight train rumbled past. A leaf fell into the water and was carried away, and the Cascade River would be flooded and Jacob would be gone and this moment would never happen again. She had to seize it or lose it.

His fingers stroked her head, following the path of her hair, root to bun, as if he were painting each strand. He enclosed the weight of the bun in his palm, squeezing, pulling, the pins tinkling onto the porch floor, the still-damp hair tumbling free.

He took a handful of my hair, she would write. *He ran his other hand along my cheek.* In the midst of these moments she tried to hold on to each sensation so she could unfold the memory and let it heat her all the days and nights he would be gone: the way he wrapped his hand around her hand, the way he bent to brush his mouth against her throat, the little explosions that skittered down her spine.

Come with me to New York.

Did he whisper it? Did she only imagine it? He didn't say it again, if he said it at all, and she really didn't know if he had. Asa and the ladies cooking in the basement of the Round Church seemed far away. The wind was humid, rich with the silt smell of the river. The spring drone of insects had begun. All was smell and texture and sound she knew she would forever associate with him, and she clung to him, greedy for the moment, even though she knew that anyone could walk into the yard and see them. Then came a soaking so thorough, so unlike anything she had ever experienced before, that she was sure she was bleeding even though that was impossible. She fumbled, one hand behind her. He misunderstood her bumbling alarm and pulled away, too, uncertainly.

Then there was true confusion: the sound of whistling, which Dez recognized in a panic as Jimmy Clifford with the afternoon mail, coming around the corner of the house.

Jimmy waved, his mailbag slung limp and slack over one shoulder. Dez was quite sure that if Jimmy had seen them, his expression, manner, something, would reveal it. Instead, he just looked happy to find two people to talk to, especially Jacob, and crossed the lawn with eagerness he tried to tamp down. "I hear you found him," he said, using a somber tone, but fixed on rehashing the facts the way people did at such times: *So you found him and then Dwight got hold of the Athol doctor. He's there at Oberon's right now.* Jimmy segued right into what would become the town's unofficial verdict: that Addis Proulx killed himself because he could not bear the thought of Cascade's destruction.

When Dez and Jacob looked doubtful, he became insistent. "The same thing happened in the 1870s when they made a reservoir out of the Sudbury River. An old man in Ashland hung himself. Couldn't handle the thought of losing his house. It's right there in black and white in a newspaper down at the library, Betty's been showing everyone. And they're moving full steam ahead, a crew coming in next Monday to get the old boys' camp ready for the engineers. That's going to be their base. Just one piece for you, Dez."

The envelope was postmarked Worcester. Payment for the portrait, finally, hopefully. She tucked it in her pocket, and through Jimmy's chatter, she and Jacob looked at each other. She put a hand to her heart to calm herself, willing Jimmy to leave, but he only kept talking, then asked for a lift back into town. Dez was the end of the line, he said, and his knee was bothering him.

Jacob lifted his shoulders in a subtle, helpless gesture. It was getting late anyway.

When they drove away, she ran inside the house and unsnapped the front of her dress in one ripping motion. She reached down. No blood. Just one trembling finger against tissue that had never felt so swollen and soft.

She rinsed her hands under the tap, not knowing what to think, how to feel. There were rules for this kind of behavior. Guilt was supposed to be felt. But she felt only agitation. She wanted to run down the road after him. She wanted to jump into his truck and drive away and never come back. What would happen between them now? What, realistically, could happen? Nothing, she knew, but that didn't stop her from wanting to see him again, immediately, now, forever. The need felt like it might possibly consume her.

We find ourselves alive here, she thought, born into a cultural set of what's right and wrong that often differs from other cultures, other time periods. You learn to trust your feelings—the sick knowledge that something's inherently wrong, or the sure certainty that something is right. The connection with Jacob felt only right.

10

She couldn't stop it. The thought of him was there when she opened her eyes in the morning; it was there when she stooped down to retrieve the newspaper, when she poured milk for Asa, when she glanced at her reflection in the mirror, when she watched her brush lay each stroke onto the tree painting, and then, finally, when she pushed it into the drying rack.

Days passed. The doctor from Athol officially pronounced Dr. Proulx's death an accident. Without a note, he said, there was no way to know what the man's intentions had been, and he had no interest in maligning a decent man's reputation. His decision allowed for a prompt funeral, which Jacob did not attend, but then, Dez reasoned, would he have even known it was happening?

A week went by, and then another, and she was barely aware of the details of the days, so consumed was she by feverish ruminations. He must have gone to New York, she decided. Something was keeping him from coming, or from letting her know his plans. Surely he'd be back, probably when she least expected it.

In town, placards were posted everywhere—on the doors of Town Hall, on the bulletin board next to the Handy's screen door, nailed to trees on each end of the common. Engineers and administrators of the state water commission would be arriving in Cascade the Monday after the holiday. Final tests would begin the first week of June.

The orioles returned, and the apple trees budded, blossomed, came into full leaf. The poppies split, one or two a day, papery splashes of red and pink amid the hardy green weeds that had grown up overnight. Dez heard people complaining in the Handy, on the streets—Jacob Solomon hadn't shown up with any of his deliveries. He let Ethel Bentonford down regarding a special red yarn order. She grew increasingly queasy.

On May 24, a Friday, Dez overheard Al Stein in the Handy Grocery telling Ethel Bentonford that he'd had a telegram from Jacob, promising delivery of the inventory Al arranged to buy. "Should include that yarn you've been on about."

Ethel grumbled that next Thursday was Memorial Day and that meant she wouldn't get the yarn for two weeks.

Dez looked down at the bar of Nason's soap she was holding. Addis Proulx had died on May 2. Twenty-two days ago. Jacob couldn't possibly be so busy he couldn't send some kind of word. Maybe he was embarrassed. Maybe he was doing what a lot of men do when they are afraid of a woman's passion, or their own, when they don't know what to do with it: disappear.

11

Years later, when Dez was hard at work on the Cascade murals, choosing the kind of storytelling details that would translate well to canvas, she would come back to this quiet Wednesday night before Memorial Day, a night so moonless and thick with clouds she couldn't see her feet as they hit the pavement, could hear only the sounds of night birds and insects, the roaring of the Cascade Falls. She would remember the shadowy, hulking shapes that were the closed-up summer homes, the empty look of the town—a single light in the police station in the basement of Town Hall, the hotel sitting dark at the end of Elm Street, with just the small flicker of a reading lamp shining from within Mrs. Mayhew's private apartment. She would paint an entire panel devoted to the dimmed, defeated look of an American small town in 1935, a night scene with one bright spot: the rear of the playhouse, glowing with amber light, like a beacon.

That morning, Asa had asked for the keys to the playhouse. He and a few men needed a private place to talk about what to do, he said, but he'd been vague about just what it was they thought they might do. And he wouldn't be pressed. "Not sure. Maybe nothing." And he wouldn't be home for supper; he'd grab something at the Brilliant.

Dez fetched the playhouse keys from where she kept them safe inside a rosewood box on a shelf in her studio, then, hearing Asa up in the bathroom, peeked into the study. A surveyor's map sat on his desk, dated 1899, depicting the entirety of the Spaulding property—forty-two acres, most of it forest, that hugged the southeastern bank of the Cascade River. Clipped to the map was a multipage chart, handwritten in faded blue ink, that noted seasonal water levels from spring 1869 until the day in July 1901 when a carriage accident ended Asa's grandfather's life.

What was Asa planning? At Dr. Proulx's funeral, she'd looked around the crowd after the service and found him in the pastor's back parlor, speaking in a low voice to a few of his friends. A week later, he'd spent Sunday afternoon tramping around the woods. When he returned at dusk, his clothes smelled of wind and pine pitch. For three or four nights in a row, while Dez was washing up after supper, instead of going back to the drugstore for six thirty, he spent time at his desk with the door closed.

The night was warm, so Dez was in luck. The men had cracked a window, one that offered a narrow view of the stage and front seats. If she strained, she would be able to hear. Bud Foster, Pete Masterson, Dick Adams, and Bill Hoden all sat in the front row in the same way: pitched forward, legs crossed at the ankles, elbows bent and hands clasped, listening to Asa, who stood at the base of the stage, talking and gesturing. A pile of small rocks sat on the stage directly behind him.

"Secret Pond," Dez heard him say. She cocked her right ear toward the stage and covered her left ear with her hand to hear more clearly. He was talking about opening the small diversion channel his great-grandfather had constructed, for assistance in dry summers, at the inlet that led to the pond called "Secret" because its point of diversion from the Cascade River was basically undetectable. The pond sat deep within a glen, hidden by giant ferns and thick pines. They had once picnicked there.

"Bud," Asa said. "You remember the dam, right?"

Asa had once explained the dam to Dez, but she didn't understand the connection, and apparently neither did Bud, who nodded, but in a confused way.

Asa explained: the Cascade River was no pebbly stream but a broad expanse of water, with an abundant flow that made it desirable to the state. But past Whistling Falls, past Pine Point, it underwent a number of twists and turns to skinny out right by his land before filling out again on its way toward the center of Cascade. Less than a quarter mile from that skinnying, Asa's grandfather had enlarged a pond on his property, and connected it to the main river by digging a narrow channel. Then he built a dam so he could flood the pond with river water whenever drought threatened. And although the flooding made it possible for him to water his crops, the leaching of the river lowered water levels only subtly, almost undetectably, the way a long drought might.

"The dam's been sealed shut for more than thirty years so there are roots and brush and trees grown up around the basin," Asa said. "The pond itself is just a dry hole right now. It's filled in with a lot of silt." He turned toward the stage and used the stones to demonstrate how he planned to pull the dam apart. "First thing, we have to dig out the pond. Then we dig the diversion channel wider and deeper."

Someone asked why.

Asa held up a finger to say *I'm getting to that*, but Dez lost the explanation as, a mile away, a train wailed, followed by faint, intrusive chugging that intensified over two minutes and culminated in a long shriek of steel and whistle.

When quiet returned, Asa was still talking and the other men had gotten to their feet to crowd around the stones on the stage. "If we divert water from that stretch of the river where it twists so much," Asa said, "we will reduce the flow into Cascade. Overflow from Secret Pond will flow toward the Whistling Falls branch of the river. On the whole, our water levels will appear lower than they should. It might look like we've got too much ledge here in Cascade. Which we do, and this will help to illustrate that."

Dez inched up the window. Someone said something she couldn't make out.

"Don't you see?" Asa was getting exasperated. "When the state performs those final tests downstream at Pine Point, they'll see all this abundant water in Whistling Falls and less of a flow to Cascade. Leaving them, I hope, to reason that west of Whistling Falls there's lots of bedrock, like at Midland. Expensive bedrock that will require dynamite, blasting, and a bigger payroll. Whistling Falls will look much more easily floodable, nothing but soft fertile valley, full of silt."

"I sort of see," Bud said. "But the idea feels sort of hopeless—too small to make a difference."

"And too complicated," Dick said. "These people are engineers, Asa. I don't think you know what you're up against."

"And they've done most of the tests already," Bud added.

Pete stepped between Asa and Dick, shaking his head at Asa's rocks. Pete had managed a large clock factory in Amherst before he lost his job, and was probably the most logical of the group. "This skinny part of the river will mean nothing once they start blasting. It's a waste of time, Asa."

"The point is," Asa said patiently, "every builder avoids ledge, and blasting, if he can help it. You can't tell me they're not working with a tight budget. If we succeed at this, it can make the decision to choose Whistling Falls easier—less work, fewer costs."

Pete considered. "Good point. But did you hear about Zeke's friend at *The Boston Evening Transcript*? They're sending a photographer and reporter out here to write about how we've been twice burned. They're going to focus on the golf course and how crazy it would be to tear it down. Why don't we just hope for a good story and put it in the hands of fate?"

"Because we should be the masters of our fate! And because this plan might work!" The passion in Asa's voice made Pete step back a little, as did Dez. It highlighted a quality of natural authority that she hadn't realized he possessed. "I'm not saying the newspaper article won't help," he said. "It might. But we've got to try everything. Secret Pond is very aptly named. If a person doesn't know about it, there's really not much of a chance he'll find it, at least not at this level of planning."

Pete picked up one of Asa's rocks and turned it about in his hand. Word had it that he spent a lot of time drinking at the roadhouse that had sprung up out on Route 13 as soon as Prohibition ended. "But is it fair to Whistling Falls?"

The question caught Asa off-guard. He pulled off his spectacles and rubbed the bridge of his nose. "No, it's not, is it?" He shrugged, accepting the acknowledgment of something about himself he hadn't known was there. "But I'm afraid it's every man for himself. And Whistling Falls doesn't have half our houses, no churches, no school, just the grange. They just don't stand to lose so much."

Maybe every person's first reaction to a problem was instinctively self-ish, Dez thought. Maybe overcoming that instinct was what differentiated the truly good from everyone else.

"It's worth a try, I think," Bill said. "How's the water pressure out there?"

"Slow and steady," Asa said, shooting Bill a grateful look.

"The trick," Bill said, "will be timing it right."

"I've worked out some calculations. I figure that opening the dam a week before they start their tests should be about right. But we need a good four days to dig. Secret Pond's more secret than pond at this point. We'll need to start tomorrow."

"But the holiday," Bud said. "What about the parade, the picnic?"

"We'll dig at dawn and you can all make it to the picnic by noontime. You can tell your families I've hired you to clear brush and work my land for me. Which is what I'm doing." He looked each man, one at a time, in the eye. "I'm hiring you."

All four men were out of work. Everyone knew that Bud had been forced to apply for the new relief program; others wouldn't be far behind.

"We all live here, Asa," Bud said. "You don't have to pay us."

"I want to pay and I insist on it. I can give you each a dollar fifty a day."

There was a shocked silence that even Dez was part of, then Dick murmured, "That's more than fair, Asa, but we can't take pay for this. If it works, we all benefit."

They began talking over one another. "No." Asa broke in firmly. "You don't all benefit. I do. You'll be on my land, giving up your time, and I'm the one who owns forty-two acres they'll have to pay assessed value to acquire if we lose."

———

So it was decided: they would begin digging in the morning, hiking into Secret Pond so as to arrive by dawn. "If we work hard," Asa said, "we can be done by Sunday. According to Zeke, surveyors are going to start first thing Monday. They'll be setting out their test sticks everywhere. That's when I'll open the dam. Seven days of water draining from the river should be enough. By the following week, when they check their levels, hopefully they'll lean toward Cascade being too full of bedrock."

Bud pointed out that Saturday was Asa's day, wasn't it, to go on his monthly supply trip to Hartford?

"I can hold off a week." Asa folded the map and laid it on the stage. "One last point," he said. "We don't tell our wives. We don't tell anybody. If the water people find out, we'll have wasted our time."

"What about Dez?" Dick said. "Won't she notice us going into the woods?"

"We'll come in from the east, near Pine Point, early. Four thirty. And I'll need her to work the drugstore this weekend anyway."

Across the common, the departing train shrieked in the dark. Dez could feel the reverberations of the rails under her feet as the train rolled away. If Cascade was taken, the rails would be lifted, the trains routed somewhere else. The river itself, which was oblivious to everyone so feverishly discussing it, would keep flowing no matter what the state decided. The Cascade River had flowed for—how long? When did the rivers begin? After the Ice Age? After a great melting to be sure, a gushing, a releasing of something central, and then all those tributaries carving new pathways. She imagined Cascade dismantled, every last house gone, imagined a dike, the river rising, rising, spilling over its sides, filling the valley. Then, what? Water. Silence.

Recording the drama of the choice—that was an idea that might sell. Maybe if the drama was portrayed in a visual way, people would want to champion Cascade. She thought back on the mural panel sketches she had jotted down at town meeting. She could scale the mural idea down to watercolor illustrations that could be printed in a magazine. She could draw a scene much like this, a meeting of determined men. She pulled her sketchpad out of her pocket, pressing it to the wall to scribble character- istics to remember: Bud's pessimism and rounded shoulders contrasted with Asa's raised arms, his zeal. She worked in a quick and focused man- ner, recognizing that she had received a kind of gift, a good opportunity— a way to achieve some notice and help Cascade at the same time. She, too, would work through the holiday—she had never cared for parades and could go to the picnic late. If Asa needed her at the drugstore over the weekend, she could bring her work and do her best to be productive between customers.

She slipped into the darkness of the common to avoid the men as they disbanded. Between all of them—Asa, herself, Zeke's friend at the newspaper—someone's plan had to make a difference. If the engineers thought Cascade was too full of ledge, if the reporter wrote a good story, if she herself illustrated the drama and managed to sell it to a magazine, if Cascade's story caught the public's attention, the public might clamor for Cascade's rescue. And there really was less work involved if the state chose Whistling Falls. The engineers might take the first new numbers they came up with and make the easy decision. The governor couldn't possibly care which town the engineers decided on, so long as Boston got its drinking water.

She was almost to Main Street when a voice called out her name. Standing in the puddle of light shining down from the streetlamp outside

Stein's, beckoning, was Lil Montgomery, calling out to ask what Dez was doing in town so late, and wanting to know if Dez would like to take in a movie sometime next week.

Dez hung back a second, observing, taking stock. Lil was transparently livelier with a man in her life, and that was a tiny bit repulsive. But wasn't she being hypocritical to think that? Hadn't she herself brightened on Thursdays?

She almost said yes. It could be a bit of fun to see a movie. But she would need time, this weekend, to work on the sample drawings, and Asa had mentioned he needed her to work the fountain. On Monday, when he opened the dam, she would start telephoning magazine editors. If she was successful, she would be busy.

"Maybe," she said, not promising anything. "I'll have to let you know."

12

The playmaster's daughter. That was what he called her—the man who showed up at the drugstore the day after Memorial Day.

First thing that morning, Dez walked to the drugstore with a bag containing her sketchbook and pencils. The town was quiet, quiet and hot. If she were to illustrate it, she would smear paint to convey the overwhelming sultriness, would use shades of unrelenting color—harsh yellows and whites that refused to be toned down.

She usually enjoyed working the fountain—people came in and talked; it was a chance to catch up, and she liked the quick pace of grill cooking. But today she needed to sketch, and the most drawing she could realistically hope to get in would be first thing and then maybe during the lull after lunch. If there even was a lull. You could never tell. And she still had to get to the library at some point, search through periodicals and telephone directories for names and numbers of editors.

She unlocked the door. Inside, the window awnings provided an illusion of coolness. The soda fountain's chrome taps gleamed. There was the humming sound of the Frigidaire, the creak and whir of the overhead fan when she yanked on the chain pull. She checked the ice supply, the lemons, the fountain syrup containers, lit the pilot on the grill. Then she sat down with her sketchbook to work on the idea she'd come up with.

Behind the railroad station, a rocky hill had been looming over the valley for thousands of years. It had watched over Indian longhouses, it had watched over settlers building homes; it would watch over any future destruction. She decided it could serve as the recognizable landmark in a series of panels that depicted different eras of Cascade history, from Indian times to the present.

Using a recognizable topographical landmark was an old idea, but one Dez had always liked. Her mother had owned a book that contained reproductions of one particular example, Thomas Cole's *Course of Empire* series. As a child, Dez had studied every detail of the color plates, mesmerized by the change that the passing of time could bring upon a place. Cole's series consisted of five paintings that traced the rise and fall of a nonspecific civilization. Each painting contained, as focal point, the same erratic boulder—a giant misfit rock, perched on a cliff, deposited randomly by a long-ago melting glacier.

Light fell through the slatted blinds onto the worn wooden floor and the overhead fan spun slowly as she worked out her first scene, an Indian longhouse shadowed by the rocky hill. She had a good half hour to herself before the bell on the door started jangling—a passerby in for a vanilla Coke, Bo Harris in for a cup of hot water, fumbling in his pocket for a tea bag. Then it was one after the other, people in for coffee and grilled muffins at first, then, as noon approached, for franks and hamburgers and Cokes.

The last lunch straggler left by two, and Dez was at the sink, up to her elbows in lukewarm gray suds, when the door jangled again. A middle-aged man wearing a much-too-small brown woolen suit that looked like it was suffocating him peered in with almost comical hope. "Are you open?" At Dez's nod, he pulled off his hat with some relief, revealing a dark red crease across his forehead where the brim cut into his skin. His face was pink and damp.

"The druggist isn't in," Dez said. "But if you leave your prescription—" she gestured with her chin toward the countertop "—you can pick it up later tonight."

"Oh, I don't need anything filled," he said. He hoisted himself onto a stool and folded his hands in front of him. "Unless a lemon Coke counts as medicine. I think it could, on such a hot day. I do think so."

Dez suppressed a sigh. Judging by the size of him, he would want at least two, as well as a big lunch and probably a slice of pie. Then the late-afternoon crowd would wander in and she'd never get back to her drawings.

She dried her hands and offered him a menu, thick plastic edged in black. He studied it as she pumped cola syrup into a glass, added fizzy water and ice, cut into a fresh lemon and squeezed the juice into the mix. She poured the soda into a paper cone and set it into its chrome support. "Are you visiting?"

"I'll be around for a while," he said. He pursed his lips and made his eyes comically round, an expression that came across as effeminate. "And I'm afraid I won't be very popular." When she didn't react, he said, "I'm from the water commission," emphasizing the word *water*, and smiling with exaggerated gratitude when she didn't then change her manner. He mouthed, as if whispering a secret, "I guess I'm already infamous. Some kid just threw a mud ball at my car."

In the space of the next two minutes he told her what had to be his entire life history: about growing up in Athol, about his wife and son and how they were living in Newton but would likely head back to Athol now that he had landed this job, about his brother in Springfield, who had six kids and was let go from the Smithfield dartboard factory. "You never think about how things like that are made, do you? Dartboards."

Dez admitted that no, she did not.

"Well, sure, someone's got to make them. Joe used to sand the edges. I do what I can to help, but it's been tough for me, too, till I got this job."

He told her too much, things most people would never talk about. Like how at one low point last winter his wife went to the welfare for some oatmeal and they gave her some but not before some grudging worker said, *You got a husband and a fine boy?*

"You might not see, out here, with farms and all, just how bad it is in the cities, but people are fighting over the garbage restaurants throw out. I couldn't say no to a job. I hope people won't hold it against me."

He seemed too thin-skinned, too concerned with whether people liked him. "No," Dez agreed. "You can't say no to a job."

His job would be to assist the commissioner, and he wasn't supposed to start work until Monday but he had decided it was smart to come early. "Get the lay of the land. The boss shows up Monday, knows I'm on the ball."

Asa and his diggers didn't expect anyone in town until Monday. What if this man went exploring? With his large frame, he didn't look like he did too much recreational walking, but you could never make assumptions. Secret Pond really was well named, but someone walking the course of the river might hear voices and investigate.

"So it's between us and Whistling Falls," she said, stating the fact to see if he might reveal information.

The last of his Coke zipped through the paper straw and disappeared. He glanced up, out of breath, and gestured for another. "Technically."

"Technically?" She set to mixing the second Coke.

"Between you and me, Cascade's the best choice, but we'd have less trouble if we took Whistling Falls."

She nodded, hoping he'd say more, and slid the drink in front of him.

"I shouldn't talk about it," he said. He studied the menu. "You wouldn't have any meat loaf, would you?" He was the kind of man whose face softened at the mention of food. "I could go for a nice meat loaf, makes my mouth water just to think about it."

"No, no meat loaf."

"I stopped in here once and there was a great meat loaf on the menu."

"My mother-in-law's, but she's passed away, a couple of years now."

He mumbled his sympathy. "And the playhouse—I saw it's boarded up. Don't tell me the playmaster's gone, too."

"My father. Did you know him?"

"He's passed on?"

"At the New Year."

He was effusive in his condolences, in his praise for her father.

"But how did you know him?"

"Oh, it's a story," he said, clasping his hands together. "One night he was playing that king who gets murdered by the fellow who wants his throne—what's-his-name." He snapped his fingers, tapped at his temple.

"Duncan."

"No, the name of the play," he said. "*Macbeth*, of course, *Macbeth*. Oops. I'm not supposed to say the name of that play, am I? It's bad luck. Right?"

"It's only bad luck if you say it inside a theater. Supposedly."

"Right. Well. I was in town selling to Stein's—I was selling then—and saw all the commotion going on, the party on the lawn. It had rained earlier and down by the river was muddy. There was a woman serving small cakes."

"Rose's madeleines!"

"Oh, they were good! She gave me one on a napkin, but I swallowed too quickly and it caught in my throat and I choked. No one knew I was choking—I think they just saw this big man doing a strange little dance—and as it came free I slipped and fell down into the mud. Gee, now that I think of it, with that kid throwing the mud at my car, I've gotten into a lot of mud in this town." He laughed. "I know I looked a sight and people were trying not to laugh, but your father was the one who didn't laugh a bit. He helped me up and brought me inside. My clothes were all muddy and he fitted me out with something to wear while that lady fixed up my

clothes. Put me in a king's cape." He laughed, then shook his head, whistling, and gazed at her. "So you're the playmaster's daughter."

"Dez Spaulding," she said, offering her hand.

"Stanley," he said, pumping hard. "Stanley Smith. Call me Stan."

"A king's cape! That's just what my father would do." She asked him
what he wanted for lunch.

"Three franks," he said. "With relish, mustard, and onions. And cole-
slaw. And beans, if you have them. And chips."

She set the franks sizzling on the grill. Two women she didn't know
sat down and ordered chocolate frappes, and she was busy for a while,
grilling and scooping and mixing.

"Hey, the franks—" Stan said at one point. The grill was smoking, the
franks starting to scorch.

She rolled them over. "I'm not much of a cook. Too bad for you you
didn't stop at the Brilliant." She let them brown, then used tongs to pick
them up and stuff them into their rolls, snugging each one into a cardboard boat. The three boats took up most of the plate, so she removed a
side plate from the stack next to the grill and filled it with a ladle of beans,
a handful of potato chips, and four pickles. She set the condiment tray in
front of him—three triangles filled with relish, mustard, onions, three
small spoons.

With the customers taken care of, she retreated to the end of the
counter with her sketchpad. The hill was sufficiently imposing, dominating the Indian longhouses below, which were covered, rectangular structures, so sensible really, unlike Thomas Cole's pretty little tipis in the first
series. Her hand slashed right to left, diagonally, making the timbers that
formed the longhouse roof. *Slash, slash*—she looked up distractedly.
Someone was clearing her throat in such a way as to be noticed. One of
the women, a dark brunette with heavy lipstick, caught her eye and pursed
her lips together. Dez hadn't noticed that both women's paper cones and
metal frappe containers were drained. She hadn't asked if they wanted
anything else, hadn't offered their bill. She hurried to help them, but they

paid with coins and took every penny of their change. When the door jangled behind them, Stan made a face at their departing shadows, visible on the sidewalk. "What were you drawing?"

"Some ideas I have for some paintings that record the town's history."

"Let's see."

He whistled when she handed him the pad. "You're a real artist. I always wished I had a talent like that."

"You like to draw?"

"Oh, I'd take any kind of talent. Music, poetry. I used to write poems. I even sent them off to the *Atlantic Monthly*. They were pretty bad when I look back on them. You know that poem 'A Psalm of Life'? Long-fellow?"

"No." She knew "The Song of Hiawatha," the poem all schoolchildren learn. That was about it.

"Tell me not, in mournful numbers, Life is but an empty dream! For the soul is dead that slumbers, And things are not what they seem. Life is real! Life is earnest! And the grave is not its goal; Dust thou art, to dust returnest, was not spoken of the soul." He reddened, as if he had forgotten himself. "That's part of it. I wish I could write a poem like that but I guess I was destined to be a reader."

"It's a lovely poem. It's the way I often feel. I'll have to look that one up." He was sweet, this pudgy man in his tight, season-inappropriate suit, reciting poetry.

"I know I don't look the type."

"What's 'the type'?" she said. "There's no such thing as a type. Some-times people in a certain profession *will* act or dress in similar ways, but I think that's part of the human need to be in a group. That can border on pretension. When I was in Paris in the twenties I noticed that—"

"You've been to *Paris*?"

She smiled.

"You ever sketch people?"

"Sure. Sometimes." Was he angling for a picture? Did he want to inspire art, did he want to be immortalized? Did everybody? "How about I do a quick sketch?"

She cleared away his plate and wiped the counter clean.

"Maybe put your hat back on," she said. "Rest this arm like that. Prop your chin in your other hand."

Then she sketched him. More than sketched—she drew a fine, detailed likeness. Her hand flashed across the paper as her eyes darted up and down, looking from his face to the paper and back again. He was a good model, showing no sign of boredom or fatigue as he perched on the stool. She captured his self-deprecating eyes, his pursed mouth. He was all curves, no angles, with a round nose and bulbous chin, but she gave his head a proud tilt and didn't include the sweat. She made sure his hat fit. She shaded in his face, remarking that it was a miracle no other customers had come in. Then she signed her name. *Desdemona Hart Spaulding, 1935.* It was a flattering portrait that she handed to him, and with the exception of the playhouse work she used to do for her father, she had never felt anyone to be so appreciative of her work.

His eyes took in every stroke, every detail. "What a kindness." He placed his fist over his mouth. "You are truly the playmaster's daughter. Thank you."

Late in the afternoon, Asa returned from digging and headed straight to the back room to wash up. Dez found him bent over the sink, rubbing a bar of Lux along his arms and hands. She mentioned Stan casually, and he set down the soap and turned to give her his full attention.

"Where is he now?"

"Checked into the hotel, I guess."

And then he told her—how they were working on something. "In the woods. A silly long shot, I suppose, but something I hope might make the decision makers think twice about Cascade." He unfolded a towel from the stack by the sink. "You can't mention it to anyone. I mean no one. If anyone finds out, the plan's ruined. What's this fellow's name again?"

"Stan Smith."

"What if he goes around snooping?"

"I don't think he will. He's a chatterbox. Seems more the type to hang around town talking."

Asa rubbed at his arm absentmindedly. "Let's hope."

13

On Monday morning, the third of June, Asa's alarm clock went off in the gray before dawn. Dez heard him flipping his calendar, running the tap in the bathroom, rustling in the wardrobe. He whispered, "Good luck with your calls," and headed off, hopeful about his own plan, and about the five sample watercolor-and-pen drawings Dez had finished and which were now propped up on top of the wainscoting in the kitchen so she could refer to them when she called the editors.

She slipped the thermometer under her tongue and tried to lie quietly but already her heart was fluttering about in her chest. It was one thing to imagine calling up editors and speaking in a confident manner. It was another thing to actually do it.

Downstairs, she looked over the drawings. The first panel depicted unspoiled Cascade land with no inhabitants, the rocky hill sitting just off-center. The next showed a longhouse inhabited by the Nipmucks who once lived along the Cascade River. In the third panel, settlers' homes began to appear in the valley, and the Nipmucks were an indistinct group moving west.

She was a little afraid that the panels were a bit too much obvious representation, a child's history book illustration, but that was what popular magazines used—pictures with mass appeal. The fourth panel was the one she liked most. It showed the stark months that were possibly to come: houses demolished, trees chopped down, townspeople slinking after the ghosts of the Nipmucks. There was such irony in the situation— though maybe that was the kind of thing that only history recognized. The fifth and final panel, she liked, too—all water, the top of the bald hill transformed to a rocky island.

———————

At nine o'clock, when the hour chimed through the house, she swallowed, picked up the phone, and waited for the operator, hoping it wouldn't be Lil, but it was Lil, who asked again about taking in a movie, perhaps some night this week while Asa was at work.

It really all depended, Dez said, on what happened with some work she was hoping to do. Then she read off the list of editors' names and numbers. She had decided to go for the less exclusive, more accessible magazines. That way, she might have more of a chance of getting a foot in the door.

"Keep your line free," Lil said.

The return calls could take hours, and those hours seemed endless. Later she would have only the vaguest memory of flitting around the house, sweeping and dusting and polishing furniture, stripping the bed, washing the sheets, and hanging them to dry in the wind.

The first call back came at eleven thirty: the editor of the *Weekly Fountain*, who cut her off as soon as she started to talk. He had no interest in paintings, only photographs, and was so closed-minded about listening to her arguments that she was surprised he'd bothered to return the call. Over the next few hours, Lil put her through to a few secretaries who said their bosses were not interested, to one editor who played with the idea, then said no. A good idea, but for photography, he said. Was she skilled with a camera? She tried to hide her exasperation when she pointed out that photographs would be interesting, yes, but only when the actual destruction, and eventual flooding—at the very least months or possibly even years away!—took place. She attempted to sell the human side of a potential pictorial, how detailed, realistic colored drawings could relay the history of the town, as well as envision the threatened destruction. No interest.

She was glum, and by two o'clock, discouraged. Maybe magazines weren't the best place—but they offered the only opportunity for color. A black-and-white representation in a newspaper would be no better than illustrations of twenty years ago. No one would care about those.

She heard Jimmy's whistle on the back step, his attention-seeking coughs, and finally, the clatter of the mail flap and his retreating footsteps. On the floor lay a single piece of mail, a postcard—a fine watercolor-and-ink rendering of the New York City skyline from Abby.

I'm living here between 7th and 8th Avenues at 267 West 33rd Street near Penn Station. The apartment has hot water, shared bath, electric light. I'm next to a grocer. Submitting an application to the W.P.A. and hanging around Union Square. I've switched to Camels. They calm me down.

Dez fingered the card, thinking how pleasant it was to get a postcard, what a nice little lift it gave a person, and then it came to her. A simple idea—so simple and right that she was preternaturally calm calling Lil again. She asked her to get Gerald Washburn at *The American Sunday Standard* in New York, and to say that it was very important, because, she thought, she might as well aim high. "And Lil," she said, "please tell him Miss Desdemona Hart is calling."

Calling herself "Miss" seemed a smart decision. Unmarried women were perceived as more reliable workers.

Then she sat down to sketch, to start all over again. The five samples she had done were far too placid and contemplative. Forget Indian long-houses. Why hadn't she been visualizing the destruction as horrifically as it would undeniably be? To create their bowl, their reservoir, the water commission would have to chop down trees, bulldoze buildings. The destruction would be complete. She rendered the splintering of wood, the shattering of windows, and even envisioned a bulldozer smashing into the playhouse. And sketching the church steeple, she had a sudden thought—what would become of the cemetery? The headstones, the bodies? Her family was buried in that cemetery. All those coffins would be moved—a disturbing detail she would have to convey without being tasteless.

When Lil rang back, it was past three o'clock. "Mr. Washburn at *The American Sunday Standard* for you."

Dez clutched the heavy earpiece. She took a steadying breath and spoke into the horn. "Mr. Washburn!" Her heart pounded and her throat was dry, but she explained who she was in a steady, friendly voice. She told him about the threat facing Cascade. She explained her proposal, though she refrained, at first, from explaining her newest idea. Let him come up with his objections first, she thought, as he did.

"Indeed, I would be quite interested in this as a story," he said, his voice cordial and crisp, like biting into apples, "but I must say that pho-tographs are what would interest people."

"For curiosity's sake, possibly, but what can you show now except what is? How can you show what was and what will be gone? You can do so much more, dramatically, with an artistic rendition, Mr. Washburn. You can convey, you can portray history as well as the present, you can convey what will be in store for the town when the destruction happens." She looked to Abby's postcard. "I'm proposing something different, a series of postcards." She suggested a "now" and "if" pair of two to start, describing the "if" illustration of the drowned town as horrifically as she could. "There will be a submerged church, only the steeple showing. Library books floating away, drowning tombstones. We can call it *Postcards from Cascade.*"

The line went quiet. She thought she could hear the sound of papers rustling, the scratch of a fountain pen. When the pause went on too long, she said, "I can draw and paint in the kind of detailed, realistic manner you see in Norman Rockwell's work, though of course I have my own style. You will see for yourself. You know people get such a kick out of illustrations that are realistic."

"I wouldn't have time to send a writer out there," he said slowly.

She was quite capable of writing, she said, her heart beginning to race. "I can set the right tone: the years of threats now coming to a head. If we start right away, we'll build tension as the town waits for the state's decision."

"Well, my dear, you interest me, your idea interests me. Of course, I'd need to see a sample," he said. "Of your artwork, your writing."

He asked her to hold the line and this time she heard the mouthpiece thump against something hard. When he returned his voice was firm. "Listen. I'm going with my instinct here. We've had to shelve a Yankees article and I've got a hole to fill. I'll give you a chance—if you get your work to me by Wednesday afternoon, and I like it, I'll run it in the Sunday issue. And maybe I'll consider a serial. *Postcards from Cascade.* I like the sound of it."

Getting a package to him by Wednesday basically meant that she had the rest of the day to do two brand-new watercolors and write the accompanying text, but if she stayed up all night, she could manage. She would do it, she said. And then figure some way to get a package to New York.

"We were just saying we need something new to capture the public's interest. Will the melodrama play out over the course of the summer, do you think?"

"It absolutely will."

They discussed how many words each card's caption would have to comprise—35 tops, but the overall text could run to 350, which they would spread across the bottom of both pages. She didn't have to worry about it being perfectly written, they could edit, but it did need to be accurate. As for the illustrations, each postcard would be seven inches across by five and a half down—larger than true postcard size, a size that would reproduce well. She could make the illustrations larger if she liked; they could scale them down. Just make sure, he said, to leave at least two inches of white space around each illustration. When he rang off, she replaced the earpiece and stared at it.

She had done it. She had succeeded not just in getting someone interested, but in getting the editor of *The American Sunday Standard* interested. Her thoughts began to soar—ridiculously, ambitiously—she couldn't help it. She imagined her postcards capturing the imaginations of readers everywhere, gallery dealers from New York calling her up. She knew, even as she fantasized, that she was being silly—fine art dealers wouldn't seek out an illustrator, a woman illustrator at that, but the *Standard* was an incredible start. It was New York. It was *The American Sunday Standard*. She let herself bask, then she called up the expressman, who said that getting a package to New York for Wednesday meant he would have needed it in hand hours ago.

That would be fine for future weeks, but did her no good now. She felt the first fluttering of panic, then, *Abby*, she thought. She could wire Abby, ask her to meet the Connecticut train at Pennsylvania Station. She could ask Boydie Shaw to ask his brother, the Connecticut conductor, to deliver the package to Abby on Wednesday. That was a lot of relying on other people, but if it didn't work, she would get on the train herself if she had to. She called Lil back, gave her Abby's address, and dictated a simple telegram that explained the situation. WILL SEND DETAILS TOMORROW.

She called the drugstore but Asa was out on a delivery, so she got to work. She owned exactly two Strathmore illustration boards and she really didn't have time to soak and stretch paper and wait for it to dry— but just in case of any mistakes, she had better prepare some paper. She carried two sheets of her smoothest and heaviest paper upstairs to the bathroom. She unfolded a clean towel, set it on the floor, set the paper on the towel, and filled the bathtub with a couple of inches of water. She pressed each sheet of paper into its own half of the tub to soak, and went straight downstairs to look over the sketches sitting on her worktable. She would use the same perspective for both scenes, she decided—a slightly elevated, all-encompassing view of the town common. Using the faintest lines, she reproduced the two sketches onto the two illustration boards.

Back upstairs, she removed two white pillowcases from the linen closet and laid them on the floor. Then she lifted each piece of paper out of the water and set it to rest on the clean cotton until each piece of paper seemed drained and evenly saturated. She carried them, one in each hand, fingers pinching each pillowcase to each piece of paper, down to her worktable and stretched each one on a wooden board, pushing a line of thumbtacks around the four sides.

They would take a few hours to dry taut, but they were backup, and hopefully she wouldn't need them.

She began to paint. She worked quickly, efficiently, with great focus, but the afternoon passed quickly, sunlight shifting east to west across the walls. *Don't panic*, she told herself. She could stay up all night if she had to. When Asa came home for supper, she didn't even hear him come in until he knocked on the studio door and asked what was going on.

She blinked, disoriented. The room had dimmed. Then she told him, and his response made it real, his shock, his "The *Standard*," his "My God, that's a big deal," made it real.

"It is a big deal, isn't it?" She stretched back in her chair, conscious of how stiff she was from sitting in the same position for so long.

It took a moment for him to collect himself. "But why didn't you call me?"

She had, she said, but Mrs. Raymond said he was out on a delivery, and then she just got busy.

He stood over her to look down on the paintings. She felt him shake his head. He rested his hands on her shoulders and massaged where they were tight from sitting. He would get himself dinner at the Brilliant, he said. In fact, he could hardly wait to get to town and tell everyone what his wife had managed to do.

By the time he returned, a little after eleven, she'd moved only twice, once to brew tea and grab a slice of toast, and once to go to the bathroom. Enough work was done that she could stretch again, talk to Asa a bit before he headed up to bed.

By one, the paintings were complete, but she had to push on and write the text. She sat down, pen in hand, body buzzing with fatigue, and stared at the lined paper. It was like being in school and waiting until the last minute to write a report—a terrible stuck feeling. *Stuck*, a perfect word, sounding how it felt. *Stuck*. She closed her eyes, remembered a teacher's writing advice. *Think clearly about what you want to say, then say it.*

She wrote the "now" postcard's text first, something similar to a postcard Zeke had been selling for years at the Handy: *Greetings from tiny Cascade, Massachusetts, where summer welcomes are extended to visitors seeking cool breezes, clear waters, A-class golf, and cultural diversions like the renowned Cascade Shakespeare Theatre.*

The "what if?" postcard was somber, and she gave the text the overly dramatic tone that the popular magazines liked, starting with: *Cascade, Massachusetts, is no more. The thirsty city of Boston has carved its own drinking bowl far west of the city limits.*

As introduction to both postcards, she summarized the long-standing threat—Boston's water demands taxing the local supply, the water commission created by the legislature in 1927, the House and Senate passing the water bill back in 1928, the months of drought. That came to 339 words.

It was two a.m. when she finished. She was pleased. The words set the right tone, and the paintings were compelling and attractive, full of the kind of tiny detail that entertained the eye. The *"now"* postcard depicted Cascade as a desirable, archetypal summer town. Boats sailed the river, pennants flapped in the breeze. A milk wagon rolled through town. There was a concert on the common, a church picnic, children flying kites above the Cascade Falls, and actors in Elizabethan costume on the lawn of the playhouse.

The *"what if?"* postcard was meant to frighten: roiling waters at window level; rising tombstones, the foremost stone embellished with an angel holding its head in its hands. A king's crown bobbed near the playhouse, and books floated from the open windows of the library. She signed both paintings "Desdemona Hart," a tribute to her father, a toss of a coin into a wishing well. Who knew? These simple works might save the playhouse.

"They're wonderful," Asa said next morning. "They really are, Dez." He was somber, studying them, and when she stood beside him to look at them again, he put his arm around her. "You showed it as bad as it will be."

The colors had dried overnight but she worried over them anyway, and waited until the last minute to parcel them up. Then she placed them securely in between thick cardboard and taped the sides all around. She double-wrapped the entire package in brown paper, tied it with twine, and addressed it, the big black letters more solid proof: her work was going to the *Standard*. The *Standard* was expecting her work.

There was some bustle at the train station, the arrival of more men from Boston, the ones who would be setting up the water board office out at the boys' camp, on the north side of river. Dez counted six of them—thin men with loose wrists and baggy trousers, peering up from under the brims of their caps, careful not to look too long at anyone. But no one really blamed them. You couldn't blame a man for taking any job he could get.

Dez found Boydie Shaw out on the platform smoking a cigarette. What would she have done if he had not been working? *You'd have gotten on that train.*

Not a problem at all, Boydie said, when she explained the situation. In fact, it was an honor. Everyone he met, up and down his route, he said, had been talking about one thing and one thing only—the absolute unfairness of it all. He took the parcel and held it close to his chest. He assured her he wouldn't part with it until he put it into his brother's hands, and that Frank Shaw would deliver it himself to Abby if she would just meet him under the big clock at Penn Station at exactly ten o'clock tomorrow morning, and if by chance Abby did not meet the train, Boydie said Frank would arrange for one of the porters to take it on up to the *Standard*'s offices. "You can make that good with me later on, if that happens."

Next door at the telephone exchange, Alma Webster was tucking into a jelly donut when Dez walked in. Alma jumped up, wiped her mouth with a Kleenex, and brushed her hands together, beaming. William Hart must be smiling down, she said. Smiling down from heaven.

Dez found herself ducking her head in mild embarrassment. She wasn't accustomed to people in town thinking she was anything special. And she was quick to point out that nothing as yet was published. Hopefully the editors would like what she had done, she said, but in the meantime she needed to make sure her work got into their hands. She filled out a telegraph blank for Abby and passed it to Alma.

"That's sixty-five cents to New York, plus yesterday's, if you want to pay it now. So one dollar thirty."

As Dez dug in her wallet, the teleprinter began to churn out an incoming tape. Alma turned away to remove, cut, and gum the message to a blank telegram form. "Will that be all today, hon?"

Dez started to say yes, then hesitated. Why not? "Actually no. I think I'll send one more." Her hand trembling with the boldness of her decision, she filled out a second blank for Jacob, a brief announcement of her news. She had never sent him anything before, but she knew his address by heart. West Bishop Street, Springfield.

"One-fifty total," said Alma.

Dez pushed a dollar bill and two quarters across the counter. She just wanted him to know, that was all.

—————

In the morning, she bolted up from sleep, certain that Abby never received her telegrams, that Boydie's brother lost the package, that Jacob—she had no idea what Jacob might be thinking. She was a bag of nerves all day until the doorbell rang at one and she raced to greet the Western Union boy—Popcorn's brother, she could never remember his name—waiting on the porch. She tore the telegram in half in her eagerness to open it and had to hold the two pieces together to read the message. Abby had picked up the package and walked it up to Forty-third Street to deliver it directly into Mr. Washburn's waiting hands. SHOWED SAMPLES OF MY OWN WORK TOO. HOPE YOU DON'T MIND.

Dez reread the last sentence, wondering exactly what kind of samples Abby had shown. She didn't think she minded, no, but Abby lived just blocks from the *Standard*'s offices; she was primed to insert herself into any particular opportunity that might present itself.

She spent the day upstairs, washing the winter's dirt from the windows, waxing the floors, scrubbing the bathroom with a bleach-and-powder combination. She tried not to visualize New York, or the *Standard*'s offices, or Mr. Washburn unwrapping and reviewing her work. She wished it was possible to have copied what she sent so she could look it over. In her mind's eye, the paintings were not as wonderful as they seemed when she first finished them. She wished that Jacob could have looked at them, advised, judged. Had he even received the telegram, and if he had, what had he thought?

At four thirty, when the telephone jangled twice, she slipped on the stairs in her race to answer it, landing on her knee, hard. She scrambled up and into the kitchen.

"Hold for Gerald Washburn," Lil said, the initial, foolish prick of disappointment swept away by the enthusiasm she heard in Mr. Washburn's voice when Lil put him through.

He liked the work, he said, very much. In fact, their entire editorial team was quite enthusiastic. "I'm thinking, Miss Hart, that your idea for a serial might be a good one. We'll build the tension and when the time comes for Cascade to be chosen, we'll have the country biting its nails."

And that was the hitch. His publisher, Mr. Washburn said, was willing to go along with the serial if the imminent destruction of Cascade was certain.

"I thought our slant might be one that would root for saving Cascade."

"Well, you made that sound unlikely. You *drew* it unlikely."

Had she?

"Is it? Because it's a great human story. The fact that our readers will be able to say to themselves, well, we may have lost our jobs, our daily bread, but we still have our homes, our towns, beneath our feet. That's the angle we want to take."

"I see."

"If it's not really a threat, if it's all going to blow over, then we'd rather not invest the pages in it. Because if they take the other town, well, there's obviously not the same kind of drama, as you yourself implied, what with library shelves emptied, and a hotel abandoned. I'm a bit confused here."

The late-afternoon sun cast long shadows on the linoleum. She rubbed her knee where a bruise seemed already to be forming. He was waiting for her response. Of course the chances were high that the water board would choose Cascade—and of course she didn't want it to, but if Cascade was fighting a losing game, there really was no sense in her losing an opportunity like this.

She hoped no one was listening in on the line. No Lil, no Alma. "Actually, Mr. Washburn, I know someone inside the water commission," she said quietly, too quietly. She was forced to repeat herself when Mr. Washburn asked her to speak up.

"This man I know on the water commission. Well, he said that the state is just going through the motions." Stan had practically said so.

"Well then," Mr. Washburn said. "I'm making a gut-level decision here to go with this, but I like what you did. I think it'll be a great feature. I'll be in touch with you, probably on Monday—let you know the reaction we get. Assuming it's well received, we'll go ahead. All right? In the meantime, draw the next set and get them to me. We'll pay you no matter what.

And if it's all a go-ahead, then when the time comes that the town *is* dismantled, we'll dispatch a photographer, too. Expand the story, make it even bigger."

She placed the receiver back on the box. It was all happening so fast. Her paintings, even now, were being rushed into production, printed and duplicated, ready to be shipped off all over America. In three days she would see her work in *The American Sunday Standard*. But the *Standard*'s slant on the story of Cascade was going to be one of impending doom.

14

The days leading up to her issue's release were the days that would, in retrospect, be hard to remember distinctly. Dez would remember agitation, and pacing, watching the sun rise over Pine Point. She would remember the banjo clock chiming the hours, the morning milk delivery turning into the morning mail delivery turning into the afternoon mail, the afternoon paper, and then the sun setting all over again. Thursday there was a slight, foolish hope that lessened as the day wore on that Jacob might show up. At sunset, she escaped the stuffiness of the kitchen and stood on the porch. A breeze blew up from the water, a strong, head-clearing breeze. It was just as well he never came, she thought. She was a foolish woman with a good husband, a husband who had suggested a celebratory meal at the Brilliant on Saturday evening, a husband who was so busy taking care of the town that he had called to say he couldn't make it home for supper.

But the empty hours stretched ahead of her. The evenings were starting to grow long. Light lingered on the lawn, which was still a soft, early-summer green, a green with bright yellow in it. She covered the meat loaf with a dampened tea towel and slid it into the still-warm oven. She pulled her hair back into a bun and slipped her feet into her loafers. A walk would be good. A walk to the falls, which felt wonderful once she was out there on the road, the breeze rippling her blouse, the pavement solid under her feet. She should walk every day. She had loved walking in Paris—along the river and up over the Pont Neuf to wander through the Île de la Cité and the Île Saint-Louis. Sometimes you needed to look up from your work, from yourself, blink your eyes—there was a sky up there, a vast expanse of air to breathe.

In town, the fresh air had brought people outdoors. A group of boys played some kind of tin-can-and-stick game on the common; a rummage sale was going on at Stein's. Al Stein would be having plenty of those once he got his hands on the rest of Jacob's inventory. Or maybe he already had it and she would never see Jacob again. It was possible, though painful and bewildering. So many people came into your life, and they were such a part of the everyday that it was impossible to imagine them gone until, one day, they were. There had been years of best friends at Farmington, and then Jane Park—eighteen months they'd lived together in Paris, close as cousins—and Pierre Denis, though she was always squeamish to remember him and how she had played at passion. It was Jacob who'd ignited something new, something hard to let go of.

At the Criterion Theater, the marquee had changed. The first feature was *Anna Karenina,* and this seemed immediately to be some kind of sign, as did the quarter she happened to have in her pocket. There, fate seemed to be saying, remind yourself what happens to wives who lust after other men.

Dez walked into the foyer. Zeke ran a Thursday night double-header every week, two movies for the price of one, and it was popular. Dez paid, took her ticket, gave it to the usher—one of Hartwell Page's boys—and walked into the lobby, where she was immediately swarmed, treated like one of the film stars, someone joked. Elsie and Bill Smith, and Zeke, and the Pages, and Rose's old friend Hazel Burns, who was there with Peter

Southwick's widowed father—they all wanted to know every detail, or more precisely, to be a part of the excitement and anticipation. The issue would be out on Saturday, she confirmed, and the attention was gratifying and a little bit heady until she realized that everyone was certain the publicity would foster some kind of groundswell of support to save Cascade. Then she was eager to slink away to the back row, and grateful when the lights began to dim. But who knew? Maybe the postcards would indeed foster a groundswell of support. Maybe Mr. Washburn would himself be surprised. What was meant to happen would happen, she told herself.

Onstage, the curtains parted to the trumpet fanfare that introduced the newsreels. Images flickered in grainy black and white as that man with the voice who made everything sound so dire narrated the news: Roosevelt speaking to Congress, recommending that the United States maintain neutrality. King George and Queen Mary celebrating their silver jubilee, smiling and waving from a palace balcony. Then, an odd bit about a mysterious woman who wore a long black veil and showed up at Rudolph Valentino's tomb in Hollywood every year on the anniversary of his death. The newsreel flashed to an image of Valentino on a beach somewhere—in close-fitting swim trunks, hands resting on his hips, hair slicked back off his face. The time he came to Cascade, he was not yet a film star but part of a traveling musical production that had used the theater for a week. Dez didn't remember him—she'd been only eight or so—but for years after his visit, people talked about him. Even her own father got caught up, lamenting that he hadn't nabbed him for a performance—what a perfect, narcissistic Orsino in *Twelfth Night* he would have made.

The bit ended with an image of the veiled woman, her arms full of roses, reaching up to place the flowers on top of his tall crypt.

Whoever she was, she was part of the mysterious passion that the man's very existence had evoked. Dez remembered the hysteria, the news of the mobbed funeral in New York, the second funeral in Hollywood. The people who killed themselves—the woman in London who took poison, the boy in New York who first covered himself with photographs of Valentino. If people could kill themselves over the death of a person they did not even know, then who knew how Dr. Proulx might have justified his own action?

Finally, the movie began, but from the start, it was all wrong. Fredric March was a stiff, unsympathetic Vronsky. Everyone except Garbo overacted, but she was too serious, too brooding. Karenin—he was simply an unsympathetic buffoon. And Dez had no patience with these movies that had people simply *looking* at each other and falling in love. *Love looks not with the eyes but with the mind.* Where was the connection, what linked them together? Common interest? Understanding of the other? In the book, Vronsky so clearly saw and was attracted to Anna's *nature*. The movie should show that, show her nature revealed somehow, should make clear that it was her soul that he loved.

Only the scenes between Anna and her child came off as sincere. Levin and Kitty, the heart of the novel—they barely graced this movie. The whole mess ended on a sentimental note, with Vronsky gazing at a photograph of Anna, remembering her well.

Nonsense, Dez thought. How would Vronsky not instead have been haunted by that image of Anna crushed beneath the train? What lover could look fondly upon the portrait of a loved one who had committed such a wretched suicide?

15

The Sunday magazines always arrived in Cascade on the Saturday-afternoon train from Boston. Walking to town to buy her copy, Dez rehearsed how she would react. She would be pleased, very pleased, but she would—*she would have to*—be objective. She would see the *Standard* for what it was: a popular magazine that entertained all types—the discriminating and the not-so-discriminating. Her postcards were not oils gracing a wall in the Met. They were not frescos on a church wall in Italy. They were reproductions in a popular magazine, a magazine that would be replaced in exactly seven days.

She felt strong, in control of her emotions, but as she turned down Main Street and closed in on the Handy, her surroundings blurred and her senses heightened. It was clearly crowded inside, which could only mean that the issue had arrived. She paused to control the flutter in her stomach, then pushed on the swinging screen door and stepped over the threshold, conscious of heads turning her way, Zeke catching sight of her and shouting, the cluster of people echoing Zeke, beckoning her in, swarming around. There were congratulations, thanks, and someone—Dwight, usually so bashful—sliding a copy into her hands and saying, *Here you go, Miss Famous Artist!*

To have someone in Cascade refer to her so. To take the magazine into her hands, to hold it, knowing her work was inside. The pages were heavy and slick and smelled of fresh ink. Her hands trembled, checking the table of contents, skimming the pages to get to 34 and 35. There they were: colorful pictorials that pleased the eye. "The colors reproduced very well," she heard herself saying. Her worry that they weren't as good as she remembered was unfounded. The tiny details—the king's crown, the floating books—were compelling and pleasing, the colors sharply rendered.

Dwight was the first to ask for her autograph, and she demurred, embarrassed. But he insisted, and then they all began teasing her until she finally said all right, and signed her name in the bottom right margin: *Desdemona Hart.*

Dwight lifted the magazine for all to see. "Look at that," he said. His policeman's badge flashed in the late-afternoon sunlight; the Handy's resident cat mewed loudly from its perch in the window. Life seemed full of light and promise and it was permissible, Dez thought, to let go, to feel exhilaration and joy, like a kite she could release and release, all the while knowing she had her hand firmly on the string. Around the country, people were looking at her work, liking it. Here in Cascade, people were proud and hopeful. It was only for seven days, so why not revel in it?

How much they pay you? someone asked, an indistinguishable voice that didn't ask again when the crowd, with a brief, chilly silence, told the voice—it sounded like Tilly Allison—that the question was rude.

But it was likely the question everyone was thinking, and valid, because she was being paid a crazy amount of money for doing something she had the time of her life doing. Seventy-five easy dollars to add to her playhouse fund. The cost of an actor's wage, the cost of printing a season's playbills. Zeke's counter was full of someone's grocery order— Wonder bread, cans of vegetables, a triangle of meat wrapped in thick white paper. At least ten dollars' worth—and to think that she would be getting seven times that.

Surely, there was more work down there for her. Abby was right—if she only got herself to New York, she would do all right. Illustration was something women had been doing successfully for years. And couldn't Asa do all right, too? If everyone in town had to leave anyway, why did it have to be Asa's decision where they would live?

Someone tapped her on the shoulder.

"I'm happy for you, Dez." It was Lil, though she didn't look happy at all, her manner begrudging. But then Bud Foster burst through the screen door, interrupting with a big hug—*Jeez, Dez, how'd you manage this?* And Bill Hoden and his twin sons hovered off to her side, waiting, wanting to know what she had in store for next week.

Dez was almost out the door when Lil cornered her again.

"Elsie mentioned she saw you at the Criterion the other night. I thought you were too busy to go."

It took a moment to process this—that in the midst of Dez's small, personal glory, Lil was caught up in hurt feelings. Dez felt herself sputtering inside, thinking of all the ways she could respond, but in the end, she voiced only the truth, that the movie was very last-minute, that she didn't even know she was going herself until she found herself wandering in.

Lil nodded. "I see," she said. But there was something else going on, Dez wasn't sure what.

At the drugstore, every stool was occupied, grill sizzling, drink blenders whirring, Mrs. Raymond refilling a glass cylinder with paper straws. Out back, Asa was bent over his mortar and pestle, grinding a prescription.

He looked up when she came in and he, too, behaved oddly—hesitating when Dez showed him the magazine. But his enthusiasm as he looked over the postcards was admiring and flattering. He pointed out details he liked and repeated how good the paintings were.

Still, his pleasure, his pride, seemed dampened. He was holding something back.

"Is something wrong?"

He shook his head in a way that said he was reluctant to spoil her moment, at the same time that he breathed in deep, ready to get something off his chest. "Well, it's this," he said, rubbing at the back of his neck, perplexed. "One of the operators happened to overhear you talking to that editor in New York. Saying you knew Cascade would be chosen."

"Lil handled that call," Dez said.

"Doesn't matter who."

"She shouldn't have been listening to my conversation."

He made a broad, forgiving gesture with his hands. "You know it happens. And that's beside the point, which is, is this true?"

"No one knows for sure what's going to happen."

"But did this man make a deal with you?"

"Of course we made a deal."

"But is it true he said he was only interested in doing this if you were positive Cascade was going to be the town they chose?"

"When did Lil tell you this?"

"It doesn't matter, I just want to know: Did you flat-out lie to that man?"

Had she? Not flat-out, no. "Mr. Washburn knows that nothing's very certain in this world right now. He's happy with the feature, and so is everyone else in this town except for my own husband and someone who used to call herself my friend."

He looked abashed; she saw him second-guessing himself. But when he wrapped her in an apologetic hug, when he said, "Just let me finish up and we'll go celebrate," she was sobered by a memory, a line from one of the plays, she couldn't remember which one exactly, and she couldn't remember the exact phrasing, but she did remember the gist: *Glory is like a circle in water which spreads and spreads and by its spreading, disappears to nothing.*

16

How quickly resolve, contrition, could turn to that eager, selfish state known as titillation. The crazy heartbeat, the wild wish: if only Asa had lagged behind. Because there was the black truck, parked in front of the Handy. There was Jacob himself walking out with a copy of the *Standard* in his hands.

"Oh, look, it's Jacob," she said, her voice somehow calm as her heart kicked against her chest.

He hesitated when he saw them, she could see that. But it was too late for him to do anything but do what he did, which was walk up and shake Asa's hand, looking him full in the eye in a way that Dez suspected meant that he was contrite. Then, to Dez, he was too overly cordial, asking how was it that in the short time he'd been away, she had managed to get herself into the pages of *The American Sunday Standard*? "I've been in New York," he explained. "I only just saw your telegram today."

She saw the look on Asa's face and hurried to explain how she'd come up with the idea. She knew she was blushing, and talking too quickly. It was the first time the three of them had shared the same space, and in the light of day, on Main Street, her connection to Jacob felt nothing like a relation-ship between two artists. He was the peddler. She was Asa's wife.

They were on their way to the Brilliant, she said, eager to break up the meeting. But first there was the sight of Jacob's palm disappearing inside Asa's handshake to endure, followed by unbidden thoughts: she had known the touch of both those hands (Asa, a little bit undone to find a bride in his childhood home, in his parents' old bedroom; Jacob, remov-ing the pins from her hair). And what kind of a woman did that make her? The kind that hoped Jacob wouldn't bring up what he did bring up: that he had one more delivery to make to Al, and since Stein's closed on Thursdays, he was hoping they could have one last meeting next Wednes-day. His manner was courteous, genial, as it had always been, showing Asa—and himself?—that these weekly meetings were faultless.

She wanted that final meeting—it might be her last chance to see him, and it would be innocent, the last time had simply been an aberration caused by the shock of Dr. Proulx's death—but she had to shrug, for Asa's sake, and murmur, "Sure," as if he had said he would deliver some apron or sauce pot.

At the Brilliant, there was distraction in the form of more congratulations. Everyone was clearly hoping that the exposure would start some kind of countrywide swell of support for Cascade. When Asa and Dez finally slid into one of the high leather booths, Dez gazed blindly at the menu Helen Whitby offered and tried to keep up a running conversation about the next postcards. There would be two: one depicting "now," one depicting "then." She had so many ideas for "then," cards, she said, wistful looks back at the 1910s and '20s—the regattas and parades. Maybe she could do a concert on the common, seeing as how the summer band concert series was about to start.

"You should put the old boys' camp in somewhere," Asa said. "All those little cabins, fun to look at."

"Good idea," she said, relieved enough to finally meet his eyes. He

looked as if he was turning something over and over in his mind, and
though he didn't seem particularly happy, he didn't seem angry, either. He
had to understand that it hadn't been easy to tell Jacob not to come. "And
for the 'now' card, I want to show how the town is fighting it—draw the
town meeting, I think. I could put Zeke Davenport in it. He'd get a kick
out of that." Let Lil spread stories about her after seeing that.

"Zeke would."

"I think I'll get the special." Her eyes sought Helen. "If I get the package to the expressman first thing Monday morning, they can promise
delivery in New York by Tuesday, and then I won't have to bother Boydie.
And I'm even thinking they might want to expand this—after Cascade,
do similar pieces on other American towns. Everyone's got a story, when
you think about it, especially in these times. Here's Helen."

Dez had never been more grateful for Helen Whitby, for her plump
good cheer and nonstop chatter as she placed their order then whistled
over every detail of the postcard spread, asking a stream of questions,
even making Asa laugh with her impressions of the humorless group of
Boston men—must have been water authority men—who had come in
a few weeks back. When Ike, behind the counter, signaled that their plates
were ready, Dez wished Helen could sit with them, keep the joviality
going. The food looked so good: the kind of delicious meat loaf Stan had
been looking for, sliced thick and studded with peppers and onions, with
Helen's hot ketchup sauce on the side. Buttery mashed potatoes, a hill of
green peas.

Asa casually picked up his fork. "So you sent him a telegram, huh?"

Dez's heart rate slowed to a thud.

"And he was obviously never told not to come to our house anymore."

Her appetite vanished, the food turning leaden on her plate. She
pushed it away. "I couldn't, Asa. The day I was going to was the day he
found Dr. Proulx."

Okay, his nod said, I'll give you that but—"That day you never shared
the news with me, you sent him a telegram."

"I called the drugstore and you were out. I told you that."

"You never bothered to call back. Yet you made an effort, you paid money, to send him a telegram."

"I sent the telegram later, after I gave Boydie the artwork, and I just did it to let him know—it was while I was already at the office sending one to Abby."

"I've been blind," he said, banging the table with such force that even he involuntarily did what Dez did—glanced around to see if anyone noticed.

But no one had. Helen was bent over a faraway booth, pointing out something on a menu. People were talking, eating, paying them no mind, and there, thankfully, was Zeke Davenport walking through the door.

Zeke, one hand shaded over his eyes to search the room, waved and headed over, sliding in next to Dez. For the next ten minutes, he was a savior, full of talk about the water authority, helping himself to the plate Dez had pushed away. She watched his fork digging in, back and forth, meat loaf to mouth, as he talked about the article his friend was writing for *The Boston Evening Transcript*—it would be published next week. Someone even came out to take pictures of the new golf course. "When I told him about Dez's postcards, it made all the difference. They really paved the way." He beamed at her and slapped the table. "Though she gave you the burn, didn't she?"

In response to their quizzical looks, he flipped open his copy of the *Standard* and pointed to Dez's small signatures, painted in the bottom left-hand corner of each postcard. *Desdemona Hart, 1935.*

"I didn't even notice," Asa said, turning toward Dez. "Why did you do that?"

As if she'd done something wrong. As if she'd done nothing right. "Because I did it for the playhouse," she said. "I did it for my father. I'm the last of the line, and I'm still a Hart even if I'm married."

Zeke slapped the table again, unaware of the tension that sat in the booth with him. "She's always been a firecracker in disguise."

It took forever to wind up the dinner, to pay, and then, on the way out, to stop and talk to everyone in the booths between theirs and the door.

Outside, Asa set off across the common, hands stuffed into his pants pockets, walking faster than Dez could keep up. Jim Carson, on his way home in his milk wagon, had to rein in his horse to avoid running into him.

Dez caught up with him at the playhouse. He was down by the water, crouching, picking through a pile of stones. When he became aware of Dez, he hurled one into the water.

"That reminds me of a line in one of your father's plays," he said bitterly, nodding toward the spreading ring the stone's entry formed. "Something about fame being like a circle in the water, getting bigger and bigger and bigger until it's nothing. Until it's gone."

Too strange that he should call that same phrase to mind! A coincidence that felt like it must mean something. Her hand closed around the magazine. "I didn't realize you paid such attention to the plays," she said carefully.

"I liked the king plays, liked seeing how men behave when circumstances interrupt their lives."

"Is that how you feel? That you're on an unplanned course?"

He rested his hands on his knees and squinted out over the water. "Maybe all men should have to fight something sometime in their lives. I'm thirty-three years old and I've never had to fight for a blessed thing, have I? And now look at me, fighting for my home, my wife. My famous wife. Fame's fleeting, Dez."

Asa trusted what his senses told him, that there was threat in the form of Jacob Solomon, threat in a wife's success. But did he imagine she was the kind of person who would run away from her promises?

"You're not fighting for me, Asa. And I'm hardly famous."

"You were in tough straits. You would have married anyone."

"That's not true."

"Look me in the eye, Dez. And tell me the truth."

She looked down into his eyes. For some reason, they always connected more intimately when she looked into his left eye rather than his right. The left eye latched on to her now.

"Would you have married me if the bank hadn't foreclosed on your house?"

She remembered a frigid autumn wind blowing the red auction flag, her father hacking away in bed, fighting the pneumonia that laid double stress on his heart. "I was frantic. I needed to find us a place to live—that was the main thought in my mind, it's true." His receptive nod was encouraging. If they could really talk and understand each other, then there was hope for a contented future, wherever they might live. "When you asked me to marry you I honestly wasn't thinking about myself."

It wasn't the response he wanted; the left eye betrayed this, turning glassy in a way he tried to hide by poking at the stones again. Maybe when people asked for honesty, what they really wanted was for you to say what they wanted to hear and for you to swear it was true. "Asa. I'm not saying I wouldn't have married you, anyway."

A branch floated past them, slowly, drifting another twenty feet before he finally spoke. "Tell me about Jacob Solomon."

Her pulse lurched, and she felt foolish and large, standing over him. Tongue-tied. The mayflies were out. "Please stand up and look at me," she said, batting at the flies.

He got to his feet. "Admit you like him."

"Of course I like him."

"No, that you really like him."

"He's my friend, of course I like him. But not in the way you're thinking." What else could she say? The truth? She wasn't even sure what the truth was—desire for Jacob ebbed and flowed, and always tussled with the desire for decency and respectability and the goodwill of others. It would be wonderful to speak freely, to admit all the conflicting emotions she felt for Jacob, but she couldn't, not without ripping apart something that likely would not stitch back together. "You're getting your wish, you know. You heard him. He's moving to New York."

He looked satisfied about that. "The mayflies are out, we better go."

They climbed up the embankment and walked along the side of the theater. Dez gazed down at the magazine in her hand. She had been so eager to see it and now it felt like old hat, like it had been out forever instead of still smelling of fresh ink. It was only an hour ago that they had set out for their celebratory dinner; now her hunger had returned but there was nowhere to go besides the Brilliant and she didn't want to go back there. Anywhere else would involve at least an hour's drive on dark roads, with a spare tire ready to go and more gasoline than you would want to use for an unnecessary trip.

"I don't know what I'd do if you asked for a divorce," Asa said.

The word itself—*divorce*—was startling, so vulgar and cheap, one she couldn't imagine applied to herself. Someone asking, "Are you married?" And having to say, "I'm divorced."

"It might be okay in some places, but around here, I can't imagine," he said, gesturing down the common to the rooftops and shutters of Main Street.

Those shutters would close up against the divorcee and her cold breeze. She didn't want to be divorced. She told him that. She meant it. The word *divorce*, like the word *suicide*, stood for intentional destruction, inherently wrong. "What I've honestly hoped for, Asa, is that if we do have to leave Cascade, that you would consider moving to a city."

There. Voicing the want made it real and uncomplicated, not a very big want at all. She wanted to live and work in a city, with people who were like her, with galleries and exhibitions and competitions and small restaurants you could go out your front door and walk to. "It doesn't have to be New York, it could be Boston. I liked Boston. Boston is small enough to feel comfortable. You liked it when you visited me."

He started to say no, then stopped himself. At least he did that. But his face flushed with exasperation.

"I love you, you know," he said.

"Do you?" She wasn't sure that the word meant the same thing to everyone. "What is it you love?"

"I love that you're you, that you're not like anyone else—Jesus, Dez, why do you have to pick everything apart?" He took her face in both his hands and pressed his lips to hers and somehow, without ever taking his hands off her, led her to the playhouse door. He still had the key and unlocked the door, throwing it open to pull her into the vestibule, his fingers swiftly, without any hesitation at all, unbuttoning her dress. It fell to the floor, a puddle around her feet that she stepped out of, aware of the slip clinging to her body, and the picture she knew she made, both of them falling to the floor together. She was probably safe, the mercury in the morning was still well over 98 degrees, and even if she wasn't, she couldn't stop. Not today, not now, a muddle of the desire she felt from this new, sure touch of his, from his urgency.

That time with Asa was good, better than it ever had been. Maybe, she thought, this kind of satisfaction had nothing at all to do with the other person, and everything to do with your own state of mind. They finished on their backs on the cold tile floor, looking up at the ceiling, past the tall empty case where the First Folio used to preside over play nights.

"I love you," he said, unable to conceal relief and pride.

She said "I love you, too" and they clutched fingers, hand to hand, eyes fixed on the ceiling. She imagined a fresco, a depiction of her life that ended here, upside down in her father's playhouse. What they had just enjoyed had been like something she might mix on her palette, an accidental color mixed from a haphazard selection of sexual challenge, lust, and a certain familiar companionship. Maybe all that added up to love.

God, it was such an ill-defined word, *love*. And *divorce* such a cheap one. A theater owner's wife out in Pittsfield had run away with the summer production's leading man a year or two back. She'd even left her children. Everyone had said the same thing: What kind of woman did such a thing?

"And what would a divorce do to this?" Asa said without warning, releasing her hand to spread his arms toward the strapwork ceiling. "I own it, whether I like it or not."

Was that his way of saying he would use the playhouse as a bargaining chip, if it came to that? She didn't know. She didn't think he did, either.

17

On Sunday night, Dez pushed back her chair and unfolded her legs—so stiff they were—and stood up to stretch. The second set was finished. She hoped the "before" postcard, circa 1912, would evoke nostalgia for that time before the war that everyone now took comfort from and looked back on as innocent. In her portrayal, an amalgam of long-ago twilit summer nights, patrons dressed in white gathered on the riverbank, where a placard announced the evening's show: *A Midsummer Night's Dream*. The playhouse glowed with amber light, a few milky stars had begun to appear in the sky, and at the other end of the common, Town Hall sat peaceful and quiet. It was a picture drawn from idealized memory, a memory of childhood nights when she had either been allowed to stay up late or else watched the goings-on, wistfully, from her bedroom window.

She had barely known Asa then. He had been part of those groups of older boys she had sometimes observed joking around and shoving one another when she was put to bed earlier than she could fall asleep, and had gazed, like a prisoner, out her window with its corner view of the common.

Sometimes she saw things she wasn't supposed to see. When she was eleven or twelve, she'd woken one night to the sound of a scuffle, to a man and woman arguing in vicious hisses. Dez lay still, hoping they would go away, feeling alone in her bed, and afraid—it sounded like they were right under her room. When she crept to the window and peered out, she saw they were in fact in the street, stopped by the waist-high iron fence that skirted the house. The man was a foot taller than the woman and gripped both her wrists in his hands; the woman tried to kick free and wrestle away. Dez was about to wake her father to go help the woman when their faces became visible in the moonlight.

It was Madelyn Crane's parents—Madelyn, one of Dez's summer friends. Mrs. Crane broke free but only for a moment and then Mr. Crane did something horrifying. He grabbed one of her arms and twisted it behind her back and kissed her as she whimpered and kicked. Mrs. Crane broke away then, and ran down the street, the sound of her shoes echoing in the night, Mr. Crane right behind her.

Dez had stared into the inky black of the hallway outside her bedroom door. She didn't know how to explain what she'd seen to make it sound serious enough, and maybe it wasn't serious. Parents sometimes had fights, of course—although she'd never seen anything like that. She crept back into bed with a sick feeling, the twisting-kissing memory playing over and over in her mind until she finally fell asleep exhausted by the whole idea of it.

The next morning, when she woke up to bright sunshine, the incident felt remote, something in the night, something that had seemed worse than it was. Later, she was on the swing reading when she heard Rose's voice, drifting through the open kitchen window, talking to her friend Hazel, housekeeper at the Adamses' house next door. Dez, out of her chair and up against the wall in an instant, heard it all, how Mr. Crane had caught Mrs. Crane with one of the summer men. In Mr. Crane's own bed, no less, and after he'd come up from New York a day early just to surprise her. He'd beaten her blind, Hazel said, and Dez shrank into herself, clutching her copy of *Jane Eyre*, inching out of earshot. Beaten her blind.

The whole family disappeared soon after, the house packed up and left empty until an Athol family moved in the following summer. The Cranes got a divorce, everyone said. *Divorce, divorce*, the word repeated around town until it sounded like a profanity.

The Cranes were the only Cascade people she had ever known to be divorced. Quite a few girls at school had had divorced parents, but those girls had come from big cities—New York and Baltimore and Boston.

Dez's life was here, in Cascade. Seventy-five dollars or not, the big cities were far away. Asa, for better or worse, was the only family she had now.

She looked down at the new paintings. The "now" card showed the town common two weeks ago. She had exaggerated the size of both the Criterion Theater and Town Hall, so as to emphasize the two streams of people heading in opposite directions to enter both buildings. On their way to see *David Copperfield*, oblivious and skipping, were young children holding the hands of more somber, older girls. In the opposite direction, their parents, bent and worried, streamed toward Town Hall, which was brightly lit and crowded. She had made quite a few people recognizable: Zeke standing on the steps, cigar in hand, Asa striding toward him in his gray pharmacist's coat. Dwight and Wendell in their police uniforms. William Hart, resurrected, his white hair blown by a breeze, walked over from the direction of the playhouse.

She hadn't painted herself in there, but looking now, she could see Asa at the depot, waiting for her train from Boston, the day she came home for good, her dormitory life finished and packed into her trunk. She could see Bud Foster driving Asa to the church on their wedding day, then driving the short distance down Spruce Street to pick up Dez and Lil and William Hart, who was too weak to walk the scant quarter-mile. She could see Asa each morning, driving down River Road, crossing the bridge, parking the Buick outside the drugstore, then getting back inside to drive it out of the boundaries of the painting—to Athol, to Belchertown, to the farms in the outlying countryside of Cascade and Whistling Falls, delivering his prescriptions, earning dollars and eggs and goodwill. She could see him driving home each night, walking in with the money he'd earned, the corn or eggs that someone had bartered for a week's dose of digitalis. It was like he was stepping right into her painting, offering it all up, a double armful of bounty that said, *Here, Dez. For you.*

18

S he sent Mr. Washburn the new set by expressman first thing Monday morning, then waited two long days to hear whether the *Standard* would go ahead with the series. During those two days it was impossible to get any kind of painting or reading or anything cerebral done. Even physical chores failed to engross her, and in fact made her restless, made her jump at every noise that might be the Western Union boy, or Jimmy with the mail, or the telephone. Late Tuesday, when the boy knocked on the door while she was upstairs washing windows, she was down the stairs and at the door within seconds.

But the telegram was from Rose: a single word—CONGRATULATIONS—followed by three exclamation marks.

Dez felt ashamed to be disappointed. Of course it was good to know Rose was proud. She folded the telegram and tucked it into her pocket and put her hand to her forehead with a little laugh because it was as if Rose were telling her what she ought to do next. Rhubarb. Harvest a few stalks, make a nice cooked dessert. She was outside cutting the thick red stalks when news finally came.

"New York on the line," Alma said, clicking the call through.

Mr. Washburn's voice boomed through the receiver. "Your postcards are a resounding success!"

It took a moment for this news to process. It was like being inside a kaleidoscope, prisms of sound and image turning her upside down and around.

The editorial office, Mr. Washburn said, was receiving feedback from all over the country. "And that's just the morning mail, and this is just Tuesday. And they are sending their feedback via postcards, my dear." He laughed. "Lots of postcards."

People were, unbeknown to one another, choosing the same method of responding to the article: by sending postcards of their own towns. "And the anecdotes!" he said. "The stories!" He was full of enthusiasm and details, yet Dez detected an undercurrent of something hesitant in his voice, too. And finally it came with a clearing of his throat. "So my heartiest congratulations, my dear. Although I must say I do have a bit of unwelcome news."

She looked down at her hands, at her fingernails plugged with dirt. She closed her eyes.

"Your friend Abby stopped by."

It was the way he said "your friend"—as if in quotes—that put her on alert. "She found her way into Harry's office—Harry is our publisher. She had some good ideas for making use of our end page, coat-tailing the postcard idea when the decision about Cascade has been reached. *Postcards from America*. She'd done up some samples and she has fair talent with a pen, though not like you—"

Dez broke in, careful to keep emotion out of her voice. "What are you trying to tell me, Mr. Washburn?"

"Well, the ironical thing is that she happened in with this idea this morning, just as we were beginning to receive all these postcards. She suggested that we *solicit* story ideas from people across the country. Have them send in their own town stories, then she could illustrate them in the postcard format. Towns would vie with one another for a bit of fame. We could start the new series once the Cascade serial turns to photographs."

The idea was exactly what Dez mentioned to Asa, a good way to expand the series once the Cascade story became a photographer's feature. "It is indeed a great idea, Mr. Washburn, an idea I planned to suggest to you myself."

"I see." He hesitated a moment. "And that is as I wondered. Well, my dear, the thing that makes Miss Hadden desirable is that she could do the work here in our offices."

"Why?" She knew, but she needed to hear him say it, needed to hear him offer what would be a tangible excuse.

"Well, for one thing, our turnaround time is quick. And Harry and I discussed the fact that we would want the subjects, and what's depicted, driven by editorial decisions. Those are the kinds of decisions that are made here, around our table."

"But Mr. Washburn." She was conscious, with her replies, that Alma or Lil or anyone might be listening. She prayed no one was, because what she said next gave her the sensation of jumping off Indian Cliff Rock. What if she passed up this chance and then they had to move anyway? When the time came, she would simply have to talk Asa into moving to New York. She couldn't worry about it now. Fate was directing her, had been directing her for weeks now. "I am moving to New York," she said.

His voice crackled through a glitch in the telephone line. "You are? Well, that's a horse of a different color. Splendid!"

"I thought I told you."

"You didn't, but no matter, it's settled. Harry himself told me he'd rather see you do the work. You have the bigger talent. The job is yours if you want it."

Her hand clutched the phone. *Please let no one have heard that, please let it all work out.*

"Miss Hart?"

He had asked her something; she asked him to repeat it.

"Just when will this decision by the state be made?"

"Word is, by July first."

"All right then. I figure that by the end of summer, we'll be at a point with the Cascade story where dismantling and construction might begin?" He paused for her affirmation, and she murmured noncommittally.

"We could go for real photographs then. When do you move? We're thinking that for the Fourth of July holiday we'll run a contest to solicit ideas, then we can sort through them and choose the most promising. Start the new series at the end of September and run it through Christmas. Can you be here by August?"

August. She couldn't possibly move to New York by August. "Most likely," she said. What was she thinking?

"Splendid." The rest of the call was talk of length, of deadlines, of the technicalities of magazine publication. She hung up the earpiece with shaky hands. What had she done? She paced the kitchen, agitated, gnawing her thumbnail. What would she do? She whipped open the icebox and began to pull everything off the shelves, sponging down the walls, wiping the milk bottles, the butter dish, the Hellman's, putting everything back in a clear, defined order: dairy, meat, vegetable. When she was done, the icebox was pristine, but it was still too early to cook and she was too wound up to clean or weed or paint. She walked over to the window and looked out at the sky, pale blue with streaks of white cloud. What if her father was watching her, somehow? *Are you? Are you there?*

This had to be fate; it felt like fate. She had a chance to make a success of this project, a success of herself. Abby had said she would look after herself. It wasn't as if she hadn't warned her.

Asa would have to be talked into it—but how, she couldn't imagine. And what if Cascade wasn't chosen? She glanced at the morning paper, lying on the drainboard, envisioning a headline: **STATE CHOOSES WHISTLING FALLS**, life in Cascade carrying on unchanged. Cars driving to Lenox when the Depression was over. Finding out she was pregnant, a baby like four sturdy chains attached to each of her limbs.

It seemed such a betrayal, to wish for the state to choose Cascade, yet—they had, all of them, been acting like taking a town went against nature. But there were ghost towns out west, weren't there? And ruins of civilizations all over the world.

Now was not the time to be sentimental. As a child, she'd been ridiculously sentimental about loss, about time passing. A holiday spent in Amherst with her mother's great-aunt would bring such grief by evening—*this day is gone and will never come again.* A child braiding daisies by the roadside, seen briefly as they whisked past in their Ford: *I will never see that child again.* Then her mother and Timon died, and sentimentality became something cheap, something too small and flimsy to encompass real grief. A daisy was just a daisy.

She didn't have to save Cascade; it didn't seem she could. She just had to save the playhouse. It was possible to move a building. She just needed to find someone to do it, to pay for it, find a place for it to go.

Now was when the eyes of the country were on Cascade. And if Cascade was doomed, then now was the time to reap exposure for the playhouse. If she could get people to care about it, she might get people behind her to help her move it somewhere. *Somebody* had to have that kind of money. The only person she could think of, who might remotely care, was the man who'd bought the First Folio, and she honestly couldn't remember the details. All she knew was that he was a collector who avoided the limelight and was known to be quietly hoarding as many Folios as he could get his hands on. He was wealthy enough to have been able to afford her father's entire collection: the two First Folios—the pristine one as well as the older, less-valuable version, and the Nicholas Hilliard miniatures, the Romney sketches, the promptbooks, all the antique, rare playbills.

She pulled the telegram from her pocket. CONGRATULATIONS!!!

Rose would remember his name. If he cared about Shakespeare so much, maybe he'd want to help the playhouse. If he no longer had the means or desire to move it, at the very least he might know people who did.

———⋙◆⋘———

It was always bittersweet to know that people you loved were alive in the world but in a place where you couldn't be with them. When Alma Webster got Rose on the line, Rose's voice came through strong and clear, so full of emotion that Dez could almost feel Rose's strong, ropy hands holding her face. Conscious of the long-distance call, Rose spoke staccato-fast. She'd bought a dozen copies of the *Standard*, she said. The story would surely change the state's mind, she had no doubt of that. "What do you need, dear?" she asked, because no one paid for a long-distance call for no reason.

Dez had made seventy-five dollars. If she couldn't spend part of it on Rose, who could she spend it on? She explained that to Rose and asked everyday questions just to hear her voice, to get her to slow down and talk as if she were in the room, sitting over a cup of tea. Rose tried, but a lifetime of being thrifty was too hard to overcome. She wasn't comfortable on the telephone. She said she liked Chicago well enough. It was cold, yes, in winter, but in summer the breezes off the water reminded her of Cascade. It was wonderful to have her sister's girl's children around and she loved Chicago's markets, the fine flour she could buy on Pearl Street, for her pastries. "Of course it doesn't have a Shakespeare theater. And it doesn't have you. Oh, I do miss you."

"I will visit you," Dez promised. "Someday I will visit you." She told Rose her plan, that she was hoping to find someone who might be interested in moving the playhouse. "If it comes to that."

"Move it! From Cascade?"

"Better than seeing it bulldozed."

Rose was silent. "Well, don't jump the gun, dear. You know it's always been just rumor."

Dez was about to tell her everything, then held back. What was the point?

"And don't even think of moving it without telling me first."

"I won't."

Rose did remember the name of the collector. "Henry Folger. But he's dead."

"Dead!"

"He died that summer before your father died. Right after your father agreed to sell him the collection. Oh, his estate still paid and all. He was building a library down in Washington, and the poor fellow died right after they laid the cornerstone. Your father felt terrible about it."

So the collector was dead. An avenue closed. Dez stayed on the line for another minute, but in the back of her mind she was thinking that the death of the person she hoped might help seemed a sign, a bad one. Yet surely, even in the midst of the Depression, there was someone else who had the means to help.

She hung up and looked around the quiet kitchen: the dishcloth folded by the sink, the dust motes swirling in the sunlit air, all the little details that challenged any idea that life could possibly change.

She chewed on her middle fingernail, and peered into the hall to check the time. Almost four. Still early, early enough to call on Stanley Smith. He had been in town a week. He might have a clearer idea of which way the decision was heading. Would it be too strange for her to visit? Maybe she could get an answer out of him, go forward from whatever knowledge she could obtain.

———⊷⊶———

The Cascade Hotel was a sprawling Victorian with a wraparound porch that hunkered down on the western edge of the common. In its heyday, summer rooms had always been reserved months in advance. The bankside lawn had bustled with croquet games, and waiters carrying trays of spiced tea. Now, although Mrs. Mayhew kept the place tidy, paint was peeling around the eaves. Clapboards had come loose. Dez climbed the wide steps and pushed through the front door, the lobby air moist with the smell of boiled cabbage. It permeated the rose-covered carpet, the heavy drapes. A distant sound of clinking pots came from the kitchen, and the registration desk stood unmanned. Dez slipped behind the desk to peek at the register. A flurry of men had come in over the past week. In the middle of the list, on May 31, was *Mr. S. E. Smith* of *Newton, Mass. Room 4.*

Room 4 was on the main floor, at the end of the long hallway in the east wing. Walking there, her footsteps muffled by the carpet, she felt self-conscious. Who was she to call on a man she hardly knew, in his hotel room no less?

She hesitated outside Room 4, knuckles poised. She'd come this far, she thought. And it was still early in the day; maybe he wasn't even in. She knocked.

The door opened almost immediately. "Oh," Stan said.

"I happened to be in the hotel," she explained. "I just thought I'd say hello." She was about to invite him to talk in the lobby—maybe he was embarrassed by her presence so close to where he slept—but he said, "I was hoping I'd see you again," and stepped backward to invite her into the sitting room with a gesture that was clumsy and eager to please. "You've become famous since I saw you last. Come in, come in."

The first-floor suites were large, originally intended for guests who traveled with servants and required space. The sitting room, entirely proper for entertaining, contained two overstuffed chairs, a divan, and a desk where Stan had been working. She noted his pencils, lined up neatly on the desk, a dozen folders. Through a far door, she spied his brown fedora sitting on an ivory bedspread.

"How do you like it here?"

"The view is nice," he said, following her gaze out across the croquet lawn to the playhouse. He liked watching the river, he said, the ducks that pecked around the bank.

"I was on my way to check on things there," she said, nodding toward the playhouse. "And I thought I'd say a quick hello. Invite you to visit my studio someday—maybe you could bring your wife and son. Since you showed such interest."

He loved the idea. In fact, he said, he'd just been talking to his wife, Ethel. "I said if there's one thing I'm going to do before this day is over it's get myself over to Stein's and buy a frame for that portrait." He eyed a stack of plans and papers on his desk. "I've been trying to get to it but I've been busy."

"How are the tests going?"

"Well, sit, sit," he said, gesturing to the window seat. Then he himself took a seat at the desk, crossing one leg over the other and cupping his chin in his hand. She imagined he was thinking, at first, that it was best not to say anything, but Dez was now more of a friend, wasn't she? That was what he seemed to decide.

"The fellows are saying that over by Pine Point the water runs funny, that it's indicative of a lot of ledge under Cascade."

As Asa hoped. Something inside her began deflating.

"We already know there's ledge east of Maple Street," he said. "Not that we can't blast it out, but if Whistling Falls is easier, why not? It would save a lot of time and money."

A door opened and shut somewhere down the hall. Out on the common, a dog barked. "You can't trust what you see up there," she heard herself say.

Stan cocked his head. "What do you mean?"

"There are funny little invisible inlets along the river that divert water. Up in that whole Pine Point area," she said, the words barely out of her mouth than she began to regret them. She couldn't interfere with Asa's plans, couldn't betray him so blatantly. She couldn't betray him at all! "But don't pay any attention to me. What do I know?"

And to her relief, Stan simply shrugged. "I'm sure the engineers know what they're doing," he said, turning his attention toward the door, where the steamy smell of the boiled-ham-and-cabbage supper had begun to drift down the hallway.

Dez walked home with her hands dug deep into the rickracked pockets of her dress. So Whistling Falls, a sparsely populated town, would likely be chosen, which made sense. The Cascade postcard series would have to be cut short. The *Postcards from America* project could still go on, but she couldn't possibly take the job. Even though when she imagined being there, meeting Mr. Washburn, working and taking classes at the Art

Students League, being around like-minded friends again, her heart raced like a train.

She told Asa she had never considered divorce and she meant it. But was she really so against it, or did the idea just seem overwhelming? They'd not been married long, but their lives were already completely blended, tangibly and legally. How did you actually go into a house and separate the life inside into objects and possessions? How did you decide what was yours, and what did you do with it all?

Dez didn't own a whole lot, but like anyone else, in all actuality, she was burdened by her possessions, by her four seasons' worth of clothes and shoes, by her books, her paintings, her studio full of supplies. By the bowls and platters that had memories of her mother and Rose all over them. Her mother's things: the pink velvet sewing box, her piano music, the Saucony lace wedding veil that Dez wore at her own wedding, the perfume atomizer, dried sticky-yellow inside but still smelling faintly of *muguet des bois*. And never mind all the big items: the sideboard that once belonged to her great-grandparents and which occupied the space in the hall under the banjo clock. The baby chair that belonged to her grand-mother and which Asa hoped to bring down from the attic—Asa, who had no idea that such calculating thoughts were going through his wife's mind. Her father's English steamer trunk, her mother's Minton vase. All of them things you didn't pack into a suitcase and lug on a train down to the YWCA. She would have to store those things somewhere—the only place being the playhouse, which legally belonged to Asa and which she would essentially be abandoning, too. Breaking promises and vows all over the place.

She stopped on the bridge over the Cascade Falls. How smooth and slippery the surface of the water appeared as it curved over the dam, yet seconds later that same water was ferocious, churning, white. She positioned herself against the rail so that the wind tossed her hair, so that the falls sprayed a fine mist on her face.

Suddenly she heard a shrieking from high above the falls. She tilted her head back and searched the sky. Two eagles, talons hooked together, cartwheeled and circled groundward, part of their courtship ritual. She'd seen it only once before; it was a rare sight. What did it mean, to see that dizzying sight now? That desire must be pursued? Or that desire was exhilarating but ultimately dangerous?

That was the thing about signs. You could read them any way you liked.

19

Asa drove away on Wednesday morning as Dez watched uneasily from the kitchen window. She rolled the washing machine, squeaking and protesting, over to the sink and fastened the hose to the tap. Water spilled into the barrel while she sorted the laundry, lights and darks. At breakfast, it seemed impossible that Asa couldn't read her face, her mind, couldn't see the turmoil there. Had he forgotten about Jacob's visit? It seemed so.

The second load was agitating and she was upstairs brushing her teeth when she heard Jacob's truck bouncing and squeaking down the rutted drive. Anxiety bloomed inside her chest. She spat out the toothpaste, checked her hair in the mirror, and rushed downstairs and out the screen door, arriving on the porch just as he opened the car door. He stepped out onto the running board, hopped down, and waved, a casual, nonchalant wave that calmed her. He stood with his hands on his hips as she walked toward him, his manner relaxed, as if nothing awkward had ever happened.

She said something purposefully neutral. "I can't believe it's your last visit."

"Actually, I couldn't fit everything for Al into the truck, after all, so I'll have to make another trip or two."

"Oh," she said. Did that mean this wasn't the last visit? He didn't say, and because he didn't, she didn't like to ask.

"I brought you a little going-away gift," he said, walking around to the back of the truck and opening the double doors. He lifted out a small square canvas and held it to his chest so she couldn't see what it was. The thought that he might have painted her portrait soothed the sting of realizing that no, he must not be intending to fit in a River Road art-talk visit again.

Inside, he set the painting on her worktable, facedown. "I've got something else, too," he said. "Just a little thing. From Chinatown." He handed her a small paper fortune.

An invisible thread connects those who are destined to meet, regardless of time, place, or circumstance. The thread may stretch or tangle, but it will never break. —Ancient Chinese Belief

"It reminded me of you," he said.

"Did it?"

"I think we were meant to meet. Don't you?"

How dispassionately, how maddeningly, he was able to say passionate things. "Yes, of course I do." She wanted more, more declaration—more sharing of what really went on inside his mind. But it was so hard to ask for more, so hard to speak.

"You enriched my life, Dez," he said, which sounded so terribly past tense. Then he turned the painting around and she recognized it, with disappointment, as the work Dr. Proulx had commissioned before he died. The subject was a grim woman sitting in a ladder-back chair, lit by a high side window. The painting was dramatic, well executed, but she knew the model was Jacob's mother, who looked as forbidding as Dez had imagined. It seemed an odd choice of gift, though the work was compelling, as she found all of Jacob's work to be—low-keyed, painted in harsh browns and blacks, with thick yet controlled brushstrokes. Its perspective was somewhat skewed—looking downward from near the ceiling, which made the focus of the painting Jacob's mother's eyes as she raised them and looked directly at the viewer: at Dez.

Dr. Proulx had wanted an example of "Jewish art." *Whatever that means*, Jacob had said. "What makes it Jewish?" she asked now.

"Nothing, really," he said. "Except it's showing the two sets of dishes."

The dark background contained two glass-fronted hutches, each filled with plates.

"One for meat, one for dairy," he added, with a look that said he realized she probably had no idea what that meant. She didn't. And she was suddenly despondent and didn't care. Whatever it meant, it illustrated the differences between them—differences she had not really appreciated. She saw that he was setting the tone, that they were not going to talk about what happened, that they were going to pretend that nothing had happened. He would leave. They would write now and again. Whistling Falls would be chosen. She would tell Mr. Washburn she wasn't coming to New York after all. Abby would take the job she decided she'd better not mention. She didn't want him thinking she had initiated it, that she was chasing after him.

"What makes it Jewish," he said, "is what makes it not Jewish."

"I see," she said, though she didn't see at all. "But you should keep it in your family. It's your mother, after all."

"No, I want you to have it. It's one of my favorites, and it was meant for Dr. Proulx so I'd like to keep it in Cascade. I want someone who will appreciate it to have it."

Someone, as if she was any old someone. He was standing right beside her but the partition between them was back and it was hard to believe he'd ever kissed and touched her.

"And what if the W.P.A. doesn't hire you? Will you come back?"

She had spoken too harshly. He stiffened. "Well, no. I'll have sold everything off."

"What about Ruth?"

He looked at her then with candor. He took off his hat and sat on the sofa; he tapped the brim against the palm of his hand. "Ruth's upset."

Of course she was. "Does that surprise you?"

"I never led her to believe that we were going to do anything more than go to the pictures now and then this past year."

"Women . . . expect things."

"I know. I know they do." His gaze met hers and flickered away briefly before returning with a look that was disappointing, even irritating, in its solemnity. "And I had no right to come on to you the way I did, and I apologize."

I didn't mind, she wanted to say.

"Honestly, I didn't think you would ever want to see me again. I was so grateful when I got that telegram."

"Really?" There was relief to hear that. Relief like rain. Why had he assumed the worst? And why did he have to look so grim now? "I wasn't sorry it happened, Jacob."

"I was, am. You're married." He dropped his head and studied the backs of his hands. "I felt so sordid when I saw Asa."

She wished he hadn't used that word. Wished he hadn't tainted the memory.

"What about before you saw Asa? How did you really feel? How would you feel if there was no Asa?" Her sense of irritation stronger than her timidity, pushing her to speak openly. *It's too easy to express predictable, socially mandated remorse. How did you really feel?*

She willed him to lift his head and look in her eyes, to speak openly, too. But the seconds ticked by and she realized he was not going to say anything.

"Asa told me he's been too modern about our friendship, that he doesn't want you to come here anymore."

Jacob jerked his head up. "What am I doing here, then?"

"I—"

"I completely understand." He got to his feet. "It's his house."

"It's my house, too."

"What if he came home right now? How uncomfortable would that be?"

"He won't," she said, his panic coming across as slightly, dismayingly spineless. She was sorry she'd said anything. "Don't leave. If this is really your last visit, we can't waste it."

"Then let's go for a walk or something. Let me move my truck. Let's just get out of here."

So that was how they ended up moving his truck down the street, behind the carriage house belonging to Richard Harcourt's abandoned summer house. That was how they ended up going for the walk in the woods.

20

The Spaulding land, all forty-two acres, most of it forest, was cool and quiet, last year's pine needles a soft, rusty carpet underfoot. The path out to Pine Point was well worn, thick with roots, the air heavy with the smell of pine pitch and river water. On the eastern trail, Jacob tried to bring up the subject of Asa; he understood Asa's position, he said, but Dez pointed out a pink lady slipper, growing quietly in the shade of an ancient oak. "Look, they're very rare," she said.

Like the subject of Ruth, she didn't want to talk about Asa.

Something rustled through the undergrowth, a flash of gray fur. "Squirrel," Jacob said. The squirrel triggered the bursting of a flock of birds from a tree, beating their wings and flapping toward the sky.

They watched until the birds were out of sight.

"I feel so contented," Dez said, "when I'm in the woods."

She wasn't really content. She said that because it sounded nice, because it fit the moment, because she wanted it to be true. She wondered if she should tell him about New York. If only she had Rose or a mother to offer advice—to say, *Yes, go ahead and tell him about New York.* Or, *No, dear, it's best not to speak. He might think you're chasing him.*

She told him how the summer before the flu came, she and her mother found a spring deep in these woods. "It was somewhere near Whistling Falls. And in the middle of the spring there was this frog, just sitting on a lily pad. He stared at us with these hooded, bulbous eyes." She paused to imitate the frog—his stillness, his watchfulness. She had been newly conscious of herself as alive, as someone with an eye for composition. "I had my little sketchbook," she said, patting her skirt pocket. "My mother was the one who got me into the habit of carrying one all the time. She sewed pockets on all my clothes. She watched while I drew him, and swore I'd bewitched the frog. I was little; I believed her." It was easier to talk while walking, to look ahead, to feel cocooned inside your moving body, inside the sound of your voice. "But the strange thing was, this frog really did seem to pose. He never moved, just looked straight at me. And as soon as I was done, he leaped off the lily pad and disappeared."

"And then just a year later, she was gone and my father was so—" She tried to summon the right word. *Morose, despairing, angry;* none of them adequately described the grieving her father had gone through. "He was staging a particularly bloody production of *Macbeth* and I was left to run wild. I spent an entire three days trying to find that spring. I tried retracing our steps, and when that didn't work, I walked a grid north, east, south, west, trying to find it. I found old stone walls and old foundations, and lots of Indian arrowheads. But I could never find that spring again."

"You were looking for your mother."

"I guess I was." She wished she could take his hand. Knowing she couldn't made her voice hard. "We people take up space, and then when we're gone, there's just the space left, and sometimes you can't quite comprehend how that can happen."

He turned to her. *"Yes,"* he said. "I think that's why so many of us are driven to create something tangible, something that will assert itself as *us* after we're gone."

This was why, Dez thought. This was why she loved him.

"Most people do it by having children, of course," she said. "It's normal to want a part of yourself to live on. But with children, I think *you* get diluted over time. Who knows much about his great-great-or-greater grandparent? Never mind farther back than that? Art, books, music. Those are the things that last."

"If they're lucky."

Well, of course, there had always been wars and natural disasters, she conceded. "But look how much has lasted already, and the world we live in, our civilization, isn't even all that old. We've got the First Folio, countless paintings. Music."

"True. But I think it might be memory that matters most," he said.

She thought about that. "Well, true. But where does memory come from? I think it comes back to the same thing. We have to record our existence somehow, some way, if anyone is ever going to remember it. Oral histories—do they really work anymore, in this modern world? People read books, they go to the pictures, they move far away from their original homes."

It seemed the right time to tell him about New York, but they had arrived at a fork, a fork marked by a giant boulder left by some ancient retreating glacier. If they turned right, they would find themselves at the parking area at Pine Point. They would emerge onto River Road. The sun would be bright in their eyes. Jacob would look at his watch and think about all he had to do and their walk would come to an end. If they turned left, they would travel deeper and deeper into the woods toward Secret Pond. She would get to spend at least an extra hour with him.

"Let's go left," she said. "It's beautiful. There's a pond up ahead that's so hard to find it's called Secret Pond."

Who wouldn't be tempted, who wouldn't want to see a place with a name like that?

So at the fork, they turned left. A simple choice, left instead of right.

21

When they entered the clearing to Secret Pond, Jacob drew in his breath, like everyone who saw it for the first time—the pond spread out like an illustration from a children's storybook, overhead branches forming a canopy that allowed golden, diffuse light to filter down through the thick foliage. High in the trees, birds called and flew among the boughs.

"Let's sit here," Dez said, heading for a nearby grouping of flat rocks. But instead of continuing with the conversation Dez was finding so exhilarating, Jacob craned his neck to peer across the pond. "What's that?"

"It's just an old dam."

"Really? Let's take a look," he said, walking off before she could reply. On the other side of the pond, he stood with his hands on his hips, inspecting the way the dam had been built. Why was it there, he wanted to know? Who would have built a funny little dam in the middle of the woods?

Dez explained its history but she didn't let on that Asa's family had built it. She didn't let on that they were on Spaulding land.

The stone-and-mortar dam stood only about seven feet tall but ran about fifteen feet wide. The top was flat, and wide enough to walk on. From the riverside, water flowed along a tributary that was camouflaged by brush and brambles. Normally, the water bumped up against the dam and flowed back to the river because a solid wooden floodgate kept the dam closed. But now the floodgate had been raised. It hung from a hoisting platform, poised between rusty chains, just below the rim of the dam.

Jacob climbed the embankment to get a closer look; Dez tagged after him. They looked down into the gap of the dam, where the river sloshed back and forth, passing through the lock and into Secret Pond.

It was clear that Asa's diversion had been successful, and was, as he had said, near invisible from the river. Stan himself had said the flow appeared stronger up at Whistling Falls.

"It's been opened recently," Jacob said, pointing out the bottom two-thirds of the floodgate, stained dark with muck from years of being closed up tight. "I wonder why?"

"Probably the water people."

"But why?" Jacob crouched to peer down into the gap. "It doesn't make any sense. Opening this took work."

"I don't know." Dez wanted to go back into the cool, quiet sanctuary of the woods, back to the conversation they'd been enjoying. "Supposedly the water men are saying the water runs funny near Pine Point. Maybe it's something to do with that. Checking water flow or something."

"Do you have your sketchbook?"

"Why?"

"I'd like to draw it."

She suppressed an urge to sigh and pulled the pad from her pocket as he positioned himself down onto the edge of the gap. He gestured for her to sit beside him, even though she had to squeeze into the space. As he began to draw, Dez was conscious of her leg and hip pressing against his.

"When I was young," he said, "oh, about twelve, I was completely fascinated by Leonardo da Vinci and all those perfect, precise drawings he did. The hydraulic machines, the tanks. Did you know he even played a part in the development of the dams and canals that made Milan so prosperous? Such genius."

"No." Dez didn't. And how could she really care, when his arm kept brushing hers? It was more than she could stand. She looked at him help-lessly.

He paused and met her gaze. Something intimate passed between them even as he continued to talk. "I loved that he was always trying to think of a better way to do things. And I love that some long-ago farmer came up with this."

"Me, too," she said. The unspoken something allowing her to prop her chin atop his arm casually, as if she always had such access to his body. She watched his fingers, wrapped around her pencil, taking such care to document each detail—the links that made up the chain bolted to the floodgate, the steel hook-and-pulley system, the rope that led from the pulley to the hoisting platform, ending in a sailor's knot wrapped around two cleats. A light breeze lifted his hair; she wanted to smooth it back in place. When he finished and put the sketch in his pocket and got to his feet, he reached down to help her up.

She was conscious of her hand in his, conscious of the way he held it a few moments longer than necessary. Then he tugged on the rope.

"I'd love to give it a go," he said. "Want to?"

"Why?"

"Why not? I'd like to see if it operates as smoothly as it would appear to."

She hesitated. She couldn't fool with Asa's dam. But was there really any harm in closing it then opening it right back up again? There prob-ably wasn't even any harm in closing it. The pond was already filled.

Jacob crouched to get a closer look at the gap. "Look at those grooves." She could see the twelve-year-old boy in him, and the sight was endear-ing. He pointed to the channels carved into the mortar on either side of the spillway. "See how carefully cut they were? I think we just need to make sure the grooves in the floodgate match up."

He took off his jacket, unbuttoned his cuffs, rolled up his sleeves and flexed his hands, then positioned Dez in front of him, five fingers on each shoulder that jolted through her like lightning. "You hold here," he said, demonstrating with two fists gripping the rope. "As soon as I've released the rope, I'll pull hard from the top, but you have to be ready. You have to be already pulling."

Dez grabbed tight, conscious of the smell of rope fibers and the starch from Jacob's shirt. His chin grazed her shoulder, the points of his collar pricked the back of her neck. She wondered if his heart was beating as rapidly as hers.

"Okay, *pull*," he said.

They pulled the rope hard to keep the floodgate from hurtling down, and it was inevitable, the way her back had to grind against his chest. Surely he was aware of what was happening. The floodgate, the act of closing it, was a contrivance, for both of them, wasn't it?

The floodgate dropped a few inches and stopped.

"It's stuck," he said.

"You're right, it needs to seat into those grooves."

"Forget it," he said. His lips brushed her ear, his voice vibrating her eardrum. "It's too much for you."

"No." She didn't want to stop. "Try again. We have to be synchronized here. I think we have to raise it a bit then be sure it slides evenly down, inside the grooves."

"I don't want you to get hurt."

She was far from hurt; she was exhilarated. She could do this forever, stand with him behind her, holding her, his mouth so close to her hair, the nape of her neck. "I won't. Don't worry. The key is to not let it go flying. Let's count to three, come on." They counted aloud—*one, two, three!*—pulling on the rope with just enough balancing leverage to position, then release it gently. The floodgate creaked and grunted, sliding reluctantly along the grooves. The rope burned into her palms but she ignored that. *One, two, three, again!* Down the floodgate came, another few inches, then half a foot, then suddenly free and gliding along the grooves rapidly, sliding down, down, until it sealed itself tight like a guillotine.

They let go of the rope at the same time, laughing, breathless. "Now to hoist it back up again," she said.

"There's not a chance the two of us can heft that back up again. Whoever did that must have done it with a few men."

That made her pause, but then she considered. The pond had filled. Asa's plan had already worked, and if he discovered the dam closed, he would think the water people had found and closed it. No real harm done.

She inspected her palms. "Look!" They were smeared with blood. She turned to show him and nearly stumbled backward into the gap.

"Careful." Jacob grabbed hold of her. "We'd better put that in place." He gestured to a wooden safety cover that rested against the embankment, pinning flat a dozen yellow dandelions, and reached into his back pocket for a handkerchief. "But first let me tend to your wounds, madame," he said, blotting at the spots of blood.

She savored the moment. The press of the clean cotton against her skin. The sound of crickets or cicadas or whatever it was that filled summer afternoons. The smell of grass and river water.

When he finished with her, she pushed open his right hand, then pursed her lips and blew the rope fibers away, pressing the handkerchief against his own scraped palms. All she could think was that she wanted physical contact one more time. If she could have that, she thought, she would be content for the rest of her life.

"Dez." He spoke firmly, but not quite firmly enough. She searched his eyes and they flickered, became less resolved even as he said, "I'm leaving. You're married. We need to help each other stay resolved."

She did not tell him to be resolved. Instead, she kept her eyes fixed on his and touched the inside of his wrist, knowing that when she did he would be weak. Her fingers traveled up the inside of his arm to the roll of his sleeve, her touch feathery so that his skin would quiver and jump. She thought, *Maybe this is the only time in my life I will get to do this, feel this, and when I'm an old lady with dry bones I'll be happy I didn't deny myself the moment.* She placed both hands flat against his chest and unfastened his shirt, fingers nimble with the buttons. He gave in then, with a barely audible sigh, and she swayed into him, knowing he would kiss her and snap open her dress and lead her, rather clumsily, because he was not big enough to carry her like a movie's hero, down the embankment to the soft grass.

As the back of her head pressed against the ground, she partitioned her mind away from her body and let the body take over, reveling in the feel of his skin, slippery with sweat from the effort of closing the dam, his bones pressing into her, the smell of his hair, everything that was new and different. They whispered to each other. *I love your hair. I love the way your skin feels. I love everything about you. Everything that is wonderful about me, you see, and everything that is wonderful about you, I see.* It was bliss, a blur of feeling, a kaleidoscope of dizzy joy, and they kissed in a languid, all-the-time-in-the-world way, rolling around the grass for so long that by the time he looked at her questioningly, asking for permission to go further, she was beyond stopping and dismissed the fleeting thought—what if a baby came of it? She was on her seventh day, teetering on the line between safe and fertile, but she gave in to recklessness, to the gamble. She wanted him. She told him that she wanted him, that she had wanted him forever, and he murmured that he, too, had dreamed of this, his lips sticking to her hair, his words muffled, his hand fumbling at his waist. When she felt him inside her she thought all the things that people stupid with love think—*this is meant to be, we are truly connected now*— stunned by the solid fact of him, and by the pleasure his body knew how to give her, the building of it, incredible and fleeting, and then that moment, very fierce and satisfying, a moment that seemed to hang on to itself as if it could never end.

It ended, that moment did. It passed. They gazed up at the branches, the birds, the patches of blue sky, becoming acutely aware of themselves, their two separate bodies, the air between them moist and hot and smelling faintly metallic.

Where a few minutes earlier, all external objects outside the boundaries of themselves had seemed blurred, now Dez saw the beginnings and ends of things: the nubby weave of Jacob's trousers, collapsed in an undignified heap by his ankles, the freckles on her forearm, the bones of his pelvis digging into her side. A dandelion, dark yellow and fragrant, tickled her cheek.

Jacob shot up to a sitting position, the intimacy of just minutes before becoming, dismayingly, a thing of the past as panic quickened on his face. He reached down for his pants. "Anyone could have seen us."

"It's Secret Pond, remember," she said, sounding more certain than she felt. But she sat up, too, and glanced around. The clearing was peaceful, undisturbed, but his unease infected her. She smoothed out her dress and tucked her hair behind her ears, feeling suddenly exposed and shy. She needed a towel. Jacob's hands moved to button his fly and she averted her eyes, again, dismayed. They had been so close and already they were apart.

"Do you feel strange?" he asked.

She wanted reassurance, talk of fatedness, not him shaking his head as if he had irreparably harmed them both. Wasn't it the woman who was supposed to be full of remorse?

She felt uncertain and apprehensive. "No," she said, false bravado that she hoped would be transmitted to him, thinking, *Let's be happy, our time is so short. Life is so short.*

"I do," he said. "I feel strange."

She wanted to take back what she said and give the honest response, which was like his own. *Yes*, she should have said. *I feel strange but there's no need for us to feel strange if only we are connected, if we are together in this.*

It wasn't like he wasn't a gentleman. He did the right things. He took her hand to help her as they picked their way back around the pond and into the woods. At one point along the path, he stopped and sighed and she followed his gaze. Another pink lady slipper, enfolded in its green hood.

"Whenever I see something beautiful, I think of you." But he looked so troubled, saying that, so bemused.

They really weren't so beautiful at all, Dez thought. Didn't they, really, look a bit repulsive, like miniature pink-veined lungs? Part of nature's repetition of patterns.

A few minutes later, he said, "If only things had been different."

"What things?"

"I was thinking of that painting I gave you. I suppose I wanted you to have a little part of my life. I suppose I wish our lives hadn't been so different."

"They're not all that different." Was he talking about his culture? His family? His mother with her two cupboards?

"I like to think I'm different from my family, more *bohemian*." He made a self-deprecatory gesture. "That first day I saw you, and talked to you, and you looked like that painting of Beatrice I loved, I thought, *My God, here's the woman who will be my muse. I've found her.*"

He had?

"But you were married. And now, I suppose when I think about settling down, having children, I'm more traditional than I think."

The acknowledged remorse coupled with his lack of clarity was terrible, made her feel all churned up. Was he saying a life with Jewish Ruth was not undesired after all? What was he saying? That an artist's life in Greenwich Village didn't have to mean giving up traditional aspects of his culture? Why was it so hard to ask? She thought of the pregnancy she had possibly risked with a quick, sharp prick of fright. It was impossible to think of what to say and have it be the right thing.

"I don't want to be sorry," she said. She wanted to hear him say that, too. But he gave her a long, sympathetic look that she recognized as regret and which irritated her. And it irritated her that she couldn't admit her irritation, because she didn't want him to misunderstand, she didn't want to drive him away. But why couldn't he just be lighthearted, at least for now, and live in the moment? In a hundred years they would both be dead, and wasn't it good they'd had this hour together?

They walked, the sound of the river flowing over rocks and up over roots, their feet moving, time advancing, River Road becoming visible through the foliage. They emerged through the trees into the bright daylight of the street, squinting at the brightness, too quickly reaching his truck.

He didn't jump right in but she sensed he wanted to.

If only he would say something, reveal what he is really thinking.

"So you said you have to make a few trips back and forth," she said tentatively.

"I do have to come back in the morning. With more stuff for Al. Probably Saturday, too."

"Asa goes to Hartford on Saturday. It's his monthly trip. He gets supplies and visits his brother and never gets back till late—"

He cut her off—gently, but still. She tried to hide how stung she felt. "Maybe we shouldn't prolong the agony," he said. "Maybe we should just say good-bye now."

Why, she wanted to ask. Why couldn't they establish where each of them stood? Why was it so hard to speak?

———⋙⋘———

At home in the kitchen, she sat with her head in her hands until she couldn't stand the silence. Then she roused herself to begin wringing out the second load of laundry. Asa's white broadcloth shirt, her nightgown, flattening between the rollers as she pushed each item through the wringer. She dumped the wet pile into the wicker basket and carried it outside, where an east wind whipped up from the river, making her eyes water as she wrestled to pin the clothes to the line, bending and pinning, bending and pinning shirts and socks and trousers to the clothesline like some numb automaton.

And then the wind ceased blowing, so abruptly that Asa's trousers did a final little dance before they slumped and hung limp.

She'd made a cuckold out of her husband. *Cuckold*—that Middle English–sounding word, more suited to the stage of the Cascade Theater than a modern house on River Road. *It is a heartbreaking thing to see a handsome man loose-wiv'd*—that line from somewhere. *Antony and Cleopatra? Loose-wiv'd.*

How could so much have happened so quickly? She looked down at the damp shorts in her hand. She had committed adultery. Adultery. The four syllables reverberating in her head. Seen objectively, what she'd done was unforgivable, so why was it that a deep and central part of her was glad she had done it? At the same time she felt hurt, because how could Jacob have been content to say good-bye like that? When he would come back to Cascade tomorrow and Saturday? She couldn't stand the thought of him coming here without seeing her again, so how could he stand it? And how could she go back to the business of living when all the hours left to her seemed to hang, suspended in limbo?

She pinned the last shirt to the line and headed into her studio, where she came face-to-face with his painting.

She wished the subject were anyone or anything but his mother with her penetrating eyes. *No one is good enough for my son*, those eyes said. *Especially you.*

She turned away from it and sat down. She had to work. The edge of the table pushed against her ribs; it felt real and hard and cold. There was a new set of postcards to conceive and complete.

She had been considering a two-card, duel-type comparison of Cascade and Whistling Falls, but had she interfered in that decision? She'd closed Asa's dam. The knowledge dropped through her the way the word *adultery* had. She'd closed Asa's dam, with none of the nervousness that billowed through her now like those clothes drying in the wind.

But the pond was already filled. Asa's plan had already worked. She told herself there was no need to worry, to concentrate instead on her work.

Which will it be? Cascade or Whistling Falls? She pressed pencil to paper. She had to start somewhere, with some line, some form, had to concentrate on the task at hand, draw one line and then another until a pleasing concordance of shapes assembled under her hand.

And that was the saving grace of art. As soon as you started to immerse yourself, even slightly, you could be swept up, absorbed. The banjo clock struck three thirty, four. At four thirty she got to her feet. She'd managed to complete the first card: a firmly honest representation of Whistling Falls's rolling farmland and fertile valley.

In the kitchen, she rooted through the cutlery drawer to find Rose's old meat hammer. Using it to pound chicken breasts flat between wax paper, she suddenly missed Rose so much she had to pause a moment, had to pinch between her eyes. She rolled the breasts in bread crumbs and fried them in lard. She mashed three potatoes. Then she rolled and dragged the washing machine back to its corner, scraping her ankle on the rusty wheel as she did so, a quick stab of pain that brought tears to her eyes and triggered a flow of them.

When Asa came home, he took in her swollen eyes and asked what was wrong. She pretended she had cramps and then felt worse, seeing the disappointment in his eyes.

It was easy to hate herself that evening. On his way back to the drugstore for the evening shift, Asa asked did she want him to bring her home some ice cream? Something to soothe her stomach? He noticed her scraped-up palms. "What happened here?"

"Brambles," she said. "From the raspberry canes."

He rooted in the medicine cabinet and found a tube of salve. "Here," he said, "keep that on there." Then he headed back to town. When the door shut behind him, Dez sank against the door frame. He deserved better, she told herself. She even said it aloud: "He deserves a wife who appreciates salve on her hands, who wants three or four babies, who isn't consumed with another man."

But she was not that kind of wife. She was the type who brewed a cup of tea and gave in to replaying the afternoon's moments over and over in her mind. Jacob had said, "*I didn't even know if you would want to see me again. I was so relieved when I got your telegram.*" He had said, "*Maybe we shouldn't prolong the agony. Maybe we should just say good-bye now.*" Perhaps she had been too sensitive, too negative. She couldn't be sure he wasn't in the same miserable limbo she felt herself to be in. She could at least inform him about the job in New York, see if he responded positively to the news.

She had never telephoned him, and every muscle in her body contracted at the thought of doing so. But she made herself lift the earpiece, even though her heartbeat was so out of control that when Lil or Alma or someone picked up, she set it down again.

She couldn't do it.

But neither could she go on like this—agitated, second-guessing everything.

She picked up the phone again. Alma came on, and though Dez knew it was best to speak cryptically, at least Alma Webster wasn't a gossip. She gave Alma the number, then waited while the line rang through. She prayed that he would answer, or that at least his sister would, but an impatient old-lady voice came through the crackle and static of the line. "Hallo? Hallo?"

Dez plowed through the moment, explaining that she was Dez Spaulding and was looking for Jacob. She expected that Mrs. Solomon would at least know who Dez Spaulding was.

"Who? Eh? Who?" she said, her accent thick and hard to decipher. "Despoldingk, hah?"

"I'm looking for Jacob?"

She deciphered that Jacob was "out in the evening."

"Oh," she said, through a feeling like wind in her chest.

"With Ruth."

Ruth. She'd assumed he was all done with Ruth. Maybe he was simply saying good-bye. Dez herself was married, for goodness sake. What kind of man would Jacob be if he had no woman in his life?

"Will he be long?" That question also misunderstood, so she shouted, enunciating each syllable: "DO-YOU-HAVE-A-PENCIL?"

The woman put down the phone with a grunt and returned a moment later. "Ah-kay, go."

Dez didn't quite trust that she really had a pencil, but she had no choice but to speak slowly, to deliver the message: that Jacob needed to meet Dez at the Pine Point parking area tomorrow morning at ten o'clock.

"For what you want?"

Dez was taken aback. "Because—I'm the painter he meets with? In Cascade? I'm sure he's mentioned me."

In reply, Mrs. Solomon said something that Dez did not understand, then hung up.

She was rattled. A mess of emotion. Mixed up. What would he think when he got that message? How was he spending his evening? Time was excruciating. It would not pass. Every minute watched another minute make its way around the face of the kitchen clock. Too early to go to bed. Asa would not be home for hours. She still had to finish the other half of the postcard set—one depicting Cascade as a lively community in contrast to the sleepiness of Whistling Falls. She forced herself back to work, blocking out a busy scene that showed children streaming out of school, Main Street bustling with pedestrians, the milk truck, the ice truck, the police car, Jimmy delivering the post.

Later, she heated milk on the stove and sipped a full cup—anything to make herself sleepy, to end the night and bring on morning.

Asa arrived home at eleven, carrying a softening brick of vanilla ice cream. He scooped Dez a sweet bowlful that tasted of guilt. Guilt was a useless emotion, she knew, her tongue on the cold spoon. Guilt was self-indulgent penance that made you feel like you were suffering for what you didn't want or plan to change; guilt didn't resolve a thing.

Asa filled her in on the day's news. Caseworkers from the county relief board had showed up at Bud's house, he said, to see if the Fosters really qualified. "It's terrible. I guess they inspect your icebox, your closets, your cupboards, everything. They walk around calculating just how poor you are and you've no choice but to accept it."

Dez agreed, thinking it was amazing, really, how people could partition themselves, how Jacob could exist in a distinct and separate part of her that had nothing to do with anything else.

22

There had been other such days—the long-ago morning her mother took sick, the afternoon the telegram spelled out the fact of her father's first heart attack. At the ends of those days, Dez had looked back through the blur of hours to the innocent mornings, which started so normally. An egg, a piece of buttered toast, plans for this or that. And if those days had stayed normal, if the flu had passed through her mother's body, through her brother, Timon's, if her father's heart had not seized, there would be no marveling at the day's normalcy, no reeling from being blindsided.

No, normalcy is taken for granted until it's gone.

⸺⸻⸺

The first sign of trouble was the car parked at Pine Point. It was a maroon Ford with big white wheels, and she did not recognize it. She peered inside, wondering if Jacob was possibly driving it—but if so, where was he? The interior was dark red leather, the long seat littered with boxes of Cracker Jack, newspapers, and a big paper bag.

She paced, kicking at pebbles, looking up at the sun making its slow way across the blue morning sky. Later she would learn that Jacob's mother had fouled up the time, her name, the entire message. But during that oversensitive half hour, she was caught between assuming the worst—that he did not want to see her—and wondering if he had somehow expected to meet her at the pond. Maybe he had indeed driven the maroon Ford, and was at the dam, waiting. So in she went.

The forest was dark and cool and smelled of pine. Walking along the gnarled root path, she heard nothing except birds and the peaceful buzz of insects, the faint roar of the falls. When she entered the Secret Pond clearing, there was no sign of Jacob, yet something somehow felt amiss.

Dez had often wondered whether there were other senses besides the established five—so far unnamed but existing all the same. How else to explain that she knew something was wrong? Some instinct sent her around the pine thicket, where she climbed the embankment and looked down the other side.

Water calmly slapped the grassy bank, and her mind flashed with quick relief because all seemed normal, yet in the same instant she realized no, there was something brown and lumpy at the bottom of the dam that the lucid part of her immediately understood was a person, a man, lying facedown in the water. She knew that brown suit, that hat so tight it did not fall off when its owner tumbled into the water.

She heard herself cry out, felt herself scrambling down the dam to get to him with the panic of emergency, but up close she could see he was clearly beyond help. His skin had already turned a translucent, mottled blue, a swarm of small flies buzzed around the back of his neck, and his ankle twisted away from his leg at an unnatural angle.

She wasn't conscious, later, of how long she stood rooted, horrified. He must have fallen into the channel, she realized, then caught his foot among the jagged stones as he tried to twist his way out. Mothers warn children they can drown in an inch of water, and here was terrible proof. Had he fallen from the dam? She couldn't be sure.

From Pine Point, he must have walked westward along the shore path. The dam was in no way visible from the shore, nor was the brook, so what had encouraged him to leave the path?

A bird shrieked overhead, accusatory. She had told him that there were invisible inlets along the river that diverted water, but he had been distracted, seemingly more intent on lunch than on what she'd been saying. He hadn't been paying attention—or had he?

She realized that she was shaking, that her hair and neck were slick with sweat. She began to run, back into the woods toward the shortest path to town, and caught her dress in a patch of brambles. She yanked it, the prickles tearing the gauzy cloth up the middle and scratching her arms. The forest seemed to be an entirely different place than the benign, bird-whistling place of peace she had perceived it to be just minutes earlier. Now she was reminded that the forest was the source of the howling she heard on dark winter nights. It was the home of fisher cats and screech owls.

She saw that there was a Dez who lived on River Road, whose husband was working in the drugstore and had no idea that there was this other Dez who suddenly had so much to hide.

She didn't want to be two people. She would go to town and tell Dwight and Wendell what she had found. She would face whatever had to be faced. She would forget about Jacob. If she was looking for a sign, then here was a sign, and it was staring her square in the face.

At home, she ran water over the blood-beaded scratches on her arms. Her hands shook as she buttoned into a new dress. She was heading out the back door when she saw what she had missed in her rush to get changed— a folded sheet of paper that had been slipped through the mail slot and which lay on the entry floor.

She recognized Jacob's graceful scrawl and her heart dropped in a way that was elation but felt exactly like fright. She looked at it with dread, as if it were poison, as if picking it up would taint her, make her renege on her resolve. But what could she do? Leave it? No. Throw it away without reading it? Of course not.

She carried the letter into the kitchen. The white creamer and sugar bowl sat atop the red-flecked Formica, bathed in light like subjects for a still life. Normal, everyday objects that emphasized that normalcy had gone out the window. With little shocks she apprehended all that had happened in the space of such a short time, the sounds of settling ice from within the icebox like vague mutterings.

Best not to phone my mother's house. Her English is poor and she gets confused. I'm not quite sure what you wanted—the message said something about "the Point" but I passed by Pine Point and didn't see you, so I'll head off. I'm due in Amherst by noon. I can check in with you on Saturday night when I deliver the last truckload to Al. Can we meet late, say seven, maybe at the playhouse?

23

Her intentions were good. She headed straight to Town Hall to the police station, entering through the side door and then down the stairs. But the big mahogany door was locked, the brass knob unmoving.

Back up on the sidewalk, she came face-to-face with Jimmy. "You hear about the water man?" he asked, disorienting and startling her.

Jimmy shifted his weight, slinging his mailbag onto his other shoulder. "Ella Mayhew says he never showed up for supper last night, and he was a no-show at breakfast. His room hadn't been slept in. So she called up Dwight, and Dwight got in touch with people in the water office and they called the state police. They're over there talking to Mrs. Mayhew right now."

At the hotel, two dozen people who had heard of the missing man, had seen the police car, and had nothing better to do were gathered outside around the old iron hitching post in front of the hotel's broad front steps. The group's main interest—entertainment—made itself clear as soon as Dez approached. Stan was a man few of them had laid eyes on. Of course they cared about the fellow, but here was Dez Spaulding, and they cared, too, about what she had to say, wanting to know what was next for *The American Sunday Standard.*

Dez described the postcard set that would be out soon, one eye on the hotel, ready to excuse herself as soon as the state policemen appeared. Minutes went by and finally Mrs. Mayhew emerged with an air of importance. A state policeman was going through Stan's room, she said, launching into the story she would likely tell for days: how yesterday afternoon Stan ate two portions of meat loaf for lunch, then went back to his room. At precisely two o'clock—which Mrs. Mayhew remembered because the bells were chiming down at the Round Church when she glanced out the window—she saw him drive off in his maroon Ford. "He was headed to Al Stein's first, he told me at lunch, to get a frame for that drawing you done of him, Dez."

Dez remembered the paper bag on the front seat of the Ford at Pine Point. He must have wandered into the woods not long after she and Jacob left Secret Pond. He could so easily have come upon them. Maybe he had.

"He's leaving," someone said.

The long blue police car emerged from behind the hotel and rolled down Chestnut Street. "Oh," Mrs. Mayhew said wistfully. "He left out the back."

The car was going too fast to run after it. Already it was turning right on Spruce Street, crossing over Main Street, heading in the direction of the boys' camp.

She vacillated, gripping the hitching post. The longer she waited, the odder it would seem that she stood there talking about the *Standard* when she knew all along that Stan was dead, that she knew where his body was. She decided to tell Asa. She would tell him she was out for a walk and happened upon him. Then they could take the Buick to look for the policemen.

At the drugstore, lunch hour was in full swing, every stool taken, grill sizzling, mixers whirring, the counter lined with Black Cows and Tin Roof sundaes and double-frank plates and ice-cream sodas. Mrs. Raymond and Billy, the after-school helper, barely glanced up. Asa was the same in the back room, bent over his table, holding up one finger when she knocked, his concentration steady as he measured liquid from a beaker into a bottle. He screwed the cap on tight and fixed a label to the front before looking up.

Billy popped his head in. "Zeke's here to see you, Asa. Says it's real important."

And then it was all too late. Asa carried the bottle out to Mrs. Raymond to ring up. Then he turned to Zeke, who stood by the tobacco counter, bent over the blue flame that emitted from the Turkish cigarlighter, puffing on his cigar to get it going. "You hear about that missing water man?" Zeke asked.

"I have. What's going on?"

"Dwight and Wendell found his car quick enough, out at Pine Point, and I guess they found the poor fellow, too, drowned."

"Oh!" Dez said, choking on the word. They'd found him so easily.

"I'm sorry to hear it," Asa said. "Very sorry. What can I get you, Zeke?"

"Wendell called in. He tried to call you direct but I guess no one's answering your phone."

"We've been backed up."

"They're bringing in the doctor from Bath to do the coroner's report here before they send him up to the funeral parlor in Athol. The doc needs me to deliver a few things for him for an autopsy. Wendell gave me a list." He pulled a folded sheet of paper from his back pocket.

Asa said that he was out of a few things since he'd put off his Hartford trip. But he adjusted his spectacles and scanned the list and said, "No, we're in luck, all set." He began to lead Zeke into the back room, then paused to turn to Dez. "Did you need me?"

But she shook her head no. It was too late to tell now. Or rather, there was no reason to tell.

———◦◦◦———

At home, she sat down with her sketchpad at her worktable. The card depicting the bustling Cascade street scene needed finishing but she had no idea how she would manage to focus on it. She wondered what was going on in town, what kind of conclusions were being drawn by the people investigating the drowning.

Maybe her remarks had set him to exploring when he might otherwise have never walked the river at all.

Still. An accident was an accident. And certainly part of his job would have been to walk the river, inspect the area.

"Focus," she said aloud. The hardest work was done. What was left was mindless enough, but instead she let her pen wander. Stan floating facedown, her mother as a three-year-old, pulled from that water. If her mother had died, Dez never would have been born. If Dez hadn't told Jacob that Asa didn't want him at the house, they never would have walked to Secret Pond and closed the dam. If Stan hadn't caught his foot, he might have saved himself.

So many contingencies marked our destinies.

She imagined drowning to be terrifying. She was only four when the *Titanic* sank, but she remembered the adults talking of nothing else, and an older neighbor boy illustrating, with a stick in the dirt, how deep the ocean was, how far the ship had sunk, adding detail upon detail until Dez was sufficiently horrified to satisfy him.

She drew the awful, last image of Stan—the breathing of water into the lungs, the gasping, her pages filling with perspectives from many angles—looking down from the top of the dam, sideways, at ground level. What was it? What was she trying to discover? She wanted to grasp the fact of his death, wanted to know that it did not matter that she might have encouraged him to walk the riverbank. An unfortunate and blameless accident could happen anywhere, anytime, to anyone.

We die, we know we must die, she thought, *and still we treat death as surprise, as tragedy, as punishment.* It was always a drama—like in that newsreel, the one about the woman in the long black veil mourning Rudolph Valentino at his grave every year. The woman joined one of the drowning scenes, black veil flowing, a slender pale hand dropping flowers into the water: long, white, lugubrious lilies.

How many painters had seized on Shakespeare's image of Ophelia floating among the flowers? How many maritime paintings had captured, for one transfixed moment, sailors going down at sea? People were fascinated by drowning—and here she herself had proof of that, with people from across the country responding to the mesmerizing prospect of a town drowned. A "great deluge" was part of the myth and legend of almost every culture on earth.

———⋙●⋘———

She assumed she would be alone until after eleven, when Asa closed the drugstore, but at eight-thirty she was bent over her postcard, inking in the final outlines, when she heard the Buick and the creak of the screen door, the sound of him walking around the kitchen—opening the icebox, running the tap.

She went out to meet him. His expression was haggard. "Swamped," he said, "from seven a.m., and there are still customers looking for Cokes. I had to get out of there. Billy said he'd close up."

"Is there any news of the water man? Were they able to figure out what happened?"

"I never had a chance to talk to Zeke. Simple drowning, I suppose."

Dez realized that Asa probably did not know exactly where Stan's body had been found. She screwed the cap onto her inking pen. "He was very big. He might have had a heart attack."

"Maybe." But he was too tired to pretend real concern. He was heading up to bed, he said.

Dez returned to her worktable; she had just a bit of outlining to finish. But when she picked up her pen, she stared down at the painting and pushed it away. All of it—the *Standard*, the job, New York—seemed remote, not quite real, and faintly distasteful.

24

They overslept, both of them, waking to full daylight, to the metal clatter of the mail slot, the harsh morning sun casting bleached light over the bedclothes. Asa kicked them off and jumped out of bed, and in her own haste, Dez forgot to take her temperature, and then it was too late—once the blood started pumping, you couldn't be sure of an accurate reading.

She slipped into a housedress, pulled her hair back, and headed downstairs, only to be stopped short in the hallway. "Asa, come down here," she called.

The morning mail normally consisted of an envelope or two tucked through the slot. Now there were at least twenty-five postcards and envelopes scattered on the floor.

Asa joined her and together they knelt to sift through the pile. There were mostly postcards, all addressed to *Desdemona Hart, care of Doomed Cascade, Massachusetts, or Soon-to-Be-No-More Cascade, Massachusetts.* Many of the cards depicted the senders' own cities and towns. There was sympathy for Cascade and the sharing of similar stories. A virtual ghost town in Arkansas: *the farms literally dried up and blew away.* Big River, Washington, an entire town destroyed by fire: *Everything was timber and everyone worked for the timber company. The fire burned for four days and consumed every splinter.*

Asa rocked back on his heels, a broad smile spreading across his face. "My God, Dez. You really started something."

They counted an unbelievable thirty-three pieces of mail, one of them an envelope from the *Standard*, which, when she opened it, contained her first check. She held it in her hands, a simple rectangle of paper that represented seventy-five dollars—a lot of money, and so much more than money. Right now there were copies of the *Standard* in every city, every backwater, every single town in the United States, her work duplicated over and over again. Why, right now, a man in California might be glancing over the article. A woman in Nebraska might be buying a postcard of Omaha, spurred into connecting with Dez, with Cascade, with the terrible idea of obliteration.

"And to think you've got another issue coming out tonight," said Asa. "This publicity has got to help."

Dez gathered up the cards and carried them into the kitchen while Asa went upstairs to get ready for work. There was nothing wrong with him getting his hopes up. Anyway, what would happen would happen. Her little cards didn't have that much control. She lit the gas and filled the coffeepot, scooped lard into the skillet, toasted bread. The response, at least, was a positive sign. She had touched people with her idea, a good thing.

She'd cracked three eggs and was beating them with a fork when she looked up, thinking she heard knocking. But there was no one on the porch when she peered through the window. She tipped the skillet back and forth to coat the surface with the fast-melting lard, and there it was again, a definite knock. She turned down the gas and wiped her hands on her apron, craning her head into the hall to look through the front-door sidelights. What she saw made her gasp. There, parked on River Road like a ghost, sat the big maroon Ford.

Her legs were quick and stiff, hand fumbling to unlatch and open the front door they never used. A haggard-looking woman wearing a black dress and black straw hat stood on the front step. Her hands were clasped close to her waist; a large pocketbook dangled from the crook of one elbow. "I'm Ethel Smith," she said. "And I wanted to meet the lady who done that picture of Stanley."

Dez stood back to hold the door open, stumbling over a string of condolences. "Such a terrible shock." "I was sorry not to know him better."

"Sit, sit," she said in the kitchen, pouring coffee, asking Mrs. Smith how she took it, then setting out the sugar bowl, a spoon, a pitcher of milk. She tried to make conversation, but Mrs. Smith answered in simple words and phrases. "Yes," it had been hard. "No," her son wasn't with her. "He's at the hotel with my sister."

The woman was thin, painfully so, with sharp, high cheekbones, and small blue eyes that sat deep inside bony sockets. Dez spread Asa's toast with butter and strawberry jam and offered it. At first, she refused it, then carefully and silently devoured both slices as Dez grew increasingly uncomfortable, hoping Asa would hurry down.

"Thank you," Mrs. Smith said, unclasping her purse and fishing out a nearly empty package of Chesterfields. She lit one and blew out a thin stream of smoke. "Stan expected trouble here, what with his job. Resentment. But you obviously befriended him, for long enough to draw that fine picture, so I wanted to talk to you, see if you have any idea what happened to him."

"But Mrs. Smith," Dez said uncertainly. "Stan drowned."

"Stanley was a careful man," she said, with a sudden, flinty look. "He'd never have gone close to the water like that, certainly not wearing his good suit and fedora. And his foot is broken, wrenched and all scraped-up."

"He must have fallen," Dez said, and saying this aloud confirmed what had to be true: however Stan died, his death was an accident.

"That's what they say and I don't believe it. All due respect, but I went up where his car was parked and it's all flat shoreline, grass and dirt. He was in this skinny little brook off the main river. No big rocks to clamber over." Her voice cracked for the first time and she slapped her hand to her forehead to stop her eyes brimming. "Now, a man doesn't just trip and fall into the water like that!"

"What are you saying?"

"There's something more here than meets the eye."

"Oh, Mrs. Smith, there's not a chance—"

"Now hear me out. I think someone hurt Stanley. A lady lives up on the common told me she saw a boy throw mud at his car." She wiped her eyes with the back of her hand in a fierce motion. "His very first day. Boys learn who to hate from their fathers, I know this, and I was wondering when you talked to him, if he mentioned getting any trouble, what with the resentment against the water board."

"I did meet Stan right after the mud-throwing incident."

Mrs. Smith leaned forward, as if she would glean extra insight from listening hard.

"That was the day I did the sketch."

"He was real proud of it. You did him proud."

"He came into the drugstore right after the incident, but it was his first day in town. He had no idea who had thrown the mud, just that it was a boy, and I don't think it would ever occur to anyone that a boy's prank would mean anything."

And here was Asa, thankfully. Dez jumped up to introduce him; she explained the portrait connection. Asa offered condolences, but looked mystified as to why Mrs. Smith was at their house.

"Mrs. Smith thinks that something untoward might have happened to Stanley and she thought I might have an idea about anyone who would have wanted to hurt him."

"There's not a soul in Cascade who would hurt an innocent person," he said, and Dez chimed in, "Of course not."

"I know Stan didn't just fall into the river."

Asa looked at Dez and she looked at him and they both looked grateful when the phone began to ring, but Asa got to it first; he turned away to murmur into it. When he hung up, he apologized to Mrs. Smith and took Dez aside. "All hell's broken loose down there. The grill's down and a fuse blew and Mrs. Raymond has to leave at noon. I'll need you to help with lunch."

He slipped into his pharmacist's coat, and shook Mrs. Smith's hand. Again, he said how sorry he was. Again, he said no one would have intentionally hurt her husband.

Mrs. Smith remained closed-mouthed. She watched him walk out the back door, her face puckering as if she might cry. Then she nodded her head to go. "I won't be taking up any more of your time."

All the words she might say caught in Dez's throat as she twisted her fingers, mute and uncertain, accompanying Mrs. Smith back to the front door. She thought about how no one knew that she had been the first one to find Stan drowned. She had seen his twisted ankle with her very own eyes. An obvious accident. But telling this woman she'd seen her husband dead in the river would do no good and only raise questions. *I found him but by the time I saw Dwight and Wendell, they already knew about him.* It wouldn't change a thing.

On the front steps, Mrs. Smith's face darkened. "I'll have to sell that, what with the funeral expenses," Mrs. Smith said, meaning the Ford.

Dez remembered Stan talking about how his wife had gone to the welfare last year, how they had grudgingly given her oatmeal. *You got a husband and a fine boy?* How had he managed to buy a spiffy Ford? He must have been a bad money manager, and now this woman had nothing.

It was an impulse. She told Mrs. Smith to hold on, then ran back to the kitchen, scribbled her signature on the back of the *American Sunday Standard* check, and rushed back outside.

As soon as she offered it, she knew it was the wrong gesture. Mrs. Smith refused it quickly, with a flat, protesting palm and disbelief that turned to deep distrust—a look that said Dez must either be positively bats or else somehow strangely guilty to give away money like that.

Dez pocketed the check but she didn't know what to do with her body, her hands. "Are you staying in town?"

"Stan paid up his room, good for a week, so we'll make use of it and head up to Athol for the funeral on Sunday."

"I'm sure you will plan some nice readings. Stan mentioned he loved a poem by Longfellow. He recited a bit. It was lovely," she said. She'd meant to look up that poem.

"He was always reciting that poem."

25

There was a commotion going on inside the Brilliant, and when Dez walked in, conversation halted for a moment. As she looked from one keyed-up face to the next, Zeke Davenport filled her in. They had been discussing Ethel Smith's suspicions.

"So there's a postcard for you," Ella said. "We all came up with it. Mysterious drowning."

Pretending to consider the idea, Dez accepted the glass of water Helen put in front of her. "But the drowning was an accident," she said.

"We can't be sure of that."

Bill Hoden spoke. "We were talking about the fact that Mrs. Smith might have a point. A man doesn't just break his ankle and fall into the river."

"And as I was just about to say," Dick Adams said, drawing out his words, waiting for the attention he'd obviously enjoyed before Dez walked in, "I thought it was odd at the time, but—" He paused, and looked around at everyone. "But I saw the Jew truck going down the road to Pine

Point yesterday, and that," he said, slowing down to emphasize the importance of what he said next, "was where this Stanley Smith disappeared
from."

There was a general murmur of interested reaction, an urging to go on.
Dez sipped her water with rising panic.

"Oh, Jacob's a good fellow, just like his father," Pete Masterson said.
"No worries with Jacob Solomon."

"He's a very fine man," Dez said. "I know him well."

"But I remember it was funny-like," Dick persisted, "it being so early
in the morning. I remember thinking, *What's he doing in Cascade on a
Tuesday?* But more curious, *What's he up to Pine Point for?* There's nothing up there."

Dez spoke calmly. "Why on earth would Jacob Solomon have anything to do with the death of the water man?"

Dick's response was to look blank. No one else was forthcoming with
any kind of reason.

"If Cascade's gone, it's one less town he can sell to!" Ella finally said.

"Oh, Ella," Zeke said. "That's nonsense, and it still has nothing to do
with why one single man dead would make a difference to a big project
like this."

"Exactly," Dez said. "Let's not try to make something more out of the
poor man's death than it is."

"We certainly don't want to accuse anyone of anything," Zeke said.

"Well, it was just odd seeing him up there, like I said," Dick said.

"He'd have no cause to be involved in this," Dez said. "The wife is
grieving. She's grasping at straws."

"And that's natural enough," said Zeke.

"Let's face it," Ella said, regretfully. "He'd take triple helpings at my table.
He was fat and a bit clumsy and probably plopped right into the water."

Ella didn't mean it to be funny, and no one thought the situation was
funny, but the way she said it was funny nonetheless and people looked
uncomfortably shamefaced.

Zeke took a stool at the counter and twirled one of the little vases between his own sausage fingers. Poking out of the vase were two daisies and a dandelion, and Dez remembered another dandelion, its fuzzy fluff trapped by her ear. She remembered, too, a wall of them, flattened by the wooden safety cover, the one they'd never fitted over the gap on top of the dam. She concentrated, trying to remember exactly how they'd left the area.

No, they'd never covered the treacherous little gap.

———

At the drugstore, Dwight and Wendell had arrived just ahead of her, accompanied by a stranger with graying temples who stood well over six feet tall. The man wore a dark suit and a smart fedora with a small red feather tucked into its dark band. He looked about briskly, clearly in charge, his poised, elegant demeanor reminiscent of the summer men who had once essentially ruled Cascade.

Asa emerged from the back room and the man introduced himself as Elliot Lowell, commissioner of the Massachusetts Water Board. He said they had come to inform Asa, as owner of the property, that someone had been trespassing on the land near Pine Point.

"People often do." Asa spoke carefully. "I don't post signs."

Lowell explained—during their search for Stan, Dwight found the pond. He'd seen fresh digging, tampering that had gone on at the dam. "Someone did quite a bit of work in there."

Asa, solid and respectable, frowned at them, giving away nothing.

"It looks like someone opened the old dam in there, then closed it," Lowell said.

"Closed it?" Asa did well, hiding his reaction, Dez thought. He turned toward Carl Treadway, who had come in looking to refill a prescription, and held up a finger, a gesture that let Mr. Lowell, however important he was, know that he, Asa, was important, too. Then he gave his attention to Lowell. "That dam's been closed for years."

"Oh, I can assure you it was opened."

"How can you be sure?" Dez asked.

Lowell turned toward Dez, eyebrows arched, acknowledging her for the first time. "Because that pond on the other side of the dam's pretty near full. It couldn't have filled up with rain since there hasn't been much. We thought maybe this Mr. Smith found it open and tried to close it, but it's difficult trying to open and close that thing, too much for one person, we think, and those of us who tried scraped up our hands quite a bit." He opened his hands, which bore abrasions similar to the ones on Dez's own.

She pressed her palms flat against her dress.

"Why does all this matter? What is your point?" Asa asked.

"I'm sorry, you mean you don't know?" Lowell said.

Asa looked questioningly at Dwight, at Wendell.

"We found his body at the base of the dam," Dwight said.

Asa took that information in. "You're saying you found this man's body on my property?"

"Yes, we found him in the channel between the dam and the river."

"What was he doing there?"

"No idea."

Wendell spoke. "This wooden cover that looked like it used to seal the top of the dam," he said, "well, it was off to the side, so there was a gap where he might've stumbled, if he'd a gone up there."

Dez pictured the gap in her mind, the cover to the side, and felt the panic of remorse. Regardless of whether Stan died because of the gap, they should have been careful to leave the site safe.

"We had to notify you because the death happened on your property," Lowell said, in a cordial, almost dismissive way. "And we wondered if you knew anything about the tampering. You obviously don't. So unless we learn anything more, we won't be bothering you again."

"Of course. And how are the water tests going?"

Lowell was vague, noncommittal. "Stan oversaw the placement of the measurement markers. Now it's just wait and see." He puffed appreciatively on his cigarette, the holder clicking against his teeth. "I was here once, myself, not too many years ago, with Governor Fuller. We saw a production of *Twelfth Night* at your charming theater."

"My father's theater," Dez said.

"Oh?" Lowell turned his attention to Dez in a manner that reminded her of the hungry fox of children's stories. "So you are the woman artist."

"Desdemona is my wife," Asa said.

"I see," Lowell said indulgently. "Bringing all of you a little notoriety. I hoped I would meet you, Mrs. Spaulding. I was sorry to hear that your father passed on." He lifted his hat. "And sorry to see that the theater is closed. Had you planned to reopen it? It would be a shame to see a beautiful building like that destroyed."

Asa's face drained of color. Had Lowell played his hand?

"I plan to reopen it," Dez said slowly.

"Well, if worse comes to worst," Lowell said offhandedly, as he motioned that he was ready to leave and pushed the screen door, "maybe we can get it moved somewhere."

Asa turned to Carl. "Could you come back in twenty minutes?" Then he beckoned Dez into the back room, where he dropped all pretense of composure.

"That area is secluded," he said. "Who would know, and go to the trouble of closing it?" His face sagged and his eyes filled at the realization that all of his labor and expense was for nothing. He dropped into his chair, dropped his head into his hands. When he looked up, he said, "Who did it," but there was no questioning inflection in his voice and she heard, "*You* did it."

She couldn't speak. She couldn't deny it, it was all so obvious. In fact, she felt something close to relief.

But he repeated, "Who did it? Who?" and she realized the fact of his confusion in the midst of her own.

"I think it was Bud," he said, finally. "He took the digging work on but I know he'd take cash for his land." He closed his fist and squinted up at the ring of fluorescent light. "I think he wants it to happen. He's desperate. And too proud for a loan, won't ever take a loan, but no, he'll sabotage me."

"It was not Bud," Dez blurted out. Life was bad enough for Bud right now without his best friend suspecting him of betrayal.

"The man's capable of anything right now," Asa said.

"We are all capable of anything, given the right circumstances, but—"

"Apparently."

"Asa, I know Bud would not do this. His circumstances are not that dire. He's got the welfare. His children are not starving."

She couldn't tell him.

She would have to tell him.

"He's desperate. Emotionally desperate. Although—" He blinked, thinking hard, retracing steps. "They said one person alone couldn't do it, and I know that's true for a fact. You need leverage, one person pulling from up high, one down lower."

"Think, Asa. Bud did not do this. Maybe, despite what everyone's saying, Stan himself did it. He must have. A big man like Stan was strong. He probably saw that the river was draining into the pond and tried to stop it, that's all."

"Why would he care, really? And even if that's true," Asa said, the fingers of his right hand splaying across his chest in dismay, "then his death is still my fault because I fooled with the dam in the first place."

And it didn't matter that she assured him that regardless of what happened, Stan's death had been an accident. He didn't reply, just got to his feet and began to assemble the ingredients for Carl's prescription.

26

They were outside the drugstore, packing up the Buick for Asa's trip to Hartford on Saturday morning, when Dez learned just how bad the idle gossip had become.

"So Bud stopped by earlier," Asa said. "He wanted to confide in me."

Dez glanced up. It was still early; the streets were quiet, just a faint sound of distant hammering coming from the direction of the boys' camp. Asa was bent over the front seat, fiddling with the gas pedal. "About what?"

"He said he saw Jacob near the Pine Point road, too, and now he's wondering, naturally, why he was out there where there are no houses, nothing, two days in a row."

Dez became conscious of her hands and arms, still in the process of fitting a box of empty 7-Up bottles on the floor behind the front seat. She looked up at Asa, who had stopped his nonsense with the gas pedal and was watching her, waiting for her response.

"What are you saying, Asa?"

"Bud was thinking he should tell Dwight and Wendell."

"Tell them what?"

"That Jacob was out there," he said. "But you know Bud. It bothers him to have to point the finger at someone."

"He doesn't have to point any fingers at all."

"True, but I told him, 'You just go and tell Dwight and Wendell. Just tell them what you saw. It's a fact you're stating, not blame. Just stating a fact.' Because what do we all really know of Jacob Solomon, anyway? Yes, his father was a good man, but that doesn't mean he is."

"*I* know him. Do you forget that? I know him very well. Has Bud spoken to them yet?" She had to curb an impulse to drop everything and run over to the police station. "Because why do this to Jacob? What possible motivation would he have to harm your dam or Stan or anything at all? This is crazy."

"It's fishy, though. Why was he hanging around there? Was he on my property? Maybe, and I don't know why, and I don't like it."

"Jacob is an honest man." She would have to try to get in touch with him, warn him before he showed up in Cascade tonight.

"Well, it's up to the boys to decide what to do with Bud's information. If he's innocent of any wrongdoing, it will come out, won't it?" He rested a hand on the car door. "Anyway, Bud got me thinking. When I get back I'm going to tell them I opened the dam, lay it all out on the line. If I'm in any way responsible, I need to own up to it."

Mrs. Raymond opened the door and called to him. "I'll be right back." He disappeared inside the store.

Dez got to her feet. The sun shone down on the top of her head. A boy ran by, calves flashing white above red socks. It was Saturday. Only a week had passed since she'd soared with the first *Sunday Standard* publication. Now she had plummeted from those heights, and it was as if it had happened to another person. Her next installment would appear by late afternoon but she felt far removed from it.

Someone called her name. Zeke, coming up the sidewalk. "Just the person I wanted to see. I need you tonight."

"Need me for what?"

Zeke ran the annual summer evening band concert series; the series would start in a matter of hours, and he and the other selectmen had decided to present her with an award. "For your efforts to save Cascade."

She tried to refuse. She had no right to accept any award. But Asa came out of the drugstore and Zeke told him the plan, and then neither man would listen to her protests.

"Here's the thing," Zeke said. He stepped closer to give her his complete attention, and she was reminded why Zeke was the kind of man who ran things. He was always warm and friendly, and made people feel included and liked, but at heart, he was a serious man. "It's about more than just you here. You're the kickoff to this hope that it's my duty as head of the selectmen to keep alive. For morale. People don't have much else."

"Put that way, I guess I don't have much choice."

Zeke smiled and shook his head. "Nope. The bandstand, seven sharp."

Seven, the time Jacob was due to meet her at the playhouse.

Zeke headed off toward the Brilliant, but Asa lingered, one foot on the running board. She saw him calculating the hours ahead—the miles of rutted roads, the meetings with suppliers, the certainty of at least one flat tire, factoring in the time to fix it. "I wish I could put this trip off but I just can't," he said. "Maybe I can get back early. Silas won't mind if I skip supper."

"Oh, Asa, get your buying done and visit with your brother." He was always grateful for a hot meal and a chance to catch up with Silas before making the long trip back. "There's really no need for you to rush back just so you can see Zeke Davenport hand me a piece of paper with the town seal on it."

"I've always liked the first concert, though. And the second issue will be out tonight."

"Buy it in Hartford and show it to Silas. I'll probably take the award and go straight home." How desperate she was, how anxious and stupid and pathetic. Desperate to grab a snatched hour with a man who was saying good-bye.

When Asa finally drove off, she didn't know what to do with everything churning up inside her and so spent a few hours in town before heading home—sweeping the playhouse, opening the cupboards to air them, putting in a grocery order at the Handy.

———◦◦◦———

The note had been tucked inside an envelope, addressed to her and left on the back porch, propped up on the threshold.

My dear Mrs. Spaulding, I would very much like to have a private word with you. Please phone me at your earliest convenience, at either the Cascade Hotel (CA-3) or at the office we've set up (CA-19). Yours, Elliot Lowell

She called the switchboard and asked Lil to put her through to the hotel. Ella Mayhew said that Elliot Lowell was long gone, and the man who answered the phone at the water-board office, when she tried there, said he was out in the field.

Dez debated with herself, the phone in hand. Jacob had asked her not to call his house, but she had little choice, it seemed, considering the circumstances.

No one answered.

She looked around the quiet house. The tick-tick-tick of the clock was numbingly slow. The hours would drag till seven. She couldn't garden—not with her chafed hands. Even holding a mop hurt. And her mind was still too rattled to focus on painting. She spent some time tidying the kitchen, then finally settled on the sofa in her studio with the book Asa was reading, *It Can't Happen Here*, fiction based on the coming election and the rise of fascism. But it was disturbing, and she set it aside to glance through the other articles in last week's *Standard*. The new weekly Roper's Poll question was, "What kinds of people do you object to?" Gossips, troublemakers, she thought. The short story was about a working girl who didn't want to give up her job to have a baby. Dez skimmed through the piece to see how it would end—though she knew from the beginning that the stock character would realize that a baby was far more satisfying than business could ever be.

Late in the afternoon, Zeke's delivery boy, Sam, knocked on the back door with the carton of groceries. Lying on top was the new *Standard*, and Sam was full of shy praise. She tipped him a nickel, and when he was gone, picked the magazine off the top of the pile. The table of contents listed the postcards on page 56 and there they were: *Postcards from Cascade*. Her eyes quickly scanned the feature, the paintings and text familiar yet startling, so slick and permanent on the page. The colors were fine, the reproductions spot-on. She reviewed each sentence: no mistakes. She read the entire copy three times, then gazed out the window, feeling relief, allowing herself a jolt of pleasure. It was good, she was pleased, but it was disconcerting, too, how within minutes her work could feel so much part of the past.

That was silly. She opened the *Standard* for another good look. The magazine fell open to the previous week's Roper Poll results, which she read with dismay. "What kinds of people do you object to?" The majority response, at 35 percent, had been, simply, "Jews." At 27 percent, coming in second: "cheap, loud, boisterous people."

She tried to phone Jacob three more times, each time wishing it was possible to make a call without an operator knowing about it. The three times Lil put her through, there was no answer. At six, she ran a quick bath and then put on a casual, soft green dress with pearl buttons. She replaced her scuffed canvas shoes with black leather flats. She pinned her hair back, applied some Precious Coral lipstick to her mouth, and walked to town to accept her award.

27

She was on the bandstand ready to receive the award—the band momentarily paused, instruments resting on their laps—when she saw Jacob's truck rolling down Spruce Street. Zeke was saying pretty much what he'd said to her on the sidewalk, that he represented the town in presenting her with a formal award for the appreciation of her efforts. The band, a quartet out of Amherst, men in the red-and-white-striped jackets and straw boaters of an earlier time, their brass instruments flashing in the waning light, looked on with courteous smiles. As she climbed the miniature steps to join Zeke on the podium, Jacob's truck turned left on Chestnut Street.

She cleared her throat, suddenly nervous in front of all the upturned, expectant faces. She imagined that people were looking at her funny and spoke too quickly, too falsely vivaciously, hoping no one would notice Jacob. She thanked the crowd and said, "As you will see, one of this week's postcards is this very scene, a nostalgic look at—" but their attention was being diverted, a murmuring spreading across the crowd "—a quintessential American summer band concert. So thank you."

The truck rolled to a stop in front of the playhouse.

Zeke waved a hand to corral the crowd. "Regardless of what happens to our beloved Cascade, we will be forever grateful to this lady artist . . ."

There was the beginning of applause, but eyes turned to the peddler's truck, to Jacob getting out of it, and Wendell breaking away from the crowd, taking off across the common, Dwight lumbering behind.

The quartet looked on with mild curiosity. Zeke was briefly distracted, too, then clapped for everyone's attention. "Thank you, Dez Spaulding!" he bellowed, clapping so heartily that the crowd, stunned for a moment, belatedly joined in, then matched his exuberance.

Dez pretended very well. She accepted the award—a piece of paper that basically reiterated Zeke's words, and which was stamped with the official seal of Cascade. She descended the steps, where everybody close to the stage and less distracted by the situation on Chestnut Street squeezed her arms, shoulders, and hands to offer congratulations. Everybody except Lil, who inclined her head toward where Dwight and Wendell were climbing into Jacob's truck.

"Your friend's in trouble."

What did she mean? And how would she know? Most eyes, either surreptitiously or blatantly, watched the truck turn around and drive toward Main Street. The quartet was starting up again, "Get Yourself a Sweetie and Kiss Your Troubles Away," popular back in the early twenties, when the easy, postwar years had seemed like relief, like respite, and everyone had banked on life continuing that way forever.

Lil stood with folded arms and a stony expression. Her marceled waves were gone, hair pulled back into its usual twist.

Did the ribbon salesman leave, Dez wanted to ask, then saw that yes, that was exactly what had happened.

Zeke, passing around his copy of the *Standard*, called her over. People congratulated her, they asked to see the award. A cluster of women bent over the magazine, exclaiming over the recognizable landmarks, the tiny, precious details.

Dez was signing her name to Ethel Bentonford's copy when she overheard, behind her, the first poison dart of gossip, heard Dot King say to Popcorn's mother, "Well, I never did care for that Jacob Solomon." It was as if Dez's ears flattened backward, like a horse's, straining to listen. Popcorn's mother said she'd heard that Stanley's widow was with Dwight when Bud told his story of seeing Jacob up at Pine Point. "And Dwight was real careful, well, he'd have to be, with her there. He told Bud, 'I'm real reluctant to go out there and start questioning a man like that. Looks like an accident no matter where it happened.'"

"I just don't trust those Jews, though," Dot murmured, in a regretful manner that said she hated having to state such a thing, but that sometimes unfortunate truths needed to be voiced.

Dez turned to see Popcorn's mother lay a hand on Dot's forearm. "And neither does Mrs. Smith! She insisted on those policemen asking him a question or two. And wasn't it fishy he drove into town tonight. Who knows what's up his sleeve?"

Dot spoke gravely. "I do believe I know, but I'm not in a position to talk about it right now." Her lips settled into a tight line. "Let's just say that poor Addis shouldn't have been so trusting, either."

Dez could not imagine what Dot was talking about. She only knew she had to get away from them all. She rolled the award up tight and pushed it deep into her pocket, edging away from the crowd until she reached a point where she could slip, unnoticed, to the playhouse. On the front steps, she looked back over the common. From this distance, the scene looked remarkably like her postcard. The styles she had drawn were twenty years past, but the elms, the evening haze, the moths, the light—all of these were unchanged. The scene looked timeless and idyllic, and every person in the country who saw it would sigh with recognition and loss.

However, those warm truths she had sketched, the truths that readers of the *Standard* wanted to see, were a fanciful product of nostalgia. The real crowd, gathered around the real bandstand, illustrated truth, and it was dismaying to watch Dot King's gossip spread visibly: heads turning, one to another. Groups of two becoming groups of four, then six. Mouths moving, and as the story spread, the pinched, satisfied looks of those telling the stories transferring to those who listened.

Or so she imagined.

What were they saying? She did not know. But she knew this: her small success, however applauded at first, would soon enough incite a certain amount of resentment and envy. Her eyesight blurred and it was as if she were seeing every incarnation of every public gathering on the Cascade Common. Those idyllic nights before a play, in the days when William Hart was the town's most imposing citizen. William Hart—educated, well-traveled, and wealthy, who could have lived anywhere and chose Cascade.

She saw the November day her mother died, the way the sound of noise built on the common, not the normal noise of the town, but the sound of something momentous and important. She saw herself flinging open the front door and running out to the street with the flu mask everyone was supposed to wear, fitting it over her face. The bells in the Round Church clanged, the fire truck blew all its whistles, rang its bells. Everywhere, people were throwing off their flu masks. Dez threw hers off, too, thinking, wildly, that the flu was cured, that somehow Dr. Proulx would be able to bring her mother back. But it wasn't the flu they were cheering about, it was the war. The war was over and one of the neighbors' Irish maids, gleefully dancing in circles, suddenly looked down and saw Dez. *Get on home with you now! Sickness shouldn't be out in the streets!*

And William Hart, hadn't his luck turned, beginning with the loss of his wife and son? But he'd suffered in the Crash like so many others, and really, wasn't that some kind of justification, a natural righting of what was wrong? Was it fair that some should have so much and others so little? And now all that was left of those Harts was the daughter who'd been overblessed with a good husband and here she was now, dallying with the traveling Jew.

That was what she imagined they were saying—or would soon be saying. Twilight deepened into true dusk, turning the air dark and soft. Lanterns were lit, strings of electric light turned on. She slipped into the dark, down the north side of the common until she was well past the crowd, searching the streets for Jacob's truck. It was parked in front of Town Hall, engine still steaming, making crackling noises. In the basement—police headquarters—light shone through the grilled windows.

She hesitated; she couldn't just barge in. But she had to barge in. Her mind scrambled for an excuse and came up with something lame but reasonable: she could ask Dwight if he'd happened to see Asa before he left for Connecticut. *Do you know what time he left? He mentioned he was going to stop in to see you.*

She picked her way down the dimly lit stairwell. The door stood slightly ajar, casting a triangular shadow on the floor. She rapped on the frosted window, turned the knob. "Dwight? Wendell?"

Silence. Inside, the two desks were empty, but beyond them, in the holding cell, Jacob was sitting on a cot, his eyes glimmering in the dim light. He sat unmoving, the door to the cell wide open.

"What is going on?" she whispered.

He lifted one shoulder in a half-shrug.

"Why are you here, Jacob? Where are Dwight and Wendell? What is going on?"

"Oh, they seem to think I may have done all manner of things."

His voice sounded disembodied, and she stepped closer, wrapping her hands around the iron rungs. "What manner of things?"

"Oh." He lifted one hand and looked at it as if he didn't recognize it. He counted off on his fingers. "One. Tampering with 'Mr. Asa Spaulding's property.' Thereby, two, causing the death of the water man. Shall I go on?"

She sat down gingerly, on the very edge of the cot. "What have you told them?"

He let a moment pass. "What haven't you told me?"

"What do you mean?"

"We were on your husband's property. You must have known."

She was quiet. "I thought if you knew we were on Asa's land, you'd feel morally obligated to leave."

"Of course I would have."

It was not the time to argue, to point out that every acre of woods out there belonged to Asa, that they would never have been able to go for that last walk. "Have they arrested you?"

"No," he admitted. "But they did ask me—and rather politely, too, I must give them credit—to stay and answer some questions. They're fetching a man named Lowell."

"They can't do this to you. You have rights."

"Do I?"

"Of course, Jacob. What's wrong with you?"

Why didn't he just get angry? She couldn't stand this part of him, this broody, self-absorbed quality.

"They wanted to know why I was back in town tonight."

"What did you say?"

"I told them the truth, that I was here to deliver goods to Al Stein. They said why so late and I explained that Al is pretty orthodox, doesn't work any more on the Sabbath than he must, to feed his family."

He saw that she didn't really understand what he was saying and added, somewhat impatiently, "Al asked me to make the delivery after sundown. And Wendell thought he caught me in some kind of lie because everyone knows the Sabbath day is Sunday. What kind of intellect am I dealing with here? No wonder I want to get the hell back to New York."

She murmured noncommittally.

"And just today," he said bitterly, "we got word from my cousin. Buying from Jews has been declared a 'treason to the people.' His own neighbors smashed his windows, the windows of his little shop. And as I was driving here, I was thinking about it, and I thought, *Well, at least I live here, where people can say things about me, but they can't do much more.* And then I drive into town and I'm accosted and accused, and I think, *Where is there a secure place in this world?"*

"There is no such place," she said. Somehow she had always known that. Only, where Jacob found that truth disheartening, she found it oddly freeing. Because what was security? It was a word, an abstract idea, grasped at by people who believed they needed it, who hadn't yet discovered their own strength. She had so wanted to believe in security that she'd married a man for all the wrong reasons. And what had her sacrifice for security gotten any one of them? A tombstone for her father two months after the marriage. A locked-in state of mind for herself and Asa. In the beginning, so unthinkingly, she had gone along with Asa's idea of security, of what was right, as if it was carved-in-stone truth: that life was about planning children, about working, and about sticking with marriage vows. But security was an illusion. Look at the bulldozers threatening the playhouse, the house on River Road, all of Cascade, and the men in all those newspaper photos in every city in the country, standing in lines, waiting for meals, for charity.

"I guess they found some kind of chain up at Pine Point," Jacob was saying. "Pine Point—now that's the very same place where two hundred people picnicked two weeks ago, if I'm not mistaken, but no one thought of that. No, they automatically deduce that the chain must belong to me."

"What kind of chain? Why do they think it's yours?"

"A neck chain, of some sort. I gather it sports a Star of David or some symbol they consider Jewish."

He should stand up to them, she thought, tell them they were being bigoted. Music drifted in through the small casement window. Ragtime music. "Asa himself opened that dam," she said. "He was keeping it a secret from everyone. He hoped the altered water levels of the river would affect the state's decision. He's planning to tell them when he gets back from Connecticut."

Jacob shrugged. "That doesn't explain who closed it."

"They'll think it was Stan."

"If they thought that, they wouldn't have hauled me in here now, would they?"

She studied the floor, a speckled, gritty cement, and stole a glance at his hands, resting in his lap. Her eyes locked there for a second before looking away, a dreadful second, because looking at his lap felt wrong and embarrassing. And then she felt sad. They'd been together in the most intimate way possible yet now they sat with a gulf between them.

"You'll just have to tell them the truth," she said decisively, brave on the outside but inside starting to free-fall at the thought of Asa finding out. "You—*we*—closed the dam, just because we wanted to see how it worked."

"I don't want people talking about you, gossiping about why we were in the woods together."

"But we can't lie to the police."

Still. There had to be a way out of this for both of them. Asa had said he was going to tell the police he opened the dam himself. If she told them that Asa had been working on the dam, they might just drop the matter altogether. She could tell Asa that there was no need to talk to Dwight and Wendell because she'd already told them all they needed to know.

That's what she would say, she decided. And she would never, ever get herself tangled up in lies again. What was that line from *The Tempest*, about making a sinner of one's own memory by crediting a lie? She'd never been a lying sort of person; she wanted to be done with lies. "There's something I haven't told you. I have the offer of a job in New York. With the *Standard*."

He looked at her, wordlessly asking for explanation. She told him about the *Postcards from America* plan, how the conversation with Mr. Washburn had come about so quickly. "He asked if I could be there by August and I didn't have time to think, I just said yes. All I know is that I want that job. I don't belong here, I never did."

He didn't say anything and she couldn't read him. "I didn't want you to think I was chasing after you. That's why I didn't mention it."

He was silent so long she began to feel impatient. Was this the man who'd said, "We belong together"?

"Are you kidding?" he said quietly. "I would love it if you were in New York." His face so serious, such a contrast to his words. "But what about Asa?"

"Asa," she said, pronouncing his name with all the anguish she felt. "I haven't told him yet. I guess I was vaguely, miraculously hoping he would think about moving there if they take Cascade." But there wasn't really a hope that Asa would consent to a move to New York. And now he would find out about the dam and maybe about Jacob, and maybe he would want a clean slate, a chance to start fresh. A new town, new wife, the children he wanted. Wouldn't there be some kind of relief in that for him?

She and Jacob had to go forward with a clean slate, too. "And there's something else. It was stupid and rash but—" She had to tell him she had known, all along, the truth about the dam at Secret Pond.

There was the sound of the outside door opening, multiple foot-steps pounding down the stairs. She got to her feet and spoke quickly. "Asa's in Connecticut till late, midnight. Come by when they're done with you."

"If they let me go—"

"They have to, you haven't done anything wrong," she said as Elliot Lowell strode in, followed by Wendell and Dwight.

Dwight set two steaming cartons of something from the Brilliant on one of the desks. "Dez," he said, almost under his breath, as if no one else could hear. "What's going on?"

She gathered herself up, ready to make all the difference with what she had to say.

"Asa himself was working on that dam. No one else was fooling with it," she said. She waited for the understanding that would follow her pronouncement, but Dwight and Wendell simply exchanged raised eyebrows.

Lowell stepped forward and looked down at her with some amusement. "Your husband told me that already." Obviously, his expression said, she didn't share confidences with her husband. Obviously, she visited men who were not her husband as they sat in jail cells on Saturday nights. "Just this morning on his way out of town. He opened it, he said, but someone else closed it." His eyes lifted and he regarded Jacob steadily. "What your husband did also has no bearing on why Mr. Solomon was up there two days in a row. That's why he's here to answer a few questions." He nodded to Dwight and Wendell. "I will walk Mrs. Spaulding out."

Dez tried to catch Jacob's eye, but Wendell stood between them and she had no choice but to follow Elliot Lowell as he ushered her through the door and up the stairs.

They emerged onto the sidewalk, to a warm wind and brassy music floating down from the bandstand, wavering in intensity—now loud, now barely discernible. In the distance, electric light haloed the air over the common, but where they stood was dark and shadowy.

"I found your note," Dez said. "What is it you want?"

"Well, I've got a man dead, and his widow clamoring to find out what happened to him."

She was silent. Let him steer the conversation.

"Now everyone's saying Stanley himself was probably trying to close up the dam, that it was an accident. And it probably was an accident. But not the way people are saying." His languid way of speaking, and looking at her, unnerved her. "Stan would have notified others before doing anything himself. That's the way we run our operation."

"You know, Mr. Lowell, regardless of who closed the dam, the act of doing it didn't necessarily cause Stan's death."

"I'm hearing there's talk about you and this peddler fellow," he said abruptly. She was glad of the night, to hide the blush she knew had spread up her face. "And I'm guessing why you were in the woods, but I have no idea why you'd want to close up that dam."

Did someone actually see them? Again, she didn't respond. Let him reveal what he knew.

"Mr. Solomon didn't want to say why he was up at Pine Point, and that got Wendell suspicious of him. Wendell's ready to point the finger at him just to get rid of Mrs. Smith. But Dwight sensed that Mr. Solomon was only trying to protect you."

"I don't see how Jacob can be charged with anything. So what if he was at Pine Point? People walk it every day."

He pulled a pipe and lighter from his breast pocket, tamped down the barrel of the pipe, and flicked the lighter. Then he told her what Dot's oblique comment must have referred to. Then she knew the real reason Dwight and Wendell were taking a closer look at Jacob. Attorney Peterson was probating Addis Proulx's will. And it was only a matter of time before everyone would know that the partners in the Cascade Valley Golf Club built the course with an eye to the money they would get when the state was forced to buy it from them at assessed value.

"The land was the doctor's part of the investment," Lowell said. "Nearly two hundred acres of abandoned farmland that wasn't worth much as it stood. The other two put up the money to build the course and they built it cheap, and how?" And now, Lowell spoke like a politician. "They built it on the backs of men grateful to earn a nickel for a dollar's work, and those two crooks—well, let's just say they know what's what. That land was assessed at fifteen hundred dollars before they built the course. Now it's assessed at thirty-seven thousand. We have to pay assessed value to all property owners. The investors stand to make a tidy sum, and when we go ahead with eminent domain proceedings, proceeds from Dr. Proulx's portion of the sale will be disbursed to the beneficiaries of his will."

"I don't understand what any of this has to do with me or Asa or Jacob," she said uneasily.

Lowell clamped his teeth against his pipe and looked up at the night sky. He put both hands in his pockets, obviously enjoying the tension he was creating. "The doctor's primary beneficiary is 'the artist Jacob Solomon.'"

No. She felt unsteady, as if Lowell had pushed her. No. Jacob could not have known; he would have told her. She knew this. And she knew Dr. Proulx. "Dr. Proulx was a generous man, a philanthropic man. He would certainly have kept such a thing to himself. Jacob reminded him of his son, Paul, he liked Jacob. You don't think—?"

"You know how talk spreads."

"Jacob had no idea, I know it."

"Calm down," Lowell said. "I'm guessing Dr. Proulx found out that the golf course was a scheme. After all, the man did, out of character, so everyone said, commit suicide and no one really knows why. If he was as honest as his reputation, then the thought that he played a role in something underhanded might have troubled him. I don't know. I'm sure there are a host of reasons why someone commits suicide."

"You do believe he did?"

"I do. And so does the doctor who attended to him, but unfortunately for Mr. Solomon and his reputation, and the reputation of his friends—" He rubbed at the back of his head. "Look, he's been at the scene of two deaths. First, he finds Dr. Proulx. And then there's the fact of him up at Pine Point two days in a row. You must see how bad that looks."

"How could closing the dam or causing Stan's accident, as ridiculous as it sounds to even voice that, possibly benefit him?"

"If he knew about his inheritance, then he might try to sway us. Choosing Cascade means buying out the golf course."

So that was the root of the gossip. It was preposterous, yet her mind turned back to Dot King and Popcorn's mother, and Lil, and people gossiping over coffee at the Brilliant, all ready to believe the worst. She thought of Mrs. Smith and her suspicions.

Lowell puffed on his pipe, the stem clicking against his teeth. "Let me tell you something, Mrs. Spaulding. This incident is, quite honestly, getting in my way and on my nerves. I've got a job here, a reservoir to build, and I want this mess swept up and behind us as soon as possible. Now, I'm going to ask you outright. Are you that man's alibi?"

She saw what was happening, saw that this politician could smooth things over, fix them. Yet the answer lodged itself in her throat as she realized how completely her "yes" would change everything. She would have to face Asa and maybe his sense of anger would be so great that he would be driven to use the playhouse as pawn.

And yet she couldn't betray Jacob.

Best to be honest and face the consequences.

"Are you?"

She looked over her shoulder, instinctively lowering her voice, as if someone might hear. "I am. We were in the woods, and we found the dam, and yes, we closed it." Her rate of speech sped up. "But Jacob knew nothing about it being Asa's land, and it would really be better if my husband didn't know either—"

He held up a palm to stop her, observing her with a lazy smile. "That's all I needed to hear."

Really? It was as easy as her word? "You'll let him go?"

"Let's just say I have some influence. I do think the whole incident was an accident and it's pointless to turn this into something it's not. We have a project to get on with and I don't want this to slow us down. I'm curious as to why you closed it, though."

"It was an impulse. He wanted to see how it worked, we both did. The pulleys. I don't know." She didn't want to explain herself to Elliot Lowell.

"Well, I am going to recommend this." He lowered one finger onto his left hand to make his point. "You go on home to that husband of yours and you take care of him. Because he's going to be upset. He opened that dam for obvious and pitiable reasons, and I'm sorry for him, but—" He lowered his voice. "We are taking Cascade."

A quick, harsh noise—a noise that sounded human—caused them both to spin around. Dez peered into the night. Wind fluttered across her shoulder blades, lifted her skirt.

"Night birds," she said, shivering and instinctively looking up, imagining, already, the water overhead. So it was going to happen. It was finally real.

"We've had to kind of go through the motions—play politics. Well, you know. Your father understood these kinds of things."

Her first reaction was bristling, naïve. She almost said, *My father understood such things but didn't approve.* Then she realized that he'd approved of every political move that had kept the state and its reservoir out of Cascade.

"Stan told me it looked like Whistling Falls would be chosen," she said.

"Well, Stan was a talker and we wanted people to believe that we were seriously weighing the two options. He wasn't really in the know."

"I see." She slipped her hand into her pocket and wrapped it around the tight roll of the award.

"So I'll do my part to quiet things down," Lowell said. "I will tell the policemen here that I'm satisfied that everything is as it seems. I'll tell them the two of you were in there sketching—that might keep the gossips from talking."

She nodded intently but she was half listening. They were taking Cascade, and if they were taking Cascade, then she wanted to go to New York. She wanted to get out while there was still a way out. Like Abby had said, *no babies means you can leave.* And wouldn't Asa be better off, eventually, with someone who wanted what he wanted? If Lowell kept quiet about her involvement in the dam closing, she could wait until the water committee's formal announcement. Then, when all would be turmoil anyway, she could let Asa know, as gently as possible, that she was leaving.

It was a relief to have come to a decision, to have a plan of action, even though her resolve was still on the raw, new side, with underpinnings of doubt and trepidation.

"Mrs. Spaulding."

Lowell was looking at her in his infuriating, mildly amused way, and it dawned on her more fully: the extent of her naïveté. "Why are you telling me all this?" she asked. "Helping me. Why me?"

"You're William Hart's daughter, and I can see that you've got smarts. And I would guess from this *American Sunday Standard* business that you are ambitious. And practical." He let his words settle while he tapped at his pipe, reached into his pocket, pulled out a plug of tobacco, relit it. "I plan to run for the U.S. Senate next year."

"Ah." So he wanted something he thought Dez could give him. Music drifted down the street. "Pack Up Your Troubles in Your Old Kit Bag and Smile, Smile, Smile," taking her beyond the common, and across the country that was so full of trusting people believing in Memorial Day and band concerts and *The American Sunday Standard.*

"We plan to announce the reservoir decision on July twenty-sixth," Lowell said. "That's a Friday. And what happens when we make the announcement? The rest of the state's happy. They're going to have water. Your issue comes out the next day, and I make you and your magazine look good because your page includes 'A Letter from the Commissioner.' Which I will give you, explaining that this reservoir is for the good of the majority, which it is. I get all those Massachusetts voters who read me on Saturday night, Sunday morning, feeling good about the fact that their state's in good hands. They've got the water they need. They remember that when they go to the polls. And there's nothing wrong or bad about that."

And there wasn't—really. Sometimes politics did make sense, because someone had to be in charge, and better it be those who made an attempt at working toward the common good.

And shouldn't she play politics, too, now she had the chance?

"About the playhouse," she said. "You said you could probably find a way to move it." With Lowell involved, Asa might not dare threaten it.

"I'll see what I can do." He removed a card from his inner pocket. "All the information you need to reach me is there. In the meantime, where shall I send the letter?"

She thought of her detour down Wrong Turn Path. Now the path itself was forking yet again, and the way to go was clear. New York. "To the *Standard*'s offices, I suppose. Care of me." How strange to say that. "One Hundred West Forty-third Street, New York."

28

At home, stepping into the familiar, the everyday, the decision to leave felt immediately implausible. It was hard to hold on to her resolve. She was rattled, too aware of herself, her presence, the sound of her footsteps moving around the house, turning on lights, fingers turning the dial on the radio and the Ben Bernie Orchestra flooding the room. Too loud, jarring. She switched it off and the room reverted to silence.

The worst of it: Asa had no idea of any of this, not an inkling. No idea that his wife had decided to leave, that another man had said, "*I would love it if you were in New York.*" No idea that Cascade had already been chosen. That Cascade would be disincorporated and its buildings depopulated and razed, its acres scooped out, flooded.

She wouldn't ask for a thing.

She could support herself. Aside from the playhouse fund, she now had the seventy-five-dollar check from the *Standard*. Seventy-five dollars could last weeks, and next week there would be another seventy-five dollars, and for weeks after that, she would get the kind of money any family man would be grateful to earn.

As for her things, all she needed were her painting supplies, a few photographs. Portia's casket. Everything else could go into storage at the playhouse.

The clock chimed eight thirty. Asa and Silas would be talking, having a cup of coffee or two, then Asa would pack up for the three-hour drive back. He would be eager to see the award. She unrolled it and read a few words—*In appreciation for your great efforts*—before letting it curl up with a snap. She was a fraud, but she hadn't intended to be a fraud.

In her studio, she stood by the east window and looked out, willing the truck to appear. Jacob would surely have been released by Dwight and Wendell as soon as Lowell went back inside. But all was quiet, moonlight illuminating the lilac hedge, making a white ribbon of River Road.

She sat down at her worktable, one ear cocked toward the road, trying to sketch some ideas, in pencil, for the next set of cards, but her mind kept wandering. When the clock chimed nine, she realized it was too late, he wouldn't come. He wouldn't risk running into Asa. And though she knew it was hopeless, she gave it another half hour.

At nine thirty she put her pencils in their cup and got up from the table. Miles away, Asa would be driving through the night, the Buick making its steady course north. It would be hard to tell him, and hard, these next weeks, until the formal announcement, to pretend.

She moved around the house, turning off lights, climbing the stairs, changing into a nightgown. As she brushed her teeth, she caught sight of the bottle of sleeping tablets that Asa kept on hand as a hedge against insomnia. Impulsively, she spat out the toothpaste and swallowed one, wanting oblivion. She crawled between the sheets, where it seemed strange to share Asa's bed, considering her intentions. That thought set up a fluttering chain of doubts and what-ifs until the sleeping pill did its work.

Hours later, she felt the panic of the drowning person—trapped, struggling. At first she didn't know where she was and who was hurting her. She knew the sheets, white with embroidered daisy-chain hems, but the man on top of her was a shadow smelling of a roadhouse, with hands that forced her knees apart then pinned her arms to the bed.

"Whore," he said, to a tumbling of memory and panic. She squeezed her eyes shut and tried to blank her mind, but his hot breath was all over her face, and when she turned from it he forced his tongue into her mouth, the bristles on his face scraping her chin. When he stopped and rolled over, she couldn't tell if he'd finished or given up. Her stomach felt wet and her ribs hurt. After a minute, she dared crack open her eyes. He was a heap in the dark, reeking of whiskey, curled onto his side, arm flung out, mouth open.

She had never known Asa Spaulding to go to a roadhouse. She wondered which he had heard—truth or gossip—and lay awake, her heart thudding, until the tablet, still slugging through her blood and brain, sent her back to sleep.

She woke to immediate dread, to a room full of sunshine, to an urgent bladder. The sheet lay flat and empty beside her, but her dresser drawers had been pulled open, her clothes tossed all over the floor. She limped over to the window and looked down. The driveway was empty.

In the bathroom, she took stock of the shiny raw red patch on her chin, the six small bruises, three on each fleshy bicep. On the toilet, she had to hunch over and wince through the stinging. There was little doubt she was in a fertile time, and the thought filled her with the kind of dread she usually staved off by shutting herself away in her studio.

Her studio.

She scrambled up and practically fell down the stairs, rushing through the parlor to fling open the studio door.

The room was a shambles, reeking of turpentine, but even in panic she focused, mind clicking, taking inventory of the exact damage. Books and brushes and tubes of paint thrown about—no harm done. Canvases pulled from the drying racks and flung across the room, but intact. One leg of her good easel kicked in and broken. Fixable. But the big jars of turpentine and linseed oil were tipped over, puddled on the floor—how crazed could he have been? A single match and that would burst into flame. She would have to sop it all up with towels and rags, and burn those rags outside.

Everything seemed to have been thrown about with such hatred, her sketchbook flung so hard it had sailed through the door and onto the parlor rug. Crouching to pick it up, she felt something cold underfoot. The key to Portia's casket. She reached for it, suddenly aware, with a prickling at the back of her scalp, that she wasn't alone. She looked up. Asa sat on the far sofa, in shadow, watching her, wearing the rumpled tan trousers and broadcloth shirt he'd worn to Hartford.

"Asa," she said.

"Do you know," he asked softly, "about your boyfriend, about the little windfall he's expecting?"

When she didn't respond, he sputtered with impatience. "Do you?"

"I heard about it last night, like everyone else. It was thoughtful of Dr. Proulx."

"Very thoughtful, for a dead man. Of course, now no one's sure if he really meant to be dead."

She told herself to stay calm. "You've been listening to gossip, Asa, to Dot King and people like her. Jacob didn't know about that will. Dr. Proulx was upset, because of the golf course, because of Cascade—who knows why, but I saw him myself not long before he did it. He wasn't himself, he was upset. Jacob had nothing to do with anything, including your dam."

"Well now." He rubbed his chin. "That's just what everyone is saying— how they've begun to notice that my wife is suddenly all over town, listening in on town gossip though she normally doesn't care two figs for that sort of thing. And she's sticking up for the peddler, making excuses for him. And now they say you're running off to New York with him."

She got to her feet, clutching the sketchbook to her chest, inching her way to the edge of the sofa opposite his. How could he know about New York? "I have no way of defending myself if I don't know what you're talking about."

He sprang off the sofa. "Do you think he cares about you? Do you think he didn't know that money from Dr. Proulx was coming? Do you know what he's done? Do you? He's gone and blamed you. He told Elliot Lowell that you helped him close the dam. He said he had no idea I owned the land."

"He was telling the truth."

"And he said you have a job in New York, a job you haven't even had the *morality* to tell me about."

Jacob would never have volunteered that information, she was sure of it. So how did Asa know? "I've been offered a job," she said. "That's all. It's just an offer."

"Were you ever going to tell me about it?"

"Of course."

"But you told him first and then you closed my dam. Why?"

She had no idea what Jacob might have said, what Asa knew, no idea what to say.

"I want to know," he shouted with such fury that she fell back against the cushions. He yanked the sketchbook out of her hands and threw it down to force her palms open, "See these scrapes? He has them, too. Something else people noticed. People notice everything, don't you know that? And they talk about what they notice."

He dropped her hands as if she were too disgusting to touch and inhaled deeply in a show of pulling himself together. "Stan Smith's hands had no scrapes," he said. He picked up the sketchbook and calmly flipped through it, then, so quickly she couldn't believe it, he ripped out a random sketch—one of the Pine Point ones, one she'd planned to use for reference—and balled it up. And then there was wrestling and yelling on both their parts and the sketchbook fell to the floor.

She felt his shock in the way his arms went limp; she followed his gaze. The pages had fallen open to one of the drowning scenes, the first one, more document than interpretation, showing Stan's position facedown in the channel, the brim of his hat submerged, his twisted foot.

Asa turned to stare at her with disbelief and horror. "You *saw* that man drowned? You *knew?*" He fumbled behind him, feeling for the sofa, and fell down heavily. "Jesus," he said. "This is worse than I thought." All of it—the whole situation—veering off in a terrible new direction.

She tried to tell him how it had been, how she'd gone for a walk in the woods. Yes, she had seen Stan before anyone else had. She'd gone to town and tried to tell.

"No," Asa said firmly. "Any normal person stumbles across a dead man, the normal person doesn't *try*, he *tells* someone."

"By the time I got to town, Dwight and Wendell were already out looking for him, and by the time I finally saw them, he'd already been found. I didn't see the point in getting myself involved."

"And why was that?"

She had no answer and he didn't wait for one. "Because you didn't want me to figure out you'd closed my dam." His voice cracked. "You wanted this to happen—the reservoir, your *Sunday Standard* glory, regardless of the cost."

"No, Asa."

"What, then? What? Dez, if that dirty Jew got you mixed up in something unsavory so he could get his hands on Dr. Proulx's money, now is the time to wipe your breast clean."

"Asa, he did not," she said vehemently. "Don't talk about him that way!"

"I'll talk whatever way I want to talk!" But to her horror, his eyes were filling with tears.

"It was just that Jacob was interested in the mechanics of it. He wanted to see how it worked, but once we closed it we couldn't get the floodgate back up again. And he wasn't even there when I found Stan. It was the next day. Jacob knew nothing about it. And also the job in New York has nothing to do with him. The only reason I didn't tell you yet was because I had no idea Cascade was going to be chosen until Elliot Lowell told me, just last night."

"I know, I know. I heard it all." He sat down on the sofa and dropped his head onto his hands. He'd rushed his trip to Hartford, he said.

Skipped supper at Silas's. But the drive back was slow-going. He got a flat tire outside Meredith, and by the time he got to the concert, the ceremony was over. Outside Town Hall, he overheard her speaking to Elliot Lowell.

"I thought I heard something," she said. "Where were you? Why didn't you say something?" And how had he known where to find her?

His voice grew cold again. "I was inside the front doorway overhang listening to everything. Lil had warned me, said they'd taken him and you'd gone running after him." He batted at his eyes, upset with himself for getting emotional. "So I went down there. When I saw the two of you talking, I hid under the overhang. I've never felt so sick in my life. Hearing that the big decision's been a sham. Hearing my wife say she's been in the woods—my woods—with the peddler, with no thought to her reputation or mine, closing my dam. After you left and Lowell went back inside, I stood there thinking what to do. I thought, *Well, Asa, you've lived with a whole pile of assumptions and none of them has ever been tested before.* I went into the station, and I didn't know who I wanted to punch first, that worm Lowell or your boyfriend."

"He's not my boyfriend," she whispered.

"You're right," he said. "He's not, not anymore. Now he knows what kind of person you are."

She turned to the window, blinking rapidly to keep from crying. Life had turned so ugly so quickly, yet the peonies bloomed, the river sparkled. "You should have married someone like Lil. I never really did understand why you wanted me."

"Yes, well, I've been wondering that myself."

He wanted to hurt her, wanted to insult her. Fine. She deserved his disappointment, his anger, all of it. *Get it all out of your system*, she thought, looking into his left eye, hoping to make the usual connection.

Both eyes regarded her coldly.

"You can get a second chance," she said. "Even if you don't think that's what you want right now."

"What are you talking about?"

It didn't matter that she tried to explain her decision to leave in the calmest, kindest tone possible, he was adamant. "You need my consent for a divorce, and I am not going to be the kind of man whose wife divorces him."

"That's just pride talking, Asa. Think. You can start over again with someone who deserves you."

"My pride seems to be all I have right now. Oh, wait. I own a play-house, too, don't I? That pile of wood you cherish is *mine*. And I can do what I want with it."

The telephone rang and she was grateful to escape to answer it. It was Dwight, his muffled voice saying they needed to see her. The state officers. A formality.

She poked her head into the parlor; he hadn't budged. He made no response when she said she had to go to town, so she shrank away and slipped upstairs to clean up. Her hands shook, turning the tap; she expected that her reflection in the mirror would be ghastly and pale. It was not. There was a flush to her cheeks; her eyes were bright and clear; she looked alive. She pressed her face so close to the mirror she could see the depths of her pupils, the ropelike vessels in the irises. She was organic matter—dust to dust—that would someday be gone, and she had to believe that this had all happened for a reason.

From the pile of scattered clothes, she chose a gray plaid shift, the dress of a decent woman, and made noise going downstairs so Asa could call out if he wished; he did not.

It was still early, nearly nine o'clock, a fresh, clear morning. In town, on the far side of the common, people streamed toward services at the Round Church. In the station, an officer she did not know, a man wearing the French-blue uniform of the state police, barely glanced up as she entered. He had taken over Dwight's desk, and Dwight stood off to one side as if he didn't know quite what to do with himself. The holding-cell door stood open, cot neatly made up with the gray blanket.

Dwight leaned in confidentially. "We were satisfied with Jacob's statements last night." He introduced her to the sergeant, an irritable man named Malvoy. Months later, Dwight would tell her that Malvoy, based in Springfield, had been put out at having to come all the way to a backwater to investigate what was obviously an accidental drowning. The man's interrogation of Dez basically boiled down to one sentence: "Did you and Mr. Jacob Solomon close that dam and in so doing, neglect to use the plank to cover the gap?"

"We did," she said, and when it was apparent that there was nothing more to say, he thanked her, shook his head, and said under his breath, "You were, after all, on your husband's property."

Dwight offered to see Dez out; on the way he picked up the copy of the new *Standard* that sat on Wendell's desk. They were silent climbing the stairs. Outside, they stood on the spot where she and Lowell had talked. She looked to the doorway where Asa had been hiding. "What happened after I left?" she asked.

What happened, Dwight said, was that Asa staggered into the station like a stunned deer. "Honest to God, like he was full of buckshot. Jeez, I'd never seen him like that."

He must have been reeling from all the news at once—the gossip on the common, the cavalier way Lowell had struck his deal, the news that Cascade was doomed, that there had never, really, been a choice.

"I thought he was going to start swinging, I really did. Jacob tried to calm things down. He was real up-front about taking responsibility. He said he just wanted to see how the pulleys worked, from a mechanical point of view."

"I know."

"And then—" He explained the rest. How Asa grabbed Jacob by the collar and said he'd paid four men to dig for four days. And his wife knew that. "And he wanted to know what Jacob had done to talk you into doing such a thing and why." Dwight shifted uncomfortably. "See—Asa was wanting to blame Jacob, and Wendell was all for blaming Jacob, too, but I have to tell you, Dez, it seemed pretty obvious, to me, anyway, that Jacob was telling the truth."

She pressed her palms to the heat of her face. Would Jacob forgive this?

"And then he tried to go after Lowell, accused him of lying to the town, already having made the choice. And Lowell denied having made any choice and said, 'I'm going to insist you arrest this man if he touches me again.'"

Asa backed off then, Dwight said. And Lowell said that whatever Jacob might have done, it wasn't anything criminal, but he told him to do himself a favor and get out of town and stay out. "And he told Asa to get himself on home."

"What did Jacob tell Asa about New York?"

Dwight shook his head doubtfully. "New York? Nothing."

So Asa lied. He knew about New York because he'd heard her tell Elliot Lowell. "And Jacob left? That was it—he just left?"

"Yeah. Gee, Dez, why *did* you want to close that dam?"

What could she say? That she'd put a single crazy longing to touch another man before her husband, her town, before everyone and everything else? She wondered how it was that Dwight could still be so kind, letting her get away with not answering him.

"After Jacob left, we kept Asa here to calm him down," he said. "We didn't want him going after Jacob."

"What time was all this?"

"Still early. Eight."

She wished she could turn back the clock—just twenty-four hours, that was all it would take. She could be there when Asa came rushing back to see her receive the award only to see his life start to fall apart instead. Or she could tell Jacob that she had known about the dam, tell him right away, the minute she walked into the station.

"What about Stan's wife? Is she satisfied that it was an accident?"

"Now there's a hard-knock life." Dwight sighed. "She's not happy we didn't find evidence of trouble, but we haven't, and Lowell's ready to sweep it all under the rug. What about you? What's going to happen now?"

She shook her head, blinking back emotion. "I don't know." She started to walk away—where she was going she did not know—but Dwight stopped her.

"Hold on!"

She turned back hopefully, as if he might possibly say something that would change anything, help anything. He held up the *Standard*. "Would you mind autographing this?"

29

S he ended up in the only place left that felt like sanctuary—the playhouse, where she paced the aisles, her thoughts a scramble, all of them edged with uncertainty. Uncertainty, the hardest state of mind to bear. She had to take stock of her situation. Jacob might want nothing more to do with her. She might have crossed the line with Asa; he might never return to being the reasonable man she knew. She supposed she would have to go stay in the hotel. She would have to be ready for the gossip, the frosty looks, the way people would cross streets and duck into doorways to avoid having to acknowledge her. She breathed in the old-wood smell of the playhouse—surely Asa wouldn't see it destroyed, just to hurt her. The only good thing about a pregnancy would be that the playhouse would belong to the child. *A child of the union*, her father had stipulated. But the thought of pregnancy made something in her rise up hysterically. She couldn't be pregnant, she simply couldn't. A woman living alone with a baby in New York, living anywhere in the world, would have a difficult time of it without family, without at the very least a nurse, and could she make enough to pay for a nurse? Would that be the cruelest manifestation of irony—that she'd end up sunk in the endless toil of baby-caring? She'd envisioned her job at the *Standard* providing the means to spend her free hours on her painting, hours that a baby would suck dry.

But maybe she was not pregnant, maybe she was worrying over something that not only had not happened but would not happen. *There is a good possibility I am not pregnant*, she told herself. The thought was like being washed with sweet, cool water, but only briefly, and she knew she would go for weeks like this, alternating between dread and the airy possibility of escape, until she knew one way or the other. And if she was pregnant, well, there were ways, early on—strong medicines you could take, though the specifics were foggy and wrapped in old-folklore feminine mystery. Rose might know—but no, she couldn't do that kind of thing, she just had to pray she wasn't. God, how had she gotten to this point? *Just one child will make a difference in your life that you can't imagine.* What was more a sign of fate than a baby? Maybe she was meant to have a baby, and twenty years from now she would know why and all would be clear to her. But oh, it was too bad children couldn't be born already school-age and independent. She might not mind that so much, might welcome the kind of little companion she'd been to her father. What would his life have been like if the flu had taken Dez along with Timon and her mother, that terrible autumn? William Hart had died depending on her to make sure his legacy lived on. She would have to remain friendly with Asa. She would have to find some way to move the building—hound Lowell, save and scrape. Once she was in New York, she could seek out people with means who might help.

She climbed up to the thrust stage and walked across the boards, each footstep echoing up to the rafters. The ceiling paint had begun to peel in small, hanging spirals. She closed her eyes, wanting to reminisce, but she was too restless for that indulgence, and put her hands to her hips and looked around. How was a building moved, anyway? Would they take it apart and put it back together? Number each board, load them onto a truck, and cart them away? Or would they chain it whole to a flatbed, drag it inch by inch, yard by yard, the many miles it would take to reach a new home?

With a start, she heard the creak of dry hinges and peered down the rows of seats to the arched entryway. A man's figure appeared in silhouette, making his way down the aisle. Asa.

"I need to talk to you," he said.

Dez slid off the stage, landing on her feet. At least the scary, out-of-character anger was gone from his voice.

"I want to make a deal," he said.

"What kind of deal?"

His eyes flickered angrily. "The kind of deal you had no problem making with Lowell, that kind. A deal that benefits both of us."

"What kind of deal?" she asked again.

"This kind: people are already talking, and maybe you don't care about your reputation, but I care about mine, and whether you like it or not, we're tied together. Now, you want to see this playhouse saved," he said. "And I can say yea or nay to that."

She nodded for him to go on.

"I want us to join forces, to present a united face as a couple over the next few days and weeks. To stop the talk in its tracks. I was just over at the Brilliant, and I let everyone who was there having breakfast know that my silly trusting wife had been talked into helping this conniver Solomon close up my dam. Everyone's already talking about how he must have known he was in for money if the state was forced to purchase Addis Proulx's land."

"But that's not true."

"People believe it. And those people will tell more people, and if we stand by that story, stick together, then our reputations stay intact."

"What about Jacob's reputation?"

"Dez. Get something through your head. I don't care about Jacob Solomon. They're already thinking the worst of him. He doesn't live here. I've lived here all my life and I will not become the butt of rumors and scandal and snickering."

"I understand your position, but I can't lie, Asa."

"You already have lied, Dez. Countless times."

She swallowed; she couldn't deny it.

"You don't have to say anything, just be by my side in the coming days and this will all die down soon enough, what with what we're all facing anyway. Can you do that for my sake, for my reputation? For the sake of this playhouse?"

"You wouldn't see this place destroyed, Asa."

"Oh, really? You forget that no one else cares about it the way you do."

She looked up at the strapwork ceiling, the painted gilt lion. *Life is a stage and all the people merely players.* He was blackmailing her, essentially. She had to make herself calm, remove emotion from the situation, gauge the long view.

"I can make things very difficult. I can go after him," he said, "for trespassing, for damages."

"You're not that kind of person, I know you're not."

"Don't kid yourself, Dez. I've been naïve, but no more. I'm done."

"Asa, why would you want to be married to me if the only way you could have me was through blackmail? What kind of a marriage is that?" She tried to tell him, with her eyes, that she was serious, serious and sorry. "I'm going to New York. I have to give it a try."

He lifted his chin. "I'm only asking you to stick by me for the next few weeks," he said. "Is that so much to ask?"

"You mean put on a show while we live under the same roof? Oh, Asa, no. I'll go to Mrs. Mayhew for the next couple of weeks. That's what I've decided."

His hand came slamming down onto the stage, even as he managed to control his voice. "This has come at me out of the blue. The reservoir, you—all of it. If you leave in the midst of all this talk, well, then, in for a penny in for a pound, so they say. You let them tear down our reputations, I will let them tear down this playhouse, I promise you. And I won't give you a divorce, if that's what you're after. I won't do it. But if you can manage," he said, jerking his head to one side to hide his eyes, gone suddenly shiny and wet, "to show some consideration for me, and let me hold my head up in this town, then I might let you decide what to do with this place. I might allow that."

She twisted her wedding ring around her finger. "It will be awkward, living together in the house, knowing it's a sham," she said.

"More awkward," he said, "to have the whole town whispering and talking behind our backs."

———◦———

Later, she would look back on that agreement, on how odd and business-like and false it was even as she went through with it, spending the next weeks parading around town with Asa, plowing through those days conscious of her inner eye observing in dismay, constantly off-kilter, like stepping sideways.

They were not apart once, and she often caught Asa looking at her with concentration, as if he was trying to figure something out. They did things they had never done. They worked the fountain together. They hand-delivered prescriptions to the outlying towns and farms. They watched double-features—*The 39 Steps, Mutiny on the Bounty*. She overheard Jacob's name on people's lips—talk that died as soon as the speaker spied the Spauldings.

The closest she came to calling the whole deal off was the Thursday night they spent at the Brilliant. It was a mild, golden evening, and the Brilliant was bustling. Ike and Helen Whitby encouraged people to congregate there, even if they ordered only water, to talk about the reservoir. Everyone was rumbling about the threat and the dismal economy and the ineffectuality, or not, of President Roosevelt. At one point, there was a squabble about the latest buzz, something Charles Lindbergh was reported to have said: that the greatest danger of Jewish power lay in their ownership and influence in motion pictures and press and radio and government. "Damn right," Dick Adams blustered as the door jangled and Al Stein and his wife, Judith, walked in. Dick's back was to the Steins, and no one took any particular notice of their entrance, though the few who did notice said hello as the couple took stools at the far end of the counter, near the big plate window that looked out onto Main Street.

"Rosenfeld's toadies are ruining our lives," Dick said, waiting for the spattered laughter that the bastardization of Roosevelt's name usually got. "They took us off the gold standard, they're printing money at will, they're manipulating everything we see and do. Decent men like Bud and I can't get a job, and this takeover of our town? It's all about money. Right, Bud?"

Bud, sitting with his wife at the counter, looked embarrassed and took a sip of his water. "I dunno, Dick."

"Well, what did you see last night?" Pete Masterson nodded toward Dez and Asa, a serious nod, as if their answer would prove Dick right.

"See?"

"At the Criterion."

"*Mutiny on the Bounty*," Asa said, looking confused.

"There you go," Dick said. "Bligh: Thalberg's version of Hitler. Thalberg's a Jew. Wants to stir things up, wants what Rosenfeld wants: renounce capitalism, sell us all out to communism."

Asa eyeballed both Pete and Dick to point out Al and Judith, who sat stiffly at the counter. Pete shrugged to show he wasn't sorry.

"You can't blame everything on the New Deal, Dick," Asa said.

"You mean the Jew Deal. But hey, at least there's one less Jew around for you to worry about, Asa."

Only Dez knew how infuriated he was, how much effort it took for him to stay calm, to rise and suggest to Dez that they get going.

During those awkward weeks, she hoped she would hear from Jacob; she did not. Two weeks after the worst of the gossip had finally died down, she gathered courage and phoned his house, praying that he or his sister or one of the children would pick up the line. Instead, the old woman answered and, recognizing Dez's voice, went into a tirade. "I don't talk to nobody from Cascade." Pronouncing it Cas-ked. "He good man, always good. You to drown, I say—" and here she said something guttural and blunt in another language and hung up.

Dez hung up herself, trembling. Jacob was most likely in New York by now anyway. She would find him when she got there. She would find him and explain and apologize. She prayed that she would not have to confess to a pregnancy.

The idea obsessed her. Every night, she held her palm over her stomach, trying to detect some sign of life. In the morning she stood sideways and peered at her abdomen in the long mahogany pedestal mirror next to the closet, looking for signs. There was no swelling. Her breasts—did she imagine they were more tender than usual? She couldn't tell. She gnawed herself into such anxiety over the possibility that anxiety became something like resignation. If she was to be pregnant, she wanted the baby to be Jacob's, and that was a wish that originated somewhere deep inside. She wasn't sure how she would get through nine months of uncertainty, but trusted that once the baby was born, she would know. A dark-haired, dark-eyed baby would belong to Jacob, and she and Jacob would manage. At least that was what she thought when she was feeling optimistic. Other times, she remembered the day he said she reminded him of Rosetti's Beatrice, that personification of purity and love. She had once searched the Cascade library, trying, in vain, to find a reproduction of that painting.

She felt so far from pure.

She kept up with her cards for the *Standard*: a historic look at an early Independence Day celebration one hundred years ago, paired with a speculative view of the proposed reservoir in twenty-five years—1960, a date that seemed as remote and unreal as 1860 seemed now.

June drew to a close. The talk about Jacob and Dez died down, as Asa had declared it would. In his desire to suppress gossip, he did not tell anyone about overhearing Lowell confirm that Cascade was doomed. Zeke returned from a trip to Boston on July 1 and mentioned that his friend at the State House thought the deal was sealed: Cascade would be chosen. People gathered in the streets, in the Handy and the Brilliant and in Spaulding Drug and the Criterion Theater to talk, to mull over what was fact and what was still speculation.

The first week of July, none of the week's newsreels were light. One delivered news of another dust storm in northern Kansas—spotted, crackling pictures that revealed a black sky raining dirt as a single car tried to escape it. Another announced that the Führer had decreed the Mauser K98k to be the main battle rifle of the Third Reich. The third posed a question: Would Japan, too, adopt fascism? The news was the sort that usually made people want to hunker down in their homes, but now Cascade faced homelessness, displacement, and for its residents, public places had become more homelike, more comforting, than wood-

and-shingle dwellings that could soon fall to bulldozers. A newsreel team filmed the Independence Day picnic on Cascade Common, festivities that were somewhat frenzied, everyone knowing that they could be the last festivities the common saw.

With focus off her, Dez felt ready to slip away to New York, but at night she couldn't quite believe that she would really go. She knew she must, that she would never get another chance if she did the weak, safe thing now. She fought sentimentality every day. *Soon I will never climb these steps again, never open this cupboard, turn this faucet, turn down this bed.* At night, she lay awake, Asa asleep beside her, her heart quietly beating. Only so many beats in one lifetime. She tried to grasp what it would be like to sleep somewhere else, in a strange bed in a building she didn't yet know. New York was real, with smells and sounds and sidewalks, but until you were actually in a place, that place felt inaccessible, static.

She vacillated, but most of the time she was afraid to go. She was afraid to board the train and head off to the unknown. She would have to find a place to live; she would have to get all her belongings there; she still had to hound Lowell about moving the playhouse. She sent him a reminder, and received a terse "working on it" note in reply. In her worst moments, she was so overwhelmed that she was close to calling off the move. It would be so easy, so safe, to stay with Asa, who had turned out to be so tolerant, in his way. She would turn her head and watch him sleep, his chest rising up and down, and marvel at how people could remain so committed to institutions and rules. To him, she was his wife in the most legal sense of the term. If he could turn back time, would he still want to marry her? She thought the answer would be no. So why did he want to hold on? He had made no move to touch her, but he wanted her in their bedroom because they were still married. He predicted she would get to New York and regret it. "You'll be home within a month," he said. In the meantime, he had no intention of letting people know the truth and planned to say that she was working on a project down in New York, a project with vague deadlines.

Dez indulged him. She packed a single trunk and conceded that he might very well be right. Asa told her that he had looked into where she should stay, and that the best place was the Barbizon, known as a safe haven for independent women in the city.

A hotel stay was temporary by its very nature. Dez had no intention of living in a hotel. She would feel settled, able to truly judge living on her own, in the city, only in her own place. But she didn't tell him that, and she turned down the money he pressed on her until he insisted; Dez was still his wife. He was hardly going to let his wife go off without funds.

Her leave-taking on the morning of July 15 was calm and without theatrics or animosity, but it was strange. Strange to have Asa carry her trunk downstairs and load it into the Buick. Strange to inhale the fresh morning air, the kind of air that promised a lazy summer day, and climb into the car thinking how unnecessary this really was. No one was making her move. She didn't have to move. She rested her hands in her lap, feeling an acute sense of embarrassment, as if she were drawing attention to herself in a way that was melodramatic and unjustified.

Asa was quiet in the car. She supposed he hadn't really believed it would come to this. He grimly started the engine and drove down the driveway. *I'm really leaving*, she thought with rising panic.

They traveled down River Road, past the decaying summer homes. Would she see them again? They could start tearing places like this down very soon. The car rumbled over the Cascade River bridge and she talked about the *Standard* to fill the silence. It was a good thing she would be able to sit in on all the early meetings, she said. She didn't know that she would be able to do the series, otherwise. "Mr. Washburn said the editorial board's been so pleased with my Cascade work that they really want me to guide the direction of the new series. It's an honor, don't you think?"

Asa nodded noncommittally. He turned left onto Spruce Street and pulled up in front of the train station. He got out and came around to Dez's side of the car to open the door. "Hopefully," he said, "the new series will do more for the country than the other one did for Cascade."

Her eyes smarted as he walked into the station to get the porter, part of her close to saying, *What am I doing? Drive me home.* He returned with Albie Ray, the stunted little porter, who hefted her trunk onto a dolly and wheeled it away. They walked through the waiting room and onto the platform. The train was already on the tracks, quivering and throwing off heat like some fire-breathing beast. Asa appeared at once stoic and resigned and hopeful and bewildered. "So," he said, his voice louder than necessary, speaking for the sake of other people nearby. "I guess you'll go get your work done and let me know what's going on," he said.

"Yes," she said, forcing herself to say no more, to make no promises. He helped her up the stairs and into her seat and pecked her briefly on the cheek, his lips cool and dry. He made a movement with his head that was both a shake and a nod, then climbed back down the narrow steps to wait on the platform.

Through the window, she met his eyes. Looking too happy would be cruel, but she couldn't look mournful. She adopted what she hoped was a bucking-up, businesslike expression every time their eyes caught until finally, blessedly, the engineer blew two long whistles, then two short ones. The train began to grind out of the station, slowly at first. Asa raised his arm, eyes fastened on Dez, his figure quickly shrinking as the train rolled forward. She waved without looking directly at him. She was too afraid she would change her mind, that she would get off in Hartford and jump on the next train back, blubbering with cowardice and guilt. The train rolled past the common, past the back of the playhouse, which she glimpsed with a catch in her throat, then plunged into the woods, running along the river, taking her with it, moving her away from Massachusetts for the first time in almost five years. Miles passed, miraculously fast, farmers' walls and birch groves a streaming blur.

She had known she would feel grief, regret, and fear at this moment, and she did feel all that, but as the train sped up, rushing and clacketing along the tracks, the woods and countryside falling away, she felt something else more fully: the lightness, the exhilaration, the chest-expanding relief of finally moving forward.

NEW YORK CITY

30

In spite of the increasingly urgent murmurings coming from across the Atlantic, Dez did not understand what had truly happened to Jacob during that brief, fluttering period of scandal in Cascade. It wouldn't be until the *Life* story came out four years later, after the success of *The Black Veil*, when her life would have already changed so vastly, that she would really recognize the extent of the isolation Jacob must have felt that night a town pointed its collective finger at him. In the beginning, new in New York, she just wanted to find him.

She was only half an hour into the train journey when Cascade and her months as Mrs. Asa Spaulding began to feel as remote as the plot of a half-remembered movie. A staid porter maneuvered a tea cart down the aisle, and Dez was reminded of her school days, when she used to travel alone, by train, back to Farmington. No matter how morose she felt at the station—her father bending down to kiss her cheek, slipping some wrapped surprise into her pocket, assuring her that Christmas was just around the corner—she would, within minutes of the train's departure, be strangely happy to be exactly where she was: in her own company and settled into her plush velvet seat, face turned to the window.

She was enveloped by that sense of self-sufficiency, arriving in New York late Monday afternoon. How easy to disembark amid the fumes and noise of Penn Station, to tip the porter, to hail a hackney cab and find her way to the Barbizon Women's Hotel on East Sixty-third Street. Easy to register, to explain that she would just be staying a couple of nights. Easy to fall asleep on clean cotton sheets, ears filled with the muffled sound of car horns and footsteps and voices. And easy to spend Tuesday exploring flats with the apartment representative recommended by the Barbizon desk clerk.

By three o'clock, she had chosen a one-room, furnished flat with bath on West Seventy-fourth Street between Central Park and the Hudson River. It cost fifteen dollars and fifty cents a week, more than she thought she would have to pay, but it was safe and clean, with three large windows that let in a steady north light. She crossed her fingers that the job at *The American Sunday Standard* would be hers for as long as she wanted it, for the first time feeling for herself the undercurrent of anxiety that had plagued people everywhere these past years: How much worse can things get? If I have a job, how long can I keep it? What will I do if I lose it?

Back at the Barbizon, she tucked inside one of the phone booths off the lobby. She perched on the small seat and counted out nickels from her purse, depositing one into the slot and waiting for the operator to take the call.

It was four o'clock. Mrs. Raymond would have gone home; Asa was likely alone in the drugstore, puttering in the back room, or mixing a soft drink for a late-afternoon straggler. Her stomach pitched with dread, waiting through the connections, until his voice came through, faint but clear, "Spaulding Drug."

His response to her announcement—"I've found an apartment"—was silence, a blind chasm that she talked into, her voice like an echo, providing the address, explaining that there was no lease, the agreement was tenant-at-will. She wasn't sure if the nonbinding agreement was for his sake—indulging the pretense that she was in New York temporarily—or if it was a means of giving herself a way out. She hoped she wouldn't resort to that, whatever happened. Wouldn't resort to the weak way out.

"Asa?" If only he would say something. "Do you hear me?"

Finally, he spoke. "I'm just wondering how long it's going to take you to get this out of your system."

She pulled the receiver from her ear and looked at it a moment. It was a thing, a piece of hard, black Bakelite. She was tempted to simply hang it up, but when she put it back to her ear, he was already gone.

The new flat occupied the fourth floor of a late-nineteenth-century sandstone building. It contained a brown plaid armchair, a maple bureau, a narrow bed. A drop-leaf table and ladder-back chair crowded the minuscule kitchen, which consisted of a sink, a single burner plate, and an icebox connected by an ice chute to the back landing that ran the length of the building. A red-and-white-checked oilcloth skirt, tacked beneath the short countertop, tidily concealed the basics that were all anyone needed: fry pan, saucepan, two plates, two cups, two glasses, and some assorted cutlery. There was a surprisingly large closet, obviously part of some long-ago bedroom, before the fourth floor was carved into apartments. The bath was old, with a plain white peg-leg sink and small, footed tub, but it was functional and private, and that was all that counted. By eleven o'clock the next morning, Dez had paid the super and moved in, her trunk dragged up the four flights by a portly, red-faced driver the Barbizon desk clerk had called. The man grunted and complained with every step until he heaved the trunk over the threshold. Dez paid him quickly, eager to be rid of him, to be alone. She listened to his footsteps fade away down the stairs then sat on the edge of the bed, surveying the tiny space. Her own little room. A fluttering passed through her chest—fear that she might regret what she was doing, hope that she was indeed doing the right thing. And like an underpinning to every thought, the ever-present, pulsating concern that she had been careless, that after all this, she might find herself pregnant. Here, in new surroundings, feeling physically no different than she ever had, the idea seemed both absurd and terrifying, so unnerving it made her jump to her feet. She couldn't be. And she simply had to stop thinking about it.

She opened the windows and peered down through the leafy trees to the sidewalk below. It was hard to believe she was two hundred miles away from Cascade, that the river light that filled this street was from the Hudson, that just weeks ago, she could never have imagined that mid-July would find her living in New York. Hard to believe that Jacob was out there, somewhere close by. Abby was out there, too, and what to do about that? Yes, Abby had tried to usurp Dez's place at the magazine, and that seemed unforgivable, but Dez was also a bit uncertain about her own role as guilty party. She had, after all, assumed ownership of the *Postcards from America* idea.

She unlocked her trunk and took stock of the blouses and skirts and carefully wrapped tools. Most of what mattered had managed to fit inside such a small space. A narrow built-in bookshelf in the east corner of the room took Portia's box and the few books she'd packed, including her collected Shakespeare, the Chinese fortune carefully tucked inside Sonnet 116. She set her tack box, her stretching tools, and her good brushes on the kitchen table, which would have to serve as workspace for the time being. She would need a new easel. Her clothes, though she had carefully rolled them, shook out all wrinkled. She would need to buy a hot-iron. Oh, and wire hangers. The hooks in the closet held only two.

She had been unsure what to do about her paintings, and in the end, lugged along her best ones, too afraid to chance their destruction. Everything else she stored in the playhouse. She lifted out *Twilight, Cascade Common*, and unwrapped it. It would look good by the door but she would need a hammer, nails. She started a list of things to buy. Sheets for the bed. Towels. Turpentine. Linseed oil. Sugar and salt and oil and tea. And Rose. She would have to call Rose at some point, confide in her.

Her wedding band flashed as she wrote—probably time to take it off. She had signed all her postcard paintings "Desdemona Hart" and it would be just as well to be known as Miss Hart once she began work. "Mrs. Spaulding" would raise questions. She didn't want the stigma of divorce imposed on her and yet she could hardly betray Asa by calling herself a widow. The benign "Miss" seemed the best choice. She slid the ring off her finger and rubbed it against her thumb knuckle like a worry stone. Of course, if it turned out she was pregnant, she would have some revising to do, perhaps let on that Miss Hart was a kind of pseudonym. But she would worry about that if the time came to worry about it.

The last time Dez had visited New York was in the fall of 1928, and as busy as the city was then, it seemed to have grown more hectic. A vast bridge, made completely of steel, now spanned the Hudson, allowing a flood of cars to pour onto the island each morning. Taxis joined the cars in clogging the streets, and their drivers all seemed to be in a contest to see who could blow his horn the longest. Dance palaces, billiard halls, and movie palaces all blazed with electric light. Street peddlers sold anything they could get their hands on—apples, pencils, neckties—and every block had its shoeshine boys, even though many were old men sitting patiently on their wooden boxes, shine kits at their feet. Everywhere was stark contrast: bread lines so long they snaked around corners at the same time that women wearing smart hats stepped out of taxis to enter the dozens of restaurants that seemed to be doing a thriving business despite the hard times.

Dez walked down to the new Empire State Building, tallest in the world, as soon as she had settled in, just to gawk at it, at its modern, stainless-steel entrance canopies, at its sleek, tapered sides, which led up to an observatory that maybe she would visit with Jacob, once she'd found him. She remembered reading about its official opening a few years back, how President Hoover was able to light up the entire 1,250 floors by pressing a single button in Washington, D.C. What an extravagance it seemed, to build such a thing in the middle of an economic depression. Dizzying, to peer up at its needle top. Much of it still stood empty, said a man who paused to join her in admiring it. "Tenants are few and far between, they say. People are calling it the Empty State Building, but you have to admire its permanence, don't you?" he said. "It's not going anywhere, is it?"

It certainly wasn't, Dez agreed. No bulldozer would ever barge in and push that aside to make way for something else.

The man tipped his hat and walked on, and she realized that she liked the un-self-conscious way New Yorkers said what they felt like saying and then moved on. Her immediate neighbors in the apartment building were like that, too, much more open than people she had known in Paris and Boston. One of them was Walter Munroe, a retired carpenter who salvaged scraps of discarded lumber from construction yards and built bookcases for a vendor down on Second Avenue. One of the first things he asked when he met Dez on the stairs her second day in the apartment was did she need a bookcase? No, she said, but she could use an easel. Within days, Walter had built her a beauty: smooth, solid mahogany with a pull-out drawer and foldable legs. He sold it for not much more than the cost of the wood, and hammered a metal plate to the back of it, on which, when Dez inspected it, he had hand-etched his name. *Walter Francis Xavier Munroe.*

Everyone wanted to put their mark to something.

Another neighbor was an older Russian woman, Maria Petrova, who spoke with a careful, lilting accent and sewed satin wedding dresses and long veils of imported lace for Bonwit Teller. She was lucky, she said, that the people who bought her gowns at Bonwit's were people who always had money, regardless of the state of the world. Her flat, bigger than Dez's by two rooms, was crammed with tall bolts of satin and silk that Dez fingered the day she was invited in to drink red tea in a glass. At night, while Dez painted or sketched or read a magazine, she could hear Maria's grandson Boris, a gawky boy sprouting first whiskers, scratch at the violin.

Every morning, she caught the 8:15 trolley the thirty-one blocks down to Forty-third Street and rode the elevator up to the *Standard*'s editorial offices on the twenty-third floor. Bobby, the elevator operator, always greeted her with compliments. "Your postcards make me feel I've gone home, Miss. You'd think you knew Alsdale, Pennsylvania, that's how much your Cascade looks like home."

It was strange to be Miss Hart again.

Miss Hart. She could almost believe in her existence. She was put to work with other illustrators, writers, and reporters in the large corner wing at the west end of the floor. Her drawing space sat around the corner from Mr. Washburn's office, adjacent to a steam radiator and a double-hung window with a view to the brick building next door. In addition to a desk, she was given an easel and a drawing table. One of the junior illustrators, a boy fresh from art school, introduced himself the first day. His name was Simon Turcott, and something about his youthful shyness, the hair he nervously pushed out of his eyes, made her warm to him. He was there to give her the pencils and paper she needed and get her to write up a list of supplies she wanted from Mason's Art Store, he said. "This place is like a dream," he confided. "They give you anything you want."

That first day, she confided in Mr. Washburn, who was as warm and cordial in real life as she had imagined, someone with whom she felt instantly comfortable. She was actually married, she said, and her married name was Spaulding; future checks would have to be made out to her in that name. The Cascade bank had no problem cashing a check made out to Desdemona Hart, but any account she opened in New York would have to be in her legal name. She let Mr. Washburn assume that her husband would join her eventually, but said that publicly she would like to be known as Miss Hart. Less invasive for her husband, she said, a vague excuse that required no real explanation.

Mr. Washburn leaned toward plumpness but somehow managed to look both compact and extremely tidy. He was delighted that she had arrived earlier than August, and especially delighted with the "Letter from the Commissioner" idea, with the fact that the *Standard* would have obviously scooped the news. He planned a two-page spread: her postcard to the left, the commissioner's letter, official seal replicated, to the right.

So it was decided. Her next project would be the "decision" card, and she would depict the scene that would likely take place in Cascade on announcement day. Lowell and the rest of the water board would speak from the steps of Town Hall. A crowd would be gathered on the common. Photographers from Boston and Springfield and Worcester would be there, flashbulbs popping, to record the moment. And around the common, everything that would soon be bulldozed—the tall pines and maples, the Round Church, the Town Hall, the library—would serve as solid backdrop, as if for eternity.

31

Where was Jacob? On buses, on sidewalks, Dez's eyes searched the streets and crowds for him. At night, when her apartment building quieted down, when Boris put his violin away, when Walter stopped his hammering, when the only sounds she heard were the sounds she herself made, she settled into her bed, ears tuned as if she might be able to discern his whereabouts by listening.

That first full week in New York, she used her lunch hours to look for him. One day she paid for a taxi to wait at the Columbus Street W.P.A. office while she ran inside to see if Jacob's address could be found and given out. The office was oppressive in the July heat, crowded with people and their smells of perspiration and hair oil and cigarette smoke and something strangely dry and dusty, like pencil shavings. There was a line, she immediately saw, a line she would have to wait in. She toyed with running back outside to tell the taxi to go, but three more people walked in; the line would only get longer. After wasting a precious twenty minutes inching forward, it was finally her turn. A harried man with sweat glistening on his forehead and spectacles sliding down his nose told her that applications were still being processed, that artists were in the process of securing their necessary paperwork—letters of approval from senators and such—and in any event (and here he looked at her with a wide-eyed gaze that said she must be insane), he couldn't simply *pore* through hundreds of applications to find the one address she was seeking. If this person was her friend, he said skeptically, wouldn't he find her anyway?

She spent a second lunch hour switching into her rubber-soled canvas painting shoes so she could run, literally, up to the Art Students League, even though she had to endure the glances and snickering that her footwear provoked. The young woman manning the front desk had no idea who Jacob Solomon was, and spent a few minutes paging through some kind of roster before looking up with a shrug of regret. Dez peered beyond the woman's desk, down a nondescript hallway that led to the studios. People shuffled in and out, carrying satchels and bags, and she had to remind herself this was the Art Students League, this was what she wanted: to be with other artists, to paint, to take classes. She glanced at the clock. No time to sign up now. She headed back to work, left with only the hope that Jacob would get in touch with her through the *Standard*. She couldn't remember if she'd told him exactly when the *Standard* was expecting her in New York, but surely he knew to contact her through the magazine, regardless.

Of course, the real fear that settled in and refused to let her relax was that he had decided not to contact her at all, that her lapse in telling the whole truth that last night in Cascade had hardened his heart.

Or perhaps he hadn't come to New York after all. She got out the Chinese fortune and ran her fingers over the words. *An invisible thread connects those who are destined to meet, regardless of time, place, or circumstance. The thread may stretch or tangle, but it will never break.*

In any case, at the very least, he had to be looking at the postcard series each week.

She spent Saturday morning in the reference library at the Metropolitan Museum of Art, requesting book after book of color plates until she found it: a hand-colored print of the Rossetti painting Jacob had seen in London. *The Death of Beatrice*, from Dante's *Divine Comedy*. In the painting, Beatrice kneels, face upturned, eyes closed in a kind of entreaty.

The plate's accompanying text explained that the painting depicted the mystical transformation of Beatrice from earth to heaven. In the background, to Beatrice's left, a figure in a red robe was Dante himself. To her right, a luminous sundial read nine, the hour of her death on June 9, 1290. A red bird, messenger of death, delivered a poppy, symbol of sleep, into her open hands.

The reproduction was good; you could see how it must, in real life, somewhere in London, glow with light, the way Jacob said it did. She studied it a long time. She duplicated its lines in a careful sketch, made note of its colors. Then she went home to rework the "decision" postcard.

On Monday, she packed a small bag with a belt and sanitary napkin and tucked it into her purse, even though she did not yet feel any cramping and, in any case, wasn't truly expecting anything until Tuesday, or even Wednesday. Each day that week, she forced herself to be calm, to sit on the toilet and expect, quietly, to see bright crimson, and each day she forced herself to remain calm when she did not. By Thursday she was telling herself that any slight delay could be due to the pressure of moving. Body functions always took a while to regulate after traveling. And besides, she felt no different. There had been no nausea, no bloating. *There is absolutely no sign that I am pregnant*, she told herself that day. She was in the ladies' washroom, and when she looked up from the sink and glanced at her reflection in the mirror, she saw how anxious and drawn she looked. She needed to relax and focus on the everyday, and that way, when she wasn't even thinking about it, the familiar cramping would return.

Martha, the afternoon receptionist, popped her head into the wash-room. "You've got a telegram," she said. "I left it on your desk."

The telegram was from Elliot Lowell, confirming that the water board would indeed make its formal announcement in Cascade the next morn-ing, Friday, July 26, at ten o'clock.

The day dawned humid and cloudless. Cascade was on Dez's mind all morning, as she dressed and rode the trolley, as she sat down at her desk. She thought, the way she did at least once a minute now, about the fact that she still hadn't started bleeding, and that if she was indeed pregnant, she would have to do something. She couldn't remain Miss Hart.

She completed her first *"America"* postcard; Mr. Washburn had chosen the story that had haunted them both the most: the town in Arkansas where *the farms literally dried up and blew away.* She painted the farm buildings sepia and ghostly, with a creek sucked dry and livestock nearly transparent, vanishing in the wind. Farm buildings, with wet sheets pinned to the windows, looked miniaturized in contrast to the giant, pulverizing dust clouds, the black sky raining dirt. Those people in Arkan-sas would consider Cascade fortunate.

At one o'clock, she got up to stretch and stood gazing out the window at the brick-faced back of the building next door. Above the roofline was clear sky, the same sky that looked down on Cascade a couple of hun-dred miles away. The crowd on the common would have dispersed, but people would have gathered in other places, to rehash, to worry, to weep, and to grumble. At lunchtime, she slipped into a telephone booth at the coffee shop on Forty-third Street to phone Asa at the drugstore. They hadn't spoken since a week ago Tuesday, since the day at the Barbizon, but he sounded better than she'd expected, almost happy to hear from her. The coffee shop was so full of noise and bustle that in spite of the closed booth, she had to cup the receiver hard against her ear to hear him.

"I was just wondering how the town is taking the news." She had to speak loudly; it was noisy at the drugstore, too. "And to see how you're taking it."

"Between the rumors and leaks," Asa said, "no one was surprised. Everyone's resigned, I guess."

She reminded him that the decision card would be published in Sunday's issue. "It'll be obvious I knew all along and I suppose my name will be mud, but you're free to act as surprised as anyone."

He was so quiet she thought she had lost the connection, and was about to click for the operator when he said, in such a subdued voice she had to strain to hear, "It's all very awkward, isn't it?"

It was. Yes. "It is," she said.

"It's all going to happen very fast." In the coming weeks, he said, representatives from the state would begin to draw up contracts with landowners. "They've already begun construction of a diversion tunnel. Over off Route Thirteen, near the golf course."

A diversion tunnel, a first step in diverting water from one place to another. "How can they get away with starting construction so soon?"

"The state was quietly buying up more land than anyone knew the last two years. Oh, there are some holdouts, people who swear they'll never move. March Pierce, the Wellses. But everyone knows eventually we'll all be history." They were both quiet a moment. "When are you coming back, Dez?"

She hesitated. "I'll be busy with this new project for weeks."

"They say we'll have a year, at least, to leave, but the sooner we start packing everything up, the better. Weed things out." He talked about relocation possibilities—a lot of people were looking at Belchertown. He had always liked Belchertown—did she?

God, no. Belchertown was a small town even farther away from Worcester and Boston than Cascade. She felt herself fill with panic and despair just to imagine living there. She couldn't be pregnant; she could never go back there; where was Jacob? *He must not want me*, she thought. Maudlin, pathetic lament. "Whatever you like is fine with me."

There was a burst of static on the line. The drugstore was packed, no one wanted to go home, she heard him say before the connection went dead.

The next day the *Standard* published the "Decision: Cascade" spread with an editor's note: now that the decision had been made, the feature would be changing format. Once a month, they would publish the *Cascade Progress Report*. Other weeks would be devoted to a new feature, *Postcards from America*. The editors urged readers to enter ideas and photographs for postcards that told dramatic stories of their own small towns.

"Decision: Cascade" hit the public consciousness at the right time. Newspapers across the country picked up the story. The announcement of *Postcards from America* added to the collective sense of anticipation. On Sunday night, *The Gallagher Radio Hour* mentioned it. Dez was leaning out her window, looking down on all the people who had escaped the humid night to sit on their front stoops, when she heard it on the radio perched on the ledge below. "Imagine," she heard one man say, "flooding a whole town like that. I grew up in a town like that Cascade."

On Monday, Bobby, the elevator boy, called for the twenty-third floor and said, "You might have been drawing Alsdale, Miss. I liked the library best, the tiny books through the windows."

"Decision: Cascade" also contained this detail: a woman standing by the playhouse, in front of a tiny easel on which was displayed a miniature reproduction of the Rossetti *Beatrice* portrait. Only in Dez's version there was no red bird. Instead, Beatrice's hands released a white bird, olive branch in its mouth.

However Jacob felt, he had to be reading the *Standard*, she was sure of it. She waited for him to send her a note via the magazine, something that would at least acknowledge her presence. She left her address with the doorman at the *Standard*'s offices, explaining that an old friend might come looking for her.

She waited through the weekend, imagining she felt a baby's presence inside her. She was now almost officially a week late and it was hard to focus on working, or reading, or even walking down the street without being consumed by anxiety. The fatalist in her set in. She was being punished; her good fortune had come to an end. Now she would have to scramble, she would lose her job, she would have to ask for help. But where? She didn't know, but she resigned herself so completely that when, on Sunday evening, in the middle of swiftly undressing, she found herself bleeding, there was such shock, and such unexpected grief mixed with relief, that she burst into tears. She sank onto the bed and gave into big, shuddering sobs even as she felt herself brighten and become buoyant with the knowledge that there was no baby.

It had now been more than a month since she had seen Jacob, since he had said, *"Are you kidding? I'd love it if you were in New York."* Where was he?

The newsreel that the visiting crew had filmed on Independence Day in Cascade played in theaters the week of July 29, and America sighed. Because what small town did not have a Criterion Theater? A Brilliant Lunch Bar? A tiny cemetery with rain-worn tombstones toppling over behind a steepled church? And who could conceive of the destruction of such permanence?

Still she heard nothing from Jacob. On Friday night, her apartment was so stuffy and hot she couldn't sleep but lay half-awake all night, slick with sweat. The apartment was an oven on Saturday, too stifling to do anything. Maria Petrova knocked on her door and invited her down for Russian *blintsi*, thin pancakes that Dez devoured, her first home-cooked meal in weeks.

She spent the rest of the day alone but not alone, sketching children at a picnic in Central Park. She made the kind of witty small talk, with people she would never see again, that is exhilarating at the time, dispiriting when recollected. That evening, her first installment of *Postcards from America* came out. She picked up the magazine at the corner drugstore and sat with it at the fountain. She ordered a vanilla Coke and studied her painting. As text, the editors had decided on a collection of real quotes from people who had lived in Macomber:

"After the droughts, the dusters came and you couldn't breathe lest you held a rag to your face."

"Every single crop was smothered by dirt."

"We might have survived the drought years if the banks and land companies hadn't bought up all the land and cleared the timber. The cleared land left us wide open to the windstorms and then they foreclosed on us."

People reacted to it, and the next week the *Standard*'s offices received three sacks of postcards, so many that Mr. Washburn had to hire a girl from Barnard to sort through them all. The workweek was busy with the new project—a fire that leveled a town in California—and editorial meetings to decide which ideas to illustrate and in which order, but the weekend itself was long, and by late Sunday afternoon, she was restless. In fits and starts, she'd spent all of Saturday attempting a new painting that wasn't amounting to anything. Now she scraped down the canvas, leaving just smeared, ruddy nothingness.

She abandoned her easel for a walk. In Central Park, fat leaves hung flat and limp from their branches. She wanted to reach into the thick, sultry air and grab handfuls of it, paint it, use it. She wanted to share her feelings. She wanted to talk. She was alone in the middle of New York. She needed to make some friends. She should probably get over her resentment and get in touch with Abby.

Back in her flat, she picked up Portia's box. She held it a long while, even getting out the key. *Something infinitely worth saving,* her father had said. She played with fitting the key into the lock until, exasperated with herself, she pushed both items back onto the shelf and leaned out the middle window. It was a perfect, hazy summer evening, heavy with an enveloping humidity that mellowed the sounds of horns and streetcars and radios. A woman pushed a giant pram down the street; a small white terrier skipped and pulled from its leash; a man strode purposefully, newspaper tucked under his arm.

She wanted so badly to look down and see Jacob, had imagined it so often, that she became oddly still when she did see him, her heart seeming to stop, not believing that the person really was him, slowly walking down the street, checking the numbers on the buildings.

He glanced up. Their eyes met, and she was filled with relief and elation, even as she marked that he did not smile, wave, or shout. It didn't matter. He could be subdued for any number of reasons. All she cared about was that he was here, finally, and she flew down the four flights of stairs to let him in.

Through the thick glass sidelight, she could see him on the landing, holding his hat, fingering the brim. He looked worried, guarded. She opened the door.

"Jacob," she said uncertainly. "Finally."

He met her eyes with a look that was apologetic and regretful. "I know I should have come sooner," he said, "but I really didn't know how to."

She pushed down the anxiety that bubbled up inside her, and led him upstairs, trying to speak vivaciously, pointing out the doors that led to her colorful neighbors. They met Maria Petrova, on the second-floor landing, who said, "Is this the young man you wait for?" Dez was embarrassed to be found out, embarrassed and relieved. *Let him know*, she thought. *Let him know I've been waiting for him.* They could handle whatever was wrong. All that mattered was that he was here, finally.

But his noncommittal, forced smile increased her nervousness. By the time they reached her apartment, she was literally queasy and had to sit down. Jacob took in the room, noting the scraped canvas on the easel, the view out the windows. His gaze fell on the bed and darted away.

"Please. Sit." She gestured to the ladder-back chair and offered a cold drink—or tea? "I don't have coffee, but—"

"Nothing. Thanks."

She folded her hands in her lap. "It was so awful—in Cascade." She was close to stammering. "I'm sorry you had to go through all that. It was all my fault. Do you remember I was about to tell you something when Dwight and Wendell and that man Lowell came in?"

He put up a hand to stop her. "Don't," he said. "Don't explain."

"But I need to."

"It's done. And maybe it was all a good thing."

Her eyes asked, why? How could what happened be a good thing?

"You find out what people are made of. You find out what you your-self are made of." She didn't like the way he spoke without looking at her. She tried to catch his eye but he looked at his hands, at the floor, everywhere but at her. "I thought I could stand the obstacles we would have to face together, if we ever were together," he said. "But when something like this happens, you realize who you are and where you come from and nothing's ever going to change that, and you think about children and raising them, and do you give in to your own selfish im-pulses?"

What was he talking about? They were both in New York. She was free. He was free.

"At first, I hoped you would call, write to me, something," he said.

"But I did call," she said eagerly. "Your mother hung up on me."

"Ah," he said, as if something had been made clear. "Well. I suppose it doesn't really matter anyway," he said. "Because what's the point, really, of all of this?"

"Of what?"

He gestured to her easel, to the city beyond the window, the approach-ing storm. "All of it." The room grew darker, she could no longer clearly see his face. "You can smell the rain."

"Yes."

"You know, on my way here I stopped in to that cathedral on Fifth Avenue. I'd never been inside a Christian church before. Have you been in it?" When she shook her head no, he described the marble floor, the vaulted ceiling, the banks of candles flickering inside red glass votives. "Every footstep echoes in a place like that. I suppose that's the intent."

She listened, waiting for his point.

"Isn't it strange, Dez, that we never see certain parts of ourselves? Our backs, our lungs, our hearts. We never know what it really is to sit across from ourselves."

"No," she said. "But—?"

"And does it matter? And does religion really matter all that much? It doesn't matter to my tubes of paint, to the canvases I manage to produce. It only matters in places like churches and temples, in homes like my mother's. That man on the cross was a Jew, and if people hadn't believed in the idea of him being a messiah, the start of something new, you and I might not have seemed so different."

"We're not," she said, shaking her head, confused. "Why are you saying all this?"

"Because it's already done."

"What's done?" *Look at me*, she thought. *Take my hand. Anything.*

"Ruth is pregnant," he said. And he didn't repeat himself, but the words echoed in her head; they rolled around in it for days.

She shut her eyes, shut them as if shutting them tight would squeeze away what he'd said. Everything receded—noise, boundaries, the sound of his voice as she counted backward in her head. If Ruth was pregnant now, then he was having much more of a relationship with her than he had ever let on. She felt suddenly nauseated, and heard his voice as if it were somewhere far outside herself.

"After what happened in Cascade, I went back to Springfield and there was Ruth. A comfort." Planned words. Words that were like so many lines in a play. "Perhaps refuge. A mistake."

A mistake. She would cling to that. He returned to Ruth and Ruth was a mistake. "So what are you going to do?"

He looked at her wordlessly.

"You're going to marry her," she said. And when he didn't reply, the obvious took so much of her voice away that she could only whisper, "You already have." She barely heard the rest of what he said, that he and

Ruth shared the same background, after all, that children were best raised that way, it seemed. Her throat closed up, so painfully tight it was impossible to breathe. What kind of grief was this? It was not what she felt when her father died. It was something new, something worse, because it was poisoned with a jealousy that made her hands clench, her nails dig into her palms, ready to turn her into the animal scratching at her insides.

"Dez," he said. "It was the right thing to do and you were married anyway, and it's all been a mess, hasn't it? And I'm thirty-two, I suppose it's high time I became a father and—Ruth is Jewish. We'll raise the child the way we know how."

Her eyes filled; she couldn't control them.

"I have to think it was meant to be, that it's for the best." But his eyes were like a cartoonist had drawn them: two dazed spirals spinning into infinity.

"You talked yourself into it," she said as if she could talk away the facts, turn back time. As if by proving that he had, he could somehow undo what he had done. "What is she like? I don't even know." Needing a picture of Ruth in her mind even as she tried to blot her out. Wanting Ruth, on some level, to be a pale version of Dez, someone he had dated only because he couldn't have the real thing.

"Ruth," he said, the speaking of her name an abrupt expulsion of breath, "is—a regular girl. She was a typist at Waterman's until the plant closed."

"A typist."

The wind was blowing a heavy branch to and fro, making it scrape the far window. He fixed his gaze on it. "Don't, Dez."

She couldn't help it. She had to punish herself, had to make the pain as bad as it could be so that she would know where its end was. "When is the baby coming? Where are you living?"

"Winter," he said bleakly. "We're down on East Third Street. A cold-water walk-up."

So they were living in poverty. "What about your inheritance?" She said the word too bitterly and his face drained of color, and she was sorry. Sick and sorry. She said that she was sorry. "I don't want to be cruel." Though a part of her did, a part of her was burning with bitterness toward Ruth. Ruth! Who was Ruth to take him away? And who was Jacob to let himself be taken? Did he never feel what she thought he felt? Or did what he feel not really matter to him? What mattered to a man?

"It could be years before I see any of that, if I do," he said. "Other beneficiaries, like Dorothy King, have formally protested the will. I don't even care, to tell you the truth."

"What about the W.P.A.? Did you get in?"

"I'm pretty sure I'll be put on the Easel Project. Thankfully." The Easel Project was reserved for real talent. Would she, if she was needy enough, be put on the Easel Project? Or was it really just for men?

"Though it won't be as much of a salary as we all hoped," he said. "Twenty-three dollars and eighty-six cents a week."

She challenged him, voice ragged. "What if I had been pregnant? What would you have done?"

His eyes closed. "I didn't even want to think that might happen."

"It could have. It might have. What would you have done?"

"Dez—" He got to his feet. "I have to go. I shouldn't be here. I just couldn't leave you wondering after I saw your message." He flushed. "In the postcard, I mean. The Rossetti? At least I thought you—"

"No, you're right." He'd seen, he'd understood. There was some happiness to know that. But it didn't matter, did it, because he was married to Ruth Sondheim—to Ruth Solomon. Ruth Solomon was pregnant.

He was actually putting on his hat, ready to close the door on her, to walk out, to leave. "So that's it?" She rose to her feet. "We no longer have a friendship, nothing, because suddenly you're married, when all along I was married, still am married?"

A pulse beat along his jaw. He didn't meet her eyes. But he also didn't move to leave. *Twilight, Cascade Common*, the painting she had painted with him, hung beside the door. She ran her fingertips over the thick layers of paint, feeling where she, where he, had laid down brushstrokes. She wanted to touch him, and knowing she couldn't was the worst kind of rejection. Here they were, two people alone in a room, forbidding themselves. "How can we live in the same city and not see each other, Jacob?"

He rested his hand on the doorknob. "Sometimes things are as they must be," he said, "not as they ought to be."

Nonsense! she wanted to cry. *Don't be so bloody high-minded.* "Just tell me. Tell me what you would have done if I'd told you I was pregnant?"

"Oh, Dez—" An ambulance wailed through the open window. He waited until the sound grew faint. "I measure things," he said finally, turning the doorknob, opening the door. "I weigh things. You're still married. Your child would have a name, a father. Ruth's would not." He looked like he had just figured that out, and that the logic of his conclusion made him feel better, more resolved. "I'm so sorry, but life is full of tough choices between less-than-perfect alternatives."

And then he was gone. She stood on the threshold, listening to his steps swiftly descending the stairs. She ran to the window and watched him emerge from the entrance and head east toward Broadway. The rain had started, hitting the pavement in fat wet drops; he hunched forward into it and never looked back, never looked up.

Ten minutes later, Maria Petrova knocked on her door, expecting to hear the excited babble of a young woman in love, and found her blubbering instead. Dez told her everything, every detail, expecting that Maria would recoil, but Maria was an old woman and had seen more in life than Dez's sorry tale. "Cry and get it out," she said. "Then get over it, because it wasn't meant to be."

Dez had spent weeks believing that fate had steered her toward New York and Jacob. She didn't want to hear that Jacob wasn't meant to be. She spent a ferocious week at the *Standard*, immersing herself in work. She had been given a week to produce each postcard, a preposterously generous amount of time considering how fast she'd worked in Cascade. In just two days, she produced her most tumultuous card to date: the twisted wrought iron, soaking rain, and spiraling wind of the tornado that spun through New Orleans in March 1934, flattening everything in its way.

32

Oddly enough, it was Abby who reminded Dez why she was in New York, who propelled her into the frame of mind she needed to be in to paint *The Black Veil*.

On Friday Dez was at work, at her drawing board, when she heard Abby's unmistakable husky chirp coming from Mr. Washburn's office around the corner. Through the din of the typewriters and voices around her, Dez's ears pricked up, hand and pen mindlessly working the paper until a shadow fell across her desk. Abby stood there, regarding her pertly. Her lips were bright red, her hair full and curly.

"Weren't you going to let me know you were in town?"

There was something hurt in her face, and Dez felt bad, seeing that, until Abby said, "You know, Dez, I didn't think you had it in you. I am shocked and amazed that you're here."

"That's quite a comment coming from someone who used to pant after me like a puppy."

Abby laughed. "But I *was* a pup then." She perched herself on the edge of Dez's desk, filling the air with the smell of her spicy perfume, her leathery handbag, her cigarettes. "Where's your Jewish painter? Did you run away with him?"

Dez's silence made Abby smirk. Then she looked at Dez more closely. "Tell me you slept with him, at least."

"Shh." Dez glanced around to make sure no one had heard. "Don't you realize what you did? You tried to take my job."

"Don't you get it yet? It's every man for himself."

"We're not men."

"Oh, don't play the saint. Look what you've done, you've gone and told them my idea was yours."

Dez glanced around again, grateful for the clack of typewriters. "It was my idea, actually. We just happened to have the same idea at the same time." As she spoke, she reconsidered. Maybe the pitch for the *Standard* job had been forgivable, what with Abby alone in New York with no prospects, anxious to earn money. You really couldn't blame her for assuming Dez would never come to New York.

"Well, that's why we're friends. And anyway, you were the one they wanted. Obviously. But I've got other things going now. Though I did just try to pitch Washburn for some work—no luck."

"What happened with the W.P.A.?"

"Oh, it's all up in the air. My credentials didn't exactly bowl them over. The ones they're choosing as easel painters are people who've already exhibited some. But, if I get my letter of approval from Senator Wagner's office, which I will, I'll be put on as an assistant to Stuart Davis, which would be the cat's meow, don't you think?" She fished around in her purse and pulled out a pack of Camels. "You want to go to lunch?"

Until that moment, Dez had no idea how good it would be to go to lunch, and with an old friend. Letters from Abby had been her lifeline for so long. What had she been thinking, all these weeks in the city without seeking her out?

They went to Conrad's on Forty-eighth, where the tables were jammed, the pitch of talk was at a high level, and Abby wanted to know everything. Why was she in New York? Had she actually left Asa? "How long does a divorce take, anyway? Is it a lot of trouble?"

Dez was conscious of the tables on either side of them. In Cascade or Boston, conversation would have paused to discreetly listen. But the women at these tables ignored them. She actually had to raise her voice to be heard over the din as she filled Abby in. "Asa hopes I'm going to change my mind, but at least I don't have to worry about him sabotaging the playhouse. I don't think. Though how I'll ever move it I don't know. I've been hounding the water commissioner. He promised to help, but so far, nothing."

"And what about your friend? What happened?"

Dez told her everything. She needed to tell someone.

"He's here and you're here and you're not going to see each other? It was okay when you were married but not okay now that he is?"

How cut and dried that sounded, exactly how Dez had felt, but now she found herself wanting to stand up for Jacob, and her confusion made her uncomfortable. She was grateful when the waiter squeezed in, pad in hand. They ordered two herring salads. A Coke for Dez. Coffee for Abby.

"So," Dez said, "are you still living over near Penn Station?"

"Oh, I'm down in the Village now." Abby raved about the Village—yes, it was romanticized, but it really was full of poets and artists. "And it's full, too, of the—how can I say it? It's full of the *world*. Every kind of immigrant: Italians and Spaniards and Germans and Jews. Oh, you must come down." She asked where Dez was living and proclaimed it dull. And too far away. "I don't suppose you've any artists living there."

"Actually, I do," Dez said, thinking of Walter's turned wood and Maria's hand-stitched gowns. "Have you joined the Art Students League? I've been meaning to."

"Oh, do. Go on over. It's all very informal." Abby laughed. "You just need an 'acceptable moral character' and the means to pay your dues."

"Which classes are you taking?"

"None. I'm modeling."

Dez stared. "I didn't think you were serious about that."

"Oh, Dez, don't be a bluenose." Abby sat back, gratified to see shock on Dez's face. The women who'd modeled for them in art school had always seemed soft and soiled and not quite real. Women and men had never painted in the same room when a live model was on display. And now here was Abby, proud that she *was* that display. "Listen, Dez, you have to do what you can. No one's opening up their arms to you down here, I can tell you that. I'm just one more artist with a little bit of talent, a woman artist at that."

She modeled for students at the League, and privately, she said, for Marco Pineda. She said his name as if Dez should be impressed, and when Dez said she wasn't familiar with Pineda, she said, "Oh, you will be. Marco makes everyone else look stale and tame. He's delightfully wicked, and when I model for him—" She closed one eye in a slow wink.

"And you've managed to survive all this time on modeling?"

Abby laughed. "I know what you're thinking."

Dez wasn't thinking anything, but Abby was grinning as if she was dying to be coerced into giving up a secret. "Of course I had it set up. Sort of. He looks after me, and don't go acting shocked, but he's married. He's got a wife and kids in Rutherford, New Jersey. I give him what he wants, and he gives me what I want, and that's fine with me. He helped me move down to Morton Street." She lit up a cigarette and tapped it between her fingernails, enjoying Dez's silent processing of that information.

So both of them had been party to adultery. Dez wanted to believe that her act was somehow more pure, but adultery was adultery, wasn't it?

"You come to New York," Abby was saying, "and you kind of see if you have what it takes. I realized I won't be put on the Easel Project. I accept that. I like modeling well enough, and I'm sure I'll like being an assistant. This fellow of mine, he's a collector, and he introduced me to Marco— too bad for him, but if he thinks I hang around on weekends hoping he'll—anyway, there's this bash down there tonight. In Sidney Orenthal's studio. You want to come?"

Dez's first instinct was to retreat, to say no. But that was shyness. What else did she have to do? This was a chance to meet people, to meet other artists. "What do I wear?"

Abby paused, emphasizing the pause by raising one eyebrow slowly. "Casual, honey. Pajama pants, whatever you like."

33

H er heart dropped at the sight of the square, white envelope in her mail cubby that she knew would not be from Jacob, miraculously telling her that he had made a mistake, that Ruth was not pregnant, that the marriage never took place. The postmark was Athol, the letter from Ethel Smith. Asa or Dwight must have forwarded it to New York. The letter rambled, pointing out that people like Dez always got away with covering things up. *All you had to do was admit you fooled with that dam and that was enough for the bigwigs. Now no one cares a fig about finding out how Stan really died.*

Upstairs, Dez sat right down and penned a restrained reply. *Stan died because he caught his foot in a rock dam. Stan liked poetry. He particularly mentioned Longfellow. I suggest you do something that memorializes Stan, something to do with poetry. You'll find peace that way, Mrs. Smith.*

But she was shaken. Would Ethel Smith be her Marley's ghost, always reminding her of her sins? The incident added to the nervousness she felt about going to the party. A gathering of fellow artists. She had heard stories of wild Village parties, but hoped, like most stories, that they were exaggerated. Pajama pants, Abby had said. Compared to that kind of thing, her clothes were hopelessly plain, but she wasn't about to spend money on clothes yet, and she couldn't imagine that a bunch of artists had much money to spend on them, either. She ended up sticking with the simple pine-green dress she tried on first, and took the Fifth Avenue bus down to Washington Square. Abby had said eight o'clock but she wanted a little time to explore the area beforehand, before dark. Since arriving in the city, she had not ventured farther south than Thirty-fourth Street.

She stepped off the bus into the bustle and confusion of a part of the city that wasn't ordered into the easily maneuvered grid of streets uptown. After crossing Sixth Avenue, she made her way over to Bleecker Street, where she paused in front of a newsstand. She could never pass a newsstand without stopping to take in the pulpy patchwork beauty: the wall of magazines nestled under a canvas roof, the intoxicating smell of newsprint. There was pleasure to know that her work was there, available to anyone with a dime in his pocket.

A horse pulling a milk wagon passed, maybe on its way home after a long day. The clopping hooves, the sharp smell of horse reminded her of Cascade, and mixed with the smells of bread and newsprint, it made her heartsick a moment, and then glad she had left, glad she had the opportunity to feel heartsick rather than bored and trapped. She followed the smell of bread down the street. In the window of an Italian shop, fat cheeses tied with twine hung from the ceiling. A sign read *ricotta tutta* and *crema*, and she didn't know exactly what those words meant but knew they had to mean something delicious. In a bakery window, crusty round loaves sat piled on top of one another like stacks of nickels. Five cents a loaf, a sign said. Dez was tempted to buy one and eat it on the sidewalk, but she thought she was going to a proper party. She assumed there would be food.

The party—how to describe it? She would never again in her life feel as intensely lonely as at that first party. She thought that if any of the loose, casual people there had ever overheard Jacob and herself talking, they would have laughed at their seriousness, at the way Jacob so high-mindedly left her.

She was later arriving than she'd planned, making a wrong turn off Bleecker Street and misreading a street sign in the gathering dusk. Carmine Street, when she found it, was mangy-looking, lined with rickety buildings and overflowing trash cans. She located number 45, four stone steps leading up to a tired-looking door in need of paint. Inside the cramped vestibule, she searched the tenant listing—Abby had said that the party was at Sidney Orenthal's, but there was no such name, so she climbed a narrow, sour-smelling stairway, following the sound of a faint din until she reached the fifth floor, where a raucous party was obviously going on behind an unnumbered door. She knocked timidly and stepped back. When no one answered, she knocked again, louder, wishing she'd arranged to go with Abby. She shifted her weight, trying to fix a nonchalant, relaxed look on her face. Someone inside laughed uproariously, and she pictured her apartment with sharp longing. She could catch an uptown bus, pick up a magazine, get something to eat at the Automat, and be home, all within an hour.

The door opened and a grizzled man barreled through, his eyes bleary and unseeing. He grabbed the railing and half-stumbled, half-slid down the stairs before lurching to a stop on the fourth floor. As Dez watched in alarm, afraid he would pitch over the railing, he swayed from side to side, then doubled over and vomited all over his shoes.

Dez shrank back against the wall. It wasn't even eight thirty. What kind of a party had someone blind-drunk so early? She didn't want to go in, but the smell was disgusting; she burst inside. The apartment was one large room with high ceilings, scarred, smudged walls, and a heady smell of paint. Thirty or forty people stood around drinking and smoking and talking and laughing. Abby was nowhere in sight, but Dez pretended to look for her, edging her way through the crowd to keep herself moving, feeling both invisible and awkward. A tall, lanky man with wild curly hair that was far too long did a double-take as she walked by, but no one else seemed to notice her and she did what people who were uncomfortable at parties do—pretend great interest in their surroundings. In this case, she didn't have to do too much pretending. Two large paintings leaned against the back wall. They were big, urban landscapes, uncontained as the studio itself, populated with hobos and bread lines. Nearby, a ratty sofa sat in a corner, two people sprawled on it, all over each other, and she couldn't tell if they were two men, two women, or one of each.

She paused at the drinks table. There were bottles of gin and a pitcher of water, but nothing else, so she filled a small juice glass with gin and stood sipping it slowly, resisting the urge to make a face at the unpleasant fizzy juniper-berry taste. It didn't matter. She could have made all kinds of faces. No one looked at her, no one even noticed her; everyone seemed to be in the middle of some boisterous group. She would slip out, she decided, even though that would mean somehow sidestepping the horrible vomit. She was about to put down her glass and edge away when a woman, the kind who invaded personal space by standing a little too close, sidled up beside her. "You going to drink that down or just look at the glass all night?"

The woman stuck a cigarette between her lips to free her hands so she could pour herself more gin, speaking through the cigarette. "You were at the Museum School in Boston, weren't you?"

Dez scanned the woman's face. She couldn't place her. "Yes," she said, aware that the gin had gone instantly to her head. She couldn't remember the last time she'd had a drink.

"Maxie Eisenberg."

"Maxie," Dez said. She didn't remember anyone named Maxie, and didn't recognize the woman, even though she didn't seem to be the kind of woman you could forget. Her hair was bottle black, her eyeliner thick, her lips slick and red. Although maybe all that was new, put on. Dez tried to look past the makeup to the original face.

"You won the Cabot Prize," Maxie said. "I was so jealous."

"Sorry," Dez said tentatively.

Maxie just laughed. "Those were the days before I resigned myself to facing what I wasn't. I wouldn't be jealous now. Now I would just try to sell that painting. Did you, ever?"

Dez's head buzzed pleasantly. "I did, actually. Do you work at a gallery?"

Judging from the reaction on Maxie's face, she had revealed her igno-
rance of the state of the art scene in New York City. Maxie was obviously
somebody.

"I own a gallery. And aren't you refreshing. Here you are being nice to
me and you don't even know who I am."

Dez's brain clicked. *Maxie, Maxie.* Then it came: Maxie Eisenberg.
Ran the New New York Gallery. In school, she must have been that older
girl, Maxine, known for having her own place on Commonwealth Avenue. Her father was rumored to own half of New York. Maxine had been
homely, devoid of the makeup that made her face so arresting now. They
had never spoken.

"Boston was dreadfully staid, wasn't it? Father thought he could polish
me up there. But you know what? I do thank Boston for helping me realize
I am *not* staid." She laughed aloud. "And I thank Paris and Venice for making me realize I'm no artist but something I like better, a connoisseur."

Dez nodded, bits of information picked up from her copies of *Art
News* coming back to her now. Maxie Eisenberg lived in Europe for a
couple of years. She moved back to New York, began acquiring pieces,
and now she had opened a gallery that showcased American modern art.
At a time when most galleries still kowtowed to the Europeans, Maxine
was rich enough and brash enough to push Americans.

"Ah, you know who I am now. I can see it in your eyes."

"Yes, of course," Dez said, perhaps too politely, because the look on
Maxie's face changed in an instant to contempt. Just as instantly, Dez
responded with a hard, short look of disinterest and glanced away.

"Were you interested in sleeping with me?"

Dez had had just enough gin that she could conceal her shock. She
could even banter. "No," she said. "Sorry. Are you badly in need of someone to sleep with?"

Maxie laughed harder. "I thought you might want to get something on
my walls."

"Surely that's not the way someone gets something on your walls."

"Damn right." She stubbed out her cigarette into a big glass ashtray and talked through the smoke streaming from her mouth. "I'd never make a name for myself if I chose art that way, now would I?" She waved at someone behind Dez. "Marco. I've got someone for you."

Abby's infamous Marco turned out to be the wild-haired man who had given Dez the eye when she walked in. He took the near-empty glass from her hand and put a full one in its place. The glass rocked, dropping a bit onto the hollow space between her thumb and wrist bone. He lifted her wrist and licked off the drop without missing a beat. Her blood pulsed, the soft wet of his tongue intoxicating and repulsive. She wanted to run home and hide, and turned on herself. *What is wrong with you? Cascade is too provincial, New York too raw and lascivious. Are you ever going to be happy?* She swallowed more gin, told herself to loosen up.

People gathered around Marco and Marco introduced Dez to Sidney Orenthal, their host. Someone came in shrieking about the "revolting mess on the landing," and everyone decided people would have to leave by the fire escape. Marco hovered attentively. Everyone was drinking and the atmosphere was animated, Sidney Orenthal leading a heated discussion, insisting that the Regionalists were irrelevant, that art needed to make social statements that were stronger than hope.

By her third full glass of straight gin, more than Dez had ever had to drink in her life, her uneasiness had transformed into soaring euphoria. She would become friendly with some of these people over the course of the next few years, and her first impression of them that night would be correct. They were most of them wild, and obsessive about creating art. Not all of them had been to Europe, and those who had were adamant that American art had to lead the way from now on.

Abby showed up and Dez suddenly understood Abby, and had great empathy for her. Abby saw that Marco was interested in Dez, and it seemed that Abby was being stunningly generous when she whispered that she would go home with Jack Borenstein.

Maxie pulled her aside, too. Abby had told her that Dez was the artist behind the *Standard*'s new series. "Those paintings are good representational art, but you stick with that stuff, you're never going to make a name for your-self. You should have used a different name for stuff like that."

Dez said she had done that, instinctively. She had used her maiden name, Hart. Her legal name was Spaulding.

"Well, stick to Spaulding if you ever show in my gallery."

Dez tried to keep her face neutral, but Maxie knew she had nudged her hopes. "I said *if.* And *if* you show, the critics will pounce on you if they know right off the bat you're that postcard girl. It's bad enough you're a girl to begin with. They'll pigeonhole you as illustrator art, not that there's a damn thing wrong with it. Lots of people—lots of men—do both, but let them praise you first, then if they want to skin you alive, they'll have to eat crow. And they don't like eating crow." She lit a ciga-rette. "Abby said you've got some damn fine paintings."

Dez swallowed more gin and thought that she loved Abby, that she had never met anyone as wonderful as Maxie.

"Come to my flat," Dez suggested. It was becoming difficult to talk. Her tongue was getting in the way. "See my work."

"I didn't say Abby's opinion was worth anything. I barely know her."

"Oh, but in this case . . ." So difficult to get the words out.

"I like this girl," Maxie said to no one in particular. "There's nothing bohemian about her. She's working at *The American Sunday Standard.* Who can blame a kid for making an honest buck?"

It seemed to Dez that, finally, all the dots were connecting, all of life making sense. At some point, Marco slipped an arm around her waist and walked with her down to the end of the loft. They didn't even pretend to look at Sidney Orenthal's landscapes but stumbled onto the ratty couch, where she gave in to exhilarating, uninhibited lust, thinking, *Fuck Jacob.* She had never been one to curse and the freedom to let herself do so made her reckless and satisfied. *Fuck Jacob.*

Marco was tall and lean with dark hair as unruly as her own. She would barely remember going home with him. The memory of the night would always be of skin slippery with sweat, the smell of gin seeping through pores, and big, blank patches of black. She remembered having the presence of mind to tell him she wasn't safe, to ask if he had anything. She woke up with him, on a mattress, barely covered with a sheet, her head the size of a small planet, her mouth sour, gut sick and strained. It all came back to her—the night, the gin, Maxie, Marco. Jacob. Marco was naked and sweaty, his mouth half-open as he slept, everything about him looking too skinny, too shriveled. Repellent. She gathered her underwear, her shoes. She stepped into her crumpled dress and stumbled out into a blindingly sunny morning with no idea where she was, every step against the pavement making the bones in her head pound. A street sign read Grove Street, but that meant nothing. She walked, hoping for a taxi, until she found one on Hudson Street. Finally, somehow, she reached her apartment building and crawled up the four flights. She drank glass after glass of water. She licked salt and swallowed four aspirin. She lay down on her bed and forced herself to sleep, wanting to sleep forever. She woke at one point to her bell buzzing insistently and dragged herself downstairs to accept a telegram. She ripped it open. It was from Lily Martin, Rose's sister, and had been forwarded from Alma in Cascade. Dez read, gripping the landing post when the solid black words made no sense. Rose was dead, the words said, dead of a stroke. She was still so nauseated, her brain fuzzy. She wasn't sure she trusted what she was reading. Lily promised a letter would follow, but Dez couldn't bear it, didn't want to hear anymore. The whole time she was living her degenerate evening, Rose was dying or already dead. Her reflection in the window glass was repulsive. She wanted to smash it, paint it, fix it.

34

S aturday was lost to her. She stayed in bed, slipping in and out of
consciousness, dreaming of Rose and Timon and crazy things—
madeleines and gravestones and Timon's tin toys, wound up and
marching over the Cascade River bridge.

On Sunday morning, she immediately tried to burrow back to uncon-
sciousness. She didn't want to be awake, didn't want to know that she
would never visit Chicago to see Rose; that she would never see Rose again.
She cracked an eye open to the quiet of a New York Sunday morning. The
sky was rosy. Birds sang. Occasional voices rose up from the sidewalk. Two
miles south, Jacob was lying in bed with his wife, an image so painful it
propelled her from her bed. She put the kettle on the gas ring and wrapped
her arms around her chest. At least she didn't feel nauseated anymore. Her
glance fell on Portia's casket and she had an urge to fling it out the window.

"Nothing is infinitely worth saving." She said it aloud. It wasn't true,
she didn't mean it, but whatever was in that casket meant going *back*. She
needed to go forward. She needed to do something large. She needed to
fill her head with work.

She sat down at the table. She drank her tea. Then she stepped out onto the landing, crossed the hall, and knocked on Walter Munroe's door to ask for some long strips of wood. Through the morning, he helped her nail a frame together. Then she stretched a large rectangular canvas, tall as herself. She pushed the armchair and dining table aside, leaned the canvas against the wall, and got to work prepping it.

Though the piece would be a product of restlessness, it found order and beauty in chaos. Her moving hand, clutching its brush, felt like an escape, like a tempest within, a feverish intensity, rising, flying, hurling upward. She painted through the day, wolfed down a couple of pieces of toast at dusk, and continued into the night with lights rigged up along the walls.

The last thing she wanted to do was go to work on Monday. She bathed and dressed, wanting only to slip into her smock and get back to her canvas. She even went so far as to consider, crazily, asking Mr. Washburn if he would be amenable to letting her work as a stringer, but she couldn't be without steady money, and would be a raving fool to leave a secure job. At work she watched the clock, anxious to get back home.

She started setting her alarm for first light, painting until eight, getting herself to the office, scooting home at lunchtime to paint what needed to be painted in natural light, then grabbing something at the Automat and staying up late. She laid down the last stroke on Saturday night and named it *The Tempest,* painting the title in a tiny scroll along the bottom of the piece. It was a spun-sugar dream of a painting, lyrical with brushstrokes suggesting *cloud-capp'd towers melting into thin air.* Harsh lines hinted at violence, but she had tempered these with luminous panels that billowed and seemed to expand beyond the boundaries of the canvas. She had never painted anything like it—not quite abstract, vaguely impressionistic. She signed it D. H. Spaulding.

She would paint a series of them over the course of that summer, six in all. And the style would be different in each one. Macbeth and Lady Macbeth were neatly interlocking figures of jewel-like color and texture, enveloped by a recurrent motif in the shape of a bloody crown. *A Midsummer Night's Dream* was a lush evocation of contrasts, of brilliance and darkness, of beauty and folly.

Except for her *Postcards from America* and the first *Cascade Progress Report*, she did nothing else those weeks it took her to paint the series. Abby called in to the office to ask her to another party, and lunch. Marco wanted to see her again, Abby said. Dez went to lunch but turned the party invitation down.

She did run into Maxie Eisenberg one morning, in a Fifth Avenue coffee shop, and said hello. Maxie nodded without recognition, so Dez reminded her who she was. Maxie shrugged with disinterest, her hands shaking as she lit a cigarette. Dez stood awkwardly by Maxie's booth until she realized that Maxie was ignoring her, then she turned on her heel and left without a word.

Weekends were gifts, two long days to paint. She often went for hours without thinking of Jacob, and when she did, she thought, *Why, this is easy. It will only get easier.* Then he would consume her thoughts for hours, bad as ever—torturous "if only" thinking. She would visualize Ruth's growing belly and have to put down her brush and pinch the bridge of her nose to stop herself from getting emotional.

She had letters from Asa. Bud Foster had already sold out but had six months to stay in the house before he moved the family to Bath. Construction of the baffle dam had begun, digging of the great tunnel to Boston was under way. Big news: a man in Sturbridge, who was buying up old buildings with the intent of creating a living museum, had bought the Round Church; they were already getting ready to cart it away. But yes, Asa wrote, he had inquired about him possibly taking the playhouse, too, but it didn't fit in with the man's vision of an early nineteenth-century farming village.

She started writing to Elliot Lowell daily. Persistent, handwritten notes, a constant barrage to remind him the playhouse needed moving. He was working on something, he replied. In the meantime, she wrote to the colleges around Springfield and Worcester, offering to donate the playhouse in exchange for its paid removal.

By late August, she had one tentative offer—from a buildings administrator at Amherst College who was truly interested and understood the need for preservation but had outspent his budget through 1936. He had no funds to pay for the removal. At the same time, Asa wrote to warn her that demolition had already started on Spruce Street; she might never see her childhood home again. They'd gotten to work so quickly. Dez's first thought was to race up there and see her old house one more time. But—what would she do, really? Stand there and look at it? Her *Twilight, Cascade Common* was the essence of her memory of her old home in a way that the actual structure never was, once they'd moved. And the painting lived with her, every day.

Another letter from Asa informed her that he had found a beautiful center-chimney colonial in Belchertown. The back of the house got a lot of light, he wrote. Did she want to train up and see it? She hesitated writing back. It was good of him to think of light, but it wouldn't do him any favors to pretend she was coming back. She wrote that she couldn't come, that she was sure whatever he chose would be fine. She didn't hear from him for a while and knew he was upset. He'd expected she would give up New York in a month. Now she had been away two months, with no sign of returning.

She wrote again. She told him about the series she was doing; she described each painting—at the time, she was on the fifth canvas. It seemed important that he know that her life in New York was work-based and austere. In return she got a letter containing only one line:

Is he there?

She wrote back: *No.*

Another day, she received a letter bearing an official return address and the seal of the Massachusetts Water Commission, requesting her permission to exhume the bodies of William Hart, Caroline Hart, and Timon Hart and move them to the newly created Cascade Memorial Cemetery in Bath. The letter emphasized that families were not to be present during the removals. *Private services after re-interment are advised.* She sat right down and signed the response form. She sealed it and stamped it and carried it down to the mailbox. She wanted it gone, wanted the imagery it conjured out of her head.

Toward the end of September, as she was finishing *Hamlet*, she arrived home one evening to another brief letter from Asa. People were starting to wonder about them, he wrote. What was he to tell them?

She knew it was time to go to Cascade, to let him know, once and for all, that she wasn't coming back, to oversee the packing-up of her belongings. She had already told Mr. Washburn that the details of the second *Cascade Progress Report* would have to be reported firsthand. And now it looked like she would have to take a good chunk of savings, get herself out to Amherst College to arrange some kind of move for the playhouse—offer to pay over the course of years, if necessary. Surely a crew of men and a flatbed truck could be found and persuaded to do the job.

She arrived at work in the morning, ready to knock on Mr. Washburn's door to ask about making the trip, but he was waiting for her, with news. "James Lawrence King has offered to move your playhouse."

The world seemed to stop.

"You know, the philanthropist, my dear?"

"Of course." It was impossibly good news.

"You'd better sit," Mr. Washburn said, directing her to the chair opposite his desk. "Because it is certainly fainting news." He filled her in: James Lawrence King planned to build a summer home in Lenox, Massachusetts, in the Berkshires. He had purchased a good deal of land there. The area was home to Jacob's Pillow, a summer dance company, and as of next summer, 1936, the town would host summer Boston Symphony Orchestra concerts. A Shakespearean theater was what Lenox needed next, King thought.

Mr. Washburn lit his pipe and puffed on it. "You should know that Elliot Lowell worked for this."

"Really." So Lowell had stuck to his word, after all.

"And I understand that Mr. Spaulding has been informed of the offer and has agreed to it. So Lowell's invited us—meaning staff as necessary— up to Cascade to meet with Mr. King next week, to record it all, of course. Quite a bit of work has already begun up there, and I think it's time to get a photographer and writer involved. Seeing as how Lowell's paying, I thought I would go, too. You've made me quite curious about the place."

So it was decided. Four of them would train up the following weekend.

35

On September 30, they boarded the northbound train from Penn Station. Joe Katz and Nancy Bracewell, photographer and reporter, respectively, traveled with them. The two were engaged to be married. Joe was obviously Jewish, Nancy a Connecticut Yankee. Dez wanted to know their story and left her seat to sit opposite them, to try to engage them in conversation. But they were young lovers thrilled to find themselves together on a paid trip. They answered her questions politely, but evasively. They wanted to be alone.

Back in her seat, with Mr. Washburn engrossed in his paper, Dez gazed out the window at the Connecticut countryside. Already, with the city behind them, New York didn't feel quite real. As if reality existed only where she existed. The metal car she sat in was real, Mr. Washburn turning the pages of his *New York Times* was real. The white fencepost flashing by, the two dappled horses in that field of clover—all real. When she left Cascade in July, Cascade seemed to become a place that existed somewhere in lost time. It was strangely disorienting to be heading back.

She wasn't sure that seeing it in the demolition stage was a good thing. If she never saw the destruction, she might always have been able to imagine that it still existed, pristine and idyllic as it had been during her growing-up years.

She was calm enough through the gauzy September morning, through lunch in the dining car—sole in lemon butter, parsley potatoes—through the train change in Hartford. But as they crossed into Massachusetts, chugging closer and closer to Cascade, her heart beat faster. How would people treat her, how would Asa react when she told him she was never coming back? And what could she do with all the belongings she had stored in the playhouse? The conductor announced Cascade Station and the train began to slow. Dez peered out the window, bracing herself for shock, but the station looked exactly the same as the day she left—solid brownstone walls, the wooden overhang, the empty bench with Albie Ray loitering beside it.

Inside, the clock above the ticket window ticked as usual. A few people sat waiting on the slatted wooden benches. The station was so unchanged that it made the view of the common that greeted them when they passed through the front doors utterly startling. Intellectually, Dez had understood that in order to turn the valley into a bowl of water, every structure, every tree would have to be leveled, but intellect had not prepared her imagination.

The once-lush rectangle of green grass was gone, transformed into a muddy stretch of rubble. Harsh, bright sunlight beat down on bulldozers parked among the stumps of trees that used to provide leaf-and-pine-needled shade. Nancy began scribbling in a notebook, Joe set up his camera. "This is what the French countryside looked like after the war," Mr. Washburn said, and they were all silent a moment, looking around, conscious of the constant thwack of ax on wood as more trees were chopped down. "Them's what we're calling woodpeckers," Albie said, referring to the ax wielders. "And look, Dez. Your old house is gone."

Dez peered ahead. Where the Hart home and three others once stood were four gaping holes. Two more houses had been bulldozed and stood in giant splintered piles that were waiting to be carted away. As Joe photographed the holes, Mr. Washburn, ever considerate, pointed to the far end of the common. "But there's your playhouse, safe and sound." It, at least, still stood, and thank God—thank James Lawrence King—the bulldozer would spare it. Elliot Lowell wanted publicity, of course, for his run for the senate, but at least he had delivered on his promise.

Down to the left, the Round Church was completely gone, its existence marked only by a cavernous cellar hole. "You'd never know it," Dez said, "but that's where the beautiful Round Church was."

"I remember it from your postcards," Mr. Washburn said. "Why was it round, anyway?"

"The Devil can't hide in a church that hasn't any corners," Dez said with a laugh. "Or so the story went. It was built such a long time ago, 1815 or so, no one really knows."

She looked around, hands on her hips, taking stock. They had done so much, so quickly! From the common, it was now possible to see past the falls clear to River Road. She could see the house, could even make out the bench where her father sat that last day of his life.

They picked their way through the mud and rubble toward the hotel. A dynamite blast rumbled through the valley, and feeling the vibrations underfoot, Dez quelled a mixture of uncertainty and regret and nostalgia. Too late, too late for any of that. There was no looking back now.

At the front desk, Mrs. Mayhew clearly wasn't sure how to talk to Dez. On the one hand, Dez was the girl who had brought—who was still bringing—celebrity to the town. But it was a small town and she had left her husband, surely that was what had happened. She left in July and hadn't been back all summer and now she was there with another man, an employer, but another man all the same. And there had been those stories about her and the peddler. Still—Asa went around town acting proper and behaving as if everything was normal. She decided to smile sweetly at Dez, at the whole New York group. She told them they were welcome, that supper would be served between five thirty and seven thirty, and breakfast from seven to nine.

Dez phoned Asa from the lobby. He was at the drugstore and wanted to come right over but Dez put him off. It had been a long day, and she didn't have the emotional strength to deal with Asa right now. She told him she was tired, that she was going to retire to her room early. She agreed to meet him at the house in the morning.

At seven the next day, she slipped out of the hotel, sketchbook in hand, to walk the route that was so familiar yet so changed. Her eye noted the kind of detail that would end up in the *Cascade Progress Report*: the gaping stone foundation that had supported the Round Church for 120 years, the orderly rows of dark patches of earth showing where coffins had been disinterred, the swath of tree stumps along Main Street. Piles of bricks lay heaped along Elm Street, waiting to be carted away by a salvage company. Abandoned chickens on Pond Street pecked the ground for food.

It was early, but she still bumped into a few people. Reactions were mixed. Judith Stein hurried by with a frosty look and no hello. Zeke was outwardly as effusive as ever, praising the postcards, asking about New York, but all the while his eyes tried to gauge just what was going on. Bud's wife was kind, taking Dez's hand and saying it was good to see her back, her placid face saying, *I don't want to know. I don't judge.* Dez caught sight of Lil coming out of her apartment above Stein's but Lil darted back inside and pretended not to see her.

Up River Road, the closed-up summer homes were more forlorn than ever. They would never see life again now. She stood for a moment facing the carriage house behind Richard Harcourt's old house, remembering for a moment how Jacob had parked his truck there that final day. Then she crossed the street and headed down the driveway.

It was strange to be able to see across the river clear into the town center. It was also strange to knock like the visitor that she was. She knocked again and pushed on the door, calling out Asa's name. The hall was cluttered with boxes. She stepped around them, bumping into him as he emerged from the kitchen.

Their embrace was a clumsy clasping of shoulders and arms, quick and polite. He had cut his hair extrashort on top, which made his face look more angular, more bony. Or maybe it was just that he had blurred for her while she was in New York. "How are you?" she asked.

He shrugged, his eyes intent on her face, reading her, sensing what was going to happen. "What'd you think?" he asked, referring to the changes in town.

"It's so bright with all those trees gone. I can't believe how quickly they got started. I guess there's no turning back now." She glanced at the boxes in the hall.

"Every night I try to do a little packing up."

"I thought you weren't moving till spring."

He closed his eyes, held them shut a beat.

She hadn't meant to be so blunt. "I'm sorry, Asa." She'd meant to wait, to break the news gently. "But I suppose you must know by now."

His face darkened, although with disappointment, not anger. "Yes," he said. "I guess we'd better discuss all that. As for moving, no, not till spring, but I don't want to feel rushed. You want some coffee?"

He filled the pot and turned on the gas. He had made the kitchen his own, cups and canisters off the shelves and lined up neatly on the drainboard, at hand, the way he maintained his supplies at the drugstore. Dez peeked across the hall into his study. It, too, was full of boxes, the bookshelves almost completely empty.

"So tell me, Dez," he said. "Are you with him down there?"

She was surprised that he was so blunt, but glad of it. "No, Asa, I'm not. And if you must know, he's married now." At least she could give him that. "He had a girlfriend all this time, you know. It was friendship between us."

"I see." He turned to hide his pleasure, making himself busy with the coffee cups. "So, then, you really are there just because you want to be there? Because you want to work like a man?"

"I guess that's the long and the short of it."

He shook his head. Her desires, her behavior made no sense to him. She looked at the kitchen sink, at the washing machine with the rusty edge. In a way it felt as if she had never really left, that she still worked that old machine, cooked on those gas rings, filled that soapstone sink with suds and dishes. Yet, at the same time, it all felt part of the past. At this point, neither Cascade nor New York seemed real. She herself might not even be real. She pressed her weight against the linoleum, feeling the strength of the floor against her shoes, remembering the early nights of their marriage, when her father was still alive and she was so grateful for Asa's shelter, for the comfortable bed, for a kitchen to cook him hot meals. After supper, they sometimes played cards, the three of them, one quick round of whist before Asa returned to the drugstore. Those were the days before Jacob came into her life, before she had known to be dissatisfied. She made herself look out at the tree where she and Jacob had kissed, thinking, *I am in control of this memory. I am in charge.*

She realized Asa was talking about the house in Belchertown. There was a drugstore there, he was saying. Addison's. Jim Addison was close to retiring; his son had no interest in the business. "Strictly a soda fountain, like most, though," he said. "No grill. Old fittings. It's a step backward, but I could sort something out." His arms hung by his side and he looked at her with still-lingering bewilderment. There were things in the air, about to be said. Obligatory things. She put a hand to his mouth and suggested that they remember their nice times together as just that—nice.

"I guess our separation is what you'd call an open secret anyway," he said. "Everyone knows, and nobody's said anything, and everyone's awfully nice about it."

"That's 'cause you handled it so well, Asa. You were right, that first week, to insist on handling it the way you did."

He looked down at her naked ring finger. Maybe she should have had the decency to put it back on before making the trip, but the truth was, she'd never given it a thought.

"Never thought I'd see myself divorced," he said.

She tried to show, with all the powers of expression her face was capable of, just how sorry she was. "But thank you so much for taking care of the playhouse, for letting all this happen."

He was incredulous. "Did you really think I'd let it be destroyed?"

She shrugged. She didn't know. It was hard enough to really know yourself, to know what you were capable of, never mind another person.

The coffeepot started its faint rumbling. "This pot takes forever," he said.

"Forget the coffee. Show me the new cemetery," she said, to take their minds off what was bad, to turn their minds to what was worse. "Drive me there, will you?"

———

The state had tried its best to make the new cemetery glorious, magnificent. The landscaping was composed of hedges and flowering trees and pebble-stoned paths named Azalea and Gardenia that connected clusters of plots to clusters of plots, each cluster presided over by leafy oaks and maples, all designed to beautify the ugly fact that souls resting for years were dug up by gravediggers, that rotting coffins were moved under cover of night to be furtively and hastily reburied by morning.

Dez fretted that she should have been there when they moved her family, but Asa assured her: the board in charge of doing the moving had insisted that families not be involved. "The digging up and the reburying wasn't always as neat as they'd hoped," he said, then apologized. "They didn't want to upset people."

Still. To think that she hadn't known where her family's remains were the last few weeks. She stood over their headstones, situated near a maple sapling on Peony Path. *William Aloysius Hart, 1864–1934. Caroline Haywood Hart, 1884–1918. Timon William Hart, 1910–1918.* Lives defined and reduced by a bracketing of numbers.

Once someone was dead awhile, it was hard to believe they'd really existed. Dead was dead. Past was past. Yet the processing of the centuries would go on. *Desdemona Hart Spaulding, 1908–*

Timon's eight years looked negligible on stone. They were slim digits that in no way conveyed that his eight years had seemed longer because they had also seemed endless. Timon's skin had been darker than his sister's, his hair white-blond with a cowlick that refused to flatten, even with pomade. He'd been a king at marbles and could run like the devil. He'd had a talent for the piano, too, just like their mother, but hadn't liked her Brahms and Beethoven and instead insisted on making up his own, short, funny tunes with lyrics to match. A whole little life that had just—stopped.

"I don't know that I want to be buried here," Asa said. "I always assumed I'd be buried in Cascade, but I don't think I want to be buried here."

Dez had never, before this day, given a thought to where she might be buried. She almost asked, did it matter? But it did matter—to Asa, to his type of person.

"Addison's will be good for you," she said. "You're still young. By the time you're ready to retire, Belchertown will be home to you. You can be buried there."

He seemed to take comfort in the idea.

On Elm Street, Asa whistled. "Will you look at that?" Parked in front of the playhouse sat a silver-blue Rolls-Royce. "That's a Phantom," he said. They caught up with Joe and Nancy, walking over from the hotel. "Asa Spaulding, legal owner of the playhouse," Dez said, making introductions. "Joe Katz, Nancy Bracewell." She felt a bit guilty, not identifying him as her husband, but she didn't want to reveal any more of her private life to people than was necessary.

Inside, they met up with Elliot Lowell, who introduced them to James Lawrence King, Frank May, King's attorney, the engineer Mark Whitman, and Dick Holt, the man who would supervise the move. James Lawrence King was not the imposing sort Dez expected but a tall, wiry man with a face set in a perpetual squint. He had a cordial yet distracted way of talking and got right down to business, his quiet authority evident when Lowell tried to orchestrate a photograph. He stopped him with a gesture. "No pictures yet."

He wasn't the type to do more than oversee a project, but he wanted to check that the building was sound before signing the deal and arranging for its move to Lenox. They toured the building for more than an hour, with King directing most of his questions to Dez. Were there ever any major maintenance problems? No. How extensive was the prop collection? Complete, as far as she knew, for all of the major plays. King's interest was focused firmly on the theater, not at all on her, but for the first time since Jacob, she felt that fluttering of mild panic, that giddy rumbling of attraction. It didn't make sense. He had a mouth like a gash; he had to be at least fifty.

They assembled back in the vestibule, where the engineer declared the building sound. King said that once the playhouse was moved, they could worry about what to do with it, how best to reopen it, and that he would be in touch then. For the first time he turned his attention completely to Dez. "I take it I shall direct all future correspondence to you?" His eyes flickered across her face and he smiled warmly, lightly touching her arm. He had charm, she realized. The man had charm. Probably everyone responded positively to him.

"You are welcome to include any personal storage, within reason, of course," he added, brushing aside her thanks. "If you would provide Dick with all of your pertinent information, I will be in touch as we move forward." He turned to his lawyer. "Let's get on with the signing, shall we? And your photograph, of course, Elliot." He and Asa signed a sheaf of papers, then they posed with Lowell. Joe's flashbulb popped, recording the moment, blinding them all.

King shook hands all around, and then he was gone.

It took Dez two days to oversee the packing-up, but Dick Holt hired locals to help her, so aside from sorting her own belongings at the house, which she did while Asa was at the drugstore, she had very little physical work to do. She'd forgotten how much easier life was with help, with money to pay people. She packed her father's old steamer trunk with mementos and added it to her personal storage. Her things would be safe in Lenox; she could worry about what to do with them one day when she was more settled.

Her last day in the playhouse, she walked around with Dick Holt. The costumes were packed away in cedar wardrobes, props wrapped in newspaper and boxed up. The drapes had come down, the autographed pictures carefully wrapped away. All had been boxed and stacked, ready to be trucked to Lenox.

Their footsteps echoed up to the rafters. "That's it," Dick said.

Dez ticked off a list of final places to check: basement, crawl space above the balcony, backstage wardrobes.

"We seem to have gotten everything," Dick said.

"There's a cupboard behind the balcony, though."

"Checked."

"How about the basement?" It was spidery and dark and pretty much empty down there.

"We cleaned the old staging out, but other than that it was empty."

"There's a big safe in the basement," she said. "Hidden behind an imposter wall."

"Found that."

"I guess it wasn't so hidden after all."

"We figured it was empty but I had it on my list to ask you. Is it?"

"It is. Plus it had a backup key and I have no idea where that is. I don't suppose we need to cart it away."

"It'd be heavy," Dick said. "Besides, Mr. King ain't the kind of man needs a safe." He laughed at his little joke.

Dez looked around one last time, then walked outside and stood on the front path, letting the years of memories wash over her. She tried not to get emotional but she knew that an era was irrevocably past, that it would be the last time she laid eyes on the playhouse in Cascade, the last time she would turn from its front door and see where their old house had once stood. Her eyes brimmed, her throat ached, and this time she didn't fight the emotion. This was what happened—when circumstances changed, when people died. Sometimes you had to give in to it.

Joe Katz took a picture of her by the front door. He had her rest her hand on the railing. He adjusted a number of settings, told her to hold her smile, and snapped the shutter. "Will it really work?" she asked Dick, suddenly nervous about the move. "I would think a building would fall apart once it's pulled from its foundation."

Dick laughed. "You'd be surprised how solid buildings are," he said.

Nancy and Joe spent the rest of the day finishing up their story and photo projects. Dez went out with her sketchpad, too. Over the course of her time in Cascade, she had jotted down ideas for the final destruction postcard, but now she realized they were too much fire and brimstone, too much the sum of all the cards she had already done. Mainly she wanted the right tone. She wanted something simple. A placard posted to the front of Stein's store announced the Farewell Ball to be held at Town Hall, which would be one of the last structures to come down. The ball would take place on the evening of June 28, 1936. At midnight, bells would toll and disincorporation would be official. That would be her card, she decided. *The Farewell Ball.*

Over dinner, she asked Nancy and Joe about their upcoming marriage—did their families mind a mixed marriage, did they foresee problems with children?

They glanced at each other with the kind of intimate, communicative look that said, *Here come the kind of small-minded questions we're ready for.*

"No, no—" Dez wanted them to know where her questions came from, that she wasn't what they thought.

But Nancy was cold, her disinterest bordering on dislike. During their time in Cascade, they had all heard the news: Germany had passed a new set of laws that imposed limits on citizenship and civil rights for German Jews.

Dez did not want to be perceived as bigoted, but the more she tried to explain, the less Nancy understood. "Never mind," she finally said. "I wasn't trying to pry." She almost didn't voice what she said next, but it felt remarkably freeing to do so, and she said it and walked away without waiting for a reaction. "It's just that I was once in love with a Jewish man and I sometimes wonder how it would have turned out."

———————

The last day in Cascade, Dez woke up early, before the sun was fully up. She stood by her hotel-room window, with its view to the common. In the misty half-light, the bulldozers and tree stumps and gaping holes took on a strange beauty, so different from her painting, and she remembered that this hour before full sun was twilight, too; twilight in fact happened twice each day.

She met with Asa once more, a quick talk, in a corner of the lobby, to work out what was next: lawyers, logistics. Asa was less friendly, more reserved now that he had had time to really dwell on the fact of her desertion. He would be in touch, he said. He'd talk to Attorney Peterson next time he was in Cascade. She caught the eye of Mr. Washburn, who was waiting discreetly on the other side of the lobby, and walked Asa to the front door. This time there was no embrace. He clapped his hat to his head and said, with a frozen face, "I guess that's it. I guess I'll see you around."

She watched him as he walked away down Elm Street, watched until he turned the corner onto Main and disappeared. Mr. Washburn appeared beside her. "When you are ready," he said kindly.

On their way to the train station, a flatbed truck rolled by, carrying a gray-shingled bungalow that used to sit near the schoolhouse. It was a bizarre sight, and though it was tethered securely to the flatbed, Dez pulled out her pad and sketched it as if its perch were precarious. She had been having a hard time imagining the playhouse making it to Lenox intact, but seeing the house, so squat and solid, making its way down the street was reassuring.

Forty-five minutes later, their train pulled away. She craned her neck backward to get every drop of the view, the last she would see of Cascade in any recognizable form. Her eyes began to water, but she squeezed them tight, ferociously. She couldn't have it both ways. Crying was terribly cheap and indulgent, and if she had to choose, she would choose where she was going: back to her apartment with its river light.

36

Why did she stir it up again, just when she was beginning to think she was on the mend? Because maybe, in a way, she was the kind of person who let her emotions inspire her art. If her life so far had been trouble-free, would it have been interesting? Would she have been moved to slash at canvases with paints and brushes? Maybe not. Maybe she wanted the star-crossed passion of a Russian novel.

Back in New York, standing in front of the empty seventh canvas, she felt herself at a crossroads. She had done six Shakespeare canvases; maybe there wasn't a need for a seventh. She walked over to the windows, looking down through the branches of the elm tree to the street. Cascade felt more fully behind her now, and with Cascade behind her, so Jacob seemed to be. And yet . . . he didn't have to be. She let her mind travel seventy blocks south and once it got there, it refused to leave.

She sat down with pen and paper and kept it simple. *Please let us resume our friendship*, she wrote. That was all. She addressed the envelope to Jacob Solomon, East Third Street. East Third Street was blocks long but it was all she had and she had to hope it would get to him.

She ran downstairs and posted it immediately in the box on the corner, even though it would not be picked up till morning. When she climbed into bed that night, she pictured it lying on the bottom of the mailbox.

She began to sketch studies for the seventh painting, letting her hand go where it wanted, lines becoming a drowning person's last blurry view through water. At first, she just drew shapes, falling shapes, smothering shapes that submerged the subject, which was itself just a shape, then she scratched all that away and tried to portray serenity—smooth stones, soft ripples, her mother as a three-year-old, struggling to stay afloat in the Cascade River. She scratched that out, too, before settling on the first view after all.

She never did finish that painting. She scraped it down and started again many times—it never came close to being part of the Shakespeare series, but remained a depiction, never quite right, of drowning.

Six felt right anyway, she decided. Six felt like a series, like half a set of apostles.

But something in her was still restless. She stretched an even larger canvas, prepped it, and spent hours pacing in front of it, making sketches, and throwing them away. It was time, she thought, to venture downtown to the Art Students League and take some courses, get involved with other people—otherwise, why was she in New York? What was she waiting for? Summer was over. It was time she settled in.

After work the next day, she walked over to the League's Fifty-seventh Street headquarters and registered for a life drawing class as Dez Hart. While she filled out the registration form, the woman at the desk asked if she had applied to the W.P.A. "For a government-funded program, it's remarkably free of judgment," she said. "Most everyone's accepted if you're poor enough." She glanced at Dez's ringless hand.

"I've got a job, fortunately. Are you on the program?"

"Well, no. Because I'm married. They don't like to hire married women. But if you ever lose your job—well, it's nice to know. You know?"

Dez stopped at the Automat for a chicken pot pie, for hot coffee, for the comfort of clean tables and bright lights. At home, two letters sat in her mailbox, and she recognized, with a certain sinking of spirits, the cream envelope, her own handwriting. But the letter was thicker than the one she had sent, the RETURN TO SENDER mark not the postman's stamp but a scribbly hand that could or could not be Jacob's. She flipped it over; it had been sealed shut with adhesive tape and she tore it open. Her letter was there, yes, as well as a second sheet of paper.

Friendship? You sat there with all of them and dragged me through the mud. We all make our choices, Dez, and then we have to live with them.

Moments passed, frantic moments, wondering why he would write such a thing. Then she knew: Al Stein. Jacob must have talked to Al Stein since the day he visited her flat. Al Stein who sat at the Brilliant with his wife, Judith, while Dick and Pete lambasted Roosevelt and Jews. She remembered Judith Stein in Cascade, frosty, quickening her pace as Dez approached.

What to do? What was it possible to do? The other envelope was crisp and white and bore an Athol postmark—Stan's wife again, a letter that was less wild, less rambling, more disturbing.

You seemed a nice woman that day I met you and all the while you knew your husband had been monkeying with that dam. Trying to fob me off with money. I won't bother you anymore but I just want to say I HOPE YOU CAN LIVE WITH YOURSELF.

I will have to live with myself, Mrs. Smith, she thought. *I have no choice.* She would have to live with the fact that Stanley Smith was dead, maybe because of her, that Asa had no children and would suffer the stigma of divorce, that she had no family left, that the man she wanted had married someone else, that they were expecting a baby, and that he thought the worst of her.

It was fall but unseasonably warm, much like the evening that Jacob had come and gone. She wanted to get a cab, or run down to Third Street and find him, but she couldn't do that. She could only write another letter and try to get through to him. She sat down and wrote honestly and clearly. She explained that Asa had been hurt and angry. *You saw him that night, in the jail. Dwight said he was like a stunned deer. Like he was full of buckshot, Dwight said.* She explained that Asa had threatened to destroy the playhouse, and that she had agreed to stick by his side until the talk died down, to save Asa's reputation. *I don't know what Al thought he heard that night, but he did not hear a single derogatory word from Asa's mouth or from mine. In fact, once all that talk started, Asa and I left. As I look back now, maybe that wasn't enough. Maybe it wasn't enough to say nothing, to not stand up for you and your people, but I was in an impossible situation with Asa, which you must appreciate. I am your friend, Jacob. Regardless of whether I ever hear from you again, I am always going to be your friend, I'm always going to admire and love you. I can live with a platonic friend-ship but I can't live without your friendship. I can't live without you.*

That last line looked melodramatic but she let it go. It was honest; it was how she felt. Then she slid it into an envelope, addressed and sealed it, and went straight downstairs to the street to mail it. She didn't hesitate; she pulled the handle down, pushed the envelope in, heard its soft fall, the clang of metal.

Back in her apartment, she flopped down on the bed, staring up at the plaster ceiling. Radios played through open windows; people lingered outside. A broadcaster mentioned Rudolph Valentino's name and she remembered that woman who mourned him every year, going to such lengths to hide, yet at the same time calling attention to herself by griev-ing so dramatically in that long black veil.

She fully planned to wallow in misery, face buried in her pillow until sleep came, sleep, that reprieve from consciousness and pain. But in spite of herself, her brain began to pluck at images—images that grew and arranged themselves in a picture that made her get up, careful not to lose it, and sit at her table. She sketched—trembling a little, eager to get the idea down, trying not to get too excited. She did only one preliminary drawing before getting out her paints. Then she faced the large rectangular canvas she had prepped a week ago. It was as if the painting were already there, that was how clearly she saw what she painted. As if her hand were just filling in.

It took her seven days to paint *The Black Veil,* and she knew it was seven days only because the day she laid her last stroke she heard a newsboy calling for the Saturday extra and she realized it was Saturday again. The week had been a focused fog. On Monday morning she meant to phone Mr. Washburn from the corner stationery store but forgot all about work until he sent Simon Turcott down to check on her. She'd told Simon she was sick, that she'd be sick all week. Simon looked doubtful—she was an obvious picture of health—but it wasn't up to him to judge, and besides, all the illustrators knew that Dez was ahead of schedule on her *America* postcards.

She stepped back from the painting for a full look at *The Black Veil.* The oblong, roughly bowed shape of Cascade's town boundaries formed the background; the shape of the river basin and its tributaries suggested the look of a wrist and a reaching hand. The painting was not completely abstract, but it included a lot more detail than had many of the Shakespeare paintings: drowning victims, shapes that suggested people covering their eyes with their hands, people stoning a small man, others turning their backs on the sight. And though it seemed done, she knew it wasn't quite finished, and knocked on Maria's door to ask if she could buy a length of sheer, filmy veil. She dyed the veil black, turning her porcelain sink purple and ensuring the ire of her super, then laid it out on towels by the window. When it dried, she glued it over the painting so that it appeared to billow and smother the paint.

She didn't hang it—it was too large to fit her space—so kept it propped against the long wall by the door. It was her private communiqué with Jacob, her *apologia* to him and to Stan, to Asa and Cascade.

She didn't receive the second letter to Jacob back in the mail. She never received a response.

37

So she settled into a new phase of life. She started Art Students League classes on Tuesday and Thursday nights. Attorney Peterson sent a petition for divorce by Asa on grounds of desertion. James Lawrence King's assistant sent photos of the Lenox site—a grassy field lined on both sides by tall pines.

It was just chance that she met Maxie again, in a hat shop on Madison Avenue in early November. Dez was looking; Maxie was buying. Dez was prepared to ignore her after their last run-in, but it was late enough in the day that the magnanimous side of Maxie's nature had started to emerge. She lifted a lock of Dez's hair. "Bronze and copper. Art itself," she said.

It was clear that Maxie was attracted to women, and if a man had said such a thing she would think he was hopelessly transparent. Maxie made the situation more awkward by insisting on buying Dez the butter-yellow hat she'd tried on, though Dez protested right through the buying and the packaging of the hat by the salesgirl. But there was something ashamedly exhilarating, albeit a little bit frightening, about being a woman's object of desire.

Out on the sidewalk, the sky was turning the color of plums. Brown leaves skidded across the pavement. Maxie lit up a cigarette. "You want to go over to the Carlyle?"

Dez hesitated. "For a cocktail, you mean?"

Maxie drew on her cigarette, amused, as if she knew exactly what was going through Dez's mind. "Yeah."

What was the harm in a cocktail? Maxie owned an important gallery. It was time Dez showed some ambition.

The new Carlyle Hotel was quiet and genteel but thoroughly modern, designed and decorated in the *arts décoratif* style that had defined Paris and the modern world in the mid-1920s. It was graceful and restrained in a way Dez found soothing. Why, she hadn't been in a nice hotel in years. They pushed through a door to a dark, intimate bar full of small, sleek tables, and a pianist playing tranquilizing music. Maxie turned out to be easy company—someone who chattered nonstop, the kind of person who really just liked to have an audience. She ordered two old-fashioneds. "They invented these over at the Waldorf. They're all the rage."

The drinks arrived on a silver tray and looked appealing, with a rich amber hue and fat cherry garnish. Dez, expecting it to taste sweet, sputtered when the first sip was surprisingly harsh.

Maxie laughed. "That's bourbon for you," she said, turning to a man who had paused by their table.

"What's next, Maxie?"

"Nothing till the end of March," she said, waving him away with a laugh. "You think I'd spend a winter here? No thank you." She fished the cherry from her drink and popped it between her lips.

"You have a show planned for March?" Dez asked.

"Uh-huh. Ciggy?"

Dez took a cigarette from the pack, and before they could light them, the waiter reappeared to flick a silver lighter. Maxie lit up. She would be in Miami in two weeks, she said. "Have you been there? No? This style"— she waved a hand—"is everywhere. Toots's place looks like an ocean liner." She might do a place of her own down there, she said, and talked about glass brick walls and Bakelite doors. Dez only half-heard. Here she was, having a drink with Maxie Eisenberg. Shouldn't she try to get Maxie to look at her work? She already knew that Maxie was contemptuous of timidity, so waited for the right pause in the conversation then said, as confidently as she could, "If you're having a new show, you need to see my Shakespeare series. After this, we could walk across the park and have a look at them."

Maxie narrowed her eyes and pursed her mouth, tugging on her lower lip while she considered. "Let's have another drink. Then I suppose we can cab over."

"Great," Dez said coolly. The next hour, she was almost afraid to breathe, afraid that mercurial Maxie would turn petulant and change her mind. And what if they got to her apartment and Maxie made some kind of pass? She swallowed hard. She would just have to take the risk and deal with that if it happened, behave the way she would behave toward any man who did that—be nice and express some thanks.

When they finished their cocktails, Dez insisted on paying the bill, to level the playing field. Outside, the night air had grown chilly. The doorman lifted a gloved hand and a cab glided forward.

At Dez's, Maxie complained about the lack of an elevator. On the third landing, she laid her hand on the banister and paused to breathe heavily. "For Christ's sake."

Dez never had visitors. She lived too far uptown and, frankly, liked keeping her small space private. "Just one more flight," she coaxed, relieved when they reached the fourth floor and she could fit her key into the lock.

As soon as Maxie entered the apartment, she turned all business, walking straight up to *The Black Veil*, folding her arms and inspecting it. "Oh, my dear," she said. One red fingernail tapped at her front teeth. "Oh, my dear."

Dez waited, watching Maxie's unsmiling face. A full minute passed.

"You weren't kidding me, were you? Well, you've got yourself a sale. I'll take this."

"Oh, no. I—" She hadn't expected Maxie to make such a fast decision. "I can't sell that one. I meant for you to see—"

"Excuse me?"

It was Jacob's painting. If Dez lost control of it, he would likely never see it. "That one's private. It's not anything I want to part with."

"You drag me up here and then tell you don't want to 'part with' it?" Maxie mimicked her. "They're not your babies. They're your full-grown adults and what you do is send them out into the world. Now do you want my help or don't you?"

"Of course I do, but you've come to see the Shakespeare canvases." Dez quite firmly led Maxie to the large closet where the Shakespeare canvases leaned, one behind the other, against the wall.

Maxie looked a long time, silently, at the first one, the interlocking *Macbeth*. Then she lifted it away and set it against the wall to examine the next one, *The Tempest*. Then *Othello, A Midsummer Night's Dream, King Lear, Hamlet*. She studied them all quietly, finally breaking her silence to speak almost languidly. "I just love that you've got a series." She fingered *Othello*—up close, a smearing of shapes and color, but from a distance: the distinct impression of towering black rage, of violated, martyred white, of crimson.

"D. H. Spaulding," she said, as if to herself. "D. H. Spaulding." She turned to face Dez decisively. "Do you want to start a stir?"

"What kind of stir?"

"How much do you care about fame, about instant fame?"

Dez had had a small taste of instant fame with the postcards. It was cheap, and it wasn't enduring, she knew that. Still, she had enjoyed the recognition.

"Because I'm thinking that these paintings could cause a stir. But it might be better if they came out of the blue, if no one really knew much about the artist, and also—" She paused. "If the artist was assumed to be male. There's something very masculine about these, such an internal, emotionally raw look to them."

Seeing Dez's reaction, Maxie softened. "It's just the way it is, hon."

"That doesn't make me resent it any less."

"Well, I like that you've signed them D. H. Spaulding."

"Spaulding is my legal name."

"Is it? Well, I like it, the initials. Very neutral. Everyone you've met at the League, everyone in town, knows you as Hart, right? Has anyone seen these? No? We could show them and leave them all wondering who the hell painted them."

Dez hesitated. The honest response was that yes, she wanted to see her paintings shown in Maxie's gallery, but she wanted to be at the party, wanted to engage in discourse about the paintings, as herself, the acknowledged artist. And yes, she wanted to bask in any glory they might bring.

But something, maybe misguided pride, made her go with the noble answer—that art lasted, not the artist. "If you think your idea is a good one," she said, "I suppose we could give it a try."

———

Maxie unveiled the Shakespeare series in the March show she called New New York News. Nobody bought any of the canvases on opening night, but they started a buzz, as did the fact that the artist didn't show up for the opening. D. H. Spaulding, whoever he was, preferred to let art speak for itself, so Maxie and the program notes, which carefully avoided the use of pronouns, said. Who was he, people wanted to know? Where did he study? "Let art speak for itself?" Was he some kind of hermit or simply pretentious?

Dez attended the opening with Abby and Amy Cantor, a new friend from the League, and it was hard to stay quiet. At first, she thought she wouldn't have to. Although the six paintings, all different, showed her reluctance to stick to a particular style, there was a common look to them, almost ineffable, but there—an explosion of color, an underlying darkness—and surely the people she studied with would recognize this.

No one did, even though a couple of them, like Abby and Amy, knew that her husband's name was Spaulding, that she used her maiden name, Hart, in New York. She expected that people would put one and one and one together.

Standing in front of the six paintings, hanging side by side on one long wall in Maxie's gallery, Dez tested: she asked Abby outright, "What do you think of these?"

Abby shrugged. "I hate whoever the hell he is," she said with a jealous, laughing-at-herself hoot, fumbling for a cigarette. "Where do you want to go after?"

Dez nudged the conversation back to the paintings. Abby really didn't know her work, but she knew it better than anyone, and if she didn't guess, she didn't suppose anyone would. "Look, it's strange. He's got my name—well, my old name."

"He does?" Abby inspected the paintings more closely. "Extremely strange. Who is he?"

"Maxie won't say."

Abby smirked. "Next you'll tell me they're really yours." She paused to eye the paintings more carefully. "Wait a minute." She laughed uncomfortably, as if she might be the butt of a joke. "These aren't really yours, are they?"

Dez pointed out that D. H. Spaulding had wielded his brush with an intensity and freedom that Boston-trained Desdemona Hart had never come close to possessing.

A tall, languid-looking man turned to Abby, hat in his hands. "I've only ever seen *Hamlet* and I'm not a painter, but how did he get that messy search for identity down the way he did? It's marvelous."

Dez wanted to kiss him. His was the kind of reaction that made the struggle worthwhile. Though now she faced another struggle: the struggle not to reveal herself.

"And get it down," the man continued, "in a way that makes me wonder who the heck I am?"

Abby edged up to him. "And who might that be?"

There was an instant connection between Abby and the man, which Dez recognized. It made her wistful. She left them alone and slipped away to be by herself, standing by a window that someone had opened to clear the room of cigarette smoke. The March night air was cold and fresh on her face, the street outside busy with cars and cabs and pedestrians hurrying by. She craned her neck to see the sky. Somewhere up there were the same stars that shone down over what was left of Cascade. Cascade, where people lived who'd never been to Boston, who'd been to Worcester only once or twice in their lives. She tried to comprehend that she had really lived there, that she could still be there, wringing laundry and pounding chicken breasts, looking up at the night sky with a longing to leave. If all the change hadn't enabled her to go, would she really ever have left? Would she?

She turned away and, with her back to the window, sipped her wine and watched the people crowding the gallery. They paused in front of her paintings, and in front of Sidney Orenthal's, James Prout's, Max Braden's.

It was wonderful. It was what she had always wanted.

⸻◈⸻

After a new critic, Clem Greenberg, wrote that the Shakespeare series showed perhaps the freshest use of interpretive color he had seen in three seasons, and John Russell proclaimed them "paintings of the soul" in *The New York Times*, an anonymous collector bought the sprightly, vivid *Midsummer Night's Dream,* and James Lawrence King himself bought the roiling, whipped-cream *Tempest.* James Lawrence King, it turned out, was an avid collector of art and well-known to Maxie. How fitting, Dez thought. And what a delicious coincidence. Or was it fate? James Lawrence King didn't know that he had bought William Hart's daughter's painting. He didn't know that William Hart had suggested the playhouse reopen with *The Tempest.*

Maxie sold each canvas for five hundred dollars and paid Dez half. She would sell the rest eventually, she said, and did: *Othello* in May, *Lear* and *Macbeth* two weeks later, and the dark *Hamlet* to a buyer in July.

It was an odd feeling to enjoy such substantial success and not be able to lay claim to it, but Maxie's plan worked. Without knowing anything about the artist, focus turned to the art. A flurry of excitement stirred around D. H. Spaulding as Dez continued to work at the *Standard*, continued to paint at the League, and continued to grow her savings account. With each sale, with each deposit, she relaxed a bit more. Though she was more nervous about putting her earnings into a bank than she had been in Cascade, the government had been federally insuring deposits since 1933 and she figured a hopefully solid government had to be safer than a strongbox under a bed in a New York City flat.

It always surprised Dez that people did not see the obvious, did not realize that Dez Hart's work was D.H.'s. Although she tended to use her League classes for practice and experimentation and paint her "real work" in her own apartment, the truth was that the work was not completely different. The assumption that D.H. was a man made people blind to what was right in front of them.

Between her job, her classes at the League, her painting at home, and her budding social life, calendar pages started to flip more quickly: November, December, January. Occasionally, she would join people for drinks after class; she even dated someone a few times, a pleasant enough editor for the *New York Herald Tribune*. But mainly she went home; she worked.

There was news from Massachusetts: in April, Asa moved to Belchertown, to 14 Elm Street, and Attorney Peterson sent a bulging packet containing the wording of the preliminary divorce agreement. Mr. Washburn sent Joe and Nancy back to Cascade to report on the June Farewell Ball. Dez pored over Joe's pictures. Cascade had become a bulldozed swath of bowl-shaped acres, ringed by shrubby watershed. The few remaining buildings—the hotel, Town Hall, the train station—stood exposed and naked amid the dirt. They looked like early photographs she had seen of New York in the 1870s. There was that same raw, new look to the landscape. The water authority's administration offices were housed in the golf course's fancy clubhouse, which, being located on watershed land, would be the only building allowed to stay intact.

In July, the playhouse moved to its new plot of land in Lenox. She wasn't there for the move, but James Lawrence King sent a picture, via his secretary, to assure her it survived the trip. She tucked the picture into a corner of her easel. In it, the playhouse was grainy and forlorn, transplanted onto the grassy stretch of Lenox land. The picture was cropped; she could not see the tall pines that had looked so majestic in earlier photographs. Still, the playhouse was safe and that was what mattered.

That photograph witnessed many late nights and early mornings of effort. In later years, the mid- to late thirties would be seen as D. H. Spaulding's most productive period. Maxie never wanted any of Dez's work from the League, but frequently, she took the canvases D.H. painted alone, at home. Dez knew it wasn't just the fact of D. H. Spaulding that kept Maxie from buying her League studies. She knew she painted differently when she was alone, with more color and more risk.

D. H. Spaulding acquired a certain mystique. It was rumored that he lived on a bee farm on Long Island, that he lived on a houseboat on the Seine, moored near Nôtre Dame, that he was really England's Paul Sandler, producing under a type of painterly pen name. Maxie, with her closed-mouth allusions, fed the speculation, and instructed Dez to conceal her home pieces from everyone else, but it all made Dez nervous. Increasingly, she began to want to lay claim to her efforts, but the kind of buildup she was getting was bound to disappoint people if her real identity was revealed. It wouldn't matter whether she was unveiled as Leonardo reincarnated or as some gifted love child of Pablo Picasso's, the mere fact of mystery uncovered always brought with it a sense of disappointment, of deflation. The fact that she was a woman would make the disillusionment total.

But the mystique grew, and every month or so, to the point where it became a running joke, Maxie asked for *The Black Veil*. She could sell it in a minute; Dez would be set for a good long time. But Dez always said no, and it sat in her apartment, hidden in the closet with her other work, for three years—three years during which she never once ran into Jacob.

For a long time she expected that she would inevitably encounter him. She knew, through Amy Cantor, that he did indeed become a member of the Easel Project. She also knew that, as a member of that project, he could paint wherever he liked and that most artists chose to work at home or in their own studios. Still, she expected she would run into him sometime. New York was a big city, but it wasn't that big. She braced for the possibility that she might even see him when he was with his wife and baby, but months passed, then a year, two years, and when she did not ever glimpse him, she grew first bitter, then sad, and then, finally, resigned. In that resigned state, she could think of him with distance, with bemusement even, until some small, beautiful thing, a reflection on a rainy pavement, or the sound of jazz from one of the clubs on Columbus, would pierce her, and remind her of what she still missed.

38

S he hoped Jacob would see it. When *The Black Veil* was so misunderstood, and when, ironically, that misunderstanding brought her such
acclaim, such incredible, instant fame, the primary reason she was
elated by the publicity was that she wanted Jacob to know that with that
painting she was telling the truth and that she had told it for him.

She finally decided to show it in the fall of 1939. The previous June,
her divorce was made final at last. She returned to Massachusetts to meet
with Asa in a Springfield court, to sign the documents that would dissolve
their marriage. Asa, embarrassed to be standing in front of a judge in a
divorce case, was cordial to Dez, but only that. Four years had passed
since the day she boarded the train at Cascade Station; he'd had a lot of
time to reflect. His eyes had faint lines around the corners; he wore a
buttoned-up cardigan sweater under his suit. He seemed to have become
a contented bachelor, and as they stood side by side in front of the judge,
she doubted that he would marry again.

Afterward, she traveled to Cascade by herself. The *Standard* continued
the project with quarterly progress reports, but used Joe Katz's stark

photographs and his wife, Nancy's reporting exclusively. There had been no need for Dez's interpretive paintings since *The Farewell Ball* in the summer of 1936.

Dez was eager to see the area now that the reservoir was complete. Enough time had passed that all the slow, transitional destruction/construction was done. The reservoir had even been dedicated, and formally named the Rappahannock, an Indian word for "swift rising river."

She traveled from Springfield to Bath and registered at the Bath River Hotel, where she hired a driver to take her out to the Rappahannock. The driver was a quiet old man who kept his cap pulled down over his forehead and hummed, but otherwise didn't say a word. He drove Dez the ten miles on leafy, tree-lined Route 13 to the reservoir, slowing down when they got to fenced-off land with signs, at intervals, that read *Massachusetts Water Authority*. At one point, Dez guessed that they were in the area of what had been the Poplar Street turnoff, but as soon as they passed through a set of iron gates, she lost her bearings. They were on a paved road through what might have been a grassy meadow, or maybe the grassy meadow had developed after the houses and trees came down. The road led straight to a small circular rotary that offered a choice: left or right. Ahead lay the great basin, a large expanse of what looked, now, like a half-filled lake. "Stop," she said. "Please. I want to get out."

The basin was vast, a bowl thirty-six square miles in size, ringed by watershed land. The surrounding land still looked scarred, disturbed, unnatural. The reservoir was about a quarter way full, slowly rising as the river, rainwater, and melting winter snow filled it year after year. Dez had read that it would take eight or nine years to fill the Rappahannock to capacity.

She peered down the road on either side of the rotary, looking for landmarks, but there were none. Back in the car, she instructed the driver to take a left, a blind choice. About a quarter mile down the road, they came to a parking lot and building—the former golf-course clubhouse. The ornate stone structure now bore a plaque identifying it as the water authority's administration office. That meant that the common, the falls, River Road, and all of it must have been down past the rotary in the other direction. They headed back and this time the road began to climb a curving hill. At the summit, a semicircular parking area allowed cars to stop and look out over the reservoir. A wooden sign read *Cascade Lookout*. Cascade Lookout, it seemed, was the ridge that once sat high above Pine Point, and it offered a spectacular view. Where once the river below flowed in from the northeast and curved around in a swooping arc toward town, now the water spread out like a vast lake.

Hard to fathom that it was the same space. The same spot of earth.

The car door opened and the driver got out to join her in looking out over the basin. "I'm guessing you used to live here."

"I did. We lived on the common, then I moved a little bit out, just right about there, when I got married." She pointed down to the left, to where the house on River Road must have stood. Asa's mother's Catholic kneelers, she suddenly remembered. What had become of them? Probably packed and moved to Belchertown.

"I bring a lot of people out here. Those postcards they did made this place kind of famous. People always want to come out and have a look."

They drove back down the hill and stopped where Dez thought the Cascade Falls used to roar and spray. Sure enough, off to the left, a road led in toward the reservoir, toward what must have been the town center, the paved roads still in place. She got out and followed the road. Strange to think it was the same pavement she had walked so many times, yet when she looked left or right or straight ahead, nothing—*nothing*—was familiar. Not a single shrub or stone. She followed the road until it ended at the water, and she could only faintly see the drowned asphalt. The town center had sat at a low elevation, so they hadn't had to do any digging here. And because the water levels were still low, the basin was shallow, the submerged network of paved roads still visible. Everything else had been painstakingly removed—every building, streetlamp, mailbox, fence.

Near the edge of the basin, she realized she was walking parallel to what must have been Elm Street, which had led to Chestnut Street, to the hotel and to the playhouse. Where buildings were razed, large cellar holes quickly filled with water. In the distance, something black, like a stick or pole, seemed to float upright under the water. At first, she couldn't make it out. Then she realized it was the old iron hitching post, still standing in front of the cellar hole where the Cascade Hotel had stood. Why had they left that? Surely not a mistake. The decision of someone who couldn't stand to totally obliterate what had once been a civilization? She could imagine so, because it was dizzying to remember the hotel in that very spot, to visualize herself as a ten-year-old, a twenty-year-old, walking in a place that had seemed so permanent and had proven to be anything but. Beside it, too far away to really see, would be the playhouse's flooded cellar hole. She stared in the direction of the hole, trying to imagine, to re-create the past, to do some kind of justice to it, to believe that the past could somehow be kept alive.

She supposed it could—through art. The past lived through a culture's art. Her postcards documented surface Cascade, a Cascade that should be remembered, yes, but *The Black Veil* recorded an episode that also needed to be remembered. She couldn't let it go to a private collection, but she could show it, send it out into the world. Perhaps now that was the only way Jacob would ever see it.

When she returned to New York, she delivered it to Maxie.

39

D ez had already found that with art, with the whole idea of "career," that getting what you wanted was satisfying only on one level. It was the same sort of satisfaction you might feel when you'd made a list for your busy day, and at day's end, ticked off each accomplishment. For example, perhaps you'd longed for, dreamed of winning, the Huntington Prize, had imagined how it would feel, but when you had actually won the Huntington Prize, you were already back at your easel, trying for something else.

Real satisfaction came when inspiration and effort magically took flight at the easel—the satisfaction that had come the submerged week of painting that she still remembered with cocoonlike warmth. Did she feel different when she showed *The Black Veil* at the New New York Gallery and it won the Huntington Prize? When the Whitney purchased it? Not really. And that was the thing about art, about any artistic endeavor where you gathered all the energy and emotion that surrounded you and tried to paint it, write it, sing it. It was never quite enough. There was always the impulse to try for better, for purer.

It was just coincidence—a coincidence Dez never noticed—that the shape of Cascade resembled the shape of the European continent, that the river and basin formed the shape of the state of Germany.

Maxie showed it in September of 1939, just after Britain and France declared war on Germany. The critics started a buzz about it, then George Biddle, the friend of President Roosevelt who conceived the W.P.A., saw it, and all of a sudden *The Black Veil* was being interpreted as an anti-Nazi painting. The editor of *Life* magazine, Henry Luce, a major proponent of U.S. interventionist policy, reproduced it in the pages of his magazine as part of his ongoing campaign to rouse public support for that policy in the press and on the airwaves.

It made her name.

Life wanted to do a story on D. H. Spaulding but he didn't exist. Maxie counseled: "You have to keep the mystique going. If you come out and take the credit for what you've done—then there's no mystique anymore. Instead you're a pretty girl and people come out with their claws. I can guarantee that there won't be quite the same respect for you, my girl, as there is for this dignified-sounding D.H., whoever the fuck he is." She laughed hard, and her laugh by then was raspy, because she smoked Chesterfields night and day.

Dez really had no one else to advise her. She sensed that Maxie was right. But what was the point of creating something if she couldn't partake in the discussion about it? And now critics were looking back at the Shakespeare series and remarking that all along, weren't they prophetic, using the universal truths found in Shakespeare to make statements about the current, earthly turmoil?

She came the closest she ever had to opening Portia's casket, thinking that if she had an idea of what her father put in there, an idea of what he had thought was "infinitely" worth saving, she might extract some wisdom from his choice, might find an answer for herself. Art lasted past the artist; she had lived by that creed her father had believed in. It almost didn't matter who she was. Like every generation, hers was likely ignoring people who would go down in history while many of those getting so much acclaim, like herself, would have their names turn to dust along with their bones.

Regardless of whether there was some form of afterlife, Dez knew that when it came right down to it, she wanted to be recognized as the artist of the work she had done in *this* life. And she wanted Jacob to know that she was who she was: D. H. Spaulding. Surely, if anyone had guessed about Spaulding's identity, he had?

She had not seen him in four years.

She romanticized him; she was aware of that. Romanticized him even when she dated other men—none of whom really interested her. One good reason for doing the interview was so that he could know, wherever he was, that she was the artist responsible for *The Black Veil*. She wanted him to see it for what it really was—a painting for him, a painting about Cascade.

And, her reasoning continued, if the painting was being seen by the general public as anti-Nazi, then there were better, purer, less personal reasons for wanting to show it, to be part of an interventionist push. The stories coming out of Europe had, with the years, grown impossible to read—most recently, the state-backed, two-night, glass-shattering storm of violence throughout Germany that had outraged the world. Germany was a black stain spreading over the continent, gobbling up more and more of the European capitals, and the threat didn't stop at Europe's borders. In winter, American Nazis had held a rally at Madison Square Garden. The rally leader turned out to be a petty criminal with big dreams, and the rally was followed by a larger "Stop Germany" march down Fifth Avenue, true, but the easy spread of the ideology was chilling, all the same.

"What glisters might be gold," she told Maxie. "I'm going to do it."

———

In November 1939, the *Life* story came out. It was a typical day-in-the-life *Life* story, and what little political commentary there was got lost in the sudsy text. Once the editors realized that D. H. Spaulding was no man, the story's political bent had gone out the window. The photographs showed Dez painting in her flat, showed her riding the trolley to the office. *She is not your average bohemian artist,* the copy said, *living in Greenwich Village. Miss Spaulding lives on the west side and shops for her hats at Macy's, like any career girl.*

Of course the whole idea was a mistake. When she saw how corny and condescending the piece was, she burned with regret. There wasn't the same respect and seriousness of tone that a piece about a man would have commanded. Or maybe it had nothing to do with her being a woman, but about her being so foolish as to allow herself to be photographed buying a hat. She should have been photographed in Camden's smoking a Lucky Strike. It was the fact of her normalcy, her hats, her job. Suddenly, D. H. Spaulding was a bore.

Although she'd finally confided in Abby and Amy, other colleagues at the League were funny—miffed, mainly—about their exclusion from the big secret. Dez pointed out that the evidence had been there all along, right in front of them. It wasn't her fault that people assumed D.H. was a man. Of course, plenty of people, like Mr. Washburn and most of her colleagues at the *Standard,* thought the *Life* story was a great coup.

Art lives after the artist. She tried to hang on to that sentiment, but it was cold comfort, and sometimes not even true. Sometimes art turned to dust: burned, lost, destroyed, forgotten. What was it all for, if not for someone with whom to share it? She understood the sense of isolation Jacob must have felt back in Cascade; she felt it now herself. What hurt most was that she heard from Sidney Orenthal, who knew someone who knew him, that Jacob had left New York City well over a year before, sometime in late 1937 or early 1938, to take a teaching post in New Haven.

Their paths were not going to cross; he had never wanted them to cross. Theirs was not some great Russian love affair. It was a small thing, tightly wound, and it had strangled on itself.

———◦———

She didn't paint anything for a while. It seemed she had nothing left to paint, and she didn't know who she was: Dez Spaulding, Dez Hart, D.H.

She realized, too, that she did not care for people noticing her, pointing her out on trolleys, asking if she was the girl artist they had seen in *Life*. Was there really a whole town under water, they would ask? Did books really float out of library windows?

It was an isolating time, but like all bad times, it got better.

In April, James Lawrence King, returning from a monthlong trip to South America, sent a telegram expressing his astonishment, and to say he looked forward to seeing more of her work. When she wrote to thank him, she mentioned that her father had said he would like to reopen the playhouse with *The Tempest*. *It is not only remarkable that you were the one who bought the painting, it is oddly fitting, don't you think?*

After all the stir of "girl artist," Clem Greenberg championed her in an article in *Art News*. He balanced the buildup and criticism by focusing attention on her paintings. *Where the focus should be*, he wrote. The tide began to turn in that way no single person can ever really control. People started looking for her work around the same time that Dez realized she had to get back to it, and take her work in a new direction, regardless of how people might receive it.

She began experimenting with eliminating color and with emphasizing line and form, producing what became her *New York Subway Series*: seven stark, simplified black-and-white scenes inspired by riding the IRT. Maxie showed the series in June and five of them sold within two weeks.

What a whim success could be, what a fluke, Dez thought. But she was grateful for that fluke. In the fall of 1940, she bought a modest but high-ceilinged apartment on Central Park West, with a sunny living room that she turned into a studio, where she plunged back into color and completed *Color Studies*: five five-foot-high abstract explorations of color that appeared to shimmer and pulse, thanks to a subtly undulating base of thick plaster that she covered with sheets of hand-hammered silver leaf. Maxie showed the series in December, and James Lawrence King bought *#4, Blue.* His note to Dez, her reply, turned into regular correspondence. In March of 1941, he wrote to say that he planned to turn his attention to the playhouse within the coming months. In September, he wrote that renovation was already under way. He was wiring the building for electricity and steam heat. He had also decided to punch out an addition—"still in keeping with the Elizabethan look of the place, not to worry"—that would add space for new, separate, ladies' and gents' rooms, as well as a drinks bar. Italian craftsmen would refinish the woodwork and build what was needed. A team of seamstresses in Connecticut would make new seat cushions. In the spirit of what was, an assistant had located a textile factory that could duplicate the gold-flecked red velvet Dez's mother had chosen for the original cushions.

Dez phoned the number engraved at the top of his stationery. A receptionist put her through to his secretary, and then finally to him, and his voice, when he came on the line, sounded genuinely pleased to hear from her.

She said she was phoning to thank him for all he'd done, for the cushions, especially. She told him how incredibly touched she had been, to hear that.

"Well, we can't forget who founded the theater, can we?" His voice was charming in a way she now, vaguely, remembered from that day she'd met him so briefly.

"I was thinking," he said, "or should I say, hoping, that you would paint the poster for the opening production. Unless you'd like me to use your *Tempest?*"

"I'd like to do a new poster," she said, realizing that it was true. "I'd like to put my father in it." She could immortalize him as Prospero. She added that now seemed the right time to mention that she had little desire to be directly involved in the production. "I've been hoping we can choose a staff—a director, all that—and let them do what they do best," she said. "I am most definitely not my father."

"I'll get someone on it, start advertising," he said. "I have to be in New York in January, and probably February, too. It's looking to be a busy year, '42. Why don't we plan to interview people then? I'm assuming you'll at least want to be part of that."

She did, of course, and during that call, they decided on a date for the grand reopening. Thursday, August 6, 1942, a little less than a year away. For the first time in a long time, Dez found herself looking forward.

———

Instead, the war came. A week after Pearl Harbor, King sent a terse telegram. THEATER PLANS DELAYED INDEFINITELY. Another week after that, a handwritten letter arrived, one of apology and invitation. *Can I make it up with a New Year's dinner at 65 Irving when I'm in the city next week?*

THE RAPPAHANNOCK

40

August 1947

D

ez rode the Connecticut Central north, early on a mild August morning. James and most of his contingent would take the Philadelphia train; Abby and the New York group were motoring up.

She wanted to be by herself on this trip. She wanted the lull and comfort of the train's clacking wheels, the sway of the carriage back and forth. She wanted to rest her forehead against cool glass and watch Connecticut flash by. The countryside was changing—there were more roads and filling stations, fewer fields. Where cows used to gape at the trains flashing by, developments of small houses were popping up.

Portia's casket and a copy of the opening-night program rested on her lap. For the program's cover and accompanying poster, she had painted a great, swirling wind blowing a ship onto an island where the lone figure of William Hart as Prospero stood with arms outstretched, in welcome, in wait, and as if to embrace infinity.

She had placed advertisements in newspapers in major cities across the country, announcing the reopening of the Cascade Shakespeare Theatre in Lenox, Massachusetts. She wanted anyone who cared, anyone who had an interest, to have the opportunity to see it again, and in truth, there was a vague hope that Jacob would see and respond to one of the ads. It had been years since that day he walked out of her apartment, since she sent that last, unanswered letter, but she'd never let go of the feeling that seeing him once again was somehow necessary, and probably inevitable.

———

At Lenox, she was met by Albert, one of James's assistants. As they drove through town, with its prosperous-looking storefronts, Dez imagined that Cascade might have looked like Lenox if it had been allowed to grow after the Depression. Shiny new cars lined the streets, pedestrians filled the sidewalks. Dez counted two ladies' dress shops, two coffee shops, a stationer's, a barber, and two drugstores.

At the Curtis Hotel, Albert handed her luggage off to a porter, then took her directly to the playhouse a short mile away. Though she had seen it in its new home many times, it was always momentarily startling to see it in another space. It was no longer riverside, but its location, set back from the road and framed by tall pines, had its own peaceful beauty. Box hedges had grown in around the foundation; the building no longer looked transplanted. Rather, it looked like it had graced Lenox forever.

Stepping inside evoked a flood of memories—of her parents, of Rose, of Cascade—but what struck her most was that her father built something so long ago, before two wars now, and it had lasted. It had mattered. The wood shone. The ticket window had been lined with new glass and brass trim. The new drinks bar was a beautiful, curved mahogany. The plinth in the display case had been covered in fresh red velvet, and on it rested a fine, imposing-looking reproduction of the First Folio, opened now to *The Tempest*.

James wouldn't arrive until late afternoon, in time for the cocktail party, but the director, the manager, and the cast were all on hand to greet her. Prospero was being played by the veteran actor Richard Leslie, now sixty-eight years old, the man who had once knelt to button her shoe when she was a child. As a younger man in Cascade, he had played both Hamlet and Macbeth. Older, he looked remarkably like William Hart, enough so that her poster of Prospero could have used either man as model. "My dear Desdemona!" he cried. "Did you ever think you would see the day?" He draped an arm across her shoulders and they looked around, necks craned to take it all in as Dez shook her head, no. No, she really had never thought to see such a magnificent rebirth.

Behind the mahogany bar, James had arranged for the construction of a concealed fire cupboard, with a paneled door that swung open when the top left corner was pressed. Dez tried it out with one push of her index finger. There was a click, and the door popped ajar. The cupboard itself was four feet high and four feet deep, lined with metal. She slid Portia's casket inside for safekeeping.

The preshow cocktail party on the lawn recalled past parties, but was, in reality, far more elegant. These days, any occasion was an occasion to dress up—men in tails, women in long gowns. Dez wore emerald satin and a rope of pearls around her neck. Her hair, grown long, fell in waves down her back.

Four musicians perched on bamboo chairs under a bank of trees, Haydn's string quartets drifting along the evening air. A long table, spread with white linen, displayed buckets of champagne and rows of crystal glasses. White-gloved waiters passed frosted grapes and tiny canapés on silver trays that glinted and flashed in the sinking sun. James, remembering Dez's stories, had ordered madeleines, platters of them; they graced a long table near the playhouse door. Dez bit into one, remembering Stan and his tale of nearly having choked to death. She never again, after that last letter, heard from his wife.

James arrived just as the party got under way, in time for the hearty hellos, the shoulder claps. When Dez caught sight of him, striding across the lawn, greeting people, a grateful shiver passed through her. How extraordinarily lucky she and her father and the playhouse had been that the planets had aligned themselves and produced James Lawrence King as savior. Fate had played a role, she was sure of it. The dots had connected—the postcards, James seeing them, his Lenox connection, his money, his desire to preserve what deserved preserving.

Lenox people arrived—local politicians and supporters—all mixed in with the current summer crowd. A small contingent from Cascade showed up, a group of about ten, including Zeke Davenport. Zeke had shrunk, turned slim and white—he would die of lung cancer within the year— but he was jolly as ever. He grabbed her in a bear hug and laughed and said, "They'll never see the likes of a Falstaff like mine, though."

Personal friends arrived, too—associates of Dez's and James's, friends from New York and Pennsylvania, all of them swarming around with congratulations, with talk. The conversation became, for Dez, a back- ground buzz, a general feeling of well-being. Abby had come up with her husband, Bill Richdale, the stockbroker she met at Dez's first show and married during the war, on one of his leaves. Abby was chic in a claret off-the-shoulder gown, and she looked around approvingly. "Now *this* is what I imagined Cascade to be, all those years ago."

Asa did not come, though Dez had invited him. He still, technically, owned the theater, and would until he died, but he had done the decent thing and turned all operations over to the James Lawrence King Philan- thropic Foundation. He sent a letter, cordial but brief, offering congratu- lations and "all best wishes." Early on, when war was declared, he'd tried to enlist, but was deemed necessary in his civilian capacity. Instead, he married a widow from Springfield, a woman with two children. She and

Asa had not had any of their own. In a movie, he would have married Lil, but life was not a movie at the Criterion Theater, and as far as Dez knew, Lillian Montgomery never did marry.

⸻

After all those early years of hoping to see Jacob, Dez never truly expected that he would respond to her advertisements and come. Yet, when she glanced across the lawn and saw him under the pines, wearing a dark suit in place of black tie, using his program to shield his eyes and scout the crowd, his presence felt inevitable.

She excused herself—barely aware of whom she was excusing herself from—and crossed the lawn. Inwardly, she was trembling, but how easy it turned out, thanks to that balm, the passage of time, to behave like he was anyone, to say, "Jacob Solomon, I don't believe it," to thrust out her hands and take his in welcome. Up close, he looked remarkably the same—a bit more chiseled in the face perhaps, the roundness of youth gone. But his dark hair was still thick, only a few silver strands shimmered through the black.

They said the things that people say when they meet after a long absence: *How are you? So good of you to come.* But underneath the pleasantries and catching up, their eyes said other things:

I thought I'd never see you again.

I missed you.

I thought of you for years.

Then why did you let all those years go by?

I don't know. I don't know why I let all those years go by.

She heard herself chattering, saying she had heard he'd ended up in New Haven and wondered why he'd gone there after working so hard to get back to New York, but inside she was willing time to slow down, to stop for just a moment so she could marvel, could drink in the fact that they were actually together, talking, after all these years.

"I guess," he said, and he was rueful, "because I'd been part of a couple of shows, and no one even noticed. They didn't even say I was bad. And then they were phasing out the federal art projects, so when that teaching offer came, even though it was only for a year, I grabbed it. I had to. I had a wife and daughter to support."

She nodded, knowing better than anyone the role of luck, of chance. But what of Dr. Proulx's legacy, she wondered?

He seemed to read her thoughts. It was tied up for years, he said. "When I finally got it, I honestly didn't know what to do with it until I realized it should be for Esther. She's bright. She'll go to college."

"Is your family with you?" She peered around, more out of politeness than any real sense he'd come with someone, because some part of her sensed something was amiss.

He shook his head. It was a long story, that shake said. "Get back to your guests, please. I just wanted to congratulate you."

"You're my guest," she said, insisting, until she finally got the story out of him: how after the teaching stint ended, with the war ramping up, he'd enlisted. How Ruth's mother, Sarah, had moved down to New Haven to help out with Esther. How he'd been in Samoa six months when he got word that Ruth had woken up one morning with a headache like a hammer; a few hours later, Sarah found her on the floor. "They said it was cerebral apoplexy. A little time bomb we never knew was there. She lasted only a few days, and everyone said it was a blessing, considering the state she was in. But I don't know about that. It's been hard on Esther."

"Of course," Dez said, infusing those two little words with warmth and concern. Esther would be—nearly twelve? Of course. Twelve. Twelve years since Jacob said, *"Ruth is pregnant. We're married."* Just a little older than the age Dez was when she lost her own mother.

"So it's been a tough road," she said.

Somewhere, a laughing voice called out, *"Where the hell is Dez?"* She slipped into the shadow of the pine tree, hoping whoever it was wouldn't spot her.

"Dez, I've taken up enough of your time. It's your big night. Everyone wants to see you."

"No, no." She positioned herself deeper into the shadow. "I see these people all the time." But the cocktail hour was ending, the sun sinking, waiters tidying up, groups of people starting to drift toward the doors.

Jacob glanced around, then spoke in an embarrassed rush. "You sent me a letter, years ago, after that first one."

She looked at him: yes?

"I found it," he said, as if he had been waiting forever to tell her. "Just a few months ago, cleaning out Ruth's closet. I found that letter. In a candy box. And there were all these other things. Clippings about you, that sketch I did of you. It had gone missing early on, when we were first in New York."

She shook her head, confused.

"I never got that second letter, Dez. I never knew Ruth intercepted it. I never even thought she knew about you."

"Oh," she said, a single, startled syllable.

The last fingers of sunlight illuminated one side of his face and she saw the lines around his eyes, saw that he was changed, after all. Of course, they were both changed.

"The letter didn't really excuse anything, but it was an explanation," she said. "An apology."

"I know." And he had written his own letter in haste, he said. In anger. It was pure coincidence that her first letter had come right after he'd spoken with Al Stein. "I'm sorry I didn't give you the benefit of the doubt."

"Well, it appears we were star-crossed, Jacob. It seems fitting, considering we're at a Shakespeare theater."

"Tell me," he said. "And I won't be embarrassed if you say no, but did you run those ads for me?"

She pressed her lips together. Across the lawn, James and Abby and the others stood in a circle. Abby leaned in to say something and the group erupted in laughter. "Partly," she admitted.

"I missed you all those years," he said. "Missed your friendship. You were right, you know. We were two people alive in the same city and not seeing each other—I don't know. It would have been wrong, I know, but in better ways it would have been right."

She heard his words as if from some great distance and wondered when he had changed his mind. Before the war? During it? He surely must have grasped the brevity of a single lifetime, even before Ruth died.

"I saw glimpses of you," he said. "The *Life* article, other mentions here and there. I went to see *The Black Veil* at the Whitney and God, Dez, I wished I could talk to you about it."

"You saw it?"

"I went as soon as I heard about it."

"I'm so glad. And you understood what I was trying to say?"

"The Nazi message, yes, of course. It was brilliant."

She looked down into her glass, at the slender threads of rising bubbles, to hide her disappointment. It wasn't his fault he didn't understand her cryptic apology, especially after all the publicity the painting received.

"It wasn't intended to be a political message." She smiled at his confusion. "That was just the way people interpreted it. It was Cascade, Jacob. It was a message to *you*," she explained, and as she did, he half-closed his eyes, trying to see the painting in his mind's eye.

"God, I wish I'd known," he said. "For years I was sure you would want nothing to do with me after that awful letter. But then I saw that ad." He rested his fingertips against her wrist and they burned. Even now, they burned. Rational thought unraveling, ready to fly out the window. Desire was so primal, so hard to control. And to think it had been smoldering all those years, when she was telling herself she could think of him with bemused distance.

Maybe an epistolary correspondence, she could say. *We can be proper, old-fashioned.*

But she couldn't do it, couldn't stir it all up again.

"I'm married, Jacob," she said. How could he not have known? "To James."

He took a single, reflexive step backward. "Right," he said, almost to himself. "Of course."

"I thought you would have known." The marriage had caused a modest amount of publicity.

He lifted his head, becoming the cordial, correct self she remembered. "I didn't."

An usher emerged from the playhouse, ringing a bell, and she was aware of James seeking her out, beckoning, striding across the grass.

Stay for the afterparty, she urged, but he didn't get a chance to reply. Something was happening, causing everyone to look around and up. There was a collective sound of appreciation, a drawn-out "ohhhh . . ." followed by applause.

On the roof of the playhouse, the gathering dusk and a flick of a switch had illuminated a row of round lightbulbs that spelled out SHAKESPEARE in white electric light.

James headed toward Dez with mild disappointment in his gait— obviously someone had switched on the lights before he intended. But no matter, his manner seemed to say. He made a sweeping, offering gesture with his arm, from Dez to the roof.

A gift.

James.

And next she thought of him, Jacob had slipped away, part of the crowd sweeping into the theater.

<hr />

The theater was a polished jewel. Its Elizabethan-style paneling, refinished and waxed, gleamed. New electrical wiring fitted out the lanterns, which glowed with amber light. The new drapes were thick burgundy velvet. Dez and James made their way down the center aisle to the stage, clutching their programs, calling out hellos and thank-yous, waiting for everyone to settle in. The sound of excited chattering was almost deafening, and it was a giddy feeling to look around and imagine her father's delight. When every seat appeared to be occupied, even up into the rafters, she turned to James. "I think we can begin."

James spread his arms and began to clap for silence. The noisy buzz turned to a few voices, then subsided. All eyes looked to him.

"Dez and I decided not to open the production with a lot of fanfare," he said. "We would like tonight's performance to speak for itself, but we would of course like to thank everyone who had a part in preserving this historic gem and we would like to thank all of you for being here." He looked to Dez. "Desdemona?"

Dez gave the audience a small wave. The rows; no single face was distinguishable. "This is the day my father trusted would happen. It's the day he talked about on the last day of his life. I know he is looking down on us with complete and utter delight. We'll talk and celebrate later, but for now—" She held up both hands like a conductor. "Let the show begin."

They took their seats to the sound of applause, clutching each other's fingers.

"At last," James whispered.

"At last."

The lights blinked off. There was a long, drawn-out moment of inky darkness and the play began with *a tempestuous noise*: a loud crack of thunder and roiling waves, a shipwreck just offshore from an island. In the background sat the stark, skeletal remains of other wrecked ships. Sailors on board cried out and abandoned ship, saying good-bye to their lives.

As the performance progressed, she imagined her father, standing just offstage, cuing actors, adjusting gowns and crowns and wings. She imagined him simply folding his arms and watching over what he had helped bring to life. Dez had to hand it to the director, his attention to detail was spot-on—sounds that set the right mood, flawless stage sets and lighting, superb performances. Ferdinand and Miranda were perfectly cast, and when they got to the part where they declared their love for each other, when Miranda asked, *Do you love me?* and Ferdinand, almost ashamed that she even had to ask said, *O! heaven! O earth! bear witness to this sound. I, beyond all limit of what else in the world, do love, prize, honour you,* Dez couldn't help but think of Jacob, somewhere behind her in the dark.

"I am a fool to weep at what I am glad of!" Miranda said, and Dez took James's hand. Their life was satisfying and good. She must not weep at what she was glad of.

During the brief intermission, swallowed up in the crush of people at the bar, Dez saw no sign of Jacob, but it was James's moment anyway, and it was her father's. The buzzing, the excitement, the glasses raised in William Hart's memory, belonged to the two men who had made the playhouse happen.

Her father would have approved of the audience's eagerness to settle back into their seats. He would be gratified to see the rapt attention they gave the rest of the play. When Richard Leslie paused with quiet fanfare, then gathered himself up to speak the play's most famous lines, everyone became still and attentive in that way Dez had forgotten.

"Our revels now are ended. These our actors, as I foretold you, were all spirits and are melted into air, into thin air. And, like the baseless fabric of this vision, the cloud-capp'd towers, the gorgeous palaces, the solemn temples, the great globe itself, yea, all which it inherit, shall dissolve. And, like this insubstantial pageant faded, leave not a rack behind. We are such stuff as dreams are made on, and our little life is rounded with a sleep."

Leslie very emphatically emphasized the *we*, which seemed to be his way of reminding the audience that they were really listening to Shakespeare talk down through the ages.

"Thank you," Dez whispered when James inclined his head toward hers. He was nearing sixty now, but he was vigorous and fit, a man who had built an empire of steel yet always found time to appreciate the three graces. Their marriage had been a successful and independent meeting of the minds. They lived weekends in Hastings-on-Hudson; weekdays found Dez in her Central Park studio.

The play wound to its end. Prospero, having relinquished his magic powers, cued the audience to clap by asking them to let him leave the island *with the help of your good hands.* The clapping filled the rafters, real and enthusiastic—real applause always so spontaneous and exuberant, hard to fake.

The production was a success. Newspapers, next day, would call it a mar-velous blend of pageantry and poetry as they praised Leslie's soaring performance, calling it both arrogant and humble. *With the addition of the William Hart Shakespeare Theatre, Lenox promises to be an arts mecca for decades to come, The Sunday Call* would write.

Everyone gathered in the vestibule after the show, the actors, still in their costumes, mingling with the guests. Dez was conscious of her eyes sweeping the crowd for Jacob, but there was no sign of him, and she told herself it was for the best. As much as she was tempted to renew the rela-tionship, she couldn't do it, couldn't walk into infidelity with her eyes open.

James, behind the drinks bar, signaled to Dez—*ready?* He pushed on the corner of the concealed cupboard and the door swung open. Dez reached in to retrieve Portia's casket, the moment almost unreal, but the lead cold and hard to the touch, quite real. She hopped up on the stool that someone had provided and signaled to James, who clinked two glasses together to get everyone's attention. When the crowd had stilled, upturned faces smiling at her expectantly, she began by thanking every-one, by reciting a brief history of the playhouse, and the tale of its removal from Cascade to Lenox.

Then she held Portia's casket up high and explained its story. "Those of you who knew my father can well imagine the glee with which he'd have planned something like this. I know he died more comfortably knowing that he would be part of this production tonight."

"So a toast," James called out. "To William Hart."

"Toast!" A hundred glasses lifted into the air. "To William Hart!"

Dez fitted the key into the lock. Her wrists trembled even as she steeled herself for a letdown. Like the unmasking of D. H. Spaulding, nothing in Portia's box could possibly live up to the excitement and mys-tery of the unknown. But as she lifted the lid, her heart thudded like hammer blows, regardless. Inside lay two folded sheets of stationery and a rolled handkerchief that she immediately recognized as her father's. She pressed it to her face with bittersweet disbelief—the smell of his shaving soap still lingered in the fabric, even after the passing of so much time.

Her eyes flooded and she looked down, blinking furiously. She opened the handkerchief, revealing the initials *WH* embroidered in small, square black letters. A sturdy iron key fell out.

She held up the key to show the crowd, and shrugged to show that she did not know what lock it fit. She unfolded the letters. One was personal. *My dear Dez—*She squeezed her eyes shut. Later. She would savor it later.

The other letter was addressed to the audience. She held it up and the room went still, everyone all ears. "It's a letter," she said. "To all of us here."

She gathered her composure, and cleared her throat and read. *To all of you assembled here,* he had written in his grand-orator, playmaster's voice.

I trust that my daughter has treated you all to a worthy production of The Tempest. The Tempest may have been Shakespeare's farewell to theater; I make it mine. I felt it was important to open a new season, a new era, with a comedy, with a light heart and a forgiving, forward-looking spirit, and I trust, by now, that the hard times are over and Cascade is once again a thriving summer community.

For every truth there is an equal and opposite truth, and Shakespeare knew that better than most. His plays speak for everyone—but his words are valuable only so long as they are preserved and passed on to new generations.

As many of you know, it was pure good fortune that Mr. Heminge and Mr. Condell collected the plays and had them published at a time when plays were not considered literature and were only just beginning to be published in folio form. Eighteen of Shakespeare's plays had never been published at all, so had the First Folio not been published, we would have lost

The Tempest and Twelfth Night. We would have lost Antony and Cleopatra and Julius Caesar. I shudder to think that these plays could so easily have vanished.

One of my treasured possessions is this playhouse, of course. These walls are part of history, a small part of the river of literacy that courses through our civilization. But I could assemble players on any grassy field and what would I have without the plays themselves, without the words?

I treasure my First Folio even more than these walls.

My daughter thinks it is gone, sold, but Dez, behold the key in your hand. It is the backup key to the vault in the cellar. I know you think it is empty, as it was. You may have even forgotten it by now. But go downstairs. Yes, now! Open it—the combination is 22, 14, 36, 2. The key turns to the left.

Dez glanced out at the crowd, the mood turned palpably awkward.

The Folio will be well-wrapped in its special cloths; the air in the vault is quite dry. It is time, now that you've done your part, to let the playgoers see this gem again.

Take good care, good people, of this book, which must endure, this little mirror held up to all that is both fair and foul in our world.

—WILLIAM ALOYSIUS HART, DECEMBER 1934

A murmuring started, and grew louder. Dez unfolded the second letter and skimmed it. It was full of words of love and sorrow that she read with a spreading sense of disappointment. She had sacrificed her independence, she had entered into a *marriage*, because she loved her father, because making sacrifices was what human beings did for each other. But he had never sold the First Folio at all. No, he had let her marry Asa, and then spent his last days focusing on this final theatrical drama, this grand, sweeping gesture that was supposed to have made a great point, but in the end, only illustrated human frailty.

The letter closed:

I couldn't let it go. You understand, don't you?

Dez thought back. Rose must have known. She must have slipped the Folio into the vault long after Dez cleaned it of the few remaining dollar bills left inside. And Rose wasn't able to warn Dez, because by the time Dez moved the playhouse, Rose, too, was gone.

41

AND SOMETHING BECOMES SOMETHING ELSE

The day after the grand reopening, after James left on the morning train, Dez traveled to the place that had been Cascade, Massachusetts, for 121 years, intending to do studies for a series of murals. She was full of determined ambition that day, and filled a dozen sheets of oversize linen hard-stock with sketches, notes, details, and color samples, intending to start on the series as soon as she got back to New York. She didn't know that she would not actually execute the Cascade Murals until the end of her life; didn't know that she would paint them not on canvas, but on the walls of the Lenox Theatre Institute, which she would endow in the early 1980s.

All she knew on that day after the grand reopening was that she wanted to sort out a few things. She wanted to sort out how she felt about what her father had done. She wanted to sort out what Jacob had meant to her. And she wanted to capture a larger sense of what had happened to Cascade.

Albert drove her up Route 13, through crisp morning air that promised an early autumn, the road dappled with light. At Cascade Lookout, he lifted her easel from the trunk—the easel that Walter Munroe, dead two years now, had built with such care, carrying it to the edge of the overlook while Dez set up her brushes and paint box on the chest-high wall that separated the lookout from the water-filled valley below. She would be good for two or three hours, she told him.

Below, the reservoir stretched for miles, its surface broken only once, by a single island. The water authority had erected a placard that pointed out that this island was really the hill that had once risen behind the train station in Cascade's town center. A grainy photograph, mounted under thick plastic, revealed the view as it had looked in July 1935.

By gauging her distance from the island and comparing it with the photograph, Dez worked out where her childhood home had stood. If she squinted, she could almost see the steeple of the Round Church rising over pines that were no longer there, could almost see the cemetery with its weathered stones and moss-covered crosses that had once been mute testament to permanence.

And somewhere to the left, far below the surface, would be the playhouse's stone foundation. Inside that foundation, behind the shale imposter's wall, locked in the Victor Manganese Steel Vault with Triple Time Lock, would be the First Folio. It would have bloated with water years ago, disintegrating year by year.

I couldn't let it go. You understand, don't you?

No, yes. There were so many ways she could answer that question, but only one made sense: too much time had passed. The players had long left the stage. She had to believe that he—and Rose, too—had truly thought she would have married Asa anyway, that she was better off married and cared for.

But she wondered if, in some afterlife, her father saw the futility of what he'd done. Because trying to hold on to things was uncertain. You lost control when you died. You had no idea whether what you cared about would go into a museum or into a rubbish bin.

And who could say whether saving anything mattered? Mightn't it be effort that mattered most? People were compelled—she was compelled—to try to mark existence, and would even if something cataclysmic happened, more of the earth blasted away, like at Hiroshima, like Cole's Course of Empire series. And the world had to start back at its beginnings.

Here, it was easy to imagine such a world. From this vantage point, there was not a sign of civilization—no car on the access road far to the left, no view of the water authority building, nor the apparatus that pumped thousands of gallons of water a day one hundred miles to Boston. The Rapahannock was as pristine and still as it might have appeared to the first settlers who found Indians living on this land.

Yet down there was the same space on earth where she had, so many Thursdays, waited for the sound of Jacob's truck coming up River Road. She could still feel that catch in her chest, that alertness. Hadn't she felt it last night, in spite of herself, when she turned and saw him beneath the pines? Before marrying James, she had confided in Abby—she still thought about Jacob, and was that fair to James? "You'll always think about Jacob," Abby had said. "Because he was forbidden. He was exotic. But if you'd lived with him, the mystique would have been long gone."

Dez had conceded that that might well have been true. That she might have been feeding a fantasy all those years. But now she and Jacob had seen each other again. The invisible thread, stretched and tangled as it had become, had shown itself to be unbroken.

She took up her brush. She couldn't think about that. Without events unfolding as they had, she would not have painted the Shakespeare series and *The Black Veil*. She might have created something equally as good, as deeply and internally satisfying, as unique to her soul as her thumbprint to her skin, but she couldn't be sure, and since she couldn't be sure, she had to be content with the life she'd lived and how she had lived it.

The light had begun to grow more liquid; she hurried to prepare her paints, laying on some fast color washes, setting rough compositions, establishing the base colors, the peculiar milky light. Now that the trees were gone, the sky was big, like the Western skies she had heard described and had seen in paintings and photographs, but not yet seen for herself.

She could capture that big sky, but how to capture the fact that water covered a town, just swallowed everyone up, encouraged people to move, to change, to do things they might not otherwise have done?

She thought of Asa, digging out Secret Pond, trying to fight off the inevitable. She thought of Dr. Proulx, breathing his ether-soaked rag to escape it. She thought of the Round Church, and all those prayers voiced into all those Sunday mornings, thought of Pearl Harbor sending neutrality right out the window.

Change was the only constant, a river coursing through the present, turning it exhilarating and unknown. Even now—though her hand and brush tried to keep up—even now the light was changing. It moved one step ahead of her, beckoning.

AUTHOR'S NOTE

I took some liberties with historic facts. In reality, a reservoir would not have been built as quickly as my novel built the fictional Rappahannock, but the basic elements, although speeded up, are true. Other truths: the Roper Poll that dismays Dez in 1935 was an actual Roper Poll in 1939. Henry Clay Folger did die soon after the cornerstone for his Folger Shakespeare library was laid in Washington DC, but in 1930, not 1934.

I used period photographs, news clippings, essays, reservoir construction literature, and art books published before 1935 to imagine myself into the time period. I would like to acknowledge those sources I found helpful:

After Picasso, James Thrall Soby (Edwin Valentine Mitchell, 1935).

American Chronicle: Six Decades in American life, 1920–1980, Lois Gordon, Alan Gordon (Atheneum, 1987).

A New Deal for the Arts, Bruce I. Bustard (National Archives & Record Service, 1997).

Changing New York, The Complete WPA Project, Berenice Abbott, ed. Bonnie Yochelson (The New Press, 2008).

Documenting America, 1935–1943, Lawrence W. Levine, Alan Trachtenberg, Carl Fleischhauer, Beverly W. Brannan (University of California Press, 1988).

Gramma Remembers New England, William O. Thomson (Old Saltbox Publishing, 1986).

Historic Quabbin Hikes, J.R. Greene (Highland Press, 1994).

Just Looking: Essays on American Art, John Updike (MFA Publications, 2000).

Modern American Painting, Peyton Boswell (Dodd Mead, 1940).

Quabbin: A History and Explorers Guide, Michael Tougias (On Cape Publications, 2002).

Quabbin Facts & Figures, Friends of Quabbin, Inc. & Metropolitan District Commission, Division of Watershed Management (1991).

The 1930s: The Hulton Getty Picture Collection, Nick Yapp (Konemann, 1998).

The Amateur Artist, F. Delamotte (Frederick J. Drake & Co., 1906).

The Creation of Quabbin Reservoir, J.R. Greene (The Transcript Press, 1981).

The Friends of Quabbin, Inc., a society dedicated to preserving the memory of the lost towns, and fostering appreciation for the unique place of beauty that the Quabbin Reservoir has become.

The Restless Decade: John Gutmann's Photographs of the Thirties, Max Kozloff, Lew Thomas (Harry N. Abrams, 1996).

Understanding Modern Art, Morris Davidson (Tudor Publishing, 1934).

www.realcolorwheel.com A comprehensive art instruction website by the artist Don Jusko.